THE LAST OF THE HEIRS
BOOK ONE

FROST AND DEATH

L. L. RILEY

M.G.M

*For those who have experienced the loss of a loved one,
may you find healing through your pain
and find your happy again.*

CONTENT WARNINGS

Explicit language, PTSD, grief, self-esteem issues, self-loathing, trauma, loss, survivor's guilt, death, murder, blood, violence, anxiety, bullying, use of magic, dark magic involving control, seduction, manipulation for one's own gain, sleepwalking, near-death experiences, thoughts of death, thoughts of dying, drowning, injuries, menstrual cycle, period cramping, self-pleasure, self-pleasure during menstruation, and other heavily depicted and explicit sex scenes.

Author's Note

While this novel is meant to take a reader into a fictional world, it also highlights heavy topics many can face in reality. This book will emphasize how heavy those topics can be for some. Do not forget it is okay to not be okay and not be a badass one hundred percent of the time. It is okay to heal on your own terms, however you choose to go about it. Give yourself grace and remember to always love yourself—flaws and all. This story focuses on character development. Should these words ever feel too much for you, please prioritize your mental health first.

Hugs and love,

L.L. Riley

Frost and Death Playlist

Deities, also known as the Makers:

Yeva, Deity of Life: yeh-vuh
Letum, Deity of Death: leh-tum
Aiyana, Deity of Seasons: eye-yah-nah
Leander, Deity of Beasts: lee-an-dur
Anwir, Deity of Illusion: an-weir
Alora, Deity of Divination: ah-low-rah

Continent:

Draymenk: dray-menk

Each kingdom and its characters:

Axidoria: ax-ah-dor-eea
(Former) Queen Asta: ah-stah
Queen Tove: toh-vah
Princess Runa: roo-nah
Lord Nikolaj (Niko): nee-co-lahj
Lord Ulrik: ul-ric
Betina: beh-tina

Palaena: pah-lay-nah
(Former) King Ivan: eye-van
King Jerrick: jeh-ric
Prince Jonas: jo-nas
Dorit: doh-reet
Ophelia: oh-fee-lee-ah
Cordelia: cor-dee-lee-ah
Viggo: vee-go
Frida: free-dah

Belmur: bel-mur
King Bernard (Bernie): bur-nard
Queen Johanne: jo-an
Princess Vivienne (Vi): viv-ee-en
Princess Marian: mehr-ee-anne

Unterkirch: un-ter-kurch
Queen Verena: ver-ee-nah
Princess Sybille: sih-bul
Lord Rick: rih-ck

Torgem: toor-gum
King Beauvais (Beau): bo-vay/bo

Northtry: north-tree
King Vinzent: vin-sint
Queen Zarina: zah-ree-nah

N
W
E
S
Thosow
Thresborn Forest
KINGDOM AXIDORIA
Velkan Mountains
Lake Iyr
Thorgur
Yadir
Yalta
Bronkirk
Kezrar
Gaith
KINGDOM PALAENA
Rorvik
Black Lake
Vilbirn
Whispering Bay
Lake Torden
Biala Forest
Silford
Weshee
Nadée
Glaston Forest
Riverdein
KINGDOM TORGEM
Harlug
Auriville
Lonar Canyon
Lake Moss
Borville
C'eaux
Essbog

Coral Sea
Malfell Mountains
Tarrgien
Lake Sellen
Dereen Forest
Vanta
Goldbeck
Fisher's Lake
Mezu
KINGDOM NORTHTRY
Corotos
Reidon
Hinbron Mountain Pass
Torrhal
Elinya Mountains
Semfeld
KINGDOM UNTERKIRCH
Lomburg
Wexkee
KINGDOM BELMUR
Oundalk
Oroheim Woods
Edenberry
Dutril
Haliver Woods
South Way
Cobalt Sea
DRAYMENK

FROST AND DEATH

1

MY HEART IS A GRAVE

The tinge of frost atop the three tombstones lying before me conceals the names of my family. Memories of how each brought joy to others are long forgotten to the world, except by me.

I am alone—living with a constant numbness weighing me down, a burden surrounding my heart.

I study each grave methodically and relive moments of love I once had in my life. A bitter sharpness of ice hits my skin when I touch their names carved on the tombstones. Even as I withdraw and rub my nose, I wish instead the cold could have proven useful in drying my tears.

I was merely twenty when I lost my family, and it shocked me and my kingdom.

First, Father, then the transfer of magic to me happened.

It was then I knew Mother, too, was gone.

The nipping air mixed with pine and cedar almost blow down the hood of my cloak, and I fasten it in place, my stare lingering most on the last grave.

I was nothing compared to the sunshine my sister was. She was my best friend—and she was taken away far too soon.

A rupture in my world surrounds me, grating and carving out fractured pieces of my heart.

I squeeze my eyes shut as the hopelessness I struggle to suppress and hide daily turns into frustration, my powers shooting out from my palm in response. Memories and failures draw out a choked sob.

"Oh, Runa."

I hunch over and clasp a hand over my mouth, unable to control my sorrow. The agonizing pain keels over, surging the frost forth, and covering her grave once more.

I *just* cleaned it free of the damned frost.

Each day without my family is another day that my pain expands so much I have convinced myself to welcome it and let it swallow me whole.

And that is the fucked-up thing about grief.

It consumes me every day.

I am grief, and grief is me.

I focus on my breathing, struggling, as I always have, to stop my power from escaping. Once it leaves, I cannot draw it back, and I cannot melt it.

I lean into the cold fury thrashing in my veins, hoping it will cease and extinguish my emotions. Instead, it does as it always has and trails soft kisses in its wake along my skin.

I don't revel in the magic I have inherited, only forge the mask of a monster, a destroyer, and smother it away into nothingness.

It deserves to be buried and locked away.

Magic only creates more problems.

The inheritance of power came from the Makers, bestowed only amongst the six royal bloodlines. And each new monarch's ability was different from their predecessor, forcing and creating secrecy between neighboring kingdoms. The concealment of magic made wielding it cumbersome, with the only source for possibly learning about one's gift being through ancestors' journals.

And for some stupid, fated reason, I am the first heir of Axidoria to inherit gifts from the Deity of Seasons, Aiyana. No journals, no resources, no way to stop this winter.

My fucking cursed winter.

The whistling air accompanies me in a somber ballad on my way home, leaves billowing with the wind as I wipe my soaked cheeks. I huff and puff through each booted step, surveying more and more of my surroundings crusting over with frost.

The light snow over grass beneath me trails back to the frozen lake along the edge of Biala Forest. My never-ending winter started there and drifted toward the rest of my kingdom, and the spasming veins of frost grow day by day, year by year, hardening everything it touches. The ice creeps further up the walls of my home, kills more crops, and increases the hatred and disdain my people have for me.

Time has proven I didn't just lose my family but doomed a kingdom I was not well-enough prepared to rule.

A random gust of wind pulls me from my thoughts, ripping down my hood and leaving me scrambling for it. Small wisps of my silver hair get caught in my mouth, and I thank the Makers the rest of it is in a plait.

"This damned wind," I grumble as the black gates come into view.

Clouds loom above me, and snow covers the spiked tips of the barrier leading to the courtyard, Aiyana's cold month-long season just beginning. Unfortunately for me, the weather will only add to my magic-touched winter. If only her blossoming springs and blistering summers melted my power away, then I wouldn't even be in this mess to begin with.

"At least the clouds aren't my fault," I mutter grimly.

Hopefully the skies will clear and save me from more scorn and disappointment before the Celebration of Spirits next week. If one thing could go right when so many are attending, I would take that as a miracle.

Passing through the threshold, my steps echo, the castle I used to love eerily silent. Rooms that have fallen victim to my magic are blocked off and, luckily, are at the back of my home.

But on days like today, where the loss and failure fester, I can't seem to care—can't seem to move.

Exhaustion tugs at me when I reach my chambers and peel off my cloak. I remove Mother's small handheld mirror from my dress pocket, admiring the grooves carved into the gilded handle. As I run my thumb across it, I glance at its paired vanity.

The mirrored set has been in the Clemmensen family for generations. They were never important until Mother used her magic from the Deity of Illusion, Anwir, and cast a glamour on them to be a method of communication. The two mirrors are the last bit I have of my mother and her magic. It is a comfort and keeps her memory strong, the only solace I can turn to on my darkest days.

I clutch the mirror to my chest before reverently resting it on my vanity and remove the rest of my clothes, draping them over the cushioned chair.

The stone hearth blazes heat across my cold skin, the warmth following me as I collapse onto my bed, plush cushions cocooning me as the clean linen scent eases my eyes closed.

Three loud knocks reverberate throughout my bedchamber, and I *loathe* the insistency behind each one.

I remain silent, wondering if the clanging will happen again.

It does.

"Tove?"

A smooth baritone voice echoes into my bedchamber.

I glare at the door, stalling, with the hope my silence will be enough to send Nikolaj, my royal advisor, away. Stilling my breath, I listen for footsteps receding down the hall and jolt when his voice booms into my chambers once more.

"I know you are awake. I can feel your stare melting through the door."

I groan despite a small smirk forming. "Go away."

"Never."

Nikolaj's voice remains distant.

His laughter rings as I roll my eyes, squeezing my pillow once before expelling the air from my chest.

I rise and slip clothes over my curvy, petite frame, lifting my hair out from underneath the dress, checking to make sure I look presentable through my vanity. Running my hand down the long length of my plait, I note my sunken features.

My small pointed nose has a speck of red yet to diminish from the cold outside, and my hooded eyes are rimmed in dark undertones of purple and pink—the singular sign of crying and lack of sleep.

Blue irises, pale and as lifeless as ice, stare back.

A crack in the mirror has me blinking, the hallucination of the monster within thrashing.

I rub my eyes quickly, dragging myself to the door to open it a fraction, Nikolaj peering through with a wide grin.

His copper hair, streaked with darker hues of mahogany, is unruly, with the waves granting him a beauty I find myself envious of. Rich colors warm his skin and accentuate the amber in his eyes, fit to match his jubilant, colorful personality.

But it's the light stubble framing his square jaw that appeals to his boyish charm and always makes my chest flutter.

"Oh, come now, Tee. Let me in already," Nikolaj insists.

I stiffen at the shortened name he uses for me. It is meant to be endearing, but it, ultimately, started as a form of payback for me starting it.

I open the door faster than I can roll my eyes.

It is easy for my guard to slip whenever he is around, especially when he beams from cheek to cheek.

Nikolaj strides into my bedchamber, knowing I wasn't going to turn him away.

Tove, you are such a fucking pushover.

Niko scans my room, his attention pausing on the untouched food on my vanity and the emptied bottle of wine lying on the dark-blue rug. He shifts his body, rising as he places his hands on his hips.

I quickly mimic his actions, preparing for a full-blown lecture, but am surprised when he turns, still wearing a grin.

Sweet Makers, I hate how much smiling reminds me of Runa.

I shudder away from the memory of her, seeking my wardrobe to occupy my thoughts with dresses.

Fashion is one of the few remaining joys I have these days. A small pleasure in how each outfit can be pleasing and beautiful, enough to hide the person wearing it. But as I touch the gowns, an impending void of darkness yearns to make an appearance.

I cough to clear the tightness forming in my throat. "What can I help you with this morning, Niko?" I fidget with a satin dress in repetitive motions, my fingertips fixating on the smooth texture as Niko comes up from behind.

He cages me into his hard chest, and heat envelops me.

Sandalwood soap and leather dances along my senses, goose bumps prickling underneath my clothes.

The longing I've had for this man has multiplied in our time spent together. From being mine and my sister's royal guard to being appointed as my advisor, Niko's dedication and compassion for Axidoria, my family, and me are truly what help keep the storm within from consuming me.

Shifting from princess to queen has been difficult, but Niko has never once left my side. Even when I believed dismissing everyone and locking myself away was the safest option, he thought otherwise.

From weekly check-ins to more detailed reports and updates on the kingdom, I knew I could always trust Niko to make the right calls for me and Axidoria. I nodded solemnly and grieved in peace until he started pushing me to learn about my magic. Even though my efforts were pointless, looking back on those first few months to now helped me find some small purpose and grow into my role.

My gratitude and admiration to Niko strengthen each new day, as I'm indebted to him for not giving up on me.

But the fear of losing him like my family has me constantly pushing my feelings down.

I shouldn't even hope for a chance of love again.

It will always be taken away.

And yet my hopeful heart pushes past fear, grief, and self-hatred, dangling those feelings in front of me with moments like this.

I wiggle out of his embrace, seeking the distance to cool my desire. But when his boyish grin remains, I instantly regret facing him, using all my strength to not touch my heated cheeks.

"Are you ready for this coming week?" He gestures to the dresses behind me.

I laugh bitterly. "This coming week? Seriously? It's not like I *want* to find a husband during the Celebration of Spirits."

The Celebration of Spirits takes part every winter. It is a week-long event filled with festivities, balls, and a lantern ceremony where people come together to honor Yeva, the Deity of Life, and Letum, the Deity of Death.

This year, it will also be where I find my future king consort.

With the disdain from my people and no signs of winter ending, Niko advised it was time for me to marry. I rejected the suggestion time and time again, not wanting to even consider it. But deep down I knew a union would be something to raise the kingdom's spirits.

If even for a little bit.

"Tove—"

"Don't remind me," I grumble and wave Niko off, walking away from him and picking up the wine bottle near my bed.

I know he means well, as he strives to help show my people I am a worthy ruler despite the rumors. But they continue to spread like wildfire, so much so even my noblemen whisper to Niko of my cruelty when I am not present in meetings.

It drew me to the point of surrendering to the monster my people claim me to be, as it's easier to pretend my indifference to everyone is due to my cruelty rather than my grief.

"I know this is not what you had in mind, Tee, but it is time to further your family's line. Your parents would want that for you and for the kingdom."

"You don't know what they would have wanted!" I snap, the words landing harsher than I intended.

The jab hits Niko enough for him to wince.

I shake my head as I twirl the bottle around the table, trying to keep my mood at bay during this conversation.

I don't like talking about *them*.

"I'm sorry," he whispers, the tenderness in his voice worsening my regret.

I avert my eyes from his speculation and pity as a knot tightens in my chest.

Niko comes up and takes my hand into his. "Tove."

His calloused thumb brushes against my skin.

It lulls me for a moment until I remember that even letting Niko get closer to me will only damn him.

"I can't." I yank my hand from his grasp.

No matter how right it feels to have him near, I can't risk losing him.

My emotions stir, a twinkle of magic peeking its eye open. A chill kisses down my spine as I force myself back a step from Niko.

Calm down, Tove.

Niko tracks the icy breath seeping from my lips as I breathe through diminishing frost desiring escape.

I sag with relief when the sensation finally dissipates.

Niko blinks away his wariness and bounces back into conversation. "Are you still set on our plan to help you with your"—he coughs—"*prospects*?"

I smirk, still not believing in our *plan*.

We sent invitations to all the noblemen in Draymenk, informing them of my search for a husband and hoping many—or even one—would be interested. Niko also suggested he and I flirt to determine who has interest and puts in the most effort for winning my attention.

"Yes, Niko, but right now, I would very much like to try to get some sleep," I say, not wanting to show how difficult flirting with him will be.

Niko regards my outfit, lips curling as he asks, "You are going to bed in *that*?"

Worried he can see through my gown, I look down at myself. He tries to stifle a laugh, and I glare at him.

Why is he teasing me over what I am wearing?

"No." I cross my arms. "I am going to sleep naked, like I always do."

Niko gapes, coughing in astonishment as realization dawns.

My own eyes widen, and I cover my mouth in horror. Damn my mouth for getting the better of me.

Niko breaks into a rich laugh. "Already practicing flirting with me?"

I slump, heat warming my cheeks.

"It's fine, Tee. If it makes you feel any better, I sleep naked, too," he teases.

I groan, envious of his sunny disposition and lack of awareness regarding my true feelings. "Back to our discussion, *Nikolaj*," I grit through clenched teeth. "No matter the plan, I don't think anyone is going to want to marry the *Snow Queen*."

His mouth thins at the nickname my people have coined for me. "Tee, every eligible male wants to marry you. You are a queen with no heirs."

I know he is trying to reassure me, but reassurance doesn't make the nickname go away.

"Oh?" I challenge, throwing my flirtation attempts back at him. "Then, I guess you must want to marry me, too."

Eyes flashing, Niko shrinks back as if I have burned him. Even as his amber eyes rake down my entire body, my heart pounds.

My throat bobs when he meets my gaze again, and I don't allow myself a chance to understand why he just looked at me like that. I feign nonchalance with a wave of my hand.

"Relax. I was joking. Forgive me. I haven't eaten yet today."

His brows furrow. "Why haven't you been eating?"

Gesturing to the bed, I reply, "I was attempting to sleep before you came knocking, remember?"

Niko chuckles. "You probably need to eat *and* sleep."

I nod, knowing he is right and hoping my compliance will end this conversation.

He turns for the door, and I follow, only to bump into him when he stops. Niko twists and catches me before I fall on my ass.

When I look up to thank him, the sunlight normally surrounding him has turned to clouded darkness. My instincts kick in, concern tugging his face toward mine.

"Niko?" I ask. "What is it?"

He pulls me close, latching on as if I am a lifeline and lowering his head into the crook of my neck. His stubble rubs against my skin as he releases a long sigh.

Deities, my wish for him to always be this close has me wrapping my arms around him, allowing this token of affection. It is just a hug.

We have hugged plenty of times, and there is nothing different about this one.

But Niko remains quiet in our embrace.

I pull away and study him. "Niko?"

Niko moves, his face dipping inward, warmth hitting my nose. "It's—"

Hanging on with bated breath, I wait for a response as the rest of my body heats at his proximity.

His cheeky grin returns as he taunts, "*Please* make sure you eat today."

I deflate as glee erupts from him. My temper defends my crushed hope that he was going to do something more.

I shove him out of my chambers, slamming my door, unable to remove the sound of Niko's laughter echoing down the corridor.

I clench my fists. "*Make sure you eat today.*"

Slinking out of my gown, I approach my bed, slumping onto it with a loud thump. The debate of whether I should remain lying on top of my covers or not fuels my anger.

I stew in my irritation and eventually tug the blankets out from under me, refusing to move another inch.

Fucking Niko.

My mind wanders over our conversation and the impending arrival of next week. I wrap one arm around my pillow, burying the unease in favor of looming sleep.

Oh, Sweet Makers, I wish I never had to leave this bed.

2

THROWN TO THE WOLVES

Guests arrive from near and far throughout Draymenk, carrying on diverse conversations scattered around the throne room.

I am tucked away in the back chamber, the safest place to peer out, while praying for the impossible feat of no one noticing my absence. But hiding for these few moments does nothing for the twists and turns of my insides.

I fuss and tug on my gown, adjusting the fabric to make my body shape look smooth. It fits tight in the bodice, hugging each curve. The sleek satin, dyed a deep emerald green, has handsewn beading and lining to depict branches woven across the center. A sequined belt tightens my waist, holding an overskirt and beautiful train. Pockets are sewn in under the overskirt, allowing me to carry Mother's mirror.

But the one thing I am self-conscious of in this gown is the plunging neckline exposing the curves of my breasts as the main attraction.

Betina, my lady-in-waiting, worked with my tailor these last few weeks, ensuring every outfit I wear is unique. While she succeeded in that aspect, she used my love for fashion to help me taunt and lure in more suitors.

Despite my modest reservations, the cheeky woman knew I wouldn't turn down wearing a beautiful dress.

Glancing back to the ballroom, I marvel at the delicate intricacy of each garment the noblewomen wear. The vibrant colors adorned in an array of beads, jewels, and sashes, pair well with the noblemen's velvet vests and leather pants, warming everyone from the chill outside.

The tension remains in my muscles as I hold the door for support. "Sweet Makers, help me," I pray, hoping that honoring them all this week might grant me fortune in finding *someone*.

I walk myself through every minor detail of how each night this week is coordinated. Grand entrance, dance, converse, repeat. And when everyone is stupidly drunk, I can sneak away to rest.

Niko and I worked diligently last week, ensuring everything was set for the celebrations. From extra staff entertaining and decorating the castle for each ball, to having the guests visit the villages during the day. We planned to narrow down my options after each night, hoping to announce an engagement by the third, with the wedding and union happening at the end of the week.

I wanted it to be a surprise while also get it over with.

I didn't want a long duration to think and grieve my family being absent on a day meant to be filled with happiness.

It is fitting I won't be marrying for love.

My stomach drops as dread looms in the back of my mind. Somehow, I know I am going to ruin this all.

Stress and the fear of failure have been rooted so deeply these last few days my night terrors drove me into sleepwalking.

The knowledge of guests and suitors coming here to my home to see the damage I've caused firsthand—

I jolt from my trance when a hand touches my shoulder, slamming the door shut in an instant. The relief of a scream not escaping vanishes as Niko stands with his arms crossed and his brow arched.

His tousled auburn hair is slicked down, the waves smooth and neat to bring out his amber colored eyes. A deep emerald vest peeks through his black jacket, matching his tailored trousers, his entire ensemble hugging and emphasizing the muscles he trains every day.

I ache to see how they might flex if I were to grip them when on my knees before him—

"You look... good," Niko rasps, voice thick and husky.

I shrivel inward at the compliment, meeting his glinting amber eyes. "You look... good, too." I gulp down a breath.

Niko chuckles, scanning me over, and I avert my gaze when his stare lingers on my chest.

Brushing my sweaty hands against the sides of my gown, I try to appear as if I am smoothing the fabric and not imagining my mouth taking him.

Niko lowers into a formal bow, grabbing my hand to brush his soft lips against my knuckles, eyes blazing. "Care to accompany me to the party?"

The fire in his stare goes straight to my core. Words dry on my tongue, but I nod quickly, trying to remember myself.

Niko rises, his broad frame towering over me as he wraps my hand around his.

My grip tightens, the tingling in my legs leaving my knees wobbly as I brace myself.

Niko opens the door, exchanging hushed words with the guard.

The man walks to the opposite side of the ballroom, alerting the announcer of my arrival.

I cringe when the clanking of the announcer's staff hits the marbled tile floor. Ice swirls to life in my chest, a figurative mask taking place as the man's booming voice silences the room.

"Presenting your host, Queen Tove Clemmensen, and her royal advisor, Lord Nikolaj Drost!"

Bile lurches in my throat as we stride forward, light and bright music filling the quiet void.

Warmth from the lanterns and chandeliers complement the beige-marbled pillars adorned with roses of red, orange, yellow, and white. Shrubbery accents the back walls, framing the high arched windows and wide glass doors opening to the courtyard. The foliage and flowers drape across the ceiling, parallel with the lush runner resting on the steps of the dais.

Niko escorts me through the crowd of nobles, who each lower their head or curtsy. But as we pass, the hushed whispers follow, the awful nickname screeching against my ears.

The walls cage and close me in, and my nails dig into Niko's sleeve as I pretend to be unaffected.

"Ignore them," he urges.

I nod to myself more than him as I keep my expression blank.

As we reach the center of the room, Niko asks, "Ready to dance?"

I beam.

Anything revolving around music is my true calling. From playing piano and swaying on my bench, to the crescendo and buildup of a ballad, to dancing to the violinists in a waltz. Losing myself to the rhythm of any song grants me a haven of joy nothing else in this world ever can.

"Yes," I reply.

Niko guides me into position, and I note the warmth emanating from him. His touch is so close to my bare skin, the hand resting on my back lower than protocol dictates.

My cheeks warm at the thought he is comfortable with me and not merely flirting.

When the music starts, our bodies touch, and I am embraced and woven into the light rhythm. We sway to the elevation of the composition, my heartbeat increasing from the movements, sweat beading along my brow.

I spare a glance around the room, noting the guests and couples paired together, smiling and conversing. But when eyes meet me, a chilling breath caresses the nape of my neck. Each scornful stare is a sharp note not intended to pair with the song.

As Niko pulls me back into the dancing, my head is swimming, and a weight pinches the tips of my toes.

I try to shield my wince.

Niko's expression turns apologetic. "Why did it have to be a waltz?" He groans, twisting me out.

"I can always lead if you want." I snicker as he loops me back in.

"How is that going to work when I have to be the one to show you off?"

The decorations in the room blur as we spin, menacing stares of guests fade away as the push and pull of the waltz settles deep in my bones. My body relaxes as the music calls to me, the rhythm twinkling with my movements becoming more expressive as I bask in the dance.

"You look radiant tonight, Tee," Niko whispers.

My heart constricts at the compliment, wanting to believe it, but my reflexes have me deflecting. "You're killing it with the flirting, Niko."

He pulls a mocking face as the crescendo builds. Niko lifts our hands, spinning me rapidly, my eyes keeping a spot on him to refrain from getting dizzy.

His boyish grin grows with each twirl, tugging my own lips to lift as the world around us quiets. Niko dips me as the music reaches its abrupt conclusion, the two of us breathing heavily. My heart skips as his face inches close to mine, and I lick my lips in anticipation.

The glow of joy shines in his amber eyes. And so does something else.

The thunderous applause draws a sharp breath from my chest, turning away from the proximity of Niko's lips. Embarrassment shrivels in my core, my feelings getting the better of me as Niko guides me upright.

His eyes remain downcast when he bows, and I want to say *something*.

But when I behold his handsome face again, it is inscrutable.

My heart wants to claw out from my chest and beg him to come back to the moment, but I sense a wall forming between us. My mind is telling me to let it go and remember the moment we shared is orchestrated.

But even as Niko reaches for my hand to kiss it, I can't help but feel that if I let him go, I will never get him back.

"Your Majesty," Niko says as the crowd nears. Amber eyes I have come to love and admire every day stare before he adds, "Good luck." He walks away, leaving me stranded amid a swarm of men.

I try to call him back, but my voice is overwhelmed by the requests of noblemen surrounding me. The voices blend, echoing in my ears, drowning me more by the second.

A rich voice says to my right, "Your Majesty!"

"Queen Tove!"

A voice to my left, deep and low, vibrates in my ears.

"May I have this dance?" each of the men ask.

I tune out the repetitive questions, knowing many could be a part of the rumors that follow me. Even though I want to waste and wither away, I have a duty to my kingdom.Finding someone to marry will lift the kingdom's spirits. Finding someone could show

I am not as evil as my people claim. Finding someone to marry will help me move on from Niko.

Now I just need to find someone tolerable enough who won't demand I be tied to their hip.

Royal protocol and manners I've known my entire life click into place, pairing with the indifferent mantle of the Snow Queen.

I greet each nobleman, stopping on a familiar face.

The lean man wears a navy suit adorned with white flowers on one side of the lapel. Short blond hair is swept back from his tanned face where his cheeks are hollowed in. The man's slightly crooked nose sniffs as dark-blue eyes peer into mine as if he can hear my own thoughts.

I greet Axidoria's wealthiest nobleman with a tight-lipped smile. "Lord Ulrik, a pleasure to see you here."

Ulrik Albertsen's family is as old as the Clemmensens. The Albertsen's lands grant them access to metals and gems, which are heavily traded throughout Draymenk. But the power and wealth from their property has gone to their heads.

Ulrik recently stepped into the role of lord, and while he has been kind when we've interacted, the man is blunt and rude, always the first to insult me in meetings Niko holds in my stead.

"Your Majesty, it is an honor to be here," Ulrik chimes in a lofty voice, the scent of leather and tobacco overpowering my nose, making it hard to breathe.

I feign kindness. "I am grateful for your presence and contributions to the festivities this week."

"I was hoping we might be able to discuss—"

"My lord," I interrupt, hoping to steer away from politics tonight. "I was wondering if you would be my partner for this next dance."

Ulrik's yellowed teeth gleam. "It would be my pleasure, Queen Tove." He extends his hand.

I inhale one fresh breath before he notices, then take his hand and follow him to an open space on the dance floor. I keep up appearances, remaining calm as I fight to tune out the whispers.

The next song is traditional, meant for all guests to dance together. Stomping feet and clapping hands surround each coupled pair. We take off to the faster tempo, Ulrik and I shuffling through partners, his stench of smoke following me.

Switching between partners in twists and spins, everyone laughs. The shared moments lift my lips, happy I was able to bring a small glimpse of joy to my people after all the wrongs I've done.

When the dancers form parallel lines, couples join hands and take their turns running down the center.

Ulrik and I wait side by side, clapping to the rhythm and preparing to join, but the pungent smell of tobacco is bitter enough to water my eyes when he leans in.

"I hear you are looking for a husband."

Despite the nausea curling in my stomach, marrying someone like Ulrik would be good for the kingdom. Many people are familiar with him and support his family. His riches could help fund extra clothing and food, and we could negotiate his resources.

Yet I cannot help but clarify, "My Lord Ulrik, I am currently looking for a good dance partner." I rush down the center of the lines with a different nobleman, laughing at myself.

The moment dissolves when I accidentally bump into someone at the end.

My brows lift in surprise at the man I collide with.

Black hair, bright blue eyes, and a scar are all I catch before Ulrik takes my hand and sweeps me away.

The showmanship of Ulrik's effort leaves me startled and amused, and his smile turns genuine as we twirl through the line of people. He does have his own sort of attraction, and I debate an arranged marriage with him again.

But then I remember the hatred he spews about me.

The music ends, and I break away, but Ulrik clasps onto my wrist before I can escape. "Was I an adequate dance partner?" he asks out of breath.

I dip my head, hoping the tightness in my voice doesn't hint at anything more. "Yes." I politely tug my hand away. "Thank you for the dance, Lord Ulrik."

"I would like to talk with you in private later."

"I will see if Lord Nikolaj can arrange something," I say with dismissal.

Ulrik's face tightens, and he flexes his jaw. "Of course, Your Majesty." His lips purse as he blinks away his resentment. "I thank you."

Ulrik departs as I scan the crowd for Niko.

Not finding those amber eyes I know so well lead me into scouring for the man I bumped into. I should apologize, but I don't see any man with a scar.

Defeated in my search, I retreat to the small dais at the edge of the ballroom that hosts a throne.

Unlike the one in the main room, now frozen, this throne is perfect for appearances this week. It stands out against the beige stones and marbled floor, but my thoughts drift back to the rooms slowly freezing over or already frozen over in my home.

Those quiet halls tug at my soul.

My old rooms, my sister's rooms, and even the piano room, my favorite room of all, are completely frozen. It hacks away at my heart bit by bit as I lower into the throne, wishing to strum a melody on my instrument rather than be here, surrounded by people.

I lean into the chair and almost forgo appearances when no one approaches. While it could be interpreted as an insult, I count it as a miracle. No one *really* wants to converse with me without Niko present.

His presence always gives them enough courage to face me.

A staff member approaches with a single glass of liquid.

I reach for it eagerly and tell them, "Thank you."

I swig the contents down, my lips smacking at the mild sweetness of the wine, and I love how it instantly warms me. Returning the empty cup, I dismiss the man.

He bows and retreats to the sides of the ballroom.

Footsteps from behind have my lips tugging upward, and I know immediately it is Niko. And although I want to revisit what happened earlier, I can't help but feel awkward.

I resist the urge to say something stupid, rubbing my clammy palms against my skirt.

The outline of my mother's mirror presses into my thigh, and I clutch it in my pocket, a slight sense of calm returning.

He stands at my side, hands clasped behind his back. "Are you enjoying yourself?" Niko asks.

Sinking my teeth into my lower lip, I bite the drying skin off at the side, trying to appear fine. "I am. The wine is marvelous."

"It's from Kezrar, the best in the kingdom."

Another staff member steps up with a newly filled cup of wine.

Eager for more of the sweetness, I reach for the glass, stopping when a warning cough comes from Niko.

I lift a brow in question. "What?"

"Are you *sure* you want to do that this early into the night?" His tone is lined with caution.

I glance back at the staff member and the glass of wine before my hand falls in defeat, hating Niko for being right.

I politely address the man. "Could you come back after a little while?"

"Of course, Your Majesty," he replies with a bow, leaving with the glass of wine my mouth salivates after.

I blow air from my lungs in frustration, and just my luck, my stomach growls. I should have asked for something to eat.

Sparing a glance at Niko, I knit my eyebrows when he shuffles his weight. "Do you need me to get you a chair?"

He scans the guests. "No, no. I am alright. It's this next part I am not looking forward to."

"This was *your* idea." My cheeks heat, and my head buzzes from the wine in my empty stomach.

Niko sticks out his tongue like a child, and I clamp my lips together to avoid snorting aloud, recovering as a group of men approach.

Niko takes a breath, folding his arms. "Here we go."

"Here we go," I repeat, mastering my features and adjusting my posture.

I extend my hand to the first suitor, praying to Alora I might find someone who could understand me and not view me as the Snow Queen everyone claims me to be.

3

A Close Call

Niko shuffling for the first hour was distracting and vexing. I ordered a chair for him for my own benefit, but peering from the corner of my eye every so often made it hard to tell if he was anxious or angry.

After a man from the northeastern village of Tarrgien leaves, Niko heaves a huge sigh, pinching the bridge between his nose.

"Is something the matter?" I ask, my cheeks stinging from plastering a polite smile all evening.

He removes his hand and meets my gaze. "I don't think any of these men are good for you, Tee."

Even I knew that going into this week of celebration.

I want to brush off his comment and tell him I will find someone, yet I don't stop myself from asking, "What makes you say that?"

His jaw works. "You need someone who is going to put your needs and the kingdom's above their own. Someone willing to make tough calls for governing this kingdom. *And* it wouldn't hurt to have them skilled in combat. But most importantly, they need to be completely devoted to you."

With three glasses of wine loosening my tongue, I am a glutton for punishment. "Huh." I pause, then lean into my poor attempts at flirting. "That sounds like you."

"No! No, that's not what I meant!" Niko's cheeks redden.

I bite back my own grin, the sight of him blushing sweeter than any wine.

"Are you sure? It *certainly* sounds like it to me," I push, wanting to keep his blush there a little longer.

"What's that supposed to mean?" Niko bristles at the bite in his voice, looking around in hopes our conversation is not being overheard.

His cheeks remain red, and I can't stop my toothy grin as I go on. "You say no one is good enough for me, but I am beginning to believe this whole *grumbling* process is because you want to be in their shoes."

"Tee."

Niko's voice comes out in a breathy whisper.

I brush off his impending rejection, reassuring him with a gentle pat on his hand.

"Don't worry, Niko, I know you don't have any interest in me." I chuckle, my head buzzing as a small truth slips through. "But I hope you understand, in my eyes, no one is like you. I enjoy your company immensely, but you are the one who told me I needed to find a husband, so you can't have me all to yourself anymore."

Niko blinks rapidly, stunned by this revelation. He latches on to my hand, all jokes set aside as he stammers through those adorably red cheeks. "You—You enjoy my company?"

A change in the air from his stutter has me inching closer, wanting to tell him yes. The lust and thought of him drown my senses.

But I swallow quickly, searching his eyes for any tells, any signs.

My mouth parts, trying to formulate words—

"Queen Tove!" a joyous voice booms from the ballroom.

I beam toward it.

Bernard Sylvaine, the King of Belmur, approaches the dais with the light of the room reflecting off him.

He is a kind man, reminding me so much of my father, except for his fading red hair and sun-kissed freckles. His beard is lighter, trimmed close to his jaw, moving, as his grandiose laugh echoes through the ballroom's conversations. His height and bloated belly can be intimidating, and he uses it to his advantage, forcing guests to steer clear of him.

"King Bernard," I say when he reaches the dais. "Thank you so much for coming this evening."

It is hard to hide my enthusiasm around King Bernard. He makes everyone want to feel loved and carefree.

"Oh, come now," he says through a genuine smile, offering me an overexaggerated bow before rising to his full height. "How many times must I tell you, Tove? Call me Bernie. We are well past that, don't you think?"

Bernie's kingdom was one of the first to reach out after my accession to the throne, offering visits and words of wisdom in every trade meeting I coordinated with him. His poor wife, Johanne, passed away a few years back, leaving his twin daughters without their mother.

Bernie's glee is purely infectious, a cathartic lightness that consumes me as I reply, "Very well, *Bernie*. But only amongst each other. No need for others to hear us breaking protocol."

I find enjoyment in the moments when he visits our kingdom because, in his presence, I don't feel like a monster—I don't believe I am the Snow Queen.

When inviting the other kingdoms in Draymenk, I knew Belmur and Unterkirch would be the only two in attendance this week. They are the ones I have the closest working relationship with.

I am on friendly terms with King Beauvais Rosselot of Torgem, but he always seems busy, given most letters I receive are from his advisors rather than him. Then there are Queen Zarina and King Vinzent Geissler of Northtry, who remain distant. But according to my parents, they have always been like that, only attending and joining meetings when all kingdoms call.

And the last kingdom, Palaena...

Stop it. Don't dwell on them, Tove. Don't sour your mood around watchful eyes.

One of Bernie's daughters, Princess Vivienne, promenades from behind her father, dipping into a curtsy.

Her tall, lean frame nears her father's height, with a heart-shaped face buried beneath long, wavy locks red as a rose. She does not have freckles, but her skin, too, is kissed by sunlight. She is polite and mindful, always keeping to herself while wearing the same inquisitive look I see now.

I dip my head. "Princess Vivienne, such a pleasure to have you here joining your father."

Her emerald-green eyes meet mine as she rises to her full stature, assessing. "The pleasure is all mine, Queen Tove." She beams.

Bernie's pride shines through as he looks upon his daughter, and I can't help but feel a tinge of pain at witnessing the love exchanged between the two.

She catches his stare, sheepishly pulling some hair around her face.

A cough from Niko at my side reminds me I am not as alone as I think. Shaking off the tug of pain and maintaining appearances, I smile back at my guests. "Is your sister in attendance?"

Vivienne is about to speak, but her father's voice booms over hers. "Oh, come now, Tove. Someone needed to watch over our borders."

"And you trust your daughter to do that for you?" Niko asks.

I bristle at Niko's question, shocked he would ask such a thing to one of our allies.

Vivienne shrinks inward as Bernie huffs.

"I trust each of my daughters wholeheartedly to look over their home with my advisors," Bernie says, his voice lowering as he crosses his arms.

"As you should!" I interject with my false smile on display. "You are the best judge of character."

Bernie laughs. "Right, you are there, Tove!"

A twinkle of amusement tugs at Princess Vivienne's face, and I take that as a good omen. Maybe we could be close friends, especially if I got her to react.

Niko extends his hand to the crowd. "We hope you'll find the music and refreshments enjoyable. We are so grateful to have Belmur represented during the celebrations."

"Yes," I blurt into the conversation. "Although I do need to converse with other guests. We shall have to visit more throughout the week while you are here."

Bernie's mouth parts, but Vivienne beats her father in response. "My father and I would love that. Thank you again for your hospitality, Your Majesty."

She curtsies again as the King of Belmur bobs his head toward me.

He extends an arm to his daughter. "I'll be sure to save you a dance, Tove," Bernie says over his shoulder as he descends the dais.

"I look forward to it, Your Majesty." I beam once more before letting my face fall and glare at Niko.

I elbow his side.

He winces and raises his hands in surrender, knowing he did something wrong. "I know, I know," he starts. "I shouldn't have said that."

"What were you thinking!?"

"I wasn't thinking. I—" He pauses. "I was distracted."

I raise my brow. "Distracted? Is everything alright?"

Someone coughs at the edge of the dais.

Our heads slowly turn, and the hair on the back of my neck rises at the tall, athletic man standing before me.

His height surpasses Niko's, his lean frame contrasting with Niko's broad stature. But even from afar, the man's muscles peek through his all-black ensemble.

His warm beige complexion is a stark contrast to his onyx shoulder-length hair. It is pulled half-back, with small wisps framing the man's cheekbones and sculpted jaw. There is a slight wave to it, making it seem messy from afar.

But I bet if I were to run my fingers through it, it would feel luxurious and delicate.

And when I catch the center of his face, my breath hitches.

One scar runs down the center of his eye, making me wish to know the tale behind it. And when I meet his piercing stare, I swear to Yeva his eyes are of the same icy depths I prefer to avoid, only rawer and more intense, like a ragged glacier.

The scarred man I bumped into earlier is more intimidating up close. Especially with his lips...

Sweet Makers.

He looks closer to a freaking deity than a man.

Niko squeezes my arm, reminding me of my role to play.

I don't know if he is someone who received an invitation about my search for a husband or a guest wishing to converse, but I beckon him forward regardless, my gaze remaining locked on his as if breaking contact will sever my chances of learning more about this stranger.

The man is silent through each intentional step forward, and I am at a loss for words.

"Good evening. Thank you for joining us in tonight's festivities."

Niko's voice grounds me as I square my shoulders.

I avoid the sensation of Niko's gaze burning into the side of my cheek as the mystery man's eyes never leave mine.

When the handsome man lowers to one knee, I lean away with alarm. But he takes my hand regardless, kissing my knuckles.

Flames erupt and shoot up my entire arm from where his lips meet my skin.

The man's eyes glint as he smirks.

I blink in astonishment.

Why do I feel like I am melting into my throne from the sheer gaze of this stranger?

Don't combust, Tove. You have appearances to maintain.

The scarred man then winks as his thumb rubs a circle over the top of my hand, the heat underneath my skin abruptly cut off by the burst of ice shooting out in my veins.

My heart plummets as the brisk kiss of frost creeps down my stomach.

The man notices something is awry and steps away, studying me with an arched brow.

I feign a tight-lipped smile, trying to calm my magic. But it stirs vigorously, not having escaped from my fingertips in such a long time. An itch needing relief.

I can't do this here.

I spare a glance at Niko, hoping my worried expression will be enough of an explanation, but he is preoccupied with studying the man instead of me.

"I-I need to be excused," I blurt, rising and disregarding a formal departure.

I rush for the back room, thankful of its proximity to the throne.

By the time I close the door, the force of the winter prickles against my skin so much I try to scratch it away... but it persists.

Shit. Shit. Shit. Shit!

I can get this to stop. I know I can. But the urge to let it out feels too good, and for a moment, I'm tempted to indulge in it. *No.*

I can't.

The hearth blazes with fire, the cracking of wood burning and shooting embers upward as I pace in circles behind the red couch.

The mantel is barren, trinkets of value removed in fear of someone untrustworthy sneaking in here during the party. But the mural painted across the back wall, depicting a gathering of people, feels as if those eyes, too, are watching me.

I try to distract myself, my fear getting the better of me at the dark thoughts even as I try to breathe. I thread my fingers through my hair, but nothing makes my magic ebb. When I run over a sore spot on my scalp from my crown, I hiss.

The door bursts open as Niko rushes in, almost hurdling over the couch. "What's wrong?" Niko demands with worry in his features.

He pins my arms to my side as he looks me over.

Shame draws forth tears, and all I can do to keep them at bay is hide from his gaze.

No one should be seeing me like this. Not even Niko.

"Did he hurt you?" He pats my arms, checking for any signs of weakness before meeting my gaze. "I *swear* I will kill him if he hurt you, Tee."

My brows furrow at his question and threat. I shake my head in earnest, hoping it is enough to warn him away.

The Snow Queen is awake.

"It's my magic," I blurt.

Niko stills as I scramble to get the words out faster than I can formulate. "I was fine one moment and then the next—I don't know, but something happened. I was warm and then I was cold."

Niko's face turns grave, and before he can flinch away, I fold into myself and collapse on the couch. I stare into the fire, studying the flickering of the light casting shadows on the wood floor while trying to stop my gifts from expelling.

"I can direct the guests outside early for the fireworks in the courtyard, and you can go down the front hall so you can be away from everyone," Niko offers, still standing and hovering near me.

I nod silently.

"It'll be alright, Tee. You've handled this before." Niko moves his hand to rest on me, but he hesitates and steps away.

That hesitation has tears blurring my vision, agony ripping through me at the monster I am.

I try to offer an explanation. "Niko, wait—"

The flash of fear behind his amber eyes cracks my heart.

I tuck my pain deep down, masking it with indifference. "Thank you," I force out.

He dips his head, promptly returning to the throne room as the first tear cascades down my cheek.

I wait a few moments, trying to calm myself, and hope that sitting while evening out my breaths will ease the power rippling through my body. The tug of control between myself and my magic is a constant war.

I rub my hands together and resume pacing. Maybe wearing down the wooden planks might make me feel like I accomplished something.

I glance between the two entrances, one to the throne room and the other a door that leads to the secret halls.

The ballroom would be faster, but I find myself incapable of waiting for the throne room to empty.

So, I brave the hidden halls that are built to run parallel with other hallways of the castle, opting for the lit path that will take me to the front entryway, knowing no one will see me escaping for the fields beyond while watching the fireworks in the courtyard.

I wait in silence when I reach the end of the tunnel, opening the door when it feels safe. A few beats pass, and I slink through, unnoticed, the threshold for the entrance coming into view. A whoosh of relief washes over me as I made it here without running into anyone.

The crisp, cold air blows in, drying the light sweat beaded on my brow. Heaviness guides my stare upward to the dark night sky.

I reach for a nearby lantern to take with me, but I hiss, my hand burning from touching the hot metal. I shake my hand in frustration, a poor attempt to make the pain go away.

Too self-absorbed that my ignorance thought it safe to play with fire.

I swear to Yeva, if I could get my powers to stop, I—

Wait...

Awareness of warmth instead of cold has me pause, peering down at my reddening hand.

Did that stop my magic?

An explosion of sound from the right of the castle jolts me back a step.

I clutch my burned hand to my chest, covering my pumping heart as each firework shoots into the sky.

They illuminate the stars and night in blues, reds, and yellows. Shapes form in the distance as the ear-piercing noise of each pop has me covering my ears.

I marvel in awe alone, grateful I could be by myself and not act indifferent to the presentation.

The staccato rhythm of each firework builds as the finale progresses, fireworks trilling in rapid succession as the pinnacle of the symphony ceases in an arpeggiated chord.

The world halts.

Applause erupts from the courtyard, telling me my distraction has run out.

Glancing down and seeing my skin welting, I wait to sense if the chill comes back. When it doesn't, I find myself amused and in debt to this little bit of pain.

I apply pressure over the burn, blowing on it with my breath, hoping to prevent the tightening sting I will feel for the next few days.

The sounds of music resume in the ballroom, and guests returning echo down the hall.

I look to the night sky once more, sending a prayer of gratitude to the Makers for saving me from disaster.

I back away from the threshold, my posterior making contact with something hard.

4

ATTRACTION IS MADDENING

Instinctively, I shield my face as I stumble forward.

But when I don't meet the ground, I glance down, noticing hands that are not mine wrapped around my waist. I am quickly twisted, and my vision plays catch-up as I come face to face with the mysterious man from earlier.

Not who I was expecting to run into.

His ice-cold eyes survey me darkly as a rich cologne drowns my senses.

I stumble through each inhalation of his intoxicating scent. "F-Forgive me, my lord."

He squeezes my sides quickly, helping me upright. The warmth from his touch expands from my waist downward.

I brush my hands on my dress, trying to conceal my skin heating.

Calm yourself, Tove.

As I tug my dress and sweep the fabric, I catch the man's shoes, noticing the dark stain surrounding the edges. Lifting my brows, I wonder who arrives at a ball with stained boots?

His low, sultry voice pulls me from my question.

"I'm glad I was able to save you, My Queen." He blatantly scans my full body, blue eyes lingering on my chest and hips before returning to my gaze.

I copy him, not letting my intimidation by him deter me.

"Yes," I say in my cold voice, but I ease my tone a bit, gambling on letting a little vulnerability through. "Thank you for that. I would have been in trouble."

A crooked smirk appears with a perfect dimple pierced in the side of his cheek. "You are the queen, right?"

"Yes?" I am unsure of where he is going with his question.

He looks around before leaning in, waving at me to do the same, as if he were wishing to share a secret.

I oblige him, dipping my head slightly.

His voice, so soft and dangerous, whispers, "Then, who would you be in trouble with?"

A snort breaks out, and I cover my mouth when his eyes widen in surprise.

Sweet Makers, I should not have let that laugh slip.

I should go back to the party and find Niko. Or maybe I should make a run for my room now to save me from causing any more disasters around this man and anyone else this evening.

The idea of hiding away tugs at me regardless of the trouble I could get into with Niko about abandoning the party too early. But obligation and everyone's happiness weighs on my shoulders, and I should cut my losses here with this man, my embarrassment killing my chances for me.

Glancing back to the party, I mentally prepare myself for my return. "I should probably head back there. Thank you again for your assistance." I move to sidestep him, only to pause by the soft touch at my elbow.

"May I escort you back?" he asks, all jokes tossed aside.

I am unsure why I agree, but his lips lift as he takes my hand and drapes it over his arm. The effort is smooth and gallant, making me wonder where he comes from.

We saunter down the hall in silence, my nerves and thoughts already ten steps ahead while I think of how everyone will take my return as we drift into the brightly lit ballroom.

Guests hover near the entrance, bowing as we stroll past.

I refrain from warning my escort of my nickname, assuming he already is well versed on my reputation. But even through maintaining my regal appearance, I catch the man sneaking glances at me.

"If you are feeling alright, would you join me for a dance?" he asks.

As much as I want to sit and forget my little mishap, I can't turn down a chance to dance. I dip my head, letting him lead me to the dance floor.

We wait on the sidelines for the music to end with the rest of the crowd when Queen Verena Lorenz of Unterkirch approaches with her daughter, Princess Sybille, in tow.

Both the mother and daughter have long raven hair adorned with small, jeweled tiaras. Their hair, pinned half up, highlights their resemblance. Pointed chin, straight nose, and sharp jawline.

The preteen Sybille is already a spitting image of her mother, save for her eyes. They are brown and doe shaped, holding wonder behind them.

Her mother, however, is stone faced and serious. She looks older than her years, with her gray eyes still reflecting the mourning of her long-deceased husband.

"Your Majesty," I extend in greeting to Queen Verena, lowering my head. My dance partner bows in kindness and echoes me.

Queen Verena politely smiles. "Queen Tove, a pleasure to be here."

Princess Sybille scoops up the sides of her dress, offering me a graceful curtsy. The princess's happiness turns giddy when she returns upright.

Princess Sybille's angelic voice sings, "Mother! You never told me arranged marriages bring together such beautiful couples!"

The Queen of Unterkirch's eyes widen as her mouth falls, and my dance partner and I stiffen.

"We—We aren't—"

Queen Verena steps forward. "I am so sorry, Queen Tove. You'll have to forgive my daughter." She whirls on Princess Sybille, anger rolling off her in swirls as she smacks her daughter's hand in reprimand.

The young girl bristles, holding her hand to her chest, lowering her face to the floor.

Queen Verena looks at my partner and me apologetically. "She hasn't been well since her father passed, and she sees the toll his death takes on me. Her hopeful heart wants everyone to be together and happy."

My heart is heavy for Princess Sybille, the loss of a parent is a mournful path. She is approaching her teenage years, and it plucks a somber song in my soul to know she has already faced grief.

Her brown eyes meet mine, water lining them.

Knowing the pain she is feeling, I hate she was deprived of the happiness she had mere moments ago. I extend my hand to the princess.

She takes it cautiously as I beam down. "No one will be as beautifully coupled as you and your future husband."

Her expression lifts from cheek to cheek as she grins. "You hear that, Mother! Another queen thinks I am beautiful like you!"

The queen smirks at her daughter, extending her gratitude. "A pleasure as always, Queen Tove."

"And you as well, Queen Verena." I incline my head.

Queen Verena glances at the man beside me.

Is he from a visiting kingdom? Maybe he is one of her subjects?

He remains still, not speaking a word since the princess spoke.

A devious smirk of what could be approval lines the queen's features as she retreats from us, and I can't hide the blush heating my cheeks.

The classical song ends, and when the dancing ceases, new couples take their places in the next dance.

My escort moves with a silent grace, drawing me close in our position and giving my hip a squeeze.

My pulse quickens.

We break into a lively waltz, my demeanor lifting when our chests press together, our gazes melting further into one another.

"That was kind of you to say to the princess," my dance partner remarks.

I shrug as we pivot around other guests. "Everyone deserves to be called beautiful, no matter their age."

"And what if someone were to call you beautiful?"

My heart swells at the question, possibly believing, for once, someone might see me as that.

His scar pinches from his closed smile, and I can't help the ease of a joke and flirtation when I say back, "I am sure I would react the same as you would if someone said that to you."

The man's smile reaches his eyes, and we both chuckle.

I replay the steps needed for this song as we move effortlessly into the waltz.

The more we dance, the more my body unwinds. My heart calls to the natural harmonic strings, wishing I could have had its paired score to play on the piano.

But reality crashes in, darkening the joy I once had for music, my piano now frozen over and locked away in the coldest parts of my home.

I falter a step, grateful it goes unnoticed by my dance partner, who pushes us onward.

Dance, spin, repeat, Tove. Do not step on his toes.

I repeat the mantra in my mind as the room spins, everyone fading into the background.

The three-step circle leads us into a lift, and horror crawls up my throat at anyone picking me up. A wave of dizziness arrives as I brace for my dance partner to drop me, but when the air shifts out from under me, I barely have time to take in how he did it with such ease.

He spins me, but it is his smooth voice that pulls me back in. "Will you tell me if this spinning makes you dizzy? Or will you maintain appearances until after the song is over?"

My face falls at his forthright question. "That's not something I am asked often."

"Did I need to ask you a more formal question?"

I contemplate a response but find myself surprised by the brazen question and enjoying it. "No, it is refreshing, actually."

"Talking with you is refreshing," he gushes with a wink.

Sweet Makers, this fucking man.

He lifts me again, this time drawing a startled gasp from me when my feet meet the ground.

I find myself wanting to return his boldness and learn more about him. "Since we are not being formal in our questions, how did you get that scar?"

I flick my attention to it.

He tenses, and instinctively, I wish I could take it back, realizing I struck a nerve. "I'm sorry, I—" I am cut off by him gripping my hip.

A dark thought has me wishing his smooth voice could talk me through vile thoughts.

"A story to be saved for next time," he says.

I scoff, unable to hide my disappointment. "What makes you think there will be a next time?"

A lone dimple makes an appearance, followed by a low chuckle that vibrates through my bones. The same tender touch of his thumb rubs circles over my knuckles, drawing a slight tug at an old memory.

Runa used to do that for me.

I frown, the energy between us souring.

The song concludes, and my question goes unanswered.

But I find myself not wanting our interaction to end. I try to think of something else to say to keep him near, but I lose my chance when he releases me, pulling all the warmth with him as he lowers into a bow.

I extend my thanks, frustrated over ruining an interaction with someone I actually enjoyed and felt myself with.

When his blue eyes meet mine, I realize I never got his name. Is it too foolish to ask after our dance?

"What shall I call you?" I ask hastily, needing to know.

His lip quirks up at the side as he takes my hand.

Staring me down through his brow as his lips meet my knuckles, he says, "Call me yours."

My heart somersaults at his words as I move closer, drawing air from my lungs. My feet remain planted to the ground as his coy smirk never leaves his face.

"Until tomorrow, My Queen," he purrs, releasing my hand and retreating backward.

My insides flex as my dance partner shifts through the crowds, disappearing into the shadows. I am about to chase after him, but a new presence from behind halts my efforts.

Niko comes up to my side, his displeasure making me wary. "I've been looking everywhere for you."

"I was dancing," I explain, my eyes still focused on the spot where I last saw the scarred man.

He remains silent, scanning the crowd beside me as I look beyond the windows, taking in the star-filled sky.

"I think I should head to bed. It's been—" I release a long, exhausted breath. "It's been a long day."

"I'll walk you back to your room," Niko offers me his arm.

I take it as we say our good nights to the guests.

Our footsteps are silent against the marbled tile as we drift past the peaked archways that frame tall floor-to-ceiling windows. The stairs leading to the higher levels of the castle are lined with dark-red rugs, and lanterns hang every few feet.

"Tee?"

Niko's voice pulls my attention from the rug up to his face.

"Yes?" I ask as we climb the stairs, heading for the royal wings.

"Who was that man you danced with earlier?"

"I don't know. He never told me his name."

I almost miss the tension leaving his body as we inch closer to my rooms.

"Ah, playing the whole *mystery man* tactic?"

I snort, knowing he hit the target. "Something like that."

A grin appears as we climb up the stairs faster than I am used to, hating the height difference between the two of us. Chest tightening at the change of pace, I grip my dress as I concentrate on my steps, always struggling to keep up with Niko's long strides.

"What happened, then? Why do I feel like you are so distant?"

I hesitate in my response, unsure of the distance he is talking about. But I replay my interaction with the mystery man from earlier, remembering his soft touches and the circles that reminded me of my sister.

Just like that, another little dose of happiness vanishes to be replaced with misery.

I deflate as the brief glimpse of joy dwindles away, allowing my darkness to consume me. I glower and find myself cracking apart at the seams as we pass up the final step to my rooms at the end of the hall.

Niko pulls me to a stop, dragging me away from the blizzard I battle internally. "Tee?" Concern weighs down on his brow as I scratch the side of my fingers in distraction.

"I was thinking about Runa," I confess, avoiding his eyes.

Suddenly, I am embraced by the soothing scents of sandalwood. I melt into it, closing my eyes and placing my arms around Niko.

Deities, he is so soft.

Thoughts wander as I lean against his chest. It is as if he holds and protects me from the world. I dream of these days so often, every day, of having him so close to me like this. My lungs finally exhale when Niko's huge arms squeeze me once more.

Why can't it always be this easy?

When we break away, he forces my gaze up to him. I still when his thumb strokes the side of my jaw.

He leans in through a hushed whisper. "I don't want you to think about Runa right now."

My eyes widen as his eyes close, lips mere inches from mine. I lick mine in earnest as lust explodes in my stomach. Nerves rapid firing, I feel as if he might kiss me.

Sweet Makers, this could be my first kiss.

I've fantasized about kissing this man for years, but an ache pulses against my chest as I hesitate.

Am I reading him all wrong? Is this part of our game?

What if he is just as tired as I am and is closing his eyes because he, too, is exhausted?

Oh, Sweet Makers, what is the matter with you, Tove? Just KISS him!

I-I... I can't.

Deities, I can't believe I am a fucking coward. I inwardly groan as I guide his hand slowly, *painfully*, away from my face. I drop my head and close my eyes, trying to sear this memory into my brain, knowing all too well I am most likely hallucinating.

This will never happen again. A memory I will have to use in future fantasies.

I avert my eyes from his gaze, reaching for the door to my chambers.

"Tee," he starts, and I halt. "Before you leave, I need you to do something for me."

Curiosity gets the better of me. "What is it, Niko?"

His lip curves up as he grabs my hand, placing it on his chest.

I swallow the lump forming when he traces along my palm, hoping he cannot see the goose bumps he is causing.

His soft voice is swiftly replaced by a hard sternness. "Don't talk to the last man you danced with."

"Why?" I tug my hand back and fold my arms.

He straightens his posture, mimicking my stance, and peers down. Somehow, I can't tell if this is coming from Niko, my friend, or Nikolaj, my advisor.

He clears his throat. "You can have anyone. Just not *him*."

My brow lifts in suspicion. "Are you... Are you jealous?"

A boisterous laugh escapes him, oscillating through my skull as it skitters down the stairs.

When he catches his breath, he spits out, "Jealous? Why would I be jealous?"

Embarrassment blooms within me, and the building lust fizzles faster than it formed. I should have known better. Of course he wouldn't like me like that. He was probably feeling pity earlier.

And now?

Now he is probably trying to *protect* me.

"Fine!" I throw my hands up in the air in frustration, fueling my anger to shield against the rejection he dangled in front of my face.

I will not let myself be fooled by him any longer.

"Tove—"

"Good night, *Nikolaj*," I seethe through clenched teeth.

I rip myself away from the hall, slamming my door behind me without a second thought.

My heart hangs on for the hope he will shout and profess his feelings for me, but the angry tears running down my cheeks tell me the harsh truth I have yet to face.

He doesn't love me.

And if he doesn't love me, someone who has known me for years, then who ever would?

I rub my eyes and sniff. I should have known better. I should have known he wouldn't care beyond our friendship. And I hate that the romantic feelings have always been there for me.

Niko has a presence and support that sucks everyone in. He reels me in every time and radiates sunshine and life.

I don't deserve it after everything I've done, but the storm clouds lessen when he is around.

It is getting harder and harder to separate emotions in our conversations. I brush the dampness on my cheeks away, wipe the excess off my dress, and slink out of it, debating whether I should ring for my staff.

No, I just want to forget this entire night happened.

Exhaustion has me too lazy to remove my undergarments, a light slip to give my body a smooth appearance with the gown I wore tonight.

Frustration has me careless of my hair and my crown. I rip it away, pins and all, unflinching, and toss it on my vanity.

I barely sigh when I kick off my shoes, the soles of my feet cushioned on the fleece rug.

I trudge to my bed, pulling the sheets back, and collapse, dragging my pillow tight. My tears dampen the linen as I find myself wishing for the mystery man's company over everyone else's at this moment.

5

ANOTHER BLOODY MOON

The sun's rays illuminate through my bedchamber, and as if right on cue, the hum of a good morning comes from my lady-in-waiting and childhood friend, Betina.

Letum damn you.

"It is time to wake up now, Tove," she says.

Squinting through my half-closed eyes, my friend serenades through her morning tasks.

Betina's coiled black hair is plaited at the base of her neck. Her hair rests over her left shoulder, while the swaying of her dress brings out the rich, glowing undertones in her sienna skin. Her graceful appearance beats mine, always looking youthful and showing no signs of aging.

She could easily pass as royalty herself.

And though her height surpasses mine, our love for pastries and wine grants us similar curves.

She comes up, lightly tapping the tops of my feet. "We must get you ready for this evening," she sings in her soprano voice.

I jerk my eyes open, scowling at her mischievous grin.

Betina's family comes from a long line of nobility and was always close to mine. In our youth, she befriended Runa and me.

But our relationship amplified when I asked her if she would move into the castle and be my lady-in-waiting.

And in becoming my constant companion, she has basked in my snowstorm, always taking my hand and supporting me through everything. Always ready to help guide me through the void of grief.

I treasure her.

Even as my lady-in-waiting, she lessens my load by coordinating my schedule, bringing me news and paperwork with any pressing issues Niko needs me to address.

But after the wreckage of last night still playing in the back of my mind, I have no care to even contemplate how tonight will fare. Smacking my hands on the sides of the bed, I lean up to rest on my elbows, giving her a pointed stare.

"Two words, Betina. *This. Evening*," I tell her, flopping on my pillow and grabbing a second one to shield my eyes.

If I could get a few more hours of sleep, maybe my mood will improve.

Her sigh of frustration forces a grin to appear as I hide underneath my pillow. I don't hear her footsteps near my bedside as she whisks the cushion out from under me.

As she hovers above me, annoyance brims in the depths of her chestnut eyes.

"*Tove*."

I give it right back to her, asserting my leadership. "*Betina*."

We remain unmoving in our stare down, waiting to see who will break first. I really want to sleep and not undergo long hours of getting ready and discussing my... *options*. I met a few nobles last night, but none took to me as much as Niko and the scarred man.

Sweet Makers, *please* don't make me resort to choosing Ulrik.

Betina's eyes soften, and I know my authority won over. It always does. She lets out a lighthearted laugh, playfully smacking the pillow across my face.

"*Fine*," she concedes. "Let me bring up some food, at least."

A chuckle escapes as I lift the pillow and coo, "And that's why I love you."

She hums and circles around the bed, passing through the threshold and pausing. "I love you, too."

The creaking sound of the door closing grants me solitude, and I savor these few extra minutes of relaxation. I slump, tossing and turning to seek comfort.

But with the sunlight draping across my bed, it limits the positions I can rest my eyes without its rays beaming in my face.

I roll to my back, staring at the dark canopy of curtain draped over my bed.

My situation diminishes any hope I have of returning to sleep.

Weight presses against my chest, and the desperation to appease everyone has tension rolling down my spine. I need to find a suitor *tonight.* No matter how badly I wish Niko would take an interest in me...

He is your friend, Tove. He is looking out for you and the kingdom.

I grumble in frustrated defeat. If only it were that easy.

As I try to rise, my lower abdomen spasms, followed by a low rumbling. *Great.*

I hover my legs over the edge of my bed as I press myself upward. Yet as soon as my feet touch the ground, I shrivel from the twisting in my stomach.

A stream of bile eases up my throat as I brace a hand against the pain. I cover my mouth with my other hand, hoping to keep it down.

Groaning, I knew it was stupid to wish everything would go smoothly this week.

My bleeding is supposed to happen monthly, but it has become sporadic these past few years, creating difficulty in planning for its impending arrival. I am lucky if I get my cycle every three new moons. Thankfully, my first days didn't involve much bleeding. Most of the time, I exhibit light spotting, and it's not even the blood that bothers me.

It's that the start of every cycle brings rigorous pain and nausea.

Every. Single. Time.

Unable to keep the bile down, I scramble to the chamber pot in the bathing room, applying pressure against my stomach. The cramping increases with each step.

I could alert a staff member for assistance and medicine through the string of bells, designed for a method of communication, but I barely make it in the privy before collapsing on the cold ground.

Reaching for the chamber pot, I empty my insides, and exhaustion weighs on me.

Ugh.

The chill of the marbled floor beneath grants me a brief reprieve before I proceed with emptying my stomach. *Again.*

Fuck, everything hurts.

The back of my eyes, my head, and Sweet Makers, my throat.

The invasion of nausea subsides, and I try to gather strength to move, but fatigue has the world spinning. Cold sweat beads down the sides of my face as I lay on my side, hugging my knees to my chest, my cheek resting against the tiled floor.

I can lie here until my energy comes back. Maybe at least till some of the pain is more manageable.

My eyes are heavy from exhaustion when the hinges on a door squeak.

That must be Betina.

Too exhausted to speak, I focus on her movements, the sound of her placing a platter on my vanity near my bathing chamber distracting my thoughts.

"Breakfast is on your vanity!" She shouts into the quiet of my bedchamber.

A few seconds pass, and her worried tone yanks me back to reality. "Tove?"

Voice scratchy, I call back, "In here."

Pain erupts, and it takes everything in me to not scream.

It's just a monthly bleeding, Tove. It'll be fine. You'll be fine. Everything will be fine.

Footsteps inch closer to the bathing chamber, and I brace myself for discovery.

"Oh, just wait till you see the dress I picked out for you for tonight's festivit—"

She cuts off with a scream, and I cringe, wincing in pain. Betina's eyes widen as they survey me. She rushes to me and places a hand on my forehead.

"Oh, Sweet Makers, Tove! Are you alright?"

The coldness of her touch has me leaning in as I try to muster words. But my abdomen spasms again, punishing me for trying to relax.

I shrink inwardly when I meet her gaze.

"Let me get some help," she says, rocking on her heels to stand.

"Wait!" I try to blurt after her, but my voice runs dry.

Caution prickles up my spine as seconds pass before the sound of footsteps fills my chambers again. And somehow, I know in my bones it is Niko.

The man I have feelings for—but try to *not* have feelings for—fills in the doorway, watching me clutch a chamber pot for dear life.

Real smooth, Tove.

Betina hovers beside Niko, apologetically grimacing. "He heard me holler your name."

He glares at her before surveying me, and it takes everything to make it appear like the floor is where I'm meant to be.

When I peer up at Niko, he isn't even looking at me.

He is looking at my chest.

My eyes widen in mortification as the slip I wear is thin and sheer. Agony explodes in my lower stomach when I try to cover myself even more.

Betina squeezes through the opening, kneeling and stroking hair from my face. "Oh, dear, the pain must be bad this time around."

"What do you mean? What is wrong with her?" Niko asks.

It is not any of his business to know the details of my cycle, so I ignore his question.

I grip onto Betina, keeping her deepened umber eyes fixed on me, trying to convey I don't want him to know anything. Especially with last night still hanging over me.

But worry lines Betina's features, and my heart tugs.

I garner my strength to reassure her, struggling to form a cohesive sentence.

Trembling through each word, I tell her, "I just need food and medicine. I'll be fine, Betina."

She combs through my hair, the soothing touch dulling the pain. I close my eyes in gratitude as she wipes the sweat from my brow. Deities, what would I do without her?

Her lips meet my forehead as she whispers, "I'll fetch you some medicine with honey to pair with the food I brought up."

Betina's warmth leaves me, taking the brief relief with her. I contort in pain, not from my monthly bleeding but from my lady-in-waiting leaving me alone with *him*.

Niko leans against the doorframe. "Is this because you had wine last night?"

I want to protect my heart right now and *not* think about last night. But anger rolls through me as he crosses his arms, and I can't even mask away my embarrassment as a twist of my insides sends me reeling.

I hiss, "It's not that. It's my cycle."

"Oh," he says into the quiet.

I blink slowly through my breath evening as Niko's eyebrows shoot up. "*Oh.*"

Spouting a laugh, I agree, "Yeah, *OH.*"

I flinch as the gnawing in my ovaries grows from an aching sensation to a punching one. I shrink into myself more, wishing it is enough of a dismissal to Niko.

Instead, his baritone voice comes out in a tender whisper. "What can I do?"

I want to let go of last night, and the damn contractions of my muscles have me admitting more than I would like to. Playing tough, I fight against my heart for wanting to let him off easy.

"Don't worry about it. I can manage," I grit out.

He lowers, his hands moving underneath my body.

I remove a hand from my stomach to push him away, but a spasm of punches rips through me. Tears well in my eyes as I lower them from Niko.

"I'm fine. Just a few minutes and then I will get up," I say, reassuring myself more than him.

He scoots his hands underneath me again.

"What are you doing?" I shriek as my weight shifts from the cold floor of my bathing room into Niko's arms.

"I'm taking matters into my own hands," he says nonchalantly.

"I said I don't need any help!"

I am completely mortified.

Nope. No. Definitely not.

He acts unbothered by my declaration as he stands with me in his arms. "Tee, you can barely remove your hand from your abdomen without crying. The least I can do is help you get to your bed."

"But I am indecent!"

His eyes dart to me, taking in every detail of my body, and arousal runs to the apex of my thighs.

I am not supposed to be feeling this, *especially* right now. It does not matter how comforting he feels.

"Like that is a good enough excuse," he scoffs.

He cradles me in his arms, walking us through the doorway to my cluttered room. Since Betina had no chance to attend to my mess, last night's attire is still scattered across the floor.

I hide my shame only for a hint of sandalwood to embrace me.

Niko approaches the side of my bed, lowering me on the mattress.

My attention focuses on his hands gliding out from under me. How they graze underneath my ass cheek.

Sweet Makers, what it would feel like to have those hands spread me.

I study him as he pulls the sheets over my body. Desire itches against my legs, and I clench my thighs tight, trying to dismiss the thoughts.

His face is so close to mine, and tenderness swirls across his features.

"Better?" he asks.

Fuck, does he melt away my fury. Gulping, I nod sheepishly.

"Good." He grins, and my heart skips.

The upturn of his lips brings one to my own as he double-checks my bedding, ensuring it cocoons me.

I reach for him. I don't want him to leave.

"Would you stay with me?" I ask, squeezing his hand once.

He arches his brow, pressing his lips in hesitation.

Remembering last night's rejection, I clarify, "Just until Betina comes back?"

Niko's eyes gleam as he streaks a hand through his wavy red hair. Looking between me and the door, he slackens his posture.

But a grin graces his features as he says, "Let me go to the other side."

His long legs help him ease onto the bed, and he lies atop the covers and scoots toward me. Niko's shoulder touches mine while I focus on holding my insides as they war with themselves.

We lie there in silence.

A loud exhale comes from Niko, and I face him, taking in his proximity and the tic in his squared jaw. "Should we announce you are not attending tonight's festivities?"

His question gives me pause.

If we do, it limits my time and options and could drive my people further into justifying their nickname for me. Suffering through the pain to prove them wrong and find someone is the least I can do.

"I don't think we should. I need to show some consistency, especially with all the shit I've pulled."

Niko rolls toward me and tucks a piece of my silver hair behind my ear.

My heart thuds loud against my chest when Niko's hand doesn't leave.

"I am proud of you, Tee."

My blood warms, and I lean into his palm. "For what?"

"It's just—it's an honor to serve you."

"Niko—"

I quiet when his lips caress my forehead.

Warmth expands, heating my cheeks, and I hate that I am blushing. But adoration forms on my face, the resentment from last night lessening even more now.

As if he, too, knows this, he beams.

"Thank you," I whisper.

"Anything for you, Tee. But the second you start showing signs of pain at the party, I am kicking everyone out."

I chuckle before another spasm explodes, hissing while holding myself for a few minutes, looking guiltily at him.

"Rest." He peels away to lie on his back. "You'll feel better when you wake up," he whispers as my eyes droop, trying to match his breath.

I lean toward the corner of his shoulder, soaking in the contact of having him nearby. My body slowly unwinds as I replay the words in my mind.

You'll feel better when you wake up.

The wind picks up, threatening to dry my tears. When I make it to the plains outside of our home, I veer right, passing the Queen's Road, hoping to reach the lake near the border of our lands.

If I can get far enough and put distance between myself and the others—I'll try to think of what comes after that.

An ache pulses against my chest as I pound my feet hard into the ground, and a whoosh of relief courses through me as water comes into view.

My feet throb when I stop running, and I hunch over, bracing myself against my knees. I study my boots in a stupor as snowflakes trickle out from where I stand, bleeding into the grass, drowning it in frost.

Blinking again in disbelief, I swallow and attempt to even my breathing.

I can't help but stare in awe.

I've never seen anything like this.

The frost amplifies into ice, stretching toward the lake.

I follow the weather, watching it solidify the water. Curiosity drives me forward, testing the lake's structure, and I chuckle at the ease of each foot moving in front of the other to the center.

A chill creeps into my bones, a peace tugging at my heart as bitterness envelops me.

My muscles relax as magic coaxes frost from my body, creating a blizzard around me and my surroundings. I surrender to the cold, closing my eyes and embracing the magnitude of winter as power surges outward.

The sheer relief of winter's kiss expelling forth from my hands and feet brings a faint twinkle of a smile to my—

CRACK!

I jolt.

Scream after scream escapes when hands wrap around me, shaking me and pressing me hard into the ice.

A voice calls.

I can't meet it.

I need to break free from whatever is holding me. I need to follow where the crackle of ice came from.

If I am pulled from this, I will lose it all.

I can't lose it all! I can't!

I flail my arms as my screams increase in volume, fighting and seeking to escape the unknown force pushing me down.

"No! I can't leave!" I shout.

Light floods my vision.

I blink at the doubled-in-size orange-gold eyes staring at me. Nose to nose in front of me is Niko. He clutches my sides, tight enough that his rigid fingernails dig into my skin.

My heart constricts underneath his worried gaze.

A defeated scream leaves my throat, and I cover my tear-filled eyes.

It's not real... This is not real...

The dream disintegrates, and I beg myself to forget the details.

But failure, an ongoing and never-ending ache, presses against my chest.

I have failed. So. Many. Times.

Is there ever a day that I will not be haunted by my mistakes?

I just want the pain to stop. I *need* it all to stop.

You will be seeking penance for the rest of your life, Tove.

My breathing stutters as the thought wedges itself deep in the back of my mind, and I cry harder.

Arms pull me to a hard chest. *Niko.*

He cradles my head, rocking me as I fist his tunic. "Shhh. You're fine," Niko soothes into my hair.

I am not fine, but I need to calm down. Yes, calm down first and then—then what?

Deities, I am stressed.

"No," I say, trying to push him away, but I am barricaded in his arms. As I wipe my tears and try to calm my nerves, I only sob more. "I-I'm so tired of this."

I am so tired of the grief, the pain, and the failure. They are constant companions mixed in with my spontaneous bleeding cycle, finding a husband, trying to make my people happy, and the ongoing nightmares.

Niko tugs me to him as I surrender to the pain and grief. Clutching his taupe shirt and drenching it with my tears, I hope gripping onto something real will diminish the dream as well as the despair. The echoing sound of my cries fills my bedchamber like a festering wound.

I can't escape this ongoing nightmare. I fear I never will.

Niko runs his hands through my hair, his arms sheltering me from the world. It feels like hours have passed before I can focus on my breathing as the different tandem of Niko's heart calms me, distracts me.

My emotions still weigh heavy on my heart, but duty has pressed itself back to the forefront of my mind. I need to keep going. I need to do right by my people. I need to do right by *them*.

Niko grabs my chin. "Tee, I think we should cancel trying to find a suitor."

I hate the pity in his eyes as he assesses me. I can't have him lose faith in me, too.

"We can't cancel," I say carefully, fighting for resolve.

He leans against the headboard, pinching the bridge of his nose. "I should have known this was going to be too much." Niko lets out a long and exaggerated sigh.

"It is not too much!" I can do this—I *have* to do this. "I need to find a husband to help my reputation with my people."

"You aren't going to find a husband if you keep acting like *this*!"

He flails his arms, lashing out and smacking his hands against the side of the bed. Anger molds across his eyes, his brows, and the vein pulsing on the side of his neck.

I lurch back in shock from the bark behind his words, clutching my chest as if an arrow plunged into my heart.

Niko has never lashed out before. And for him to say those words—he must be losing faith in me. He is probably also exhausted with everything I've thrown at him as he's helped me run my kingdom.

Have I taken his role for granted? Have I blurred the lines between friendship and duty, even the flirtation we've shared to the point that it has altered something for us?

For me? For him?

"Shit, Tee, I didn't mean—"

I raise my hand to silence him.

I withdraw, processing the pity and resentment he holds against me. I squeeze my eyes shut, struggling to bury my emotions.

But the harsh truth of my situation lies bare between us.

I know my grief is bad, but... I thought I was doing better. Clearly, I have been manipulating those closest to me, dragging them along with my grief and draining the joy out of their life, all because I don't have joy in mine anymore.

Niko's words repeat in circles, cutting through me like a knife.

I fight myself repeatedly to not let anyone in. But my hopeful heart clung to Niko like a lifeline, and I should have realized this entire time he wasn't a lifeline...

He, too, was only another grave I will eventually mourn over.

A deeper, jagged rooting of heartbreak seeps in, eternal loneliness looming over me.

No one wants to be around someone with this magnitude of grief, and I should never have convinced myself it was alright to lean on others.

The disdain in Niko's voice is evidence enough that even those I have fallen for and trust will eventually reveal their true sentiments.

I tremble with frustration at my own stupidity for hoping he might share the same feelings. Casting aside the adoration, affection, and friendship I have for the man before me, I plunge my entire self into the monster I am.

I speak with lethal calm, knowing what I must do. "We will not cancel or postpone any of the festivities, Nikolaj. Now, please *leave*." I fight through my monthly bleeding pain, fueling it into anger.

He looks as if I slapped him. Niko reaches for me. "I think you should reconsider, Tee—"

"I don't care what you think, Nikolaj!"

He flinches.

I don't care. I can't allow myself to care. I must push him away if I am to save him.

He tries to speak, but the ice inside of me is awake and growing.

The Snow Queen is here.

I mirror the disgust he's holding on to his face. "I will *not* reconsider, *Nikolaj*."

Clinging to the fury, I use the torment of his words to fuel my wretchedness. Even though heaviness seeps into my chest, rage isn't hot in my blood. It's frost.

The chilling caress at the top of my spine is gladly welcomed, as is the frigid winter washing over me.

Niko gapes at my breath turning visible.

My tear-stricken eyes strain to focus on him, but I lean into rage rather than despair. I have never been one to display fury around others, but I enforce it now as my gaze pierces through him with coldness.

"As you have so *kindly* reminded me, time and time again, I need to do this for the kingdom. I need to find someone to marry, and it's like you said."

He eyes me silently, aware of the visible breath escaping from my lips.

"Any man I choose will be *honored* I chose him," I say as I fight against the spasm exploding in my stomach.

I stare at Niko, seeing the hint of fear and disgust behind his eyes. I lean in, venom lacing each syllable, driving the statement home.

"Because I am a *fucking* queen."

He is completely still, the person standing before him, someone he, too, has never seen.

Good.

I point to the exit, breathing deep and fighting against feeding my power what it wants. "And no matter how much I might have wanted it to be you, it won't be. Now, *leave.*"

We stare each other down, my heart pulsing in tandem with either my magic or loneliness, but ruination lurks over me.

Niko studies me for a few pauses, looking as if he wants to say something, but I keep my finger pointed at the door.

He rises—leaving my room without even looking back.

I remain glued to my place, listening for his footsteps to recede before dropping my hand. Kneeling over, I clutch my stomach in agony, my power flickering away from the full force of pain radiating throughout my body.

I crumple to the floor, my head falling forward on my bed as more tears dampen my sheets. I fight against prying apart Niko's words, trying to convince myself he didn't mean what he said. Maybe I needed to hear him say those things, needed to put to rest the feelings I have for him and do my duty.

It doesn't make me feel any better that I lashed right back.

Betina's sweet voice enters the room. "Tove?"

My beautiful friend holds a tray of medicine. As she sees my pained face, a choked whimper escapes me, and heartbreak returns, knowing I should push Betina away, too.

"Oh, Tove."

Her voice cracks as she hurries to me, holding me close.

She helps me into bed before giving me medicine.

Betina holds my hand, a quiet force of support I am unworthy of.

I finally work up enough courage to tell Betina everything said between Niko and me, my heart breaking again when I apologize for dragging her into my problems.

She leans over, hugging me tightly. "Friends help each other on their good days and their dark days, Tove."

My lip quivers. "Thank you."

She pulls away, with a shift in her entire demeanor.

I cock my head in confusion.

A smirk appears as she rests her hands against her hips. "Now, let's ensure every person in attendance tonight recognizes the *honor* of being in your presence."

I shake my head as she leaves to help with preparations for tonight and to ensure Niko keeps his distance before the party.

With the pain dulling, I pray once more to the Makers I will be able to live up to my word and muster enough confidence to get through tonight's ball.

6

LEAVE THEM WANTING

"A re you serious?" I blanch as Betina wiggles her eyebrows, holding up *another* revealing gown.

It is made of sheer fabric, with the darkest shades of red layered delicately atop one another. Embellishments of maroon roses and forest green shrubbery start beneath the neckline and cascade downward as the tiered material, thickest in the bodice, becomes more transparent as the full skirt reaches the floor, framing a thigh-high slit on the right side of the dress.

Inching forward, I run my hand along the fabric, admiring the beauty of it.

While I wish there was more cloth to conceal the monster wearing it, my stomach flips with a small gleam of excitement in dressing in the best of our kingdom's fashion.

"Does it have pockets?" I ask.

Betina's expression falters. "Unfortunately not."

I press my lips together, unable to formulate words over the lack of pockets. Not only do they hide my nerves, but they keep my hands warm and allow me the opportunity to carry Mother's mirror on rough days. Having it yesterday was a comfort, and to have it taken away for tonight has my stomach churning.

Betina is quick to cast my worries aside when she rests the gown on my bed. "All will be well, Tove."

She, of course, chose her own dress to be the opposite of mine.

Hers is modest and tight around her bodice and shoots outward from her waist. The deep rust-colored tulle accentuates her skin tone while complementing the chestnut highlights that brighten her hair.

I look back and forth between her and my own gown, my mind wandering with varying scenarios that could unfold tonight. I replay my conversation earlier with Niko, and my chest aches.

As if knowing my mind wandered to him, Betina says, "Fuck Nikolaj."

I snort.

She holds me, her voice gentle as she says, "The entire purpose of this week is for you to find an eligible suitor. Don't dwell on him."

Betina has never judged me for falling for Niko and was supportive of whatever decision I made regarding my affections. But she is right.

I need to make the best of tonight regardless of the pain I am in. Physically and emotionally.

Flashing her a hint of amusement, I offer some small news. "Well, there was a suitor—"

"And you didn't think to tell me?"

A small laugh escapes me. "I am telling you now, aren't I?" I huff as her eyes squint, thinking I wouldn't tell her.

Maybe I shouldn't.

"Who is he? What does he look like? Is he a nobleman? From another kingdom?" Her brown eyes glimmer at the prospect of details.

I wave off her questions as I pour a glass of water, eating a snack to help my cramps be more manageable during tonight's event. I might need to sneak away through the night for another dose of medicine.

"I don't think I should tell you."

Her posture stiffens and she braces her hands on her hips. "Why not?"

I finish my snack and rest at my vanity.

There is kohl on the left side, meant for lining the eyes. I can never master it and always need Betina's assistance, but it doesn't hurt to practice. *Especially* as I withhold information from my friend.

I reach for the kohl and direct my attention to it rather than my own reflection staring back.

She repeats herself. "Why won't you tell me?"

Her nose wrinkles near her eyes, her cheeks bunching together in a perfectly annoyed face.

I almost break into a fit of laughter, peering over to meet her doe eyes. "Because I have no doubt you if you saw him, you would chase after him yourself."

She clicks her tongue. "That's no fair."

I snicker, choosing to keep him a secret.

Betina rolls her eyes at my deceit, still approaching to help style my hair. The soft tug on my scalp has kohl dragging across my eye. Now it is her turn to laugh.

"Don't worry. I'll fix it later," she says.

She swivels me around after finishing my hair, fixing my eyes, and adding rouge on my cheeks and lips, matching my gown. When she finishes, she grips my shoulders with a gleam in her eyes.

"Dress next."

I nod as she helps me change, apprehension looming over me as the gown drapes out across the floor. The thought of keeping up with royal appearances, avoiding Niko, and managing my cycle makes my skin crawl.

How am I going to avoid Niko all night?

Will any of the noblemen slip in maintaining protocol like I often do?

Stepping one foot at a time into the dress, my thoughts drift toward the scarred man and his easy mannerisms. It hints that he could be from a neighboring kingdom, but which one?

I wonder if he will be here again tonight.

I press the bodice of my gown to my chest as Betina fastens the laces into place. When she finishes, she claps with glee.

"You are going to be the center of attention tonight. No one will be able to keep their eyes off you." Betina twirls me toward the mirror, and I gasp at my outfit for the night.

Stepping closer and inspecting its intricacies, I marvel at how the gown complements my curves and feels lightweight. I run my hands all over the soft fabric and look at my image in the mirror, and a dark thought chimes in my mind.

This dress is going to leave men imagining.

If they even want to fantasize about being married to the Snow Queen.

I flinch at the imaginary ice cracking around me, a rumbling thunder echoing in my heart. My attention remains on the gown, reluctant to face the monster staring back.

The moment Betina places my crown on my head, it pinches above my ears, a figurative transformation taking deep root. Betina regards me carefully and extends her elbow to me.

I tilt my chin and latch on to her in a death grip as we make our way from my chambers and down to the ballroom, relying on her support with each step.

After my announced arrival, I enter the ballroom gradually, marveling at tonight's theme.

Tonight's festivities feature decorations adorned with oranges, yellows, reds, and browns. The hanging chandeliers project an orange hue, while red and yellow drapes adorn the outer walls, creating an appearance of fall. Floor-to-ceiling curtains and arched windows are also fitted with lush cherry-red fabric, accentuating the brown branches wrapped around each pillar as the dark rugs spread across the tile.

"Make tonight memorable," Betina whispers as we approach my throne.

She guides me to it, light shining across her features before breaking into a curtsy. As she leaves me to rest, I sense everyone's attention.

Carefully, I scan each face, stopping when I meet Niko's deep golden stare. I knew he was taking me in as I was him, but I cower away from his gaze, hoping he takes it as a dismissal.

Luckily, a staff member is nearby with a platter, holding one cup I can only hope is wine. I extend my gratitude as I take the glass and swallow down the contents in one gulp, my head immediately swimming.

"May I please have another?" I ask.

He nods and disappears when I pivot to the crowd.

Niko is gone, and I hope it is the last I will see of him tonight. I don't know how strong I can be if he comes near me.

My body contracts, and I drop my head, tensing and placing pressure over my abdomen.

Deities, I should have taken more medicine.

"My Queen," a deep voice I recognize whispers.

I shoot up to the real-life deity standing in front of me. My mouth runs dry at the sight.

He is drenched in all black, from his tunic loosely held by his vest to his trousers and a pair of gloves placed on the side of his hip.

The scarred man's deep glacial blue eyes study me through his contrastingly devious grin.

I shrivel inwardly, the reminder of how I thought about him last night heating my cheeks.

He extends his hand, asking, "May I be your first dance of the evening?"

The hair on the back of my neck rises at the richness of his voice, forcing me to bite my lip before speaking. "I would like that very much, Lord... ?"

His dimple appears through the small wisps of his black hair. "There is no need for formalities when all I need is your hand in mine."

While I am aware of his deflection, I do not have the energy to keep pressing him for his name. I need to maintain my regal appearance and mask the pain attacking my insides.

Deities, I should have asked Betina for extra medicine before she left.

I take my time rising, clenching my muscles so they behave. If I can get through one dance, I can get this man's name and then find Betina.

A warm gentleness soothes me as I place my hand into my dance partner's—a small comfort I focus on as knots are twisting and pulling in my stomach.

He loops it around his arm, guiding us down the dais.

A rupture of spasms explodes in my pelvis, and I clench my teeth as we reach the dance floor.

I drape my hand over his shoulder as his intoxicating cologne clouds my senses. But when a rush of pain shoots inside me, I pinch my eyes closed and cling to the scent as a welcome distraction.

The musicians play a slow melody, the required soft swaying another blessing that will allow the chance to conserve my energy. But when I look upward, the scarred man's handsome features furrow.

"I am sorry. Did you say something?" I ask.

"I asked if you wanted to be here," he replies. "I know I am not the best dancer."

Embarrassment crosses my features as I try to come up with a good excuse, but nothing comes to mind because the only thing driving me right now is the soft caress his thumb does on my hip.

Oh fuck, that feels so nice.

I whimper a soft moan of pleasure as the slight rubbing distracts me from my cycle pains. I close my eyes to the soothing contact, and my thoughts drift to the tune of the music.

The melody is euphoric, passionate, and slow, begging each dancer to dance in rhythm with the same vigor.

I loosen as it calls to me, finding the music's reprieve.

"Tove," my dance partner says, drawing me closer, breaking my stupor.

I scold him through gritted teeth, protocol slipping. "You should not be addressing me so plainly."

His charm cracks when our gazes meet, blue eyes peering into me with pure annoyance. "I can leave if you'd like."

The following spasm is unbearable, and it takes all my strength to not show weakness.

I want to apologize, but the music begs for us to part.

Drifting away to spin into him, I am winded and wiped clean of energy.

The room gets heavier, readying to collapse around me as another pang of cramps reverberates through my gut.

Strong hands reach for me, and it is all I can do to lean on them for support. They are the only thing I can focus on.

My vision blurs the light from the chandelier with the people surrounding me.

I feel... like I am in the sky.

My grip slackens as I whisper, "I don't think I am feeling well."

"That's a wonderfully good excuse to get out of—"

The room collapses.

7

THAT IS NOT A CUSHION

A foreign warmth caresses the side of my cheek as I adjust. The burning of oak wood dances along my nostrils as soft lips trail along my forehead, drawing a small smirk from me.

Hopeful this is reality, I keep my eyes closed and allow myself this peace.

When leaning to the side, a warm, solid cushion provides me with the best of comforts. I wiggle closer to it, burrowing deeper into the scent of an addictive cologne.

"Mmmm, I will be thinking about this all night," I mutter into the supportive cushion.

But a low chuckle comes from it—

I jolt my eyes open.

"There you are," the scarred man says, a small glimpse of relief behind his gaze.

I am draped across his lap, his arms cradling me close. My hands rest near my torso, intertwined with his black leather vest.

Humiliation swims through my thoughts as I take in our compromising position on the couch in the ballroom's back room.

I try to move from him, only to have him pull me closer when a searing pain pierces through my stomach.

His eyes are lined with concern. "Are you hurt?"

Worry clouds over that my personal health is further damaging my reputation. "How did we get here? What happened in the ballroom? Did anyone see?"

"Why don't you answer my questions first? Are you hurt?"

I stare into his blue eyes, my breath rattling against my chest, not only at our proximity but in relief this happened with him rather than anyone else. Still, I'm sheepish in divulging my health.

"It's honestly embarrassing to tell you."

"It can't be as bad as what I am imagining."

I chuckle, knowing my cycle is the last thing he would consider. "What *are* you imagining?"

His arms tense around me briefly, and I swear I hear a low rumble come from him. The dip of his voice is so low it tempts me closer.

"I thought someone was hurting you, as well as other things."

I have no idea what he means. All I do know is I find safety in his strong hold.

I take a bite of his sweet lure, grabbing his leather vest and tugging him close. Watching his lips, I lick mine at the thought of what he would taste like.

I reassure him with a small admission. "I am alright. And that is the second time you've saved me."

But I remember where we are, hidden away from prying eyes. Concern over if anyone saw has me stifling my pain, needing to do damage control if there has been any.

I ask, "What happened in the ballroom? Did anyone see?"

He touches the side of my face, drawing my breath taut. This man stares intently in my eyes, full of seriousness and concern.

"You don't have to hide your pain from me. Tell me."

Sensing I am not going to get answers by deflecting and making up excuses, I opt for the boldness he had last night. I surrender to laying the truth bare to him.

"It's my cycle." The scarred man's face relaxes slightly, and I continue, "When it mixes in with a lot of stress, it can be—debilitating."

I am about to tell him more if only to better explain, but I stop short when a laugh escapes him.

"I never would have thought bleeding would be debilitating," he jests.

I know a joke when I see one, but for the life of me, I don't laugh. Rather, I'm pissed.

Another man who does not understand the vicious cycles women face and glosses over that pain with humor.

At least I have a better reason for hiding my pain from people. I have a duty and an appearance to maintain.

Asshole.

The spell of lust breaks, and I release his vest, shoving myself away.

Shame and anger thrum against my blood as I seek to escape from him and this dreaded room. But my muscles pinch in my abdomen, sending me falling forward.

And again, the scarred man catches me.

So. Fucking. Infuriating.

I'm braced against his hard chest, a repeat from last night.

He applies pressure exactly where my cramps coil, and it is enough to bring relief rather than hurt. When he leans in, my breath hitches.

His aroma drowns me as his lips tickle my ear. "Forgive me. I should not have jested."

I shudder as his words sweep down my neck, goose bumps spiking across my flesh. I inch toward him for a moment, something hard pressing against my back end, and I *really* want to dwell on it.

A low groan from him coaxes me back into a tangled web of intrigue.

"I-I should go," I say, needing to get back to the party and fighting my body's desire to remain next to him. "I need to ensure I didn't cause anyone alarm and find my lady-in-waiting for medicine."

"Rest, My Queen. I was able to sneak back here without drawing much attention. Let me go fetch your lady-in-waiting for you."

"How did you—"

"*Rest*," the scarred man repeats.

He peels his body from mine, the fight leaving me as he reclines me against the chaise.

I study his black hair falling in front of his face as he fans my dress out, ensuring it is in place and not exposing anything. His touch is tender, and I find my irritability diminishing as he pulls away with a warm smile and his dimple on full display.

My lips tick up as I cradle my stomach. "Thank you."

He halts. "Rick."

I grin at the small piece of information. "Thank you for saving me from humiliation, Rick."

He winks. "Pay me back when I return, My Queen."

My heart flutters, and my cheeks heat as Rick vanishes back into the party.

I do not have very much to offer him. Except... Maybe I could approach the idea of marriage with him. He is the only one who is bearable to be around. My options are already limited, and I would *really* like to avoid choosing Ulrik.

Surely, Rick seeking me out both nights is why he's here. He must be one of the suitors we invited.

But Niko warned me against dancing with Rick.

I thought Niko warned me against it because I was drawn to another person, and like an idiot, I exploited that, thinking he was jealous. Then he laughed in my face but also took care of me while I was clutching my chamber pot this morning.

Niko pointed out my grief, and Rick made fun of my cycle.

But Niko stayed with me through a nightmare.

Would Rick ever do that if I chose him?

I barely know him, yes, but unions have happened between two people with less information. Rocking my head up to the ceiling in frustration, I hate how both men, despite being crass, have caused such a reaction from me.

Is this what relationships are always meant to be like?

I scoff in annoyance and massage my throbbing head.

The door flies open, and my hands shoot to my side as Niko's booming voice enters the room. "Tove! Are you—"

He notices my position on the couch and lifts a brow.

"What do you want?" I lace the question with venom.

It does not help that his stupidly handsome face still drives my heart into wanting him, regardless of his hurtful words from earlier.

He clenches his fists as he steps forward. "I-I came to check on you after I thought you had been back here too long with that man."

"What?"

How *did* I get back here? I don't remember anything beyond dancing.

Niko glances around. "Oh, he must have left."

When our gazes meet again, his words from earlier repeat in my mind and fracture my heart.

He sees the hurt.

"I-I need to apologize, Tee," he states. "For what I said earlier."

Brushing down my gown, I cross my arms and wait.

Niko relaxes before running his hands through his hair and exhaling. He comes to sit next to me, and I try to keep the hurt from my expression.

But when he reaches for my hand, selfishly, I let him take it.

I hate feeling beside myself with the hope that he truly is sorry.

He pulls my hand to his chest, resting it over his heart. "I can't stop thinking about what you said earlier."

It is my turn to look away. I know I said a lot of things earlier. Some were harsh, and some gutted me.

He needs to be more specific for this to be a two-way conversation.

His thumb rubs the upper side of my palm. "Tove—" He pauses, drawing my attention back and taking a long breath. "You said you wanted it to be me? What did you mean by that?"

Panic grips my heart at his question. I can't go admitting my feelings for him now.

Damn my stupid emotions for letting my mouth run rampant.

I build a wall over my heart, trying to conceal everything as I navigate myself around the real issue of him throwing my grief in my face.

"I said a lot of things because I was upset, Niko. I am sure you can understand why," I tell him in a clipped manner, trying to not explode on him.

Niko turns sullen, but his words revolve in circles in my mind, wanting me to keep him at a distance.

And yet my heart is pleading to stay and hear him out.

His hand twitches, and our proximity weighs in. "I know, Tee, and I am so sorry I said that. I meant to tell you—"

"Tell me what?" Anxiety and anticipation lace every word as my insides clench.

Is he going to tell me his reasoning in saying what he said?

Is he going to warn me away from Rick again?

"You don't know?" he asks.

The softness of his voice only creates more of a puzzle.

Niko glances toward the fire, subconsciously rubbing my hand still resting on his heart.

Desperately, I want to shift closer and take his face in my hands and kiss him senseless. I would gladly push past his callousness just to have my husband be him and only him. I *need* him.

My pulse quickens when he rests his head against mine, and Sweet Makers, I *want* this.

I *want* him.

His sandalwood scent soothes my anger while fueling my desire.

I bite my lip, falling deeper into the essence of him as he kisses my forehead.

"*Please* forgive me," he pleads.

My eyes close at the contact, hating how much I want him to kiss my lips. I am too much of a coward to put my heart at risk again without understanding his intentions.

"I can't bear it when we are at odds with one another." He pecks my right cheek.

Heat blooms underneath my pores, as if fire has jumped from the hearth and is now burning through my skin. I swear to Yeva I want this to be real and not a game of flirtation.

He kisses the other cheek. "I can't bear to lose you."

He inches closer, eyes closing. Niko's nose brushes mine so delicately, and the slightest sensation of his lips hovering over mine sends me into a frenzy.

My lips eagerly seek to touch his—

"Am I interrupting?" a low voice asks.

I propel my entire body in the opposite direction of Niko as my eyes widen, stunned to see Rick leaning against the doorway.

His arms are crossed, with a small bag perched outside the crook of his elbow, music entering the silent back room as my own shame takes over.

Stupid, stupid, stupid, Tove. Deities, take me now.

Niko coughs as mortification reminds me I should not remain frozen this long.

I wrap my arms around myself, ignoring the blush running across my cheeks as Rick closes the gap between the three of us.

Both sets of eyes plaster themselves to the back of my head.

I hug my stomach in protest, forcing myself to look into the fire and pray to the Makers this nightmare will end soon.

My efforts in getting to know Rick more and learn of his intentions for being here are wrecked. Not to mention he might spread the wrong word and sully my reputation.

Fucking Deities.

The silence is deafening as Rick approaches the couch. "Your lady-in-waiting was preoccupied, and I offered to bring you the medicine myself."

He drops the medicine pouch on the table.

I cringe at the loud clang it makes, forcing an echo throughout the room. I avoid his stare, so torn over my disgrace that I don't even say thank you.

Rick takes the silence as a dismissal.

Footsteps recede behind me, and each footfall forces the wedge to grow deeper.

I almost thought I could marry someone other than Niko.

I've failed...

Everything I set out to do this week is ruined.

"Oh, and, My Queen?" Rick asks as the door creaks.

I meet his gaze, knowing it will be the last time I would ever set my eyes on someone so handsome.

Rick smirks. "I'll be sure to fetch your advisor instead of medicine the next time your *aches* return."

8

BREAKING DOWN WALLS

Humiliation heats my cheeks as Rick leaves, my proximity to Niko shattering any chances I had of finding a suitor.

I bury my face in my hands as Niko laughs.

"What a dick."

I flick my head up, stunned he finds humor in this. "What the fuck is your problem?"

Niko's eyebrows rise in question before he gives me a reply. "Nothing is my problem. I was trying to—"

"You were trying to what, Nikolaj?" I demand, fury crashing against me.

He isn't the one who looks compromised. I am. He isn't the one needing to marry. I am.

"I was trying to—"

"Trying to *what*?" I'm too impatient to hear another excuse. Everything is ruined now. *Everything.*

It doesn't help my feelings for Niko are tangled together in the midst of it all. I agreed to him pretending to show an interest in me in hopes it would lure in more men, but with his actions last night and this morning and now—fuck!

Desperately, I seek to have him be a part of my life, but I can't interpret the differences between when he is flirting with me for the sake of our plan and when he is being my royal advisor.

A heavy weight presses on me.

I fight against my failure sending me down the same tear-filled spiral. Anger is easier to lean into as I trudge through, voicing the flaws he threw in my face earlier.

"What were you trying to tell me? That I am not good enough? Or that I need to work on myself?" I sneer, standing and reaching for the medicine bag.

Snatching the herbs, I stuff them into my mouth before throwing the bag down and clenching my fists. I scrutinize him as my magic jolts to life.

My breath is visible, and Niko's eyes widen.

My heart crumbles.

I fight against showing how much it hurts to see, but my voice cracks as I half laugh. "*Oh, yes,* let us not forget they also wouldn't want to marry me like this!" I gesture to my hands through my anger turned defeat, opening them to emphasize the frost plaguing my kingdom.

Niko studies me, his chest rising and falling.

Closing my eyes, I inhale a deep breath, reveling in the power.

I sink into it, seeking the familiarity of my magic to comfort me. Basking in that aid, I surrender to the bitter cold soothing me before nullifying itself.

The silence in the room is an added blessing, which assists me in calming the blizzard raging within.

When I open my eyes, the visible breath is no more.

Niko's amber eyes, still wide, study me, even as I lower my hands with exhaustion.

Just break my heart already and let me be.

I ask again through my blurred vision, "So what else are you trying to say, *Nikolaj*?"

My ferocity falls away underneath his stare.

The muscles in his jaw tics as he breaks contact, the side of his face dancing with light from the fire.

Tension increases my heartbeat, as I brace for his rejection to finally be voiced.

But Niko rushes for me, his hands gripping the sides of my face, lips meeting mine.

My heart leaps out of my chest.

Nothing and no one is here in this beautiful moment but us. I've always dreamed my first kiss would be with Niko, the man I've loved for years. But it is nothing like I had imagined. It is nothing like the almost touch from earlier. Rather, it is fervent, and I meet his lips in response.

Grabbing the nape of his neck, I tug his red hair slightly.

I drive my anger, exhaustion, and entire heart into our kiss.

His tongue clashes with mine, becoming needy, and it drives me *wild*.

He breaks away, his chest panting as his voice lets out a low rumble. "You drive me crazy, Tee. I am lost when it comes to you."

"*Don't* lie to me."

"I am not lying to you," he promises against my skin as each graze of his mouth drifts lower and lower down my neck.

He bites onto the base where my neck meets my shoulder, my hips grinding into his in response.

My head falls in ecstasy at his bite, and I want his body to meet mine.

"I've always cared about you, Tee. And I've always wanted you," Niko says.

I forget to breathe, and I clench my thighs as he drags his lips up my neck. I grab his shirt, untucking it to touch his bare skin. I scratch his lower back as I pinch and squeeze, pulling his body to me.

He lunges into the kiss, forcing a moan to escape me. His mouth moves from mine, trailing more kisses down the side of my neck.

"I *was* jealous when I saw you dancing with that other man," he confesses through each kiss. "It drove me crazy because I *knew*, just by looking at the two of you, that you were considering him."

I try to comprehend his admission, but selfishly, I nibble the side of his ear, eager for any bit of him I can have in case the world comes crashing down.

He lowers to kiss my chest, his fingers tracing down the length of my spine.

Our eyes meet, his full of desire and hunger.

"And then I fucked it up," he says.

The silence hangs thickly between us, and he does not wait long before lowering to the floor, his fingers digging into my ass.

He leans in, inhaling my scent between my legs and looking back up. His gaze melts my body, and I can't stop myself from admiring him on his knees before me.

He swallows thickly, his smooth, baritone voice lined with regret. "I should have never said what I said this morning. I should have never denied my jealousy."

My nerves ease at his words, especially as he runs his hands up and down the sides of my gown.

But through the apology in his eyes, a slight peak of irritation rises when he continues, "You drive me *insane*. And I am so sorry, Tee." He removes himself completely, his hands falling to rest on his thighs.

Niko lines each word with desire and lust. "I want you. I need you and only you, *please*."

"Why did you never tell me?"

My voice cracks.

He rubs his sides nervously, with something like shame shrinking his shoulders inwardly.

My heart hammers, wanting his answer, but I sense him fighting against telling me.

Carefully, I lower to my own knees, grateful I can even do so with the minimal dulling of my cramps. I reach for his hands, holding them before guiding his chin to meet my gaze.

His amber eyes are lined with tears.

I rest my palm on his cheek as he blurts, "Because I never thought you'd see me like that. You are *royalty*, Tee. I've wanted to be yours since I was tasked with being your guard. Why do you think I kept checking in on you and helping you? It wasn't because I wanted to be promoted and granted the title of Lord. I-I couldn't stay away from you."

I lower my head, thinking back to when life was different. Where I wasn't fighting grief, where, each day, I would compose a new song and where I was surrounded and embraced by those I love.

But I am still being embraced with love. Through Niko.

"You *want* to be with me?"

I still disbelieve that this is real.

He holds my face as his eyes peer into mine. "Of course I do, Tee. I have fought my feelings for as long as I have known you. I crave your company, your attention, your touch, your *everything*.

I'm fucked with jealousy over you. And I know I am fucked up for trying to hurt you alongside hurting others who draw your interest. But I am a selfish man, Tee. I only want you."

"Is that your attempt at an apology for stringing me along this long?"

He laughs and leans in to give me a chaste kiss.

I return it hungrily, loving his stubble scratching me.

Straddling him, I grind my hips, letting the friction drive me mad. It's one thing to have our pelvises touching, it's another when our entire bodies mold to one another with each movement.

My body takes complete control, my lips racing to meet his and craving his touch everywhere imaginable. My heartbeat races as our bodies compose their own melody.

Our mouths intertwine, present and alive in this moment.

This pure, blissful moment.

I can't help the titter escaping my lips as we kiss.

Niko notices and slows the kissing to being soft, languid as if he wants to savor this. His lips perk up as well through each touch, and I can't help a true laugh from escaping me.

It's extremely embarrassing.

His face moves at the sound, and my lips tuck into themselves as I turn bashful. He leans forward and rubs his nose along mine as another laugh escapes from him.

The glow of the fire illuminates his skin and teeth so much I am utterly lost in the haze of his beauty.

My cheeks pinch upward as he takes me in with the brightest grin I have seen from him in years.

His laughter quiets, and he pulls me in to rest his forehead against mine. "Tove, Tove, Tove. Please forgive me."

I meet his in kind and close my eyes at the rich woodsy scent of him. "I thought kissing you was enough of a sign."

My quip earns a snort from Niko.

Niko turns sheepish as he wraps his hands around my hips, holding me tightly. He looks into the fire as his throat bobs.

"Do you remember when I told you every eligible male wants to marry you?" he asks.

I have to think of the conversation where he told me this, and I only remember the never-ending list of preparations and meetings I have attended as of late.

My mind goes blank, and I shrug, shaking my head.

Niko bites his lip, debating speaking again.

My arms, draped around his neck, give him a tight squeeze in reassurance.

"I was trying to tell you I, too, am an eligible male," he whispers.

I try to maintain indifference, suppressing my hope.

From whatever expression I have plastered on my face, Niko hurries to add, "It's why I kept bringing up marriage. Not only for the kingdom but to see how you felt or *could* feel about me."

Niko runs a hand through his auburn hair as a blush creeps along his cheeks. "I know it was a very subtle way of... *expressing* my feelings, but—Deities, I thought this would be easier to say."

I break away from his words, noting the muffled voices and the lively music. Beyond the door, hundreds of guests are here in attendance, and only a few of them are here for my hand. And Niko is here right now, hinting at the one thing I have wanted for *years*.

Has our push and pull all been because of fear of rejecting each other? And if it is out in the open now, *does* he mean what I think he means?

No, Tove. Don't get your hopes up. This is all a farce.

Doubt prickles along my spine, and my hope of happiness dies with it. Heaviness presses on my chest as I withdraw. I can't help but feel as if the Makers are hoping to make another spectacle of me and my heart.

But Niko's grip tightens, and I stop, hesitant to look upon him. If I do, I am afraid I will wake up from this beautifully torturous nightmare.

He tilts my chin up to meet his gaze, something wholesome and warm twinkling around his irises.

I touch his face, his stubble softly prickling me.

He stares into the depths of my eyes. "Tee, my friend, my—"

I am so taken aback by the gentleness of his voice my eyes well. A laugh escapes me. I try to hide it, but Niko forces me to stay in his line of sight.

A tear falls down my cheek as I sniff, trying to get a hold of myself, and he waits for me patiently, smiling.

His eyes have a sheer gloss forming. "Will you give me the rest of our lives?"

My lips tremble as a whimper escapes at the question. Is he... is he asking?

"Will you grant me the greatest honor anyone could ever be given by becoming your forever friend, protector, husband, and king consort?"

I am weightless as my heart skips beat after beat. I've always wanted it to be him, yet I can't believe this is happening.

Tears of joy cascade down my face as I cup his cheeks and kiss him deeply. When I pull away, his amber eyes scan mine as I cry through my happiness.

"Of course, Niko."

He engulfs me and my heart bursts. Niko squeezes my hips, and I shudder in pleasure at the steady grip of him and his presence.

I break the kiss, my forehead resting on his, enjoying this moment I have been hopeful for, not believing it could happen to me.

"When should we make the announcement?" Niko asks, his voice quiet and low.

Inhaling his scent, I soak up the perfect atmosphere, hoping to commit this to memory as I consider the next steps.

I move away and rest my hands atop his shoulders. "Tomorrow." I beam, knowing nothing can take this moment from me.

Niko nods in agreement, then kisses my brow. "Let's say we go enjoy the rest of the evening amongst *our* people?" he suggests, giving me an option to do my duties or remain here.

Instinctively, I want to stay in this room in hopes of preserving this night, but duty calls. My lips curve upward at the word choice Niko used.

"I think *our* people would like that very much."

He helps me off his lap, and I adjust my gown, brushing the sides of it to smooth the wrinkles. Niko tugs his vest, making sure to tuck his shirt into his pants before extending his arm.

Niko and I do not part from each other the rest of the evening, save for when I escaped with Betina to tell her the news.

The only moment of loneliness looming over me is now, as I lie in my bed, fingertips tracing my lips in the aftermath of Niko kissing me good night after escorting me to my chambers.

Rolling side to side in bed, I try to diminish the building desire that was left unsatisfied this evening. I stare at the vaulted ceiling, and my thoughts expand tenfold as time drifts by.

My insomnia shines bright tonight.

Politics, grief, and lust take turns swimming to the surface of my thoughts, and as my arousal grows, I cave to my urges by teasing my body for a release. My fingertips trail down my neck in slow, methodical movements, as I imagine Niko's touch instead of my own.

His phantom touch around my hips from earlier draws my hands lower, circling my pebbling nipples.

I pinch one of my breasts at the thought of Niko's breath mingling with mine.

My hips buck as I drift further down my body.

I roam my hands around my lower stomach and coast up and down my thighs in anticipation. When I find my center, I shudder at the wetness.

I rub in a steady rhythm, images of amber eyes studying me drive my hand to move at a faster pace.

I want him here with me now, in this moment, driving into my body, fulfilling each one of my fantasies. I flick my pussy, sending a light flicker of frost from my fingertips to breeze along my clit.

The switch in temperature draws a deep, guttural moan from my chest.

My chest rises and falls from the pleasure and magic coming to life. I breathe through the energy of my power, hot and heady but cautious when I feed my powers alongside my arousal.

I could never do this with another, knowing it could backfire on them. But I've mastered this little glimpse of power, allowing me to hate my abilities a little less.

The sensation of cold on my pussy warms, and I flick my clit one more time, inserting one finger, throwing my head back in ecstasy.

I focus on the ceiling as I work myself, the slow buildup sensually teasing me in my lower abdomen.

Niko's image comes to my mind as I insert a second finger, trying to imagine the lustful words he would whisper in my ear. I pinch my nipple then move my hand down to join the other at my center.

The dual stimulation only gets me so far as I buck my hips, wishing wholeheartedly for Niko to be the one doing this to me.

I pinch my center and envision his thickness driving into me. My mind and hands work in sync to the fantasy playing in my head, and I ride my way to a long, needy orgasm.

I relax as I remove my hands, catching my breath as I come down from the high I finally scratched.

A coppery stench drifts to my senses, and my nose pinches.

Sighing at the mess I made, I rise from my bed to examine the magnitude of my disarray.

Pulling the bed sheet off, I crumple it up, dropping it on the ground near my bathing chambers.

I grab a dressing robe and reach for the bells connected to the staff's rooms, alerting them for a bath and a change of sheets.

9

A WEDDING PRESENT

The Celebration of Spirits revolves around honoring Yeva, the Deity of Life, and Letum, the Deity of Death, through a tradition of a lantern ceremony. During the lighting of each flame, one chooses which deity to honor. If choosing Letum, you whisper your gratitude for knowing and loving the ones passed on. If choosing Yeva, you wish for the blessing of new life.

The lantern ceremony has become one of my favorite celebrations these last five years. The beautiful beacons of light filling the winter sky feel as if my family's spirits are the closest they'll ever be.

Every year since their passing, I have lit three lanterns and honored Letum, but as I turn toward my staff and light the first one, I decide I am going to honor Yeva.

Ahead of me in the courtyard, guests are bundled together, seeking warmth from the frigid, bitter breeze while waiting for me to speak.

My hands are shaking despite holding a flame. While it could be due to the weather, it is really because I'm terrible when addressing a crowd.

Swallowing a gulp as I steady my breathing, I take a step forward, and the guests slip into a hush.

"Thank you all for attending the past week of celebration that we have dedicated to honor our Makers." Looking toward Niko, I am met with an encouraging nod.

His sweet presence shines through the onyx leather jacket and trousers. Gold accents line his vest, complementing my gown, but not enough to cause questions.

His auburn hair is combed into place, and his eyes gaze into mine, dropping down to my lips.

I square my shoulders, my own mask of indifference slipping when his grin sends heat into my cheeks.

As I veer to the guests, I scan each individual and attempt my shot at smiling. I want to show them there is more than what they whisper. Regardless of their feelings about me, the people will be overjoyed in my choosing of Niko.

But my brief burst of delight fizzles when I stop on a familiar face.

Rick.

He studies me carefully, but I shake off the grip his blue eyes have on me.

Announcing my engagement now will leave no room for Rick to speak out against me and Niko. I hold on to that thought.

I continue, "Many of you know, on this day, we shall light these lanterns to honor Yeva and Letum, the creators of all living things, but I have another reason for celebration tonight."

The crowd's voices grow into hushed discussions, and I thank the Makers that today my cycle is more manageable. If I had started my cycle today, I would have fainted and vomited on the spot while giving this speech.

"My hope for tonight is that you, the people of Axidoria, not only honor the Deities but also join me in celebrating my marriage to Lord Nikolaj Drost of Thosow." I extend a hand to Niko, my friend, royal advisor, and soon-to-be husband.

Cheers rise from the crowd as a huff of air escapes his lips. Their yipping and hollering are nothing but a muted noise in my ears as Niko steps forward, smiling and holding my hand.

His smile warms my entire body, my heart overjoyed to call him mine.

He raises his hand to silence them. "Queen Tove and I will wed at the end of the week and would be honored if you would join us in our union."

The head of my guard stands to attention, forcing the others to follow suit.

They withdraw their swords, angling them to the sky, and chant in unison, "All Hail, Queen Tove Clemmensen and future King Consort Nikolaj Drost!"

The chant is repeated by the giddy crowd as Niko and I look at each other, beaming from cheek to cheek.

Niko takes my hand, bringing it to his lips and kissing my knuckles.

A wave of heat crashes against me when he leans in, placing a gentle kiss on my lips.

I giggle when the crowd coaxes him on, and our lips meet again.

He pulls away, sunshine itself lighting up the entire courtyard.

Facing the crowd, he says, "Now let's really celebrate!"

Our guests sing their praises again as I send my first lantern dedicated to my father into the sky.

Inching forward on the steps above the courtyard, I whisper my reverence to Yeva as well as a wish.

My father taught us about the Makers and believed that wishing gives us extra luck in our future. Keeping the tradition, I wish for my kingdom to be blessed.

As I turn to begin my second and third, guests light their own lanterns, releasing them into the sky.

My second lantern goes to my mother. Honoring her and loving her was always difficult, but since she blessed me with magic, my second wish is to harness my magic for my people and find a way to end the ongoing winter.

But when Runa's lantern is lit, I hold it close, counting my breaths and trying to settle on a wish. Smiling slightly, I think of one that will always be my wish from here on out, to heal, to love, and to find my happy again with my husband by my side.

My lips lift as my final lantern tilts up to the sky.

The clusters of lanterns soar upward, illuminating the darkened purple night.

Niko holds my hand tight, and he leans in to kiss my cheek. The heat he naturally radiates lures me in.

We stand arm in arm as the lanterns soar higher and higher in the sky.

The crowd starts trickling into the main ballroom, and Niko turns to follow, but I hold him in place. "Just a little while longer."

He says nothing as he faces the courtyard and observes the lanterns.

The ballroom entrances echo lively music and cheery laughter, and while many would want to join in the fun, I can't seem to move from this spot.

Niko asks, "What did you wish for?"

I swat his hand. "Like I am going to tell you!"

He knows telling wishes is bad luck and surrenders with a boyish laugh. "Fine, fine. I thought husbands earned that right."

"You're not my husband *yet*."

"*Yet*." He chuckles, earning a laugh from me.

A shiver shoots up my spine as I squeeze Niko's hand.

He responds by huddling nearer, guiding me back into the ballroom. Heat bombards my pale skin when we pass through the threshold, and we are met by guests hovering nearby.

The entire ballroom is drenched in sheer black fabric, climbing up every pillar, across every wall, everywhere adorned with baby's breath and white roses. The intertwining of darkness and light is a beautiful sight to see, and even everyone's ensembles reflect the decorations.

Guests are dressed either in the darkest of hues or the palest, creating more contrast between Letum and Yeva. Many tilt glasses up, extending their salutations.

Niko and I bob our heads in gratitude, knowing that, while many appear to be happy, others who were potential choices glare through their masked happiness.

The power-hungry bastards, no doubt, as Niko would say.

Approaching the dais, I barely have a moment to sit down before Lord Ulrik approaches with a scowl. Like many of the guests tonight, he is dressed in warm fabric, but instead of opting for the colors of black or white for Letum and Yeva, he is adorned in a deep navy.

I grit my teeth through my false smile, knowing pleasantries with him are important with so many watching Niko and me now. Extending my hand forward, Lord Ulrik's scowl alters briefly, the side of his lips ticking up when his dark-blue eyes meet mine.

He bows, kissing my knuckles as the stench of tobacco stings my nostrils, forcing me to clench every muscle to not gag.

Sweet Makers, I would take my menstrual pain from yesterday to avoid the headache his stench brings.

A small piece of hair falls from his blond slicked-back style when he rises. He runs a hand over it to smooth it into place, a grimace slipping when he gazes at Niko.

"Your Majesty," Lord Ulrik drawls, his speech slurring from a few too many drinks. "I must offer my felicitations to you and your future *husband*."

I swear to Yeva, if he wasn't intoxicated, maybe he would not have verbalized his true feelings to my face.

But Lord Ulrik's blue eyes darken as he looks between Niko and me. "Had I known you were going to choose someone that works with you so closely, I would have inserted myself into your good graces sooner."

Niko inhales sharply as my blood heats.

Ulrik narrows his gaze at Niko, and all I can do is squeeze Niko's hand as my own fury flares to life.

I cannot believe I almost considered him. He and so many other noblemen are the reason my entire kingdom knows of my powers and why they all whisper my nickname.

Niko opens his mouth, but I raise my hand, stopping him, remaining intent on my clash with Lord Ulrik. Whether he is drunk and whether he is a noble, I am not going to stand idly by, letting others think they can step over me and my future husband.

"Lord Ulrik," I jeer, "had I not known you were so heavy on the drinks and tobacco, I might have given you a second glance."

A startled scoff erupts from Lord Ulrik, and I smirk.

Lifting a brow, I challenge him to try to push me further.

He can say whatever the Oblivion he wants, but I am not going to play nice and be docile anymore.

Staring him down, I wait for him to break.

A low, rich voice comes from behind Ulrik. "Who knew the queen had such balls?"

Our heads snap to Rick, a few steps behind Ulrik, as the rest of the guests dance, drink, and converse, completely unaware.

Rick's attention is down, inspecting his boots, as if none of us heard what he said.

I am stunned that Rick said something so blunt. Surely, he knows of Lord Ulrik's social standing.

I watch in curiosity as Ulrik levels his anger on a new person.

Lord Ulrik raises his voice. "Who are you to say such a thing in front of a woman?"

Rick straightens to his full height as he steps into the lord's vicinity, eyes raking up and down Lord Ulrik as if he could swallow him.

He leans in, too close for comfort, and Lord Ulrik arches away slightly.

"I'm the man who will chop off your balls and give them to her as a wedding present if you insult her again," Rick threatens.

My eyes widen, my heartbeat thumping loud against my heart, stunned.

Sweet Makers.

A blur of black covers my view of Rick and Lord Ulrik.

"Alright, gentlemen," Niko says, hands raised as he separates me from the two men. "Let's not start anything tonight."

I peer over Niko's shoulder, the three men fallen into silence. I glance between them, trying to predict who will take down who.

Niko is well trained with weaponry and blades. Runa and I used to watch all the castle guards train when we were in our teens.

Niko still trains every day. That, I know.

And Lord Ulrik, while he is nobility, I don't find him as skilled as Niko.

But Rick?

I inhale. I do not know what he can do. But I would wager he is at least capable of following through on his threats.

Ulrik breaks first, whirling to me and offering me a short, brief bow before storming away.

I sag in relief and Niko matches my actions, smiling.

Rick watches Ulrik depart before directing his attention to Niko and me, offering a subtle bow.

Niko laughs, waving him off. All signs of jealousy are vacant from Niko's demeanor as he addresses Rick.

"How can we extend our thanks, my lord?"

Rick's eyes meet Niko's, fleeting before finding mine. His eyes appear darker, less blue and more black, as they give me a once-over.

He blinks, and his features soften, offering me a kind smile. "If My Queen allows it, I'd like to have the next dance."

Niko grins, patting him on the arm and gesturing to the dance floor. It is reassuring to see Niko unbothered by this man, despite the mishap Rick witnessed last night.

I don't necessarily need Niko's permission to accept a dance with another man, but he still offers me a quick nod.

Last night is still fresh between Rick and me, but in using this dance to explain myself and thank him, maybe I could make a friend. I cling to the idea, hoping that leaning more into optimism might also bless my future.

Warmth surges up my body as I take Rick's hand.

He drapes my arm along his elbow, inclining his thanks to Niko. When his eyes meet mine, they are brighter and filled with blue.

As we drift to the dance floor, my guilt festers in the back of my mind that I still find him attractive.

I should not be feeling anything for this man. I have Niko, yet my gut still clenches when heat radiates from Rick's every touch.

The ensemble plays a harmonious ballad, and my steps falter after a few movements. My only saving grace is Rick's hand placement, gripping me tighter to keep embarrassment at a minimum.

He chuckles at my misstep as a blush explodes on my cheeks.

"In need of saving again so soon?" he chides.

I don't answer his remark, avoiding his gaze as we sidestep and spin.

The silence is suffocating, his gaze penetrating, as if he is waiting on me like prey to respond.

I feed him the silence as my emotions simmer down, waiting until I am ready to engage as a queen. I need to keep my features calm and cool and converse with him, as I would any other person here tonight.

Like cutting the tension with a knife, I jump into making amends for the awkwardness of last night. "I never did thank you for retrieving medicine from my lady-in-waiting yesterday."

"You are feeling better, I take it?"

"Yes, very much so."

I smile lightly, and Rick grins with a nod, his one dimple pinching his scar, making my stomach somersault.

Sweet Makers, please don't let me be blushing.

I need to think of Niko and only Niko.

Not one thought should drag me back to Rick.

We lift our hands above our heads as we turn in circles, our gazes holding as our breaths sync. Twisting and twirling, Rick spins me out, then draws me back in, his touch setting the skin beneath my onyx velvet gown ablaze.

"I find it amusing that many of your guests are congratulating your future husband instead of you. I would have imagined they'd be singing your praises, not his," he states nonchalantly.

I find Niko on the dais surrounded by many noblemen and women who clasp his hands and raise their glasses to him. I am happy to defend him.

"The people love him. It is to be expected to offer good wishes to the betrothed."

The small symphony builds the ballad for the last few bars of the song.

I try to ease into the music, but I can't stop dwelling over Rick's comment. If the people didn't know of my abilities, if they didn't succumb to this ever-growing winter, they might feel differently about me.

My mood darkens, and I wish I had not gone down that path of thought.

"Relax, My Queen," Rick coos. "Or you'll freeze over the whole ballroom if you keep that up."

What the fuck?

I blanch at Rick, stunned into silence as the song ends. I assumed he had known about my nickname, but for some reason, I wasn't expecting him to voice it so bluntly.

Coldness drapes over my features as the men and women surrounding us bow to their partners.

Rick and I hold each other's gazes.

I don't know whether to react or stay silent.

Instead, I break away harshly, returning to Niko and not giving Rick another glance.

I had not expected our conversation to end that way. I had hoped to make a friend, but I should have known Rick would be like the rest of them.

I don't dwell on the thought for long because the entire world blurs when Niko's face comes into view.

Niko tilts his head in concern as I rush to him. But when I reach him, I rise to my tiptoes to kiss his lips.

It catches him off guard.

He hesitates, unsure of how to react, but I have already lowered back down as he asks with a shocked breath, "What was that for?"

I take his hand, guiding him from the guests to sit with me. "You. You just make everything better."

Niko's eyes flash as he leans in, caressing my hand. His lips are soft against my knuckles.

"You make *me* better," he says.

Niko scoots his chair closer to the throne, and pure joy erupts.

I am compelled to keep touching him for the rest of the night.

10

MARRIAGE IS WHAT BRINGS US—

"If you keep up with that pacing, you'll run down the stone, Tove," Betina chimes when she enters my bedchamber.

I ignore her. I barely slept, fearful Niko would change his mind at the last minute.

Every person dreams of the day they get married, but here I am, crippled with doubt and believing I will fall face-first onto the marble floor.

Sweet Makers.

Every sensation devours my nerves, making me incapable of calming my own racing thoughts. They drift to the other reason I couldn't sleep. Images of how today might have gone with my family.

My mother would have picked the perfect crown and jewelry accessories to wear while she and Runa would argue over how I should style my hair.

They both would be filled with joy as I revealed my wedding gown.

Then my father would check in, and his entire face would light up with excitement at seeing me.

I can almost feel his arms wrapping around me now as he would whisper, *I am so proud of you.*

A teardrop cascades down my cheek, followed by another and then another. They blur my vision as my head slumps, my hands covering my face.

"Deities, why can't I feel the one emotion I'm supposed to feel on my wedding day? Why can't I stop thinking of them?"

A warm hand touches my arm, Betina easing me to her. Her aura lights up the entire room. Her dark skin glows in the sunlight from my bedchamber window as her voluminous black hair, pulled half-back, frames her face with tight curls.

I don't resist wrapping my arms around her and squeezing tight.

Her steady heartbeat in tandem with her sweet, spiced scent soothes me as the panic quiets in my head.

"They are watching you from above, my dear friend," Betina soothes. "I loved your sister and parents as much as anyone did, and I know they are beyond proud of everything you've accomplished here. You have been given a kingdom and magic none of your ancestors have had. And you're doing the best you can regardless, still getting out of bed every morning."

I sniff, always finding it hard to believe someone truly means that. Every time anyone says something encouraging, it sounds like pity or is just a reminder of how terrible a queen I am.

"But I am unable to remove my magic or melt the ice. I am still hurting my kingdom. It is no wonder everyone hates me. My parents would share the people's sentiments, too."

She shakes me. "Stop. You are doing everything in your power to accommodate your kingdom. Those who are closest to you know that. Those who are not close to you can fuck right off. Let them try to harness magic when they find themselves alone after learning their last family member is dead. You are growing into your role with each new day, and I know the same will happen with your magic. It's going to get better."

Betina's brown eyes stare into mine with deep intensity. Compassion oozes from her, and I grimace, uncomfortable with where this has escalated.

"It's your wedding day, Tove. Be happy."

I stare out my window at the sun beaming through a few clouds and shining into my room. My lungs expand as my sobs slow, allowing my breathing to regulate.

"I know they are watching over me," I whisper softly. "I just wish they were here."

Confessing my grief is always difficult, but Betina takes it in stride, holding my hand and squeezing.

I meet her fierce gaze.

"I know, Tove. I know. But we have done everything together to honor their memory for your special day. You look beautiful, and you will be even more beautiful when you bring a smile to your face. I doubt Niko wants to see his future bride sad," she soothes.

"I don't think anyone wants to see me sad."

Betina snorts and squeezes my hand as we face my vanity.

She reaches for my mother's small mirror, her violet tulle gown dragging lightly on the floor. Her bell sleeves are sheer with tight cuff links threaded with silver. The bodice enhances her curves, and the full skirt draped with purples and periwinkles.

It's truly a masterpiece, and I'm half tempted to ask her if I can wear it.

She extends the mirror to me, and I tuck it in my pocket while I take in my appearance for the first time.

Pure white lacework lines the bodice, with a rounded neckline around the chest and bound by buttons on the side. The gown descends outward from the waist, allowing the layers of varying shades of pale blue to glimmer in the lining, creating an illusion for those viewing it near and far.

"It is exquisite," I breathe out, my love of fashion impressed by my wedding gown's beauty.

"It's meant for you."

Betina's voice wobbles thick with emotion.

I nod slowly, unable to remove my eyes from the gown itself. I know my own features and have no desire to ruin this moment gazing upon them.

If I do, I might start crying again.

I graze the fabric of my dress delicately, seeking to commit this image to my memory. My nerves fight between staying in this room and walking down the aisle.

Even when Betina gathers my train and tulle cape, anxiety cripples my heart in a teetering, taunting melody.

I clench my mother's mirror, holding it for support, wishing Runa were beside me and my father was here to walk me down the aisle.

I brace myself against the tremors rippling through me as we exit my bedchamber. The arched hallways reach a shorter intersection, showing the pathway down the stairs.

Betina remains behind me, encouraging me onward, anxiety growing with each step as reality sets in.

I am getting married.

I peer over my shoulder at my lady-in-waiting.

"Betina? Do you—do you think this is right?" Fear and doubt are circling my mind, trying to convince me to run in the opposite direction. "I—I don't know if—"

"Tove, it's going to be alright. Remember what I said earlier." She eases my concerns.

I rub my hands together, fidgeting with my cuticles as we continue.

Dread still sinks deep into my gut as we pass portraits of my ancestors.

As we inch closer to the ballroom, I come to a stop in front of the painting of my family. Gazing at it, I take in the stoic gaze of my father's hazel eyes and his graying hair.

My mother's silver locks are up, similar to mine, as she also wears the look of stoicism.

Runa and I, in our younger years, haven't seen the toll royalty would take, and we plaster huge grins on our faces.

I walk up to the portrait, touching each face, wishing they could see everything now.

I wonder what they *really* think of me.

Betina is quiet, and I am grateful for her silent support as I fight through my grief.

I pray nothing comes of today. I haven't had a magic scare since the celebrations, and I can only hope it stays that way.

I want my parents to be proud of me for not fucking *one* thing up.

Lingering on Runa, my entire body cracks from missing her.

Dropping my head, I veer away from my mourning, approaching the doors to the ballroom.

I tilt my head in surprise when I catch Bernie and his daughter, Princess Vivienne, lingering at the entrance.

They turn, the king beaming and extending his arms for an embrace. "Queen Tove, you look absolutely beautiful!"

"Thank you, Bernie. Not as beautiful as your daughter, though," I admit, smiling in his embrace.

Vivienne bows her head in thanks as her father speaks, "You both are beautiful in my book."

Betina lowers my train, fanning it out as she asks the King of Belmur, "Do you have her from here?"

I lift an eyebrow in confusion, Bernie's features turning stoic.

"I have her from here," he says.

Princess Vivienne and Betina curtsy to me, then bow to the King of Belmur before they enter the ballroom, smiling.

"What do you mean, Bernie?" I ask in confusion.

"Exactly as it sounds. I am going to walk you down the aisle," he says, pride shining through his words.

My heart warms at the notion, but I lift my hands to reassure him. "Bernie, you don't—"

He hushes me, squeezing my sides gently. "I knew your father was an honorable man, and he wouldn't want you walking down the aisle alone. Now, are you ready, Your Majesty?"

I am caught off guard by the gesture. Unable to fight the emotion, I break softly as I embrace him again.

He wraps his large body around me, and he squeezes me twice, patting my back as my father would if he were here. "My dear Tove, all will be well."

I sniff through the tears, wiping my eyes when we drift apart. I muster all the calm I can, patting mother's mirror in my pocket as Bernie loops my arm in his and the staff attendants open the doors to the ballroom.

The heavy floral scent crashes against me as guests rise to the musicians playing Axidoria's anthem. White roses weave through green shrubbery plastered through the entire room. Silk drapes across the ceiling with flowers and foliage, spreading along the walls, over the ends of each bench, and wrapping around every pillar.

I clutch Bernie's arm as the doors close behind us, the only path onward being straight down the long aisle.

Each step and each set of eyes gnaw at me, devouring me.

I forgo the cold ruler they believe me to be, opting to show happiness that this day is finally here. Inclining my head as Bernie and I pass each row, I admire the ethereal aesthetic while being careful to not let my crown fall.

That would be an utter disaster.

But when my damned line of sight catches Rick in the crowd, I curse myself before darting my gaze away from him, hoping I didn't linger on him too long.

Bernie coughs lightly, my grip on him getting the better of me, and I direct my apprehensiveness to rubbing the worn grooves of Mother's mirror in my pocket.

Drifting closer, I allow myself to meet Niko's gaze, and my cheeks flush.

His sand-colored trousers complement the accents of baby blue lining his white doublet designed to match my gown. He wears a beige sash that matches his sword belt and medals, achievements he earned in serving Axidoria pinned neatly in place.

My heart leaps at the dedication he has for our kingdom.

He is everything Axidoria needs right now.

And while I want to move faster to get to him already, my mind wants to commit his boyish grin lighting up the entire room to memory, as if this will be the last time I see him like this.

Niko's gaze is intense, his amber eyes never leaving mine.

My own smile grows underneath his stare, enough reassurance that this is real and this is happening.

I am marrying Niko, and I could not be happier.

He extends his elbow when Bernie and I reach the end of the aisle at the foot of the dais.

Looking beyond the Alorian priest and Niko, I admire the lone throne, soon to have a partner.

I keep my feet planted on the floor for a few more brief moments, so that I may wrap my arms around Bernie.

He covers me entirely, the sun shining over me as if my family is watching.

I lean close to Bernie's ear. "Thank you for *everything*, Bernie."

His muscles tighten around me, giving me two squeezes before releasing me and offering me to Niko.

When our hands touch, a shiver rolls up and down my spine.

I am tugged closer to Niko, and a startled laugh escapes before the Alorian priest clears his throat and addresses the crowd.

"Ladies and gentlemen, Your Majesty." He looks at me, and I give the go ahead to continue.

"We are all gathered here today in celebration of the union between Her Royal Majesty, Queen Tove, and our very own Lord Nik—"

The priest coughs.

Mumbles from the crowd increase, and Niko and I arch a brow at each other as the priest's coughs turn frantic.

Niko eases forward to help the man—

The priest collapses.

Gasps escape throughout the crowd, and I peer over my shoulder, seeing the panic and horror. I turn back as Niko approaches the fallen priest, squatting and touching the man's throat.

"Is he—"

Someone claps.

Niko and I turn, everyone gaping at the man stepping into the aisle, wearing a devilish grin.

"Dead?" Rick asks coolly as he stares between Niko and me. "Yes."

Startled shock erupts through the ballroom as Niko rises, stepping away from the dais.

I glance around the room, not a guard in sight.

Where are all the guards?

"Sir, did you do this?" Niko asks.

Rick viciously sneers, releasing a low laugh. "Of course I did. How else would I have gotten your attention?"

My own eyes widen in shock, glancing back to the dead priest on the floor as a hushed silence fills the room.

I hurry to Niko's side, asking in a low whisper, "Where are the guards?"

The exit blocked by Rick clangs in response.

My blood runs cold at the hollering from beyond, staff and guards screaming for the doors to open.

Rick chuckles darkly. "It pays to be rich enough to bribe one of your staff members *handsomely* to keep any guards from coming in."

Niko and I share a glance.

My eyes flick down to his sword, the only one in the room besides Rick's.

Weapons and weddings are not meant to go together, and yet here they are, on my wedding day, with no guards in sight, a murder stopping my marriage, and guests to watch everything unfurl.

The Makers are set on ruining my existence.

Everyone waits with bated breath as Rick prowls down the aisle. "Now that I have your attention, I regret that I must inform you Queen Tove is already betrothed. And thus, I cannot allow this marriage to happen today."

Annoyance drives to the surface.

The fact I can't have one thing go right for me, including this *psychopath*, has me seething.

"I am not betrothed to anyone."

Rick's blue eyes pierce mine. "Yes, you are."

I hold Niko's hand, wanting to show a united front. "And *who* am I betrothed to if not Lord Nikolaj?"

Rick rests a hand on his heart, a huff at the slight as if I sought to offend him. But his offense shifts to smirking as he says, "Why, me, of course."

"Bullshit," Niko and I say in unison.

I do not want to hear anything Rick has to say. And somehow, Niko can tell because he angles himself between me and Rick, unsheathing his sword and pointing it.

I squeeze his hand, trusting him to handle this better than I can. He is challenging Rick, and no one, not even the crown, is to intervene when a blade is drawn.

A stupid rule amongst all swordsmen not to disrupt any party's honor.

The back door wiggles against the hinges as Rick looks over his fingernails, bored. "I would suggest against what you are insinuating, Lord Nikolaj," Rick warns in a dark tone.

My insides pinch at the warning, but the fire in Niko's eyes tells me he is not going to stand down.

Niko lifts his blade again, a reminder of the challenge to Rick, and I pray to the Makers they will protect my fiancé.

Ricks sighs, drawing his own sword and swinging it with flair. "Fine, but expect this to be over sooner than the guards can break down the door."

Guests closest to the aisle veer backward, no one able to escape.

I catch Bernie, Princess Vivienne, Betina, and her family, they too cannot do anything but watch.

Niko charges Rick, my chest plummeting fast when their blades lock.

The swords clash and drive, the clang of each hit filling the room. Fighting in an aisle puts both fighters at a disadvantage.

My eyes track every lunge, hit, and pivot.

Rick blocks and dodges each one of Niko's slashes with grace.

I haven't seen this man fight, but Niko is one of the best swordsmen I've seen.

Yet Rick looks bored.

Blades compose their own melody with the mix of feet sidestepping, everyone locked in place, staring in awe as the fight unfolds before us.

The sight of Niko's exhaustion has me wishing I could do something to stop it, but I remain frozen in place, watching and forgetting to breathe.

Rick's blade slices through the side of Niko's jacket.

Niko shrieks in pain.

People gasp as he applies pressure to the bleeding wound.

Rick pauses, a sinful grin hardening his features as he taunts Niko, "Might want to dismiss the guests. Don't want them to see you meet your demise."

Niko's eyes flash, and Rick laughs wickedly. "Oh wait. You can't, and you will."

Niko roars and charges Rick, neglecting the blood seeping down his arm.

Rick pivots away, a gleam of amusement hinting in his eyes as he fools Niko, swinging his sword arm in a swift attack.

Niko turns, barely able to fend off Rick's offensive strike.

"Please, my lords, stop this!" I exclaim, trying to command the fighting to end. "We can talk through this, I am sure."

My plea is ignored as Niko lunges for Rick, a dagger drawn from his other side.

Rick sidesteps him again, as if he anticipated it, forcing Niko to roll down the aisle, giving the enemy his back.

No.

A scream rises. "Wait! STOP!"

Rick moves faster than my words, drawing his own dagger and bringing it around Niko's throat.

I muffle my own scream, and the guests gasp.

Rick kicks Niko's sword and dagger from his hands, twisting to me. "Or what, My Queen?" Rick laces every word with menace.

Niko struggles to free himself from Rick's hold.

My heart stops when Rick's dagger pierces Niko's skin, a small dribble of blood trickling down.

Niko winces as I reach out.

Fear of losing another person I care for has a frigid crackle kissing up my arms.

Panic surges in my core, and despite my magic waking up, I somehow manage to plea, "Please, no. I can't do this without him."

But my own magic does not expel as it cascades through me. Instead, a bitter chill prickles against my skin, forcing me to look down at myself.

Frost blooms to life in my pores, specks of ice swirling across my hands and arms.

My own terrorized shriek is muted as terror explodes in the ballroom.

Screams bounce off the walls, fear driving people toward the exit as noblemen gape in horror and scorn as guests bang for the door to open and get away from the Snow Queen's power.

The symphony of alarm filling the room does not dampen Rick's rich tone. "Fascinating."

Niko collapses against Rick's hold as a guttural scream escapes me. Terror draws to the surface as Rick steps over Niko's body as if it is nothing, inching closer to me.

I stumble backward, my arms feeling dense as magic grows thicker in my veins, snow weighing me down.

I keep looking beyond Rick, toward Niko. Begging, pleading for him to—

"Relax. I will not kill your lover. Now let me help you," Rick says calmly.

"What did you do to him?" I hiss, shivers running through my body, unsure of how this man is going to help me.

Rick ignores my question, stalking after me.

I fight against my fear, managing to lift my heavy arm and strike him. But the effort goes unheeded.

Rick catches my hand before it meets his face and tugs me close.

I fight against his hold, trying to get my magic to attack him somehow and not whatever it is currently doing to me.

But Rick closes his eyes in concentration, heat erupting from where he touches me.

Warmth spews up my arm and throughout my entire body.

I don't know if it is rage or my magic, but when the frost coating my veins slowly vanishes, my eyes widen in horror when they meet Rick's gaze. I fight to escape his hold again, but my body is molten enough to faint.

"You are coming with me."

"I will *never* go with you," I spit, rage rising to the surface as the dizzying heat spreads through me.

"If you don't come willingly, I will kill your lover right here, right now." Rick tugs me, and my heart breaks seeing Niko injured.

I am left with no choice. To save him, I *have* to go with Rick.

I turn to Niko, watching him move slowly.

A few noblemen hurry to Niko, trying to help him up.

My heart leaps in relief and tears line my vision when his eyes find mine.

"Tove," Niko gasps.

The entire room is filled with terror and screams.

The doors finally open.

People and guards struggle against each other, trying to break through the tight threshold.

Noblemen abandon Niko as he reaches for me while scrambling toward his weapons.

"*Niko.*"

My voice cracks.

Amber eyes meet mine when he stands, almost falling forward from blood loss.

I half smile, a lump forming as I command, "You are the royal proxy in my stead."

Niko roars, "*No!* Get away from her!"

Niko attempts to follow us to the back room, but his steps are sluggish.

Rick laughs and opens the door with ease, and no guards wait on the other side. He pushes me through the back chamber and down the castle's secret halls.

Niko screams in agony, then cries after me. "I'm coming for you! I will find you!"

Tears stream down my cheeks. The heat and heaviness still flows through my body, keeping all cold from me. It feels as if my magic is draining from me.

I can't sense it.

I barely hold together my surprise at Rick's knowledge of the secret passageways as he pushes me. I lose my balance, stumbling over my dress.

The dress tangles between my legs as I struggle to get up.

The tearing of fabric rips.

I whip my head over my shoulder to see Rick cutting the long train of my wedding gown with his dagger. "You asshole!"

My. Wedding. Dress.

"There are prettier dresses in the world."

"*Prettier* dresses!?" I darken as rage sharpens my tone. "You motherfuck—"

Rick lifts me up. "You'll live." He brushes off my insults without a care in the world as he resumes in dragging me along.

I make my body heavy in each step to fight against his hold.

Gone is the man with charm who saved me from embarrassment, danced with ease, and flirted with me. Now the man addresses me as if it all meant nothing.

Fucking. Asshole.

We reach the back door of the castle, the closest to the stables, as shouts and raised voices fill the air.

The terror of never riding a horse before has me digging my feet into the ground as Rick ignores the sound of soldiers' boots hurrying toward us.

We approach one horse saddled with a few packs. The surprise of how large the saddle is, as if it was designed for two people, has me wondering how far in advance Rick planned this.

He gives the black steed a solid pat before directing his annoyance to me. "Your little lover is *resourceful.*"

"He is my fiancé," I spit.

Rick rolls his eyes as he grabs a rope and ties my hands together.

I wince as he finishes the last knot, the rope rubbing uncomfortably on my skin. When I try to make a break for it, he tugs me, hands tightening around me enough to change the color of my skin.

His black hair blows in the wind, and I hate how it makes his scar more stunning. "Don't even try it," Rick threatens.

I cease my efforts as he lifts me, placing me on the back of the saddle, patting his steed again as he says, "Can't have you trying to steer us in the wrong direction."

I wouldn't even know how to do that. I've only ever been in a carriage.

Rick smirks before mounting in one swift motion.

I barely have a chance to find something to hold on to when he whistles, his leg brushing against the steed, clicking his mouth twice.

The horse surges into a gallop, leaving the stables behind.

I lurch forward and seek Rick's shirt for support.

Riding is uncomfortable, the wind slashing across my face and ripping my crown and veil off my head.

We inch closer to the castle gates, and my body rocks back and forth, struggling to peer behind to my home drifting farther and farther away.

Guards fill the bridge at the gate, arrows nocked and pointed at Rick and me.

I yell into the wind, hoping to command them for fear of their arrows hitting me and not Rick. "Hold your fire!"

I don't want to get shot, but I also worry that Rick might do something drastic if my guards attack. No one else should get hurt. So many people are already affected by my dreaded winter.

I put my heart and trust in Niko that he will take care of the kingdom while he comes for me.

Faces of each soldier on the bridge become clearer, and a familiar person takes shape.

Niko.

My heart skips a beat at the relief he is safe. But knowing Niko, he is not going to let Rick get away with this.

The shouting of "Close the gates" comes from Niko as we approach.

Rick utters a command to his steed, and our speed increases.

My stomach drops as the gates close.

We aren't going to make it.

But the large black stallion's pace picks up even more, a chuckle vibrating from Rick's chest. We fly through the gates, mere inches left between us and the guards failing to stop the horse.

My faith in being saved ceases as I crash into Rick's back when he tugs on the reins. I peer over my shoulder toward my guards on the bridge, seeking Niko's face one last time.

But I clasp Rick's vest, shaking him when my guards all nock their arrows. "Rick, my guards—they aren't standing down."

"Sure," he replies, whisking the reins once more.

I brave another glance, my heart lurching from my chest when Niko's red hair separates him from the rest of the guards, my eyes widening as he grabs a bow from the guard beside him, notching it himself.

Is he... *No.*

He wouldn't!

Niko releases the arrow aimed toward us, and the fear that a weapon is headed directly for me overpowers my trust in Niko and his skillful aim.

I am unable to suppress my sheer terror. "ARROW!"

Rick tugs the bridle, guiding us to drift as a sharp searing pain pierces me.

My screams erupt at the invasion, squeezing my arms around Rick as I breathe through the arrow puncturing my shoulder.

"Fuck," Rick hisses, as the coppery smell of blood clouds my senses.

It takes everything in me not to vomit.

Rick tugs the straps again as we pass Yalta, pointing his steed northward. A stinging sensation burns hotter from my injury.

"We should reach the trees leading to Biala Forest soon. Once we pass them, I can remove the arrow," Rick tells me through the scattered winds.

My insides clench, and my shoulder throbs. The idea of removing the arrow only drives the pain more. Warmth streams down my back, ruining my wedding gown.

My *precious* wedding gown.

I shriek in pain when the horse hurdles over a wooden gate.

Rick reaches an arm behind, holding me.

"I-I can't feel my arms," I seethe as exhaustion rips through me.

I crash into his back when the horse leaps over another fence, rampaging through a small field of crops, lightly frosted. These fields are essential and are being damaged and will hurt my people come spring.

The world swims around me as I plea, "Please, my people need these crops. Can't we take another path?"

Hearing my request, Rick tugs the reins to the right, the steed leaving the rest of the crops undamaged.

A small reprieve drives my vision to soften, the hues of the blue sky blending with the lightly sleeted plains we ride through.

"R-Rick?" I ask, my head lolling and voice quieting.

"Stay with me. We are almost there."

Heaviness expands from my scalp down to the rest of my body. Trying to fight it, I tighten my hold on him, but my strength falters.

I slump forward against a warm, hard cushion.

Rich cologne dulls the sense of agony, dipping into my veins and soothing my body as darkness takes over.

11

Who's to Blame?

My eyes flutter open.

Biala Forest surrounds me with the soft light of the upcoming sunset peeking through the tree branches and leaves.

Memories force their way to the surface, remembering my wedding, Niko, Rick, and an arrow to my shoulder.

Bile coats my throat at the searing pain and begs for escape. Deities, why doesn't anything ever play out right for me?

I must be cursed.

"I should have known you'd pass out," a voice sighs.

I glare at my kidnapper as he tosses a swig of water from his pack while a small fire warms near me. I try to move my body, stopping when raw pain explodes. Hissing at the tenderness of it, I look down.

"This is *your* fault," I seethe through gritted teeth.

A jacket covers me as I lie on my side. I try to lift it, struggling through each breath. But my eyes widen at the amount of blood covering my gown, the sensation of tearing echoing in my head and body.

A groan escapes as Rick's rich voice chuckles. "You could at least say thank you for reviving you after fainting for the *second* time in my presence."

All I can think to do is stick my tongue out. Warmth blooms behind my cheeks at the childish behavior, but I cannot even contemplate moving another inch with the arrow still lodged in my upper back.

Of course, Rick laughs again, and I wish I could smack the amusement off his face. His expression turns conniving as his blue eyes meet mine, the fire illuminating his features.

"Better watch what you do with that tongue of yours, My Queen, or I'll be forced to do something about it."

"Fuck you," I lash out.

He will sorely regret saying that.

I might not be able to do anything—but if word of me being injured gets back to Niko, he will unleash Oblivion upon Rick.

His eyes grow hard and heavy, deep with desire as he clicks his tongue. "Oh, we will get to that eventually... after we wed, of course." He shrugs with nonchalance, and I scowl deeper. "I'm a gentleman, after all."

Anger rises within me. "Your idea of marrying me will never count in my kingdom."

Rick cocks his head, leaning in as he asks, "Who said anything about your kingdom?"

I roll my eyes with annoyance. "You can't be serious. There is no way you'll get away with kidnapping a queen. Niko will—"

Rick applies pressure to my right arm, a wave of new torturous pain rippling through me.

I shriek in frustration and agony and annoyance that my emotions, my body, always take the lead over my mind.

Will there ever be an occasion, a day, or a time where I won't be consumed by pain, distress, and grief? Will I ever learn not to cry?

Everything *fucking* hurts.

He removes his hold and pulls me upright, forcing another roar of pain from me.

Rick chuckles darkly. "Who said anything about *your* kingdom?"

My eyes widen when a shadow descends over Rick's features, his darkened gaze growing knowingly as his lips lift.

Fear sinks in.

I scan my surroundings once more.

Biala Forest is at the border of Axidoria, and that means... *No.*

The only other kingdom close enough is—

No. No. No. No. NO!

This isn't happening. My heart slows, and the hair on the back of my neck rises.

This *can't* be happening.

Rick's stare remains intent on me as the pieces fall into place, and my mouth runs dry.

"Y-You're—" I gulp down air despite my throat closing.

Goose bumps prickle against my skin as Rick stands, offering me an exaggerated bow. He remains bent at the waist, but those ice-cold eyes flick up to meet mine.

"King Jerrick of Palaena."

The King of Palaena...

His dimple appears. "It is a pleasure to officially meet you, My Queen."

I am *such* an idiot.

Fury reverberates beyond the tingling in my shoulder as rage boils over. Anger latches around my heart, dismissing the interest I had to this man—this *monster* who calls himself the King of Palaena.

Fuck attraction.

His kingdom is behind my family's deaths.

Hatred oozes to the surface in the presence of my enemy.

I always suspected Palaena was behind their deaths but never proved it.

The rumors surrounding my family and their early graves follow me as much as my dreaded nickname. But everyone in Axidoria was told my family's deaths involved traveling on business.

When my mother and sister died, we used the same explanation. For all we know, they could have died during travel, gotten attacked by animals, or murdered by bandits.

Or taken prisoner and assassinated by Palaena.

But I could not say that aloud without backing my claims up for fear of the Makers' wrath.

I had Niko lead the investigation. We sent our best spies and many letters, even resorted to mercenaries. No word ever came back, and neither did the people.

The false hope, the cost of that while trying to feed my kingdom, plus the pressure of seeking answers took a toll on my heart. My grief, my powers, and my attempts to rule a kingdom were already unbearable, and I needed to make a choice.

Without any proof, I knew I would not be able to do anything. And as much as I wanted and *needed* that closure, I called it off.

I couldn't bear to look into it anymore but hoped, one day, I could.

The same thing happened when Mother believed Palaena was behind Father's death. She tried to convince our priests and the other kingdoms to help go against Palaena.

But they all knew this was a serious accusation and could not be taken lightly.

It was the first potential attack against a neighboring kingdom, and to avoid the wrath of the Makers, the priests and the other four kingdoms required proof.

It would gain Mother support, so she left with a plan for trade to grant an audience with the King of Palaena.

She, too, never came back.

I tried to argue the disappearance of my family was evidence enough. But Niko, the priests, and the other kingdoms agreed it was not.

But through this *monster's* smugness before me, I know they are behind my family's deaths.

My heart falls into a frenzy, my mind calling forth my magic with a sense of urgency. I plea, leaning into resentment and vengeance to awaken my power to keep this monster away.

Winter sings in my bones, caressing a chilling breath as it creeps up my spine. Exertion from anger and pain leave me heaving. The sharp, bitter cold forces my teeth to chatter as a numbing sensation runs down my arms.

I yelp in alarm, staring in shock at the frost glimmering on my skin. Gasps of panic escape over the terror of my magic working against me.

Rick—or *Jerrick*—squats in front of me, covering my arms with his hands, warmth dissolving the swirls of ice on me.

Despite his assistance, it does nothing to suppress the vengeance I wish to seek against him and his family.

Recoiling from his touch, I pray to the Makers my magic will sync up with my rage and help me.

"Get your hands off of me," I demand.

"Feeling warmer yet, Frostbite?"

I clench my jaw, hatred seething through my teeth. "Don't call me that."

His onyx hair blows in the wind, softening his features. "Then, get a hold of your magic and breathe like a normal person, or I'll be forced to distract you."

I sneer underneath his gaze, perplexed by what he could mean by "distract me."

My magic continues to manifest along my skin, and even the tinge of frost causes more pain. I fight against his hold still trying to warm me, unsure of how he is doing this.

Fury and fear intermingle with one another, pairing together in a dance with my magic that could actually kill me if I do not get it to stop appearing on my skin.

I glance down at my arms, my breath visible. Slowly, I struggle to calm my anger, my fear, and fight through the pain.

Sections of my arms thicken in frost, causing panic to take root, sending memories rushing to the surface. I flinch, closing my eyes to the memory of snow turning into ice and cracking as it expands.

"Get a hold of yourself," Jerrick commands.

Panic grips my heart as the cold refuses to quiet, slowly taking over.

My visible fear meets Jerrick.

He springs into action, shooting forward and clashing his lips to mine.

My eyes widen in shock, his hold on my arms squeezing tightly, but his forced kiss warms my cheeks. Heat streamlines across my face, drifting underneath my skin as more warmth envelops me. Lightness takes over my body, relaxing.

I close my eyes, falling into the kiss as the pain ebbs away. It's warm and soft and deepens as his cologne intertwines with the bitter cold of my breath.

Sensation returns to me as Jerrick peels away, lingering for a final peck before withdrawing completely. My skin burns up, and it isn't until Jerrick releases me that the feeling lessens.

I open my eyes, stunned and staring into beautiful ice-blue eyes.

Jerrick winks as reality comes crashing in.

"Did you just fucking kiss me!?" I exclaim, bringing my good hand up to rub his lingering essence from my mouth as it remains open in shock.

"It worked, didn't it?" Jerrick flicks his eyes down to my sides.

I glance down at myself in wonder.

My arms are no longer coated with frost, and the well of power has completely vanished. My magic has always had its moments, but this is the second time it has directed its powers internally instead of outwardly.

Could it be because of this man?

My eyes linger on my wedding gown. A wedding gown that was tailored and designed for my wedding day. My wedding day to Niko, my fiancé.

And here I am with my enemy kissing me.

Guilt swirls and gnaws in my core, and I might vomit at my own realization.

I can't believe I did this to Niko. Kissing another man on my wedding day.

Deities, take me now.

Damn him for stealing that when it could have been Niko's mouth on mine all day today. I reach for my mouth, tempted to force myself to vomit and remove his scent still lingering on my clothes.

"I warned you I would be forced to distract you," he taunts as he rests on one knee, still too close to me.

"Kissing me was your version of distracting?"

I am furious that whatever he did worked. I roll my eyes in annoyance when his smirk turns wickedly delicious, and a damned dimple appears, making him stupidly more attractive.

"You kissed back, and your magic stopped," Jerrick teases.

"You can't kiss me!"

"And why not?" He tilts his head, as if the logic I give him is confusing.

"Because I am engaged!"

His crooked grin appears. "Yes, to me."

I scrub my face and drop my head, groaning in defeat. "Not this again."

The stretching of my emotions and body are beyond the limits of comfort. Bit by bit, my heart fractures, as this never-ending nightmare continues.

"Magic is different for most everyone to harness, but you are going about it completely wrong." Jerrick directs our conversation elsewhere.

I am minimally grateful, even when he waves his hand, as if I didn't already know I am using my magic wrong. *Of course* I am using it wrong. No one has ever had these abilities before!

"I don't want my magic," I grind out.

"Why not?" He rests a hand on his hip.

"It's a curse."

Jerrick slackens.

I attempt to wrap my arm around my body, and I hate how refreshing it is to admit that to someone. I *hate* that the someone was him.

Glancing away, something glints.

Recognition dawns, and a defeated whimper escapes as my mother's handheld mirror reflects in the firelight.

My heart fractures when I grab it, inspecting it to see a small crack in the upper corner.

No.

"What is that?" Jerrick asks, observing me.

Clutching the mirror to my chest, I protect it. "None of your business." I scowl.

He reaches toward me, and my anger kicks in. "Don't touch me!"

Pain and fear intermingle inside at the thought of him touching me again. Hurting me again or kissing me again—I don't want any of those things.

I prepare for the pain to explode, but Jerrick holds my waist, forcing me to stop. I meet those fierce eyes I am growing to loathe, only to be met with his soft chuckle.

"There's the little Frostbite."

"I swear to Yeva if you call me that one more time—"

"You'll what? You'll freeze me over like you have your kingdom?" He bounces back.

I clench my jaw in silence.

He smirks at my lack of remark, but I stick to it, fearful of saying anything that could have him take my mother's mirror away. It is my only hope of reaching home.

Let this monster who calls himself a king think he knows everything there is about the Snow Queen of Axidoria.

I clutch my mother's mirror tighter.

Jerrick studies me in silence, rolling his eyes in exasperation and stepping around to examine my injury. He mutters "Dammit," and I turn to him in question, the movement pinching down my neck.

"You've lost a lot of blood. And because of that, I cannot—nor do I want to—remove the arrow, or you'll surely bleed out. We need to keep going if you want to live." Grabbing me, Jerrick adds, "This is going to hurt like Oblivion for you."

I attempt to shake from his hold, but he leans in, whispering softly, "I've got you."

An odd comfort from the tenderness behind his words reminds me of the charm and compassion I'd seen from him before today's catastrophe. Putting aside our differences, I tell myself to live now, fight tomorrow.

If you can even make it that long, Tove.

Knowing I am out of options, I exhale one long breath, fitting Mother's mirror back in my pocket before placing my hand in my captor's and bracing for the pain.

He shifts his weight to stand, allowing me something to hold on to.

I fight through the dizziness and the yelp of agony from the movement of my joints.

Expelling the air from my lungs, I push forward as my hold tightens on Jerrick. I make it to my knees, and my head rocks, fighting the vertigo threatening to steal me under. I let my body play catch-up.

Jerrick holds my hand, waiting patiently. It is thoughtful and makes despising him harder. He gives me a signal to move again, and I respond in tune, rising fully upright.

Heaviness begs to take me down, but Jerrick reaches around me carefully, holding me close and allowing me support as he guides me to the side of the horse.

Black dots mesh with the lightly frozen forest in front of the beast. I focus on blinking the darkness away as I clutch Jerrick, hating the need for his assistance.

I bite my lip as we approach the horse, my lack of experience with animals making me wary, along with trying to figure out how to even mount the steed.

"You'll be riding sidesaddle in the front," Jerrick says, already ahead of my train of thought.

My mouth falls.

Being this is the second time I have ridden a horse in my life, I do not have any desire to ride sidesaddle. Why couldn't I have been kidnapped in a cushiony carriage?

"I-I can't—"

"It is the only way for the arrow not to be jostled during transit."

I dart back and forth between the reins and the saddle, fear turning my palms sweaty.

"You'll have me to lean against for support," he says with a taunting smirk.

That is not comforting. But my own cowardice must be shining because Jerrick helps my leg into the stirrup, leaving me hanging in an awkward position as he turns to smother the fire, jogging back and mounting the steed with ease.

He pulls me up faster than I anticipated, my muscles stretching and my arm almost dislodging.

"I don't need to lose another limb!" I scold.

He laughs and eases me back against him. "There, there, Frostbite."

I bristle at the nickname, seething. "Stop. Calling. Me. That."

Jerrick's lips tick upward as I awkwardly wrap my left arm around him, abhorring myself for leaning into my enemy for support.

12

THE VOID

The front of the saddle rubs against my right hip, causing me to wiggle and lean into Jerrick. In my pain and out of a need for comfort in what could be my last moments, I pretend that I am here by choice and Jerrick is someone I could trust.

His body is muscular and wide enough to circle me in, providing me warmth as the side of my head rests on his chest, hiding my winces through our passage into Biala Forest and closer to Palaena's border.

The further we trek from Axidoria, the more distinguishable the differences are between my cursed winter and Aiyana's season. Aiyana's weather is light and delicate in the forest, my observant eyes noting the areas kissed by her nature and killed by my touch.

My heart constricts, seeing the harsh ice and dead trees showing no signs of life all because of my powers.

The thought of dooming animals as much as my people makes my skin crawl.

The crisp breeze blows against me, drying some of the blood that has soaked through. Small shivers reverberate through me but none for Jerrick.

The damn man is so fucking warm it pisses me off.

As if he senses my irritation at his perfection, he hums under his breath, breaking the silence between us as we rock in and out of sync on the saddle.

I glance at him, and my vexation takes deeper root at his chiseled jaw, the perfect scar, the small dimple coming to life as he glances down. How could I—

"Something amusing you?"

I dart my stare from Jerrick, knowing I got caught but hoping my blush doesn't surface. Damn him and his good looks.

His gaze bores into me, and I squirm further into myself.

"Oh, come now, what else do we have to do with our time together?" he asks, trying to antagonize me more.

"I'd much rather ride in silence than be stuck speaking with you."

"And here I thought we were getting along so well."

"We do *not* get along. Your family killed mine," I spit.

"Says who?"

His denial only furthers my own beliefs. But I cannot predict what he will do if I piss him off. All I do know is he charmed me, killed a priest, fought my fiancé, and kidnapped me. He very well is capable of killing my family.

Him and the entire wretched Mikkelson line.

To keep from goading him, I bite my tongue hard, drawing blood. I hate my inability to protect myself and my stupid reliance on him to stay alive.

If I knew how to harness my abilities, I could protect myself.

And if you knew how to harness your abilities, your people wouldn't hate you, and *you wouldn't be in this mess to begin with, Tove.*

Jerrick weaves his way through Biala Forest as night sweeps across the sky. The light from the sun diminishes, the trees clear, and a cloudless sky illuminates the white glow of the moon.

With the temperature lowering, the wind picks up, swishing and whirling around us, and more shivers take hold of me the longer I remain on horseback.

Not even the heat emanating from Jerrick can stop my teeth from rattling and my exhaustion from tugging at me.

The horse slows to a quieter walk as Jerrick says, "We need to camp for the night."

I nod curtly through trembling teeth, and he guides his horse down an unworn path leading to a small clearing in front of a cave.

I look at Jerrick.

"It'll keep us warm and keep us away from any creatures here in the forest," he says.

The closer we get, the more I shake uncontrollably. It is dark outside, but the cave itself is a void.

My anxiety rises as Jerrick halts the steed and dismounts from behind me, removing all I had for warmth.

"What if something is inside?" I blurt.

"Am I to believe you are worried about me?"

I know my face is contorted with worry, alongside the pain and coldness, but Jerrick's warm hand squeezes my legs, sending heat into my chest.

Jerrick guides us into the cave.

The moonlit night is bright enough to provide us with minimal light, and there is a slight chill, but nothing compared to outside.

He gestures his hands up to help me down.

"This is probably going to hurt, but you can't scream. We don't want to alert beasts," he warns, emphasizing the last word.

Fear and the impending pain make me hesitant about dismounting, knowing my shoulder won't be the only thing hurting. The blood loss is evident even through my drained body and wheezing breaths.

I secretly hope I could pass out again just to skip the agony of getting off this horse.

I attempt to rock my hips off the horse's side. Pain sears through me as I lean forward, but Jerrick grips my waist, pulling me away from the steed, allowing the least amount of contact with my back.

It still doesn't prevent the misery exploding.

I muffle my scream by biting my lip hard enough for copper to coat my tongue. Nausea roils in my gut and in my chest, and I squeeze my eyes shut, hoping to avoid vomiting. The fight is unbearable, and I hurl to my left, barely pulling away from Jerrick in time.

Dry heaves stick as I wobble, fighting to keep the bile from coming out. But even my own body loses control.

Jerrick holds me by my sides, keeping loose strands of hair from falling in front of my mouth.

My skin is an inferno, yet the sweat on my brow is cold, and the tremors refuse to abate. It's freezing in the forest and in this cave, but I am confused by the sudden heat. I internally plea for this to stop.

"Don't look," I manage to wrench out hoarsely. Bile escapes as my body begs to crumple. "*Please.*"

This is another embarrassment for him to keep score of and throw in my face at a later time.

But Jerrick is silent, holding me steady.

Whether he holds me for minutes or hours, I don't know, but when the nausea subsides, I am spent. I want to rise and push myself through the waves of exhaustion, to show I am alright, but my knees give out.

Jerrick catches me before I scrape up my legs from the rocks on the ground, putting my weight against him and tenderly guiding me into a sitting position.

I hiss through each movement, dreading this endless cycle. I exhale, trying not to be loud, but I am so fucking drained.

My head is reeling. My throat is raw. My legs are throbbing.

And I am still in my wedding gown. My torn and *bloodied* wedding gown.

A tear falls down my cheek as defeat sinks in over how my wedding day turned into a disaster.

I can't stop sniffing, the sound of it echoing in the cave, while wishing for my bedchamber—wishing for Betina—wishing for Niko.

Jerrick notices me slumping, and he eases me down on my left side.

The cold floor crashes against my body, but the second my head is braced on something, I exhale a small shudder of relief.

Jerrick's footsteps tell me he is walking away, and only then do I fall apart.

I wish I wasn't here.

I wish I knew what my parents thought of this predicament.

Tears stream down my cheeks as Jerrick's approach earns a gasp from me as something touches me. I flinch at the contact, bracing for pain—

"Relax, it's only a blanket," he says.

I nod silently, too tired to fight him and grateful the night is shielding me from his scrutiny.

But Jerrick lowers to the floor, and when he faces me, the damn moon grants us enough light to see each other.

I blink away my tears as he studies me closely, the woolen blanket granting me heat. I want to relax, but I can't with him analyzing my every move. I grunt and wiggle, trying to find a way to hide my eyes.

Jerrick shifts closer, combing loose strands of my silver-blonde hair away from my face and forcing me to halt.

I want to revolt, but his touch is warm and tender.

"I'm not here to hurt you," Jerrick whispers.

I scoff. "Not here to hurt me?"

My eyes flash with fury only to be met by his own.

Jerrick withdraws, shifting himself into a comfortable position as he exhales an exhausted command. "Sleep, Frostbite."

Frost escapes from my fingertips, winter beaming on the light air that expands from my lips.

I wish I could stop sprinting away, but I break through the courtyards, and I keep hurrying beyond my home.

A kiss plants itself in my core, blossoming into more swirls of ice, which drifts outwardly from each step that touches the semi frozen grass.

Wind blows my hair out of my face as I come to a hard stop at the lake, relief flooding me.

I marvel in awe as frost from my feet hardens the lake.

CRACK!

Dread anchors me down as the cracking noise continues more harshly—more brutally—more violently.

CRACK! CRACK! CRACK!

"NO. Please. STOP!" I plead.

"Frostbite, wake up!" a voice screams.

I blink awake to meet the man leaning close to me.

My kidnapper.

My enemy.

I try to push him away, shrieking from moving my damned right arm.

"Easy," Jerrick says as I scan my surroundings, seeing I am still in the cave.

The wool blanket feels constrictive with Jerrick holding my side. My brows furrow at his proximity, hating that he saw me in my most vulnerable state.

I hide my torment. But mostly in avoidance of his stupidly beautiful eyes that are the same color as my own.

"Do you *have* to be next to me?"

"Well, you *did* ask." He smirks.

"I did not!"

"Oh, I must've misheard you, then."

The richness of his voice coats my skin in goose bumps as he releases me, rising to retrieve something from his pack.

He tosses it, letting it collide with my face.

"*Ow.*" I awkwardly attempt to rub the tender area.

Jerrick sighs and saunters toward me.

He lowers into a squat, dropping a few small pieces of dried meat and nuts into the palm of my hand. His scent is lighter, mixed with the dampness of the cave, as I place a nut in my mouth, crunching down softly.

"We have a lot of work to do," he grumbles.

"There is no *we*," I bite back as I swallow another helping of food.

Something dark lingers beneath his gaze, wicked enough to make my skin crawl.

"There's been a *we* ever since our parents decided to play with fate," Jerrick says coldly.

My eyes widen. "Our parents?"

He heaves an annoyed sigh, pinching his brows. "Sweet Makers, stop pretending you don't know anything."

"What are you talking about?"

He waves me off in dismissal as he rises. "Never mind. Let's get on the road before we tackle another problem."

"What. Are. You. Talking. About?" I ask again, anger lacing each word.

I wait for his reply, but of course, he decides to stay quiet, packing up the woolen blanket before coming back to reach for me.

I scoot away from him, wincing in pain. I am not going to let this slide. I need to know what the fuck he is talking about.

He tries again, and I wiggle out of his touch. His face flashes with anger as I contort mine into seriousness, waiting for him to bite.

The muscles on the side of his jaw tic, and I know I've got him.

But he surprises me when he shrugs, turns, and goes to mount the horse without me.

I panic. "Where are you going?" He can't leave me here!

What kind of person kidnaps another, just to leave them to die simply because they want answers?

Jerrick turns his frame to the side, lifting his brows. "Do you want to come with me?"

My jaw works, watching the sunbeam beyond the cave, illuminating the asshole like the deity he is.

The psychopath smiles viciously. It is cruel, meant for me to realize I will meet my demise if I do not go with him.

I am not the one in control here—he is.

Letum damn him, this cave, and my fucking shoulder.

"You aren't leaving me here," I demand, the reminder to live ringing clear as a bell through my mind.

"I'm not?" he asks knowingly, using my injury and helplessness against me.

Fucking bastard.

I am not going to die. Even if I beg the Makers to let me reunite with my family, I cannot leave Niko and my home at risk from this monster.

The frigid winter is better for my kingdom than being left in the hands of Palaena.

If playing along with his whims allows me to live and get to the bottom of what he meant, then so be it. I clench my fists, everything in me trying to not spew a remark that could make him truly leave me to die.

"*Please* take me with you," I grind out.

He leans back, laughing in feigned joy, and jumping off the horse to approach. "Oh, I am so glad you chose right, Frostbite!" He extends his hands yet again.

I wiggle and grunt through each breath. "Stop calling me that," I snarl, torturously rising with Jerrick's help.

I haven't been standing for a full minute as the world falls out from under me. Swaying side to side, my weight slips enough for even Jerrick to scramble to help me remain upright.

You can't die when he hasn't answered your questions, Tove!

My brain runs in circles despite sleeping through the night. Trying to push myself and be coherent, I grunt through the entire painful experience, pulling in my shoulder as Jerrick and I make it to the horse.

But as exhaustion sweeps over me again, I swear there are two Jerricks holding onto my leg. I huff a laugh at both of them.

"There are two of you," I remark faintly.

"Fuck," Jerrick mutters as my head lolls.

The person before me blurs and disappears, and suddenly, I am on the horse, a force guiding me to lean into Jerrick's embrace.

My mind is spent, the few steps of walking disintegrating my emotions and feelings toward my captor.

Or were there two?

I can't remember anymore.

"I feel cold," I warn the two blobs.

Jerrick puts his hand on my forehead—it is so warm. Relief tugs at my lips over the heat coming off him.

"You're burning up," one of the two blurry people comments.

"Jer—" I try to say, but I am freezing, and my body is so heavy.

I blink as everything grows darker.

Warm cologne and leather mixes into the air. I lean into a solid cushion, faintly aware of the memory from a few days ago. That was such a different time, filled with dresses, wine, and dancing.

And a handsome man that rubbed my hand in circles in the same way my sister once did.

A glimmer of a smile twinkles against my lips at the thought as I settle, eyes closing and black dots pulling my consciousness away.

A melody played with the soft, tentative touch of keys on my piano dwindles in the back of my mind.

"Mmmm. Home," I hum, rubbing my nose into the warm pillow, hearing a low, rich chuckle repeating in my mind.

13

IS THIS HOME?

Basking in the infinite abyss of slumber is, for once, peaceful to my dreams. It isn't often when I am deep in sleep that the darkness swallows me whole, protecting me from my past and from my night terrors. It is freeing to be in this harmonious pit of nothingness.

Yet there is a rustling to my right.

I try to turn away, hoping to shake off the growing noise lingering here in the dimness. Muffled voices join the sounds, nearing where I lie.

Fluttering my eyes, I squint when a fleck of light beams through the void. But something covers the light, allowing my eyes a brief relief, only for a shadowed figure to fill my view.

The peace of sleep comes to an abrupt end.

The prominent scar is on full display as the face hovers over me, blocking me from seeing anything beyond him. Gone is the shadow of a beard on his jawline, replaced with stubble that has grown out a little.

Deities, he looks as if he hasn't showered in days.

Jerrick still smells of the forest, with only traces of the cologne I find myself longing for.

His features soften. "Looks like you made it, Frostbite."

My temper flares at the damned nickname, but it is forgotten as he pulls away, allowing me to take in my surroundings.

Red satin sheets are spread and rumpled, blending in with a chaise at the foot of the bed. Gilded bronze frames the bedposts, the hearth, and the small chandelier illuminating the room.

There is a working table with a dark maroon lounge chair next to three tall windows, and to the left of me is a bathing chamber, wardrobe, and entrance.

The room is larger than the queen's chambers in Axidoria, yet it feels more homey—more cozy.

But that comfort is stripped bare as my gaze remains glued to another man leaning against the door.

His tall, lean frame is sculpted enough to make the muscles in his arms visible as he crosses them. He offers me a tight expression. His hair is black like Jerrick's but grown out beyond his ears rather than to his shoulders. No dimples and no scars on his cleanly shaven honeyed skin.

Just deep russet eyes studying me through a suspicious squint.

Beside the man is a woman. She is petite and slender, with wavy dark-brown hair and an olive-beige complexion. But it is her small pink lips and golden chestnut eyes that hold my attention the longest. She wears a tight smile compared to the two men staring at me skeptically.

She is probably a staff member. Maybe a healer. Or maid?

My gaze returns to Jerrick, braced against the bed with his hand lingering near mine. The urge to hold it hits me like a wave, seeking comfort in the only person I know.

How pathetic.

I swallow down a gulp of air, trying to rise, and I am surprised by how fast Jerrick springs forward to help me.

His arms are tense and strong as they guide me up slowly and carefully, which I am thankful for as soreness spreads along my body.

"I'd be careful if I were you. You've been in and out for a while," Jerrick comments.

My mouth falls. "Wh-What?" I inspect my right shoulder and see it bandaged.

I don't remember how I got here. All I remember is seeing two Jerrick's and pain.

I bristle at the phantom sensation of tearing and pulling, clinging the satin sheets.

"It's alright," the man from the door says, stepping into the room.

His tanned skin is accentuated by his sharp features, but his brown eyes hold a promise behind them, sending an optimistic feeling into my chest.

Jerrick stands, moving toward the foot of the bed and crossing his arms as the man comes up and takes my hand.

"It is wonderful to meet you, Queen Tove. I am Prince Jonas, but you can call me Jonas. I'm Jerrick's brother and head advisor." He kisses my knuckles, and heat rushes to my cheeks at how genuine he seems.

Trust rings true as the prince offers me a kind smile.

I palm my cheek, hiding the heat blooming and masking myself as I say, "It is a pleasure, Jonas."

The woman near the entrance walks further into the room, and her eyes meet mine as she curtsies. Her long wavy hair billows forward before rising, sweeping loose strands behind her ears.

"Hello, Your Majesty, I am Dorit, and I am to be your lady-in-waiting," her high, soft voice chimes.

I tilt my head in acknowledgment.

Jerrick claps his hands and startles me. "Wonderful. Now that you are awake, let's discuss our arrangement."

Jonas scoffs, eyes rolling. "*Arrangement.*"

I fight to suppress a laugh when Jerrick shoots Jonas a hint of annoyance.

Jonas waves his brother, the *king*, off as he glares. "I am still pissed you didn't stick to the plan we discussed."

"I only tweaked a few things," Jerrick replies.

"A *few* things? You were *supposed* to talk to her and show her the decree! What kind of *idiot* kidnaps their *betrothed* and leaves a mess in his wake?" Jonas sits in the lounge chair, crossing his legs and folding his arms.

It is surprising to hear their strategy did not involve my kidnapping. But this argument could be part of a plan laid within a plan.

I glance to Dorit, who shrugs as if this is typical behavior for the two of them.

It does nothing to help me.

"You know that plan was shit! Besides, it's not like anyone knew who I was," Jerrick dismisses.

"King Bernard and Queen Verena were there! Not to mention their children! They know who you are, you imbecile!" Jonas lectures Jerrick, and a little puff of laughter escapes Dorit's mouth.

I muddle over the knowledge. Neither of the other kingdoms sought to warn me about my interactions with Jerrick during the celebrations, but maybe they assumed he was also invited.

Jerrick's scowl melts into Dorit as her lip curls inwardly, hiding her amusement.

He takes a breath, meeting his brother's gaze.

"Bernard and Queen Verena could not have said anything. They have not seen us since you and I were young. Besides, I thrive in making a little show of things," Jerrick says, eyes twinkling with mischief.

Jonas lifts his head to the ceiling, pinching the bridge of his nose as he sighs with exhaustion. "Our plan was better than you going about kidnapping your fiancé and leaving blood everywhere."

Jerrick rolls his eyes, then inspects his fingernails. "I didn't kill anyone."

Jonas covers his face as my protective instincts take hold.

"Excuse me," I start. "You *killed* my priest!"

How many of my people were hurt by this psychopath?

Another failure of ruling thrown into my face and will surely be used against me.

"Easy there, Frostbite." Jerrick lifts a hand in warning.

I clench my fists with frustration. "You killed my priest. That is not something I take lightly. And what did I tell you about calling me *Frostbite*?"

His lips lift in challenge as my anger boils. "What are you going to do about it?"

My rage thrashes and a jolt of ice awakens. I open my palms, hoping to shoot frost at him.

His eyes widen in surprise, and he ducks away as Jonas and Dorit's mouths drop.

A smug expression tugs at my lips, but I frown when nothing comes out of my hand.

Jerrick's eyes flash with haughtiness, knowing my magic won't summon itself forth.

"That's enough!" Jonas interjects, looking between us pointedly.

I drop my hands faster than my magic dies out.

What is happening to me? Why didn't my power stretch outward?

It did not even manifest along my skin.

I break away from Jerrick's stare, meeting Jonas and Dorit.

"My king, Your Majesty," Jonas says, hands raised in surrender.

Guilt festers as anger resigns in my blood, even as Jerrick rolls his eyes at his brother. The fear I've caused and the people I could have hurt cracks my heart open.

I might have just made matters worse for myself.

I could be forced to remain a prisoner, locked deep in their keep. Then I would never see my home, my family's graves, my people, Niko, or Betina ever again.

My face falls.

Mother's mirror.

I pat my body, frantically searching for the one thing holding me to my family and to my kingdom. I could try to reach someone on the other side from my bedchamber's vanity.

Glancing and moving around carefully, I lift bedsheets without hurting my shoulder, feeling for the one hope I have of home.

"What are you doing?" Jerrick asks.

"My mother's mirror, did I lose it?"

My voice cracks as panic rises.

I look toward the sides of the bed, hoping a bedside table or something is keeping it safe. Desperation twitches in my fingers, and I comb through my hair.

"It's here, Your Majesty," Dorit offers, walking toward the wardrobe. She pulls out a small item and approaches.

Tears flood my eyes, locking on Mother's mirror. I rip it from her hands, cradling it as a small speck of conviction blooms to life.

I blink rapidly, offering Dorit kindness the two men do not deserve. "Thank you."

She grins, further illuminating her beauty.

"Your Majesty," Jonas says, drawing my attention. "I know you do not trust us, but you need to hear us out."

I dart my attention back and forth between the King and the Prince of Palaena.

Jonas pulls a piece of rolled parchment from his vest. Jerrick takes it from his brother, waiting to place it in my hands.

Skepticism makes me hesitant, but Jerrick waves it again.

I rest Mother's mirror down, curiosity getting the better of me, as I grip the parchment and unfold it. I skim through the document, noting it is a royal decree of some sort.

My eyes widen in shock as I read the last few lines.

> *The kingdoms of Palaena and Axidoria hereby approve and document this decree as binding law. This agreement is joined and composed by the two kingdoms acting with the discretion of the Makers. The signatures below, by each of the ruling monarchs of Axidoria and Palaena, agree to the arrangement of marriage between...*

My mouth drops as I read my name and Jerrick's and our parents' signatures at the bottom of the document. I note the fancy penmanship of King Ivan, the previous King of Palaena, shining brightly on the page.

Yet Mother's signature is small and tentative, stamped with her signet ring, the only evidence proving she did this.

I run my fingers over her name, questioning her actions.

I'll never forget the sound of Mother's screams, her constant words repeating that Father was gone, and she knew he was dead.

I wished I could have known—could have done something to stop it.

Mother took on Father's responsibilities but was still unable to forget they were separated. She would wail and weep, long into the hours of each night, distraught and broken that her love was taken away.

Mother fought with her advisors, claiming Palaena and King Ivan were behind it, insisting he needed to meet his end. She only backed down when she was advised repeatedly that she needed evidence before making such an accusation and that a fight would only bring more tragedy.

Not only that, but attacking Palaena would be the first time a kingdom disrupted the peace the Makers, and all kingdoms had upheld for *generations.*

But Mother was more adamant than I ever was.

She traveled to other kingdoms to seek help, especially Unterkirch, building a relationship with Queen Verena when her husband passed. And then Mother decided to draft a trade proposal between Axidoria and Palaena, one that would grant her an audience with King Ivan and a chance to find Father or get answers.

But when she packed her bags and never returned, I was left to believe Palaena was behind it.

But why is my name on a *marriage* agreement? Was this the trade proposal Mother devised?

It couldn't be.

The parchment in my hands falls as eyes bore into me, waiting to drag me further into my demise.

I look at the window.

The room remains silent as my thoughts twirl in chaos, trying to connect this information with everything I know.

Surely, this is all a sick, twisted nightmare.

"Did you force my mother into this and then kill her?" I demand, meeting Jerrick's face.

Jerrick's arms fold while his stern gaze regards me, choosing his next words very carefully.

"We did not kill her."

"You're lying!" I scream, tears forming from the blunt discussion of her death.

My mother is dead because I have inherited magic. If they *claim* they didn't kill her, what the Oblivion happened to her?

The men know exactly where my thoughts are because they glance at each other briefly when Jerrick repeats, "We did not kill your mother."

"You're all liars!" I shake my head.

Jonas's voice fills the void. "Why would we lie when *she* was the one that came here? *She* was the one who drafted this document and convinced our father to sign it! Why would she—"

Jonas stops, staring at the arm wrapped around his. The brothers silently communicate.

Jerrick shakes his head as Jonas heaves.

The hold lessens when Jonas nods, shaking his brother's lingering touch off and facing me.

"We didn't kill your mother, Queen Tove. We swear it," Jonas vows, frustration making his promise sharp.

He and Jerrick clasp a fist over their hearts and lower their heads.

The inside of my cheek scrapes against my teeth, and the tale they tell forces me to break away from their stares.

My mother *leaves* me like this. She knew how much I wanted to marry for love, like her and Father.

My jaw works as the three strangers linger in this bedchamber, knowing there is nothing and no one to trust here.

This is all a lie. A game for them to have more power. It has to be.

Mother would not do this to me. Yet denying her involvement does nothing to remove her signature and signet ring on this damned agreement.

A monarch's decree is law. Living or dead, decrees drafted by monarchs have always been handled with the utmost care because they are viewed as being a message passed down from the Makers.

Laws like this are always followed, never broken.

To disobey what another monarch created is viewed as denouncing the Makers. And if I myself, being a direct descendant of the Makers, were to ignore this decree?

The unknown forces fear to crawl up my throat.

I don't even want to imagine the consequences I will receive from the Makers when I die for not heeding this law for five years. Worry surges over me, my heart cracking with fear that my abilities could be a result of this.

But I had no knowledge of this.

I look once more at the decree, questions still running. This does not even grant me answers about what happened to my father.

I can't believe Jerrick and Jonas are telling me the truth. It does not make sense I am hearing about this five years *after* the death of my family.

Why is Palaena deciding to reveal this now?

The thought of more unanswered questions makes my head pound.

Jerrick rustles into the void. "We need to honor this agreement. A monarch's decree is law."

"Shut up," I mumble in anger, annoyed at how he is able to voice my own thoughts.

Happiness was out of my hands before I even considered marriage. My mother's betrayal and dismissal of my wishes sinks my heart to the floor.

I rub over my heart earnestly, desperately wishing to be anywhere but here, wishing none of this was real.

Another stabbing sensation digs into my chest at the memory of Niko. I could be home right now in his arms.

"What if I sweetened this marriage arrangement for you?" Jerrick offers, knowing I'm backed into a corner.

I've been kidnapped, I'm in enemy territory, and now I'm being told I have to marry because of something my mother drafted when she was still alive. I remain silent, knowing whatever offer he has would do nothing to improve this situation.

I have to follow this regardless of whether I want to or not.

If I refuse, I might never have the chance to see my family again in the afterworld.

"If you agree to marry me and agree to help unite the kingdoms of Axidoria and Palaena as your mother and my father orchestrated with this decree, I will help you train your magic."

I flick my gaze to him, and sarcasm crosses my features. "And what makes you think you know anything about *my* magic?"

"Sweet Makers," Jonas mumbles out, earning a chuckle from Dorit and a scowl from Jerrick.

They both squirm inwardly, elbowing each other like a band of misfits before Jerrick turns to me, ignoring them.

"You aren't the only one with magic, Frostbite," Jerrick says.

Trepidation pulses in my fingertips, the idea of harnessing my power comes with a great reward. If I learn more about my magic, I could stop Axidoria's ongoing winter, and if I stay here, maybe I will uncover the truth about my family.

I drag my teeth across my lip as I think of the news reaching Niko.

A thickness builds in my throat, frightened at the thought of not being with him.

I blink rapidly, forcing my emotions to remain at bay until I am left alone in this dreadful place.

"Trade and new routes will need to be better established between our kingdoms," I demand, meeting Jerrick's smirk as he takes the decree and rolls it up, tucking into his shirt.

"We will work it all out." Jerrick turns toward Jonas, issuing his command. "I am sure plenty of our people will be excited to have expanded trade routes."

"You are going to be the death of me," Jonas mumbles as he rises and adjusts his tucked shirt and vest.

He swishes his belt around, making sure his sword and dagger are properly displayed.

"Don't tempt me," Jerrick warns.

I look between the two and see Jonas wave away his brother's threat, facing me and lowering into a bow. "It shouldn't be a problem, and we will talk soon, Your Majesty."

"You might as well go ahead and start calling me Tove," I say to Jonas, choosing to play along with this charade for now.

"The wedding needs to happen within the next week. *Privately.* I don't want this to get out to the people until the other kingdoms have been notified," Jerrick says.

"That can be arranged," Jonas replies.

My face falls. In a week? I just woke up.

I try to interrupt, but they are already walking toward the exit.

Jerrick holds the door for Dorit and Jonas, extending his arm to the latter. They clasp each other at the elbow, smiling.

Dorit offers me a small curtsy before turning to leave with Jonas.

They are leaving to make everything happen while I am stuck here in bed.

"What do you get out of this?" I call back to Jerrick, halting his steps.

He peers over, those blue eyes tracing down the entire length of my body. A sinful smirk splays on his lips.

"*You*," the King of Palaena says in a low voice full of lust. He winks, sweeping the door closed and leaving me alone in a new nightmare.

14

CONNECTIONS

The brush prickles along my scalp as I drag it through each strand, massaging my head while detangling every knot my hair has accumulated. The past week, I've been tucked away in these chambers, allowing my body to heal and interacting with few.

I've tried countless times to use Mother's mirror in hopes of someone hearing me, but nothing. I won't give up, though. It is my only chance to let Betina and Niko know I am okay.

I pray to the Makers they are okay.

The brush snags on the blue robe I wear, too lazy to dress with my shoulder still on the mend.

Dorit is the only one I've seen this past week, and I find her company a blessing despite these red walls being my prison. She brings me food, helps me bathe, and assists me with moving my body a few times a day. And when she greets me every morning, she reminds me each day I am here is another day I wish it were Betina's voice.

Betina's warm spiced scent would always linger in my chambers, lending a sense of comfort that would kill me each time

I was dragged away from it, whereas Dorit leaves with gardenia and roses in her wake.

She smells so flowery that it can feel stuffy.

It makes me want to be outdoors.

I *loathe* the outdoors.

Of course it isn't her fault she smells different from Betina, and it isn't her fault I am a prisoner here. I make sure to thank her every time she aids me. I know it is not a luxurious job, and my injuries don't help either.

But Dorit is kind and helpful, and her company is not unbearable.

I have made huge strides in my healing lately, being able to rise from the bed alone and not get dizzy. I can't hide the joy from knowing my body is improving.

Dorit's soft, lyrical voice drifts in from the hall. "Your Majesty, I've come to drop off a gown for tonight."

Dorit enters, donning a simple, bold magenta dress.

The fabric extends from her hips, secured at the waist by a vested corset tied neatly on her back. Matching ribbon weaves through her plaits, highlighting more color around her and her fragile body.

She holds a package, and I grumble at the thought of wearing another wedding gown. *Especially* one I had no role in choosing. But she offers me a curtsy, resting the dress across the chaise at the end of the bed.

Rising slowly, I walk over and gasp.

The dress is not the tight bodice and flared gowns I am used to wearing, though. The fabric is satin and of the palest of blues.

The sleeves are thin, held together by rows of the whitest of pearls. The beads glimmer in the light.

I turn it over, revealing a low and see-through back with the beading draped from shoulder to shoulder, allowing my skin to shine through the pearls. It looks more like a sleeping gown, with its simplicity and lack of layered fabrics.

But the satin is so soft and delicate the quality exudes luxury.

"This is stunning," I marvel in awe.

"His Majesty picked it out."

I linger over Dorit's words, but when she turns her gaze from the dress to me, her features turn distant.

"I was hoping we could talk," she says.

I raise my eyebrow. That was not what I was expecting.

"What do you want to discuss?" I allow her to proceed, turning toward the vanity to resume brushing my hair.

In the reflection, she looks down and fidgets with her hands, and I halt my brushing, noting the signals of nervousness. Maybe she and I could have more in common.

Her chest rises and falls as she makes eye contact with me.

I try for reassurance. "It's alright."

Dorit's eyes drop to the floor. "I've been practicing this conversation since you've arrived, not knowing how to explain myself to you. I know you do not like it here, and for that, I am so sorry. And I know you don't want to be here, and I know that—"

"*Dorit*." My heart softens as her rambling gets the better of her. She stops when I face her. "It is okay."

She twists her hands as the ribbon in her plaits begins to match the color of her cheeks.

"His Majesty and I were briefly—and I mean *briefly*—involved with one another prior to him becoming king. We have known each other for years, and it was when we were young and stupid," she blurts.

I arch a brow, tilting my head. Why is she telling me this?

Dorit paces forward a few steps. "But I swear to the Makers what we shared was fleeting for the two of us. I truly do not have any deep affection for His Majesty, nor does he for me. He is the king I serve, and I am head of the house staff meant to help him and the prince where I can."

She moves toward me, but she hesitates, her lips quivering. "I *need* this job, and I know of the rumors that circulate. Deities, there are so many. But I didn't want you to learn this from anyone else and have you dismiss me before I have a chance to prove my work ethic and commitment to you."

She spoke so fast it took a minute to register what she was telling me. Dorit crumples, and she collapses to the floor, burying her face.

My heart breaks with the fear showing through this poor woman.

Are the rumors about me that scary?

Her cries are the only sound in the room as I stand very carefully, making my way to her. Reaching for her chin, I grab it gently, tilting it to meet my eyes.

Her tears have drenched her cheeks, and her nose is red.

The visible sorrow tears at my heart. I can't bear to see how much worry she has over this.

Who am I to judge her for something that happened years ago?

I can't bend over well, so I nudge her on the knee with my foot, beckoning her to stand.

She pushes off the lush red rug, brushing off her gown when she rises. When her eyes meet mine, I cannot help myself from pulling her in for an embrace.

My damned empathy—always getting the better of me.

I rub her back gently. "Thank you for sharing that with me. I know it must have been hard."

Dorit returns the hug, her sob causing her to shiver. "Th-Thank you, Y-Your Majesty."

"*Please* don't be afraid of me, Dorit."

She is careful with her hands around my back, thoughtful and not nearing my bandaged shoulder. Bless her.

I pull away from her, and tears still run down her cheeks. "You are the only one that has visited me for an entire week. I consider you more of an acquaintance than the others. *Including* my future husband."

She laughs, and I continue, "You've made me as comfortable as I can be here, and I am thankful for that."

She sniffs, bobbing her head in agreement.

I pull away and force her to look at me.

"I have no animosity toward you for what you had with the king," I reassure her. "It happened before we met, and who am I to judge you or him for exploring that adventure?"

A tear falls down her face as I give her arms a light squeeze, smiling gently.

Sweet Makers, she reminds me of Runa.

Swallowing the memories of my sister, I bury them deep for only me to experience. I cannot go dragging another person into my grief.

"Thank you for having the courage to tell me. It can be intimidating speaking your thoughts. Deities, I am a queen, and I can barely do that," I joke.

A slight chuckle escapes from her, and she covers her mouth.

I wonder at the outburst but find it refreshing to be around another person slipping with protocol.

"I am so sorry. That was rude of me to do," she says quickly.

I pat her hand. "It was a joke. It was meant to be laughed at."

We watch each other sheepishly, then laugh together for the first time as she wipes the tears from her cheeks, eying the vanity.

"Would you like me to help you get ready later this evening?" she asks.

If I get ready alone, I will probably sulk and fight against all the emotions sinking me down. Having someone here could be a welcome distraction.

But when I look at her, I cannot help but voice my immediate thought. "I don't want to marry him."

I was supposed to marry Niko. I am *supposed* to be married to Niko.

I turn away, crumbling gracefully on the chaise, my head falling into my chest. Deities, I wish I could get a hold of Niko or Betina.

I have to try again before tonight.

I almost laugh at the irony of marrying Jerrick, someone I had considered when I believed Niko was not interested in me. But words from the decree repeat in sentences, the joining of me and Jerrick... not Niko.

I do not understand why or how my mother's name is on a decree. Yet here I am, following through with it for fear of being separated from them in the afterlife as well as Jerrick's promise to help me with my magic.

Dorit sits beside me, grabbing one of my hands. "Whatever happens, I will be here for you. I've been there—literally."

I cackle so fast, surprised I even did.

Dorit joins in on the laughter.

I am grateful she is making light of this situation. It reminds me of a time Runa or Niko would do that for me. I am lucky to know someone who knows Jerrick.

Maybe she can give me tips on things he likes, and I can twist it to my advantage to piss him off and keep him at a distance.

"I wasn't expecting to say this, but thank you, Dorit." I smile.

She returns the smile, my chest constricting from her pure kindness. "You are most welcome, Your Majesty."

I squeeze her hand, hating the formality used. "Call me Tove."

Dorit inclines her head. "It's an honor, Tove."

15

THIS IS A FIRST

Holding Mother's mirror, I run my hand over it in three circles, projecting my reflection to my chambers. The image ripples and glows as my old room comes into view.

My heart remains hopeful, taking what could be my last chance of seeing Betina or Niko before Dorit returns in a few hours to help me get ready for the ceremony tonight.

"Niko? Betina?" I speak into the mirror, only met with silence.

I grip the stem of Mother's mirror tighter, trying for their names again, once more met with nothing. Irritation swims over my features, and I go to sever the connection but halt when a door opens on the other end, a voice calling for me.

"Hello?" the smooth, baritone voice asks.

I whimper, weeping through pure joy. "Is that you, Niko?"

Footsteps sound, and the image of my chamber is filled by Niko's loving gaze.

"Tove! Sweet fucking Makers, you're alive!" He holds the sides of the mirror.

I croak out a sob, unable to stop myself from touching his reflection. Wishing he was near, I bring my forehead to the mirror.

"Tove, the arrow—" His eyes turn from relief to tortured, filled with tears that are pleading and remorseful.

I lift a hand to stop him, shaking my head as my own tears fall. I don't want to think about that damned arrow. I just want to be here with him.

"I'm okay, Niko."

He swallows thickly as a single tear cascades down his cheek.

Taking in his appearance, his amber eyes are dim, riddled with bags, and his hair is disheveled while his face shows signs of a beard.

"When Betina told me you had your mirror with you, I thought you might try to reach out. I've been worried sick, thinking the worst—" He pauses, looking around my profile and noting my new surroundings. "Where are you?"

I turn, taking in the bedchamber around me. A lush black blanket hugs the sheets on the bed, and light traces of frost crest across the tall arched window beside me.

I swallow thickly, hesitant over relaying the bad news. As I rub the stem of the mirror, the jagged edges of the engraving massage my palms.

I brace myself for his fury and meet his amber gaze.

"Niko." I bite my lip, knowing my heart is going to break in telling him this.

It is already breaking the longer I look at him.

"Tee, tell me where you are *now*," he demands, each word desperate yet full of anger, not toward me but to the man who took me on our wedding day.

Niko's protectiveness is driving the demand behind his tone, but it does nothing to stop the shredding in my chest.

I grimace. "I-I'm in P-Palaena," I whisper.

"What?" he bellows, and I wince.

He steps away from the vanity, his fingers running through his hair as he paces. "I'll kill that bastard—"

"Niko," I call, trying to reach him through his spiraling thoughts.

He is willing to risk anything to find the best solution. He faces me, coming into view with anger expanding from his amber irises.

"I am coming to get you, Tee. I am going to call the banners and come for you."

"*Niko*," I breathe with warning.

"I am going to. Tee, I know it will take time. I will go to each village and call the banners, have them march to the castle and train under me."

His emotions falter momentarily, noting the change in my demeanor. Calling the banners risks upsetting the Makers.

"Or not. I could come and get you myself right now."

Another reason why war has never happened is because monarchs could never predict what abilities the other had. It would be a gamble to fight to gain more power, only to be usurped by a monarch more powerful than anticipated. And regardless of success or failure, a ruler would still invoke the Deities' wrath.

I scrape my lips against the edges of my teeth as I contemplate my options, knowing, deep down, if I ever want to return home, Niko is right.

This is the only option.

There were witnesses to my kidnapping and the death of my priest at my wedding. That should count for something and help Niko get support in organizing an attack.

I rock my head back to the ceiling, noting the framing around the bed as I send a humble prayer to Alora, begging her for mercy in the afterlife for the path I am about to go down.

Leaning against the pillows, I fold my robe over my body as I try to justify hurting others. I hate that the guarantee of my return home, being with Niko, and protecting my kingdom all boil down to a battle.

I don't want this, yet I can't help but exhale my thoughts aloud.

"You cannot come here alone, Niko. I don't know what threats lie here. There is too much at risk if we show up unprepared. And if Axidoria is going to march into another kingdom for a fight, I want you and my bannermen prepared."

Niko stiffens at my declaration, his emotions clearly rushing his decisions more than his logic, and I need to guide his intentions strategically.

"Winter will spread more in Axidoria, so take this time to gather men and train. We can set forth in the summer when it is warmer, and that should give me enough time to handle everything here."

Niko scratches the side of his cheek, a muscle ticking in his jaw as he thinks over my plan. He falls into pacing again.

When his steps falter, he turns and raises a brow. "Wait, what are you going to do?"

Hesitating momentarily, I reply, "I am going to marry their king."

Niko's eyes widen, recognition dawning. "The man who kidnapped you is the King of Palaena? And you are going to marry him?" Niko fumes, anger lacing each word.

"Yes."

"Tee," he breathes, "you *can't* marry him."

Tenderness leaves his breath and fractures my heart. It cripples me knowing we are so far apart, and I can't embrace him and comfort him.

I would hold him and lather him by kissing every inch of his body. I pray he knows it is him I want, and no one else.

I meet his gaze, assuring the finality of this decision. "I *have* to. They showed me a marriage decree drafted and signed by my mother."

Niko grimaces at the thought, disbelieving me, but I press on, "Trust me, I didn't believe it at first either, but her signature was there."

Looking through the reflection, the tension in Niko's jaw works. The despair in my chest grows, even as I try to offer a fragment of hope.

"They are hiding what really happened to my family. So, while men train for a battle, I'm going to learn what I can and follow through with my other arrangements."

Jealousy ripples down Niko as he stomps toward the vanity mirror, smacking his hands on the table. "What *else* did you agree to?"

I swallow thickly, not knowing if Axidoria could make this work or not. "We agreed once we marry, I'll help set up trade between our kingdoms, and the king would train me to wield my magic."

"But, Tee." Niko sighs, the hope draining from him. "I don't care about trade or the winter your magic caused. I care about you."

His soft words torture me as I face his amber eyes, wishing he were here to hold me.

"I know you do," I say softly, the pain of everything breaking my heart. "But I *have* to do this. I have to find answers while I am here. And there has to be a way to remove my magic or melt the ice. That way could be here. You know how difficult it has been to learn and understand my gifts without any resources at home."

"Have you already married him?" Niko asks, betrayal stinging in his question.

I shake my head, and his shoulders relax until I add, "It's happening tonight."

Niko is silent, his face reddening from the tears he, too, is shedding. He touches the mirror, and I brush it with my fingertips.

We stare silently at each other, wishing to be in one another's embrace but instead are being thrown into an Oblivion of Palaena's making.

A long exhausted sigh escapes from Niko's lips, and he rubs his eyes softly.

Realization breaks my heart that Niko may not want me after I've been married to Jerrick... Is he getting ready to tell me that?

Niko's head remains downcast. "I understand honoring the agreement your mother drafted, and I understand harnessing your abilities, but Tee—" He looks up, jealousy simmering behind his eyes.

His throat bobs once.

He exhales a promise burning deep in his gaze. "Helping the future of your kingdom isn't going to stop me from coming to get you. I'm going to kill that man for taking what is mine."

The thought should make me feel sick. Instead, it pulls a wicked idea of what Jerrick will be like as a lover, but I don't dare voice that.

I don't want to give myself to a stranger, but consummation comes as part of the marriage arrangement.

I know that.

Niko knows that.

And even Jerrick knows that.

But despite having to share a bed with Jerrick, I can't help but seek reassurance Niko will still want to be with me after all of this.

I squeeze the mantle of my mother's gilded mirror, holding on to the hope of his declaration. "You—you'd still want me? Even after marrying—and *being*—with another man?"

A lift of his features, one of the first I've seen in over a week, appears, and my heart skips, seeing the desire flash behind his eyes.

"I want you right now."

His voice lowers, deep and sensual.

The desire from his statement has my thighs clenching.

"Y-You do?" I ask, my heart rate increasing as those golden eyes simmer with the promise of pleasure.

He nods slowly, his hands bracing the mirror. "I want to fulfill every fantasy I've ever had of you."

I glance around, unsure of how he intends to fulfill such a declaration.

Embarrassment has me stating the obvious, hating to dampen his mood while also hating myself for saying it aloud. "B-But you aren't here."

"Yes, I am," he says, tilting his head to the side with a sensual smile.

His mahogany hair moves with him, and he shakes it away from his face. "And I want you to take your clothes off right here, right now."

"Let me have this."

My mouth falls as arousal thickens Niko's voice.

The blood in my veins turns hot and heavy underneath his gaze, and I bite my lip.

Niko licks his lips, a hand drifting down to rub himself. "Deities, I want this with you *so* badly."

Niko's words drive me into glancing around, a cold sweat breaking along my brow as I search for something to rest Mother's mirror on. I find a few candlesticks and grab my emptied chamber pot, carrying Niko with me as he palms himself.

"Sweet Makers, I wish that was my hand," I confess.

His eyes meet mine. "That's what I'm imagining and have imagined ever since we met."

"Deities, same," I admit as I brace the mirror against the chamber pot, as well as the candlesticks, giving Niko a full view of me and I a full view of him.

I'm breathless as we study each other, unsure of what to do next.

Niko seems to feel the same because he says, "I never imagined our first time like this."

I nod, my words running dry, not knowing what to do—what to say. All I do know is I would love to be chased into ecstasy.

Staccato notes flutter in my pulse as I sit, my hands clammy and sweaty as I rub them up and down my thighs.

Niko braces one hand against the mirror, his other still rubbing himself through his clothes, and I itch to see the fullness of him.

The thought has me clenching my insides.

"Lean back, Tee," Niko commands.

I do what he says, dragging my dressing robe up the length of my legs.

"Open your robe. Let me see you," he urges as he leans into the mirror, his lips almost kissing the glass.

I keep one hand on my leg, bunching the fabric up around my hips as I drape my sleeves down my sides, revealing my breasts.

Niko chokes out, "S-Sweet Makers."

I bite my lip again, a little shy and embarrassed, self-consciously almost covering myself, but Niko hisses, "Deities, please touch yourself."

His words run straight to my pussy, wetness forming between my legs.

My center is free from my dressing robe, the open air cold, enticing my desire more.

Niko watches me as I rub my hand up the column of my legs, down to my apex.

I moan with delight, imagining Niko's touch.

"Good," he says with a lift of his lips. "Now pleasure yourself."

I insert one finger and gasp, my chest tightening. When my head lowers, I gaze at Niko watching me, studying me. I bite my lips again underneath that hooded stare.

Power creeps along my spine. But not my magic. A different sense of power. One that has me wishing, wanting, needing to please him as he pleases me. It leaves me hungry for more, and I rub my clit.

Niko moves his hands faster than I can follow, the length of him popping out from his trousers as he lowers them to his knees. His shirt covers his cock temporarily, but he lifts it over his head with one hand, intent on keeping one wrapped around his hardness.

My mouth waters at the sight of him shirtless and broad. Muscles curved and shaped into perfection, with hair covering his chest and down his toned stomach and even further.

Pleasure oozes from me when Niko licks his lips, twisting his cock in his hands as he pumps himself.

"Fuck, I want to taste you," I moan.

His shoulders tense, leaning into the mirror for support as his head falls down. His red hair covers his face, but I pay no attention to it, my eyes refusing to vacate his nakedness.

All for me.

I shudder in pleasure, my own arousal thick at the thought of being on my knees for him.

"My cock wants it just like this." Niko shows me the movement, his eyes meeting mine as he adds, "And then you can suck me dry."

I nod, committing the lesson to memory. "Yes, I can do that."

"Pinch your nipples," he commands.

I do as he instructs, closing my eyes and reclining against the chair, my head falling back.

Lust coats his entire face, driving him to buck his hips. "Fuck," he groans as his hand remains wrapped around his cock.

I pinch my nipple harder, my hips bucking.

"Yes," Niko breathes heavily, the sound of my wetness the only thing filling the room.

Niko grunts, but I am too preoccupied with grinding harder into the lounge chair.

"Are you close yet?" Niko asks through the sound of his own pleasure filling my ears.

I struggle for words as I insert another finger, moving my hand from my breast to rub my clit as I pump my other in and out of my pussy.

"Mm-hmm," I hum, concentrating on myself.

I open my eyes, catching Niko's ragged, distraught breathing. But his strokes match my own hands.

Niko bites his lip, and I stutter through my own buildup, my stomach muscles tightening.

"Fuck," Niko growls, eyes shutting.

Seeing him getting there keeps me going.

"Yes," I pant, watching him struggle to remain upright.

Niko loses control, chasing his own pleasure. He grunts, his moan deep and satiated, the sight of him coming drives me to orgasm.

"Fuck," I groan, my hands leaving the center of my legs, falling to my sides in exhaustion.

"Yeah, something like that," Niko adds.

I rub my hands on my robe then rest one on my head, my eyes still regarding the ceiling as my breath evens. Movement has me glancing up to Niko cleaning himself with a towel, pulling on his trousers, and finding his shirt.

I study him as he bends and retrieves his tunic.

His muscles flex in the light as he faces me, giving me one final glance of his nakedness before covering back up.

I take that as an opportunity to pull my robe over my body, leaning forward and taking the mirror with me to my bedside.

Part of me wishes we could stay in this beautiful moment, but I am asking him to do a lot while I remain here—*married* to another man.

"Thank you," I whisper as he faces me. "Thank you for letting me have this with you before—"

"Tee," Niko raises a hand, cutting me off.

His eyes drift to the floor. He runs a hand through his hair, sighing and glancing out the window.

I remain patient, knowing there is a lot at risk not only for my kingdom but for us.

He meets my gaze. "I know what tonight means for you and— their *king*," Niko spits, his eyes squinting with disgust.

Weight clamps down on my chest, hating that I have done this to Niko and that my hands are completely tied right now.

"But..." Niko continues, and his anger shifts into tenderness. "But I will always want you. I will always need you. Nothing will stand in my way. I am coming for you."

I close my eyes and nod, grateful to have Niko as mine and mine alone.

"I want to be with you, Niko," I sniff, unable to help the tears forming and falling down my cheeks. "This is all but a test for our relationship and for Axidoria. We will call the banners, and I will find answers and learn more about my magic. I will find my way home to you and save our kingdom."

His handsome features illuminate, and a lustful thought sends shivers down my spine.

We watch each other, chests rising and falling, hands reaching to touch the reflection.

"I know you will do just that, Tee." He grins, pure and filled with hope.

The perfect image to cling to while I remain here, and he remains in Axidoria.

"If I have to call the banners, I won't be able to see you as often. Sweet Makers, it is already arduous being your proxy while you are gone," Niko says, changing the conversation.

Calling the banners is a strenuous task. Niko will have to trek to each village during this winter, facing some heavier iced-over areas than others. Many of the nobles will join the call, especially because they prefer Niko to me, and the prospect of having a future king will instill hope for our people.

"I know I won't," I say, steering him and his mood into better spirits. "But I trust you. You are my fiancé and my royal advisor. Think of this as practice for the real thing when I get home."

Niko nods, and I know he can handle it. He has already done so much more than a proxy before, and this time, he has our engagement and witnesses to solidify his claims and the call.

"How is everything, though?" I ask.

Niko shoots me a warning look, and it drives my need further.

I wait for him to concede.

He takes a seat in front of the vanity, and I don't know what to brace myself for. "Since you've been gone, there have been reports of new areas seeing frost and ice appearing without any warning. And Ulrik Albertsen is trying to gain the favor of enough nobles to go against you and the crown's wishes."

Rage thickens my blood, building a wall of fury around me. Winter, Ulrik, being stuck here, and forced into a marriage I didn't want.

"He is going to regret that," I vow.

"Tee, we still need him for trade."

I roll my eyes, hating how he is right. We need Ulrik for trade because he helps keep Axidoria's funds full enough to pay other kingdoms for resources we have depleted. I can't wait for the day I'll be able to remove the thorn in my side that Ulrik Albertsen is.

"But when I said he is trying to, he is trying *and* failing." Niko laughs, knowing I fell for it, and shrugs. "What can I say? The people love me."

I give him a knowing look with my eyebrow raised. I'm met with his grin on full display. While I want to smack him and scold him for teasing me, I can't help the small tug of my smirk, the Niko I have fallen for peeking through our predicament.

Annoyed but in happy defeat, I appreciate having such a man in my life for myself and for my home. I touch the reflection, and I wish with my entire heart to have him here beside me, facing this together instead of apart.

It will be hard, but in the back of my mind, I pray to the Makers there is a way to avoid a fight and save my kingdom from my own magic.

"I miss you. *So much*," I confess.

He smiles again, sending my heart skipping a beat. "I miss you too, Tee."

16

WEDLOCK

I opted to get ready for tonight alone, remembering the quiet and bliss from my time with Niko.

Staring out the window as nightfall takes over the skies, I note the lake near the town reflecting the moonlight into my room. Lights lit in the village are visible from where I observe, dreading the rest of this evening approaching.

The only reprieve the Deities blessed me with was seeing Niko. Reuniting with him and forming a rescue mission was not what I planned, but somehow, through it all, I am filled with hope. I have replayed our time together over and over in my mind as the hours tick by, dragging me further into this nightmare.

With Niko trekking throughout Axidoria to call the banners, reaching out to King Bernard and Queen Verena for support and extra supplies and handling the Ulrik situation, I firmly believe that, by the end of this, my people will rejoice in having a king and queen together again.

Even though my heart aches for him, I need to do everything right on my end to ensure I find answers and learn about my magic.

A strong, short knock comes at the door.

Looking down at my dress, I wipe my sweaty palms on it, adjusting my features and putting on my regal smile. "Come in."

The door opens, and I turn, expecting Dorit, but am surprised to see a different face.

Jonas offers a tight smile, bowing. "Your Majesty, are you ready?"

He is dressed in warm, bold colors that match the reds and browns of my room, his jacket a dark burgundy lying on top of a cream-colored tunic. His pants and boots blend into one another in a chocolate brown. A sash drapes over his vest laced and adorned with jewels that complement the small crown resting on his head.

He wears royalty handsomely, knowing he is well outfitted for tonight.

"Right," I mutter to myself more than him, mentally preparing for what's to come.

As I turn, Jonas scans me appreciatively. "If I may, can I say you look radiant this evening?"

My cheeks redden, genuine shock from his compliment turning my insides into mush. Compliments are weird and unusual, yet his made my stomach somersault.

Jonas then takes a step forward, reaching down to help hold my train in one elbow while extending his other toward me. "Allow me."

I exhale in awe of his manners, almost forgetting he is an enemy. "Where were *you* when I was looking for a husband?"

Shit. Did I really *just* say that?

I squint my eyes closed in embarrassment. This is because he complimented me. I should have just bristled at his words.

Jonas laughs. "While I appreciate the honesty, I am afraid I'm not up for grabs."

His blunt confession draws my gaze, watching him adjust my train in his elbow.

"Care to expand on that?" I ask.

We make our exit from one physical prison and press onward, where I'll enter a legally binding one, too.

"Let's just say I enjoy my sex." Understanding lifts my brows as he continues, "I know it was not acceptable for a long time in Axidoria, which is why I was hesitant to mention it, but if we're family, you should know."

Appreciation for his transparency has me hopeful that my time here might not be bad. Maybe I'll work alongside him more than Jerrick.

"Thank you for sharing that with me. My lady-in-waiting in Axidoria, Betina, prefers *all* sexes." I hope Jonas catches my play on words, trying to appease and get to know my jailors.

He does, patting my arm in amusement, a gleeful laugh perking up his mood.

"I've tried hard since stepping into my role as queen to ensure everyone has the freedom to love whomever they wish. Axidoria's customs were old, abhorrent, and outdated anyway," I tell him.

We chuckle and stroll through a sleeping wing, venturing into a new hallway. The castle's walls are stained a cream color, matching the floor we walk upon.

Darker shades of red, orange, and brown in the décor mounted on the stone walls remind me of fall as the colors are intertwined and woven into rugs, paintings, lanterns, and curtains.

The drapery is tucked and tied together, allowing the tall arched windows to shine with the sun or moon.

The soft, plush rug unfurled beneath us is so full, my feet sink into each step in my thin-soled slippers. It is so soft I could sleep on it.

Jonas tilts his head before he speaks. "It wasn't acceptable in Palaena either under my father's rule, but Jerrick worked hard to create acceptance for everyone when he ascended."

We pass by some pictures of ancestors, dust collecting on the older ones, while the newer ones depict the strong features of Jerrick and Jonas.

A sense of evil prickles along my skin as I gaze at the painting of Jerrick.

Despite Jonas saying something nice about Jerrick, a darkness lingers in the shadows, making me feel even more wary of the man I am set to marry.

"I never would have expected him to do something nice for his people," I admit.

He snorts, almost missing the last step down the stairs, and we both stumble awkwardly, bumping into each other.

I grunt through our mishap, feeling the tightness of my injured shoulder.

Thankfully, we land on the ground in one piece. We pause, check my injury, and when Jonas inclines his head quietly, all worry and laughter masks his royal appearance.

He wears his manners well, escorting me as if our little stair-tripping never happened. "Jerrick might be complicated, but he does care."

I huff my disbelief, baffled to think Jerrick, a man who forced me to leave my home, cares about anyone other than himself. Sure, he helped make me comfortable when I was injured and on my cycle, but that was because I was a problem to him and our stupid marriage arrangement.

"You don't know, do you?" Jonas asks.

I flash him a skeptical look to give him reason to continue as we step farther down to the lower floors of the castle.

"Jerrick didn't leave your side the entire time you were unconscious."

That gives me pause, halting my steps and causing Jonas to do so as well.

Why would Jerrick do that? I'm only a means to prevent consequences from affecting him and his kingdom.

He has no reason beyond that to care.

When we met in Axidoria and I fainted, he was there when I woke up, too. He went out of his way to bring me medicine and even apologized for laughing over my cycle.

Doubt prickles an eerie composition in my mind from his actions at the ball versus when he kidnapped me.

I can't stop myself from asking, "Why did he do that?"

Jonas throws me a smirk, telling me he isn't speaking more on the topic.

Anxiety rushes into my bloodstream, gripping me and leaving me utterly confused. Jerrick is attractive, yes, and we are supposed to get married, but how will I be able to push through this relationship and make it seem realistic if I don't understand the person I'm tied to?

Deities, I wish this never happened. I wish I was with Niko, already married, and thriving in the bliss of being with someone I wanted.

A small slither of frustration stems up from my gut, a clanging of incorrect keys banging on a piano and making me bristle. The

Deities, my mother, and fate play a never-ending game of torture with me.

I sigh through the vexation clawing and digging at my chest.

What did I do to be thrown into such chaos?

I grumble as Jonas and I approach dual wooden doors stretching up to the ceiling of the main floor.

He reaches forward, opening the door and allowing my sight to behold a magnificent courtyard.

A rush of air escapes my lungs at the beauty of it.

The sides of the courtyard have pillars holding up sections of the castle, creating shaded areas to sit and enjoy the beauty of the plants. Rose bushes and lilies line the pathways with tall neatly trimmed hedges filling the gaps between them.

There are other entrances to the courtyard down each pathway, telling me this is a main focal point of the Mikkelson castle.

At the center of the area stands a water fountain of a man holding a woman in a tender embrace. Water trickles down the statue as we come closer, and my heart pulls, the sculpture reflecting what I wish for most.

Jonas and I pass the water fountain where Jerrick, a few household guards, Dorit, and an Alorian priest stand.

Jerrick wears a dark-blue jacket sewn with pearls that match my gown. The sides of his trousers are embroidered with silver, tucked into black boots.

Jerrick and the priest are speaking too quietly to make out what they are saying, and Dorit stands nearby, still in her magenta dress, greeting Jonas and me with a sweet smile.

I give her a nod in greeting, and she returns it with a small curtsy.

Jerrick silently meets my gaze, and my breath catches at the contrast of his blue eyes to his deep navy ensemble.

I do not know if I will ever get used to his sharp features.

His eyes scan me from head to toe, and it sends a wave of trepidation through my system, praying I look alright.

Jerrick extends his hand.

I look at it, begging my inner strength to ground me for what I am about to do.

On my wedding day to Niko, I was a mess of emotions, worrying and pacing so much that Betina had to give it to me straight. I couldn't stop thinking about my parents or my sister, yet here I am with thoughts barely drifting to them.

Am I still in shock? Deities, what if this all goes to shit? What if this is all a trick and it's going to backfire?

Chills erupt across my skin, and I find myself gripping onto the safety of Jonas's elbow.

Jonas grabs my hand, squeezing it gently and leaning in to whisper, "It will be alright."

I clench my jaw, fearful of saying anything that could make my predicament worse.

Jonas unhooks my hand from his elbow and places it into Jerrick's, then removes the train of my gown, fanning it out across the pebbled ground.

Touching Jerrick burns at first, an odd sensation streaming up my arm and down to my core. I look at Jonas for reassurance and am met with an encouraging smile.

I swallow down my fears as I meet Jerrick's gaze once again.

It has been a week since we last saw each other, and my heart picks up speed in his presence. The man is wicked, awful, yet handsome and flirtatious.

My mind and my heart fight to remain disdainful of him, trying to not swoon at the fact he is better looking than I remember.

His eyes are a brighter blue this evening, contrasting with his scar and giving his features more symmetry. The grown-out stubble I remember when I woke up is trimmed away, and his shoulder-length black hair is tied half-back, combed neatly into place.

And his scent—Sweet Makers, it is better than I remember. It waves off him along with the arrogant smirk he wears.

And I know if I keep staring, he is going to say something that will piss me off.

It still doesn't prevent me from taking in his tall stature, dark thoughts shifting to what he would feel like hovering over me.

You should be thinking about Niko, Tove. Not this monster.

But as we stand there, hand in hand, staring at each other, I find myself wondering if he is worrying about what is going to happen after we are wed. The idea of us being alone should repulse me, and I seek the memories of my time with Niko for comfort.

But my mind drifts to when Jerrick kissed me. How soft his lips were and the tentative need behind the pressure of his touch.

Heat boils in my core, and I clench my thighs, trying to shut out the thoughts.

When the Alorian priest begins, Jerrick's dimple makes an appearance, and I pray to the Deities I am strong enough not to be affected any more by him.

Nerves erupt throughout my entire body as I try to pay attention to everything the priest is saying, but I am too distracted by the odd comfort of Jerrick's hand warming me, as if it will set me on fire.

I try to take in the courtyard again, observing the stars above sparkling in the deepened onyx night. The winter weather should be causing me to freeze over, but I am covered in sweat by everyone's gazes and Jerrick's touch.

The priest stops, guiding us to face each other before taking a step back.

Jerrick takes my hand, turning it upward as he withdraws the dagger from his belt, pointing the tip toward my palm.

Swallowing at the coldness of the blade, I brace for the pain.

"Just a little cut," he says.

The first words I've heard my future husband speak in a week, and they are soft and gentle in reassurance. They pull me from my fear, beckoning me to look into his eyes.

As the blade pierces my skin, I can't stop the cringe of pain across my features from the slash in my palm. The blood rises and Jerrick looks at the priest, waiting for his approval before speaking the vows of marriage.

When it is received, Jerrick's eyes melt into mine as his honeyed voice drowns my ears.

"To the Makers above, I vow and pledge in this bond of marriage to protect and devote my life to my wife. This I promise to Yeva, Letum, Aiyana, Alora, Anwir, and Leander, the creators of this world and the gifters of our magics. This I promise to you, my wife, Tove Clemmensen."

My name sounds rich and sweet coming from his mouth, better than being called *Frostbite* or *Snow Queen*.

I watch the blood pool in my now cupped hand as a soft cough breaks my daydream.

Offering the priest an apologetic look, I swallow down more fear as Jerrick offers me the dagger.

I take it into my shaking hands, my blood coating the hilt, ruining the glimmer reflecting off it. I bite my lip as I concentrate on his palm turned upward.

"Don't try anything, Frostbite," Jerrick says.

I expel my irritation; he thought I would hurt him before I even had considered it.

I make a smaller slash on his palm. Hating that I am repeating the words, I avert my gaze away from Jerrick's.

"To the Makers above, I vow and pledge in this bond of marriage to protect and devote my life to my husband. This, I promise to Yeva, Letum, Aiyana, Alora, Anwir, and Leander, the creators of this world and the gifters of our magics. This, I promise to you, my husband, Jerrick Mikkelson."

"Will you both join hands?" the priest asks.

Everyone's eyes drill into me as Jerrick answers, "I will join hands."

I am still examining the blood in Jerrick's palm as I repeat the words after him. "I will join hands."

Jerrick folds his hands over mine.

The priest turns to a table with a goblet and two crowns. He grabs the king's crown first, holding it with such tenderness as he pivots back.

Jerrick lowers his towering height so the priest may place it on his head.

The priest repeats his steps, and when I behold the queen's crown, my heart stops momentarily.

It is silver, like the king's crown, but adorned with bright blue jewels too pale to be considered sapphires. They are clustered in the center, surrounded by diamonds varying in size. This crown placed upon my head is so surreal I can't believe this is a wedding and a coronation.

The priest grabs the goblet, lowering his head and gesturing for us to each take a drink.

Jerrick offers it to me before helping himself, finalizing the marriage between Palaena and Axidoria.

The priest joyfully claps. "You are now bonded in marriage. All hail, King Jerrick and Queen Tove."

The guards stand to attention as Dorit and Jonas applaud from the sidelines, and I can't help the brief smirk along my lips as I watch them, knowing they didn't have to pretend to be excited.

Everyone here *knows* it is arranged.

I shake my head at their amusement and swivel back to Jerrick's hard lips suddenly on mine, sending my blood rushing to my cheeks.

He pulls away, leaving me in complete shock, and lust rests heavily deep in my core.

Fuck.

His eyes open, desire shining behind them.

I take a step away, stopping the tension at his proximity. I should not be feeling anything for this man—this monster. Exhaling and closing my eyes, I try to sear his kisses from my memory and replace them with thoughts of Niko.

Jonas runs up, touching my shoulder. "Welcome to the family, sis!"

Something about the way Jonas says that sends a wave of chills down my spine.

Politely, I thank him, then look for Dorit, only to see she is socializing with a few of the household guards.

I face Jerrick, who studies me cautiously.

He extends his elbow. "Are you ready, Frostbite, or is it too soon to call you *wife?*"

Both nicknames do nothing to improve my mood as disgust churns in my gut. I can't stop from hoping it might ruin his mood, too, knowing we are tied together and absolutely despise it.

Taking his arm, I lean in and offer a sweet, sardonic reply. "Only if you are, *husband.*"

17

A Night to *Not* Remember

We take a different path from the one Jonas and I did from my rooms, hinting we are going to Jerrick's chambers instead of mine. We walk in silence, and I don't know if I am the only one dreading the arrival or if Jerrick feels the same, too.

I try to keep my focus off what lies ahead by taking in the castle, admiring its beauty and intricate details as each step clacks against the rugs and stone floors, the only noise between us.

"Do you like it?" Jerrick asks, pulling me from examining the walls.

"What? Oh! The castle? Yes, it is beautiful," I blurt, not realizing how awkward my response is.

Sweat beads down the sides of my brow. And while my gown is a thin layer of fabric, it may as well be the thickest woolen coat.

I fear my body is giving off a rank smell, and I clench my arms and thighs and bite my lip in concentration.

Come on, Tove, pull yourself together.

The hallway we walk down is narrower than the others, with fewer decorations adorning the walls and no guards. Every few feet, there is an elevated archway that brings the spaces together, but the blackened rugs, dimmed lanterns, and the lack of windows create a moody atmosphere.

We inch up more stairs, which ruins my controlled movements. I haul myself through every step, and mercifully, Jerrick doesn't make a remark.

He matches my pace, and I appreciate it.

There were never this many stairs in my home. I need to find an excuse not to be locked up in a room and build my endurance, so I don't pass out while ascending or descending.

When we make the final clearing my heart is pounding so hard, I can hear it accompanied by Jerrick's small chuckle. I snap my head to him, scowling at his judgment.

"What is so funny?" I demand.

He glances down briefly, *still* chuckling.

He is *such* a bastard.

"You must be imagining me dead or something."

"And why do you think that?" I retort, caught off guard and pissed I wasn't thinking about it.

"I can practically feel you strangling me with the grip you have on my arm."

Baffled, I look down, noting the vise grip I do, indeed, have on him.

I release my white-knuckled hold. "Sorry," I mutter, realizing I might have been relying on his support to climb the stairs.

Illuminated at the end of the hallway is one floor-to-ceiling door, beckoning for us to open it. As our steps guide us closer, spikes of anxiety tug and rip at my chest, gripping me violently.

Jerrick inclines his head and guides us inside. As he closes the door behind us, I delve further into the rooms, taking in the lightly ruffled bed, cluttered tables, and lounge area.

The lock clicks, and Jerrick's attention focuses on me.

We stay in the quiet of the night as his footsteps move around me.

He grabs a lit candle and disperses more light to other candles throughout the bedchamber.

I fold my arms while I stand there, letting him do his work.

The room brightens with light, shining on the reflective sheer fabric of the curtains Jerrick pulls closed before turning to a worktable and adjusting some papers.

I follow his movements, noting he is tidying up as he goes, earning a crooked smirk from me.

He turns, allowing me to take him in again. Scanning him head to toe, as he does me, I note the rapid rise and fall of his chest telling me I am not alone in my worries.

I don't know what to expect, as I haven't gone beyond the passionate kisses Niko and I shared and pleasuring myself in Niko's presence.

I gulp at my lack of experience of the real thing, finding myself contemplating my value to Jerrick once again. The thought of that alone sends sweat down my spine, and I rub my sweaty hands together.

My heart sinks into my stomach as panic rushes through me.

Can I even let this happen?

I know we are married, but...

Jerrick steps toward me, throwing my fears into rapid repeat, and I instinctively move back and turn to the window.

I touch the glass, the bitter cold from outside chilling the glass and my body. I dip my head and try to let the cooling sensation numb me, but I can't relax.

Thought after thought, memory after memory, emotion after emotion. My mind is reeling, replaying anything and everything, all while I fight for air to return to my lungs. If I could manifest my magic at will, I might be able to conjure up a reasonable excuse to get out of this night.

I laugh at my stupidity, knowing nothing seems to work out when I need it to.

Cologne and leather cling to me, and I fight not to break away from the cold window to gaze at the man who is the source of all my troubles.

He fucking kidnapped me.

No matter how handsome he is, the fact he is a king, or how he *was* a little nice when we first met.

I hate how the last thought tempts me into believing I might enjoy tonight. But I shun those thoughts, feeling as if I am letting myself and Niko down.

Jerrick reaches across and tucks a loose strand of hair behind my ear. It's cold to the touch, and I want to lean into it right now to simmer down the looming feeling of failure.

I close my eyes as emotions surface, trying not to react.

"Are you in any pain?" he whispers, sending a rush of goose bumps down the side of my neck.

I exhale a long, shuddering breath, and my eyes meet his. "Do you really want to know?"

He peers out the window, and the muscles in the side of his jaw tic. Jerrick glances at his bed, then he takes my hand in his and guides us to it.

Everything tells me to fight against his hold, but I follow willingly.

The bed is large, almost bigger than my old one at home, and when we both sit on the foot, the bed dips and cushions me tightly.

Jerrick releases my hand, and I rest it on the sheets.

The black velvet rubs between my fingers, wiping away more of my sweat.

I hate that I want to sink into the comfort I know this bed is going to bring me.

"How about a drink?" He gestures to a small hutch, with petite glass doors and a countertop holding a few spun glasses.

Too nervous to speak, I nod and gulp down air the second he rises. I fan myself rapidly, hoping the sweat will abate.

The hutch creaks, forcing me to jolt to my original position as Jerrick turns, eyebrows lifted in question. "Whiskey?"

My face sours at the phantom burning sensation whiskey gives whenever I drink it. I wish it were wine, but I think any liquid courage will help me get through this night. I shrug before nodding.

A low chuckle from Jerrick escapes while he pours the whiskey. Jerrick's steps are delicate when he turns and extends the drink.

I grasp the cup, hoping he doesn't notice my trembling hands. I swig down the small amount before Jerrick even has a chance to lift his glass to his lips.

"F-Fuck!" I croak out, regretting swallowing the whiskey in one gulp as Jerrick's lips touch his glass, hiding his amusement. "Don't laugh," I rasp, rubbing my chest as the burning sensation warms me.

Jerrick scrutinizes me as he downs his entire glass, never once breaking eye contact with me.

My eyes widen at his lack of reaction.

He lowers the glass and smirks. "Now that's better." Jerrick takes my cup and turns to his wooden furniture.

I am about to protest another glass but pause when he sets them down.

He leans against the hutch, placing one foot on the bottom drawers, observing me as I grip the velvety sheets.

Jerrick clicks his tongue, and his dimpled smirk appears. He pushes off from his leaning position, stalking toward me slowly. A predator hunting its prey.

The thought alone should send me into a fit of nausea, but something dark within me is pleased by his movements.

I drop to the blanket as he sits next to me.

My breath catches at the closeness of him, the liquor warming me internally, while, externally, his gaze sets my skin ablaze.

He sweeps his hand over mine, rubbing in sweet, antagonizing circles.

I watch the rotation of his calloused thumb roam the same spot.

Jerrick leans close, kissing my upper arm far more gently than I thought he would. He is hunched over me awkwardly, his chin resting on my shoulder as his hand crawls up my beaded sleeve, sending goose bumps to prickle along my skin.

"I'm not going to hurt you," he says.

"How do you know you haven't already?" My features pinch in embarrassment, blaming the whiskey for loosening my tongue as his hand dwindles in circles.

"Allow me to rectify that," Jerrick says as his lips land on mine.

I melt against him, sighing at the rich cologne mixing in with the taste of whiskey on his tongue. It is intoxicating, and his lips are soft.

He cups my breast, and a shuddered moan escapes my throat. Oh, Sweet Makers, that feels good. *Too* good.

A low rumble vibrates against my lips as he kisses me deeper, playing with my breasts and catching me off guard with a pleasurable pinch over my nipple.

Gasping through the pained turned pleasure, Jerrick hums in approval.

"I knew you'd love that."

My nipple pebbles as he pinches tighter, twisting it between his fingertips, sending wetness straight to my center. I hiss and close my eyes.

Fuck, I want more.

Jerrick's hand drifts down, gripping onto my waist and squeezing in need. His eyes meet mine in question, the paleness of the blue in his irises darkening into a warmer gray-blue, and I can't stop from admiring the contrast between his eyes and his scar.

"Do you trust me?" he asks.

I snort. "Do you *really* want me to answer that? For Yeva's sake, you kidnapped me."

A snarl escapes from him, and I shrink in fear.

I clutch my chest, and a sudden apology forms along my lips, but his movements are faster than I can follow as he darts up to leave.

The force of him yanking the door open sends a sweep of air into the room.

He whips his head to me, fury and his pupils removing all the blue as he laces venom behind his words. "I'd rather deal with this *fucking curse* than be stuck in here with *you* any longer."

My mouth drops, and I'm stunned, speechless, as the door rips air from the bedroom, sending a loud slam to echo in the bedchamber.

The click of his boots against the stone floor recedes down the hallway.

I gasp for air as I sit on Jerrick's bed with one question repeating in my head.

What fucking curse?

18

SO MANY FACES

Small flickers of light peek in through the curtains, hinting morning was near, yet it did nothing to force an ounce of movement. Worried my whereabouts would be noted if I left the room, I remain on my side, curling into myself with my knees tucked close.

My thoughts wander over everything that *almost* happened, including everything Jerrick said prior to his harsh departure. I fell deep down into my thought's own Oblivion, hating the sense of rejection. I was left wanting from Jerrick's touch, desperately trying to remember Niko. Instead, I was teased and starved from Jerrick pinching my nipple and kissing my neck.

But that wasn't what kept me up all night.

No, it was what he said that had forced the world to stop.

Why did he say *curse* with such hatred?

He couldn't think that his magic is a curse like me. Could he?

A lifting latch sweeps away the thought, and my heart leaps at him returning, of seeking answers from him.

Yet I am let down when Dorit's form fills the doorway.

She wears a day gown dyed deep blue, with the seams lined in a pale blue, and her hair is in thick plaits, taming the enviable waves. She rests her hip against the doorway, her arms folding in concern.

"Are you alright, Tove?"

The pity in her voice should make me upset, but it only increases my guilt over ruining everything last night. I was nervous, confused, and angry. But I can't seem to shake the dooming thought of Jerrick breaking his word.

My heart sinks at the thought, realizing I did not even last a day in this arrangement before ruining my chances of helping Axidoria. I can't fight the emotions taking over me.

I break, turning away from Dorit when she catches the first tear falling.

Her touch on my shoulder pulls me to face her, pity lining her features. She wraps her arms around me, holding me as I tremble.

I work through each tremor, erring on the side of caution so my magic won't awaken.

The normal overpowering scent of roses suffocates me, and I am thankful for the inhale of fresh air when she helps me stand. "You don't have to tell me anything you don't want to."

"He just... *left*," I confess, careful of sharing more than I need to.

Anything I say can always be reported back to him.

Dorit presses her lips together, as if she, too, is unsure of what to make of his actions. "Let's get you to your chambers, alright?"

I nod and hold her hand, too exhausted from thinking. I want to leave this room and the memory of failure behind.

Dorit keeps me close. While she might be trying to console me, I can't help the suspicious thought of her being near is a way of keeping figurative chains around me.

When we make it to my chambers, the small comfort eases my racing worries.

"Do you want me to check your wound?" Dorit asks.

I nod, knowing it needed to be checked sooner rather than later.

"Let's see if we can get away with having the bandage off from now on," she says as I remove my dress, allowing her to lift the bandage.

She touches me close to the healing area, and I flinch at the contact of her fingertips. "Did I hurt you?"

I shake my head. "No. Your hands are cold. They startled me is all."

She hums, resuming her examination of my back, peeling away the bandage more. "I think you should be good to not wear the bandage. Try moving your shoulder around. Let's check the stitching to see if it bleeds."

I proceed to shrug, rotating my arm carefully, and a slight tug pulls the stitching on my back.

She nods in satisfaction. "Yeah, let's do without the bandage." Dorit turns, grabbing a day gown for me to wear today.

The black gown is modest, with long sleeves and grooves on the sides for pockets. I move tentatively as she helps slip the dress over my body.

Reclining in the chair, I seek a brush for my hair. I lower my head as I work through the knots, annoyed my arm is exhausted so quickly.

My lady-in-waiting steps up, opening her hand for the brush, and I surrender it.

Dorit takes over, detangling my silver locks. Her features brighten as she explains how she came under Jerrick's employment.

I learn her parents are a baker and a florist, and she is the oldest of her siblings.

She helps make ends meet for her family as well as encouraging Jerrick and Jonas to favor them, always giving her mother business whenever there are celebrations. Her father, though, missed the opportunity to work in the castle.

"He didn't want to work for the Mikkelsons?" I ask, my brows pinching in confusion.

"Oh, don't worry, my dad might be the best baker in Yadir, but Cordelia and Ophelia are younger and more flexible cooks for the castle. My father was glad he didn't have to sell his shop," she reassures me. "Speaking of, let's go meet Cordelia and Ophelia. Oh, you will *love* them, Tove. They are an absolutely adorable couple!"

I beam at the thought of food but grab Dorit's hand. My thoughts seek some reassurance that I have not failed my kingdom yet.

"Will Jerrick go back on his word?" My lip quivers, trying desperately not to fall apart.

Niko and Betina are back at home, and I am betraying my family by abandoning their graves. The thought of that hurts.

"Jonas won't let that happen," Dorit says.

"How do you know?"

She returns to brushing my hair, styling it into a neat plait.

I study her reflection in the mirror as she says, "Because Jonas helps the king more than I think he realizes. He won't let the prospect of trade go to waste over something petty and stupid Jerrick did, and he, most certainly, will not let Jerrick fall back on his word to you."

I contemplate that information, tucking it away. Maybe I can work more with Jonas then, and sending resources to Axidoria will help for Niko's plan.

"Dorit, would it be possible to arrange a meeting with Jonas?"

Her features brighten as she squeezes my shoulders. "He is one of your subjects now. That can easily be arranged."

I flash a grin, the Makers answering my wishes and prayers for once.

When she steps back, I spare a glance at the reflection in the mirror. My skin looks ghostly and dull, my features dark and brittle.

The chair scoots away from the vanity, preventing me from staring further into the monster I am.

"Now let's eat," Dorit chimes.

The stone arched doorway into the kitchens is darkened in color from the rest of the gray stones in the castle. Constant smoke and ash permeate out and down the hall, no doubt due to the fire always running in the kitchen. A hint of metal hangs in the air as we enter the large room.

A tall, curvy woman hovers over a slab of meat, cutting through bone and marrow, separating it for multiple meals. With each plate of ingredients, she moves to a new area of her workstation. I get a view of her strong jawline tinged with sweat, and the small baby-haired wisps escape her chestnut hair, plaited into a bun she wears at her nape.

Beyond the copper smell, rosemary and thyme accompany the yeast in full force as another woman's petite frame removes bread from one of the stone hearths. A wide grin expands across her face as she places the pot on the workstation, dusting her hands on her apron and wiping sweat from her brow. Flour sprinkles on her cheeks and the bridge of her nose, which, somehow, accentuates the hundreds of freckles gracing her warm skin.

The woman's bright green eyes meet mine, and she lights up at the sight of Dorit and me. "Dorit! We weren't expecting you until dinner!" the cook sings, but the clang of a knife falling on the table has us all startling toward the taller woman.

The blonde cook glances between us. Realization flashes in their eyes, and they both break into a deep curtsy.

"Your Majesty," they say in unison.

Dorit gives me a knowing look as the two cooks remain lowered.

I speak up, "Please, please, there is no need for curtsies."

The two women look up, hesitating. They glance at Dorit, who adds, "She is nice, I promise."

Dorit's words should not have so much effect on me, but they do. I smile my gratitude at her kindness as the two women brush off their cooking aprons.

The blonde cook steps forward, taking my hand and beaming. "I am Cordelia, Your Majesty. It is an honor to serve you."

I extend my gratitude. "If you should ever feel comfortable, you may call me Tove."

Cordelia's features soften as if sunlight itself would illuminate around her.

The other cook approaches, and I greet her before she can introduce herself. "You must be Ophelia. Please know the offer is the same for you as well."

She nods, looking breathless and full of anxiety.

Glancing at Dorit, I say to them, "Dorit has said wonderful things about your food that I can attest to myself since my arrival. I wanted to meet and personally thank you for providing such delicious meals."

They grin, Ophelia resting her hand at the small of Cordelia's back. Pure love shines between them, and they are so precious my heart wants to burst.

Ophelia faces me and Dorit. "Would you like to have some of the rolls we made?"

"Do you also have wine?" Dorit asks, and I salivate at the thought.

Cordelia snickers. "When do we not?"

Dorit claps quickly, reaching for the basket of rolls as Ophelia fetches cups and refreshment.

A small dining table is on the opposite side of the kitchen, and after I take two rolls, I join the women.

The liquid hitting each glass fills the void, and I quietly take a few bites, trying to mask my distaste for Palaena's bitter alcohol. Nostalgia for sweet wine has me focusing more on food, listening to the three women converse with one another about fellow staff members, bustling news from the market in town, zoning in and out when their discussions drift to gossip.

My eyebrow lifts in question when they talk about the staff members who ran away when Jerrick and I first arrived.

Not remembering my arrival in Palaena, I almost choke on my bread when Dorit says, "I heard that Jerrick threatened anyone who mentioned or questioned his arrival back home."

"He *threatened* his own people?" I ask, and Dorit nods.

My brows pinch in confusion as to how she heard this information.

"One of the stable hands was ordered to tell every staff member of the king's order," Cordelia adds.

Ophelia agrees as if the order remains fresh.

No wonder they looked afraid of me and filled with worry when I showed up in the kitchens. Here I thought it was due to my magic's reputation, but part of me senses their worries were based on what their own king threatened to do.

"Wh-What did he say?" I ask with trepidation, wondering how dangerous Jerrick could be.

A thrill flashes in Dorit's eyes, as if this is a ghost story rather than a possible end to her own life. "He said, 'If any staff member speaks ill of our new guest, I will end their life quicker than they will know their next heartbeat.' I've never seen him so tense!"

Shock still widens my eyes at the thought of a ruler intentionally killing his people.

Dorit attempts to brush off my own fears. "Relax, the king won't kill anyone."

I tilt my head, knowing very well he killed one of my priests in Axidoria. Dorit was there when he admitted it. So why is she dismissing his demand and claiming it to be a bluff?

"You know this how?" I ask.

She shrugs. "Jonas."

I pinch my brows. As if naming the king's brother is enough to convince me that Jerrick is not a ruthless ruler.

She waves off my concern, remaining unbothered. "Jonas tells his partner Viggo everything, and Viggo tells me everything."

I laugh. "Deities, I never thought I would hear castle gossip."

Dorit's eyes twinkle with excitement, opening her mouth to tell me more.

I lift my hand to stop her. "I don't want to know anything else."

"Not even what they say about *you*?" she teases, thinking I want to know what people here think of me.

"Please, no. I can only imagine the worst."

The mood shifts around the four of us as I grip the stem of my goblet, bristling at the wretched nickname *Snow Queen* ringing in my ears and following me from Axidoria. There is no doubt word of my arrival in Palaena has already reached the entire kingdom, despite the king's threat.

Scornful, hateful gazes of people will follow me everywhere I go.

My powers and the dreaded winter threatening my kingdom as well as other kingdoms put everyone's lives at risk. I hate that the fate of controlling my abilities lies in the hands of my enemy.

Ophelia breaks my dark thoughts, seeking to raise my spirits. "Dorit has told us of your kindness, and we have seen it firsthand, Your Majesty. Along with your beauty."

I inwardly cringe at her compliment, turning from the compassion she offers.

The harsh truth of beauty is all but a lie. There is no beauty inside of me.

Only a monster.

I force out my thanks. "I appreciate your sweet words, Ophelia."

Cordelia adds, "I have no doubt in my mind everyone would love to celebrate your and the king's union."

I bristle at the word *union*, my failure of not seeing it through last night hitting me thicker than Dorit's perfume. Smiling tight and nodding, I try to hide how close I am to breaking.

I already lost it with Dorit, but she has been the only constant here.

I can't lose it with these two women right now.

Sweet Makers, I need to do something.

Glancing out the window, I feel as if time itself is slipping. I sag with exhaustion, my head partially swimming from the wine I've consumed.

Dorit picks up on my mood. "I think it might be time for Tove to return to her chambers. She has a lot to do since recovering." Dorit rests a hand on my arm, the touch warm and comforting, and I meet her gaze, grateful for her awareness of my demeanor in such a short time.

Ophelia and Cordelia push away from the table, taking the cups and basket of bread back toward their workstations.

"We should do this again, Tove." Cordelia lingers on the use of my name rather than my title, and my cheeks perk up.

Ophelia says, "We would love to get to know our queen more if she will allow us."

Dorit beams at her friends, a blanket of comfort wrapping itself around me in their presence.

While the Mikkelsons are the enemy, their people are not, and the ease of conversation between these women has me wishfully thinking I can make acquaintances here.

I rise, inclining my head to the women who have been themselves in my presence, save for when they first saw me. I hope their authenticity may continue with and without Dorit, should I ever be allowed a chance to visit without a chaperone.

"Thank you for allowing me into your work area, and thank you for the wine and rolls," I tell them.

Dorit and I head for the archway, but I peer back. "Rolls are my favorite, and the ones you've made each day, somehow, are better than the last day's."

Ophelia pats her partner's shoulder, Cordelia looking as if she could cry at my words.

Dorit escorts me to my rooms, agreeing to a tour of the castle and setting up meetings with Jonas and Jerrick. The mention of Jerrick makes my skin crawl, hating that, eventually, I will have to face him again.

But I cannot pinpoint whether it is because he is my enemy or because he left me alone last night. I choose not to dwell on the thought, letting my mind wander to trying to reach home again today, seeking Niko or Betina.

My lack of sleep from last night tugs at my eyes along with today's physical exertion. It's been the most exercise since my arrival, and Dorit catches on quickly, offering me her arm for support.

I sag with relief when we enter my chambers, passing my thanks to Dorit as she peels away the top sheet of my bed, lifting the thick sheets over my exhausted body.

She hums as the door slinks shut, leaving me alone once more.

Despite being tired, I scramble to peel the sheets off me, seeking Mother's mirror. I rub it thrice over, the ripples happening in quick succession.

I plead desperately for a figure to be on the other side of the reflection, and my heart fractures at the body laying across my bed. I cover my mouth as Betina twiddles with her fingers, unable to sit still, much like me.

Her mannerisms bring a nostalgic smile to my face.

"Betina?"

My voice breaks.

She jolts upright, finding the exact direction of where my voice came from, relief on her face.

"Tove!" she exclaims, the gleeful sound lingering as she jumps out of the bed and rushes to the vanity. "Oh, Sweet Makers, I am thrilled to see you!"

Unable to stop her concern, she blurts, "How are you? Are you okay? Are you hurt? What about your shoulder? I heard what happened. Are you—"

"Betina," I cut in, a laugh escaping at the naturalness of her presence.

She shrugs. "Sorry."

I take in the reality of her being here and that I'm talking to her. My heart fills with hope, knowing I am not as alone as I think. But when I study her, I notice the dark circles under her eyes.

"I think the more important question is, how are you?" I ask, gesturing to my under eye.

"Oh, that." She touches her face softly. "I've been in here, waiting for you to appear again. When Nikolaj told me, I slapped his arm, pissed that he got to speak to you without me present."

That earns a chuckle from me, and blood warms my face at the memory of when I last heard from Niko. "Sorry you missed me the first time. So much has happened, and I can't use this communication all the time."

"That's why Nikolaj told me to move in here until you come back. That way, I can be here when you call," she says, gesturing to her new bedchamber. "Now, please tell me what's going on?"

My face falls in defeat. I summon the courage to push through the most recent events with her.

Betina's expressions shift from sorrow to anger as I summarize everything. By the time I finish, she is quiet.

It takes a lot to make Betina quiet.

"Tove, you aren't coming home until *summer*?" she asks, her voice a soft whisper.

I know she worries for me and also our kingdom. I mask away my pain and defeat to console her.

"I just have to bide my time here. I don't want there to be a fight, but Niko feels this is the only way. And it is not too bad waiting here. I have met Prince Jonas, the king's brother, who *seems* kind, along with my lady-in-waiting, Dorit."

Betina's expression darkens, and I snicker. "Don't worry, Betina, you're still my favorite lady-in-waiting."

She hums before her features turn solemn. "What about your magic?"

I shrug, the stitching in my right shoulder pulling. "I am not sure. Everything is jumbled and scattered. I am supposed to be training with the king, but I don't know about that now, since he stormed out during our wedding night, mentioning a curse—"

"Wait, a curse!? What?"

I lift my hand. "I doubt it is even real. I honestly think he was trying to say anything to get away from me."

The realization of my words, the memory of his touch, and the intensity of Jerrick lingers in my mind. I hate that his attractiveness lures me with need.

I could try to reach Niko later and seek his company and find release with him, but the thought of violating my marital vows, no matter that they are with Jerrick, turns my stomach into knots. Morally, I don't want to even consider that again.

That doesn't even beg to touch on the punishment the Makers could bring if I violate my marital vows and the decree.

Guess I will be using my hands from here on out.

Betina pulls me from my thoughts. "Well, then, bide your time, earn their trust, and then wreak havoc on the bastards when you are able to hone your abilities."

"I don't want to hurt anyone, and I want there to be a peaceful solution," I say, and Betina scoffs.

I stop her train of thought. "But what I want isn't something I think can be achieved."

She sighs, plopping onto my chair in my old chambers. Betina studies me through her solemn chestnut eyes, her chest shrinking as she hunches on her knees.

"I can't believe there will be a battle."

I sink farther into the bed before offering her a nod of finality. When it comes to returning home to Axidoria and marrying Niko, I know Niko is right. A fight is the only choice.

We sit in silence, my mind dwelling over the potential outcome of a battle between Axidoria and Palaena and the possibility of the plan falling apart before I can make any headway.

The anxiety trills deep in my bones, forcing me to clench my jaw as I debate if the path I've started down is one the Makers know of already and are watching, waiting, to see how badly I will doom myself. Part of me wonders if they are planning the best time to enact the most wrath upon me.

But a glint of amber eyes smiling reminds me everything we are going to do will be worth it.

"Is there anything you want me to relay to Nikolaj?"

Betina's voice enters the void of my thoughts.

"The last time he and I spoke, I told him to communicate with King Bernard and Queen Verena. Make sure he follows through with that, and I'll see about trying to send supplies from Palaena in our upcoming trade discussions in hopes of getting Lord Ulrik to back off," I tell her.

She grimaces at the mention of Ulrik, telling me he, too, is a nuisance for Niko. "Thank the Makers you didn't marry him. Nikolaj is even talking about dragging him around with him when he calls the banners, just to keep an eye on him," she blurts.

Niko would, in fact, follow through.

I laugh lightheartedly. "Sweet Makers, there is no way I could have. I would've been suffocated by secondhand tobacco stench."

She howls, slapping her knee in amusement. She inches forward, wiping a tear from her eye.

"Fucking Deities, Tove, I miss you."

I voice my tear-filled goodbyes, hoping to speak with her soon, as my eyes grow heavy with the need to sleep. I drag my hand around the mirror once, breaking my connection to Axidoria. To Niko. To Betina. To my family.

The heavy weight of grief lingers in an ominous composition, a reminder of the graves I have not seen since coming here.

I seek their love, their advice, and *them*.

Rubbing my chest doesn't ease the ache of missing my family, and I choke on my own sobs, grabbing a pillow and pulling it close. The brittle pain of being alone and separated not only from Niko, but my family as well is what drags me back into my own Oblivion, night after night, nightmares never seeming to leave me.

19

REASON OR *EXCUSE?*

The beauty of Palaena's castle is astounding and different from Axidoria's. Each floor stretches to entertainment wings, the royal library, study rooms, eating halls, and sleeping chambers. With its multiple levels, one would think that the decoration would alter. Instead, it remains unwavering throughout the entire estate.

Gilded framed portraits line many of the walls, varying from ancestor paintings to art depictions of creatures, forests, and life. They are paired with tall arched windows that are curved to a point, surrounded by black, red, and gold woven by the hanging chandeliers and lanterns.

While I knew there was more to explore, I lingered longest near the training arena, near the kitchens to chat with Ophelia and Cordelia, and near the courtyard to take in its beauty once more.

Dorit drags me to my meeting with Jonas and Jerrick in earnest, as if she does not wish for me to roam alone or converse with the castle's staff.

While I would like to learn names and familiarize myself with their faces, I stop my intentions abruptly, remembering I do not intend to remain here. I keep my resolve tight in my chest, only to lose all sense of it completely when Dorit and I drift down the study wing, catching sight of Jerrick at the opposite end.

His blue eyes seem dark and distant. But they flare when they meet mine, the same rigidness he had from our wedding night evident in his entire demeanor.

My skin turns cold underneath his stare, fear gripping me like a vise, and I pull Dorit to stay in place. My heartbeat thrums in my ears while the walls close in around me.

Darkness and hatred roll off Jerrick in waves, confusion furrowing my brows over what is wrong with him.

Jonas tentatively touches his brother's elbow.

Jerrick jerks away and snarls, Jonas flinching as Jerrick scowls back at Dorit and me, promptly leaving without any word.

I spare a glance at my lady-in-waiting, shock in her eyes as Jonas runs a hand through his hair, turning back to face us.

The rage from the King of Palaena still feels thick in the room, and whatever I just witnessed means getting Jerrick to help train my magic is going to be more difficult than I anticipated.

Nausea rolls in my stomach while I try to suppress defeat.

"Give him some time." Jonas smiles tightly.

"He can take all the time he needs. I much prefer your company," I retort as Dorit leaves us with a bow.

A hint of approval is evident in Jonas's grin as the two of us enter a study hall to discuss the future of our two kingdoms as they merge into one. Jonas pours me a glass of wine, while I take in the map of Draymenk stretched out on a long wooden table.

I've debated and planned out most of my excuses, compiling compromises that will not let the joining happen faster than I can control. I cling to a mask of lies, striving to build trust and appear willing in these negotiations, knowing it will be arduous and tiring.

"Here you are," Jonas says, handing me the wine.

I take a sip and seek the courage it will give me to function through meetings. But it is bitter and dry, nothing in comparison to the sweet wine from home. My features scrunch as I swallow the burning liquid.

Jonas studies me through his glass, unfazed by the harsh drink. He places it down as he takes a seat, jumping straight into business.

"Axidoria does have a few resources to offer, but your trade with other kingdoms and the routes your kingdom has maintained for so long are what really interest us," Jonas says, and I nod.

He continues, "We already have sent word to the other kingdoms explaining the situation, along with notifying them of the union between you and my brother. We also mentioned hosting a meeting regarding territories when the warmer seasons grant every kingdom safe passage to travel."

I relax slightly at the mention of other kingdoms being involved around the time Niko seeks to fight. The information is mercifully granting me time.

"I think it is wise to host a meeting for the merging, but I also know King Bernard will not believe everything simply from a letter."

Excitement dances in Jonas's brown eyes as he chuckles, lacing his fingers together. "Oh, I know he does not. Which is why I want us to throw a masquerade to celebrate your marriage and then host a meeting with the others."

I cannot interpret if it is for the celebration or the meeting, but I ask, "And what does the *king* think?"

My brother-in-law reclines in his chair, sighing. "He agreed to them all before he left."

"And why *did* he leave?"

Jonas shrugs dismissively. "He had other duties to attend to."

The words are short and evasive. It does nothing to ease my suspicions of Palaena and their intentions.

I plaster a light smile on my face. "I will need to write home after each of these meetings to alert my advisor, who is acting as our current proxy, of what we intend to do. We will also need to visit Axidoria."

Jonas claps, startling me. "That gives me another idea!" He wiggles his eyebrows with delight as he says, "We can host two celebrations! One here in Palaena and one in Axidoria, where the people from both kingdoms can attend both celebrations to create and strengthen the unification!"

The prince's brown eyes twinkle, his pure joy infectious.

I want to smile along with him, and I do, knowing this grants Niko a chance to enter Palaena with welcome. With him and the bannermen in attendance, the paradigm will shift.

A smirk plays along my lips. "Let's first get through trade routes and then we can plan the celebrations."

Jonas's tall frame eases into the cushioned seat, agreeing with my feedback. His brown eyes are bright and excited for this new challenge. With similar features as his brother, I can't wrap my mind around how one of them can be accommodating, charming, and kind while the other pretends to show those traits.

He glances down at the map between us, pinpointing the trade routes and goods we plan to exchange. With wine, wheat, fish for crops, and new metals, my heart leaps at the resources supplied by Palaena and not Ulrik.

The gratification at removing the Albertsens' power over my family is unparalleled. With the new trade and the planned ball, I am almost convinced this alliance could be a good thing.

Almost.

Jonas is rambling ideas aloud, unable to curb the thrill of planning this celebration of my marriage to Jerrick. "It'll be a challenge to make the arrangements, but it'll be fabulous." Jonas beams.

The relief of removing one small stress from my agenda is short lived, the added weight of scheming already taking a toll. I go along with all the suggestions Jonas mentions, too tired to expend anymore on plans for the day.

When I leave his study, I find myself heartened by the solitude of being alone for once. My footsteps take me to one of my favorite areas of the castle, grateful the figurative shackles I wear feel lighter—if only a little.

Jonas is open and forthright during our trade discussions, but each day I walk down the hall with Dorit is another day I do not see Jerrick.

It strikes me as odd, given he was the one I was supposed to be with while here. I had believed meetings would involve us both along with training my gifts.

But it is as if he is a figment of my imagination.

Each day I don't wake up beside Niko or don't have Betina greeting me is a cold slap to the face. My situation is real, not a dream.

I've fought my homesickness alone, clinging to my pillow and crying through nightmares. My grief and my failures seek to drown me each day, but I cannot even allow myself to feel the sorrow. No, I need to bide my time, wearing this false mask to find answers and return home.

Being tucked away with Jonas should be exhausting, but it's granted me chances to peel information from the prince about Palaena after a few glasses of wine. He still managed to remain tight-lipped whenever I would bring up his brother, seeking answers about him as well as my family. But Jonas listed excuses, claiming he was forbidden to discuss such matters until the king had.

It left me vexed, hating that I would have to wait for Jerrick to approach me.

Jonas diverted my questions, mentioning how he and Viggo, his partner, met. The adoration shining on his face whenever he spoke of Viggo lifted my mood despite the pang of missing Niko.

The story led deep into the night, and it was the first time I genuinely felt my time with Jonas was a delight rather than an obligation.

I've worked hard at remaining closed off, yet I found myself blurring the lines between deceiving and being myself.

Matters only remained worse, though, because I could not sense my magic.

It hasn't manifested since my injury, and part of me fears that, somehow, being here, healing has taken away my capabilities. It is another jab at my failures, reminding me that Axidoria is still plagued by my destruction.

I fidget with my fingers anxiously, still trapped in this disaster of my own making.

I seek out the courtyard after today's meeting, discussing wine as one of the first resources exchanged between Palaena and Axidoria. And as it comes into view, my breath catches, and tension leaves my body at the sight.

The sun sets behind the Velkan Mountains, with a cloudless sky covered in light hues of pink and lavender surrounding the blue of day. No sign of night has taken over the sky yet, and my arms hold my midsection, leaning against one of the courtyard pillars, enjoying one of my new favorite pastimes.

Chords and a light melody come to mind, and my fingers twitch lightly, circling movements of composition as I imagine a soft, lyrical ballad coming to life on the keys of a piano. An ache pushes against my chest from the lack of access to music, and I fight through it, trying to allow the song to uplift me. But tears line my vision.

I miss Niko and Betina.

I miss visiting my family's graves.

I try to hum the songs I've composed in my heart, but its call has disintegrated.

"How is your plan for world domination going?" a dark, low voice grumbles from the shadows.

I gasp, my hackles rising to attention at the sound of Jerrick's rich tone, paired with amusement. I bite back a retort as he stands beside me, leaning against the opposite pillar.

He hasn't approached me since our wedding night, and it has my defenses up, worrying he has been spying on me this entire time and is aware of my intentions.

I note his appearance is more dressed down than usual. A rumpled gray tunic, black leather trousers, and a belt holding his sword and dagger with matching hilts. His hair is damp, and tied half-back, displaying his square jaw and that damned dimple.

Jerrick turns when he catches me looking, and I bristle, darting my attention back to the sunset. He chuckles, as if he knows I still need him to teach me about my magic and that this is only a game of who has more willpower to not rip off the other's head.

It takes everything in me to hold my tongue, to *play nice* with this monster rather than lash out. I wish I could hide the blush creeping along my cheeks, making me feel hot and needy from his inspection.

He steps into my personal space, cologne and leather rippling off him in waves. A dangerously intoxicating scent.

I staunch my breath.

He murmurs, "I'd like to give you a tour of the grounds."

I keep my focus on the lake, scouting for any signs of wildlife as a distraction from meeting Jerrick's gaze, nerves building in my stomach from his nearness.

I am not as ready to see him again as I thought.

"I've already had a tour of the castle," I say flatly, trying to mold myself into the pillar.

He steps closer. "I bet you haven't seen the training arena." His chest touches my arm, the hardness of it and his body warmth melting into my skin.

I huff in annoyance at my own body's betrayal, fighting the urge to give him an ounce of my energy and time, knowing I can't show my desperation for training. I reach for my anger over his avoidance of me and remain focused on the sunset.

"I'd like for us to talk."

His velvet voice caresses my skin.

I grip harder for my frustrations, delaying my response to his comment. Holding my dress and fumbling with the fabric, I seek *something* to ground me and calm me. The satin skirt of my blue dress glides along my fingertips, the soothing relief of its coolness relaxing in my touch.

A warm hand grabs mine, and a calloused thumb rubs slow circles.

I meet those softened pale eyes, hopeful for my response. But a hint of remorse is behind them, too.

Jerrick's hair is pulled away from his face, one small dimple appearing while we examine one another. His mind-numbing touch calms me, reminding me of the need to work with him.

"Talk," I manage, slipping my hand from his.

I step away, needing distance and space.

Facing back to the sunset, the mountains already tease glimpses of spring. The normality of the seasons in Palaena throws me off, emotional exhaustion sweeping over me. The periodic dark cloud of my grief surfaces, looming over my mournful heart and souring my mood.

I try to keep my head held high, maintaining a regal appearance, only to turn away from Jerrick and leave, my own cowardice in my full wake.

Jerrick's footsteps follow me, the clink of his boots catching up with my steps in a hallway of the castle. When he reaches me, his strides slow to complement mine.

I want to appreciate the small gesture of not having to match his long-legged pace, but I keep walking, trying to pretend he isn't beside me.

He grips the elbow of my sleeved gown and tugs me to a halt. "I am sure you have many questions, and I promise I will answer all of them, but first, I need you to come with me."

I sigh before gesturing for him to lead the way, only for him to extend his elbow to me. My mind and body are at war from the offer, and my body wins.

We drift close as I take the king's elbow, the crisp scent of his clean tunic mixing with the air as we walk toward a closed door.

Jerrick guides me into a room I have not been in, and relief courses through me that this room is not a bedchamber. The memory of his raised voice and rejection still stings, despite him being my enemy.

I shudder as I step farther into a large study.

The room is surrounded with books stacked high on built-in shelves, and I remain quiet in my conflicting thoughts, touching the oak bookcases that hold volumes of history, art, journals, and maps of Palaena and Draymenk. Scanning the titles, some deal with religion, trade, and stories—even dabble in composition and music.

Joy lifts my mood as I trace my fingers across each music book, craving to read and memorize every score of Palaena's artists.

"You play?" Jerrick's whisper sends the hair rising along my neck, his presence made known.

My hand falls away from the texts, feeling like I was caught doing something wrong.

But his question brings back memories of my past and how it used to be surrounded with harmony. My resentment wavers slightly.

"I used to," I confess.

"Used to?"

"Before I froze over my piano back home." I, again, seek distance from him.

I ease into a high cushioned chair across from another, separated by a table piled with paperwork. I cross my arms at the small vulnerability I offered, unsure of why I even admitted that.

But the memory of playing on each key of the piano sets my determination straight, another thing capable of being fixed if I train with him.

Jerrick's sits, leaning back. He studies me carefully, tenderness leaving his features, replaced by that cocky ego I so easily remember.

"Your powers are what bring us here today," he says.

The kernel of calm and peace drains from me. "Maybe if you had upheld your end of the deal, my abilities wouldn't have to be mentioned."

His face hardens at my venom, and he inches forward and rests his arms on the table. It trembles as he says, "Oh, I still plan to train you, Frostbite. But all in good time. I, first, had to see how bad your winter was coming into my kingdom."

I never considered it affecting Palaena. The veins of snow and ice from the lake near my home sprouted in the opposite direction of their borders. But traveling through Biala Forest showed me that my powers were spreading.

I did not get to see how bad it was, my injury speaking for itself. But my own negligence and lack of awareness of it to begin with coats my throat with nausea.

My skin heats, and my palms turn clammy as I reach out for something else to focus on. I lean into the lack of an apology from him about our wedding night, aware he is seeking to brush his outburst under the rug, blaming everything on me, like everyone does.

I scoff. "Is *that* your reason for avoiding me this entire time?"

"Who said anything about avoiding?" he coos dubiously.

I roll my eyes at the taunt as he adds, "It is heartwarming to see you've taken your new role seriously. But I have returned and have cleared your schedule to work with me."

"I still have to work with Jonas and send correspondence to Axidoria. I can't simply ignore those duties to work only with you." I run my thumbs through my eyebrows as a dull ache forms in my head.

The meetings with Jonas are already long, and while I've grown to enjoy his company, it doesn't make the *unifying* of two kingdoms any easier. Not to mention the masquerade.

Will I get any time to reach out to Betina and Niko?

I might have to sacrifice time with them if I am going to get the answers and training I need from Jerrick. Darkness and misery cleave at my chest at my decision when footsteps recede toward the exit.

I lift my head as Jerrick reaches the door.

"Then you mustn't be trying hard enough," he says.

The fury coursing through me moves faster than my words.

I grab a rumpled piece of paper to throw toward Jerrick and his *tousled* onyx hair. But the harsh reality of my terrible aim and awful strength shows as the crumpled parchment hovers in the air for mere seconds before dropping to the ground—*far* away from the door.

The monster himself laughs cheerfully, haunting my thoughts and sending my rage to unravel even more. I stand, needing to expel my anger, and shove everything off the study table.

20

CONFIDE AND MORTIFIED

Betina stands next to Niko in my old bedchamber, both bundled in warm clothing. The flames from the hearth are still bright and luminous in the morning light. Winter in Palaena has eased, the season drifting by to allow the long plentiful spring and summer to flourish in their lands.

But back home, it looks as if winter has only just begun. Axidoria is cursed by my magic that nibbles away each season, significantly shortening them.

From the looks on both Niko and Betina's faces, I know my time in Palaena has done nothing to improve my kingdom's situation.

"That *fucking* asshole!" Niko says, folding his arms.

I did not want to reach out to them last night, my own anger evident from Jerrick's harsh words on a constant loop keeping me awake.

Then you mustn't be trying hard enough.

My lack of sleep allowed me to reach out to Niko or Betina in the early hours of the morning. I'm lucky Betina was awake and I caught Niko between trips around Axidoria.

But Niko's fury-filled gaze unsettles both me and Betina. His chest rises and falls, his emotions tense and dark.

I try to offer him hope. "At least he agreed to help me with my magic."

Betina says, "Yes, at least there is that."

Niko's golden eyes flash, his body relaxing a little, and he lowers his arms. He glances between us, a long sigh escaping him before he pinches the bridge of his nose.

"Forgive me for my outburst. I did not sleep well last night."

"Neither did I," I admit, and he gives me the briefest of smiles.

The stress I have thrown at him dims his normal lighthearted demeanor and shows in his lackluster skin, dark circles, and stubble.

"How is home?" I ask, hoping for a status report on everything.

Niko shifts into seriousness, his jaw flexing and fists clenching. "Fine."

It feels like he is hiding something from me. And whatever he is keeping could be in regard to the bannermen or my winter spreading. Perhaps he is withholding the details to protect me and grant me a chance to focus on training my magic.

I try to peel something more from him. "Did you receive the extra supplies sent over from Palaena?"

Niko is distant when he gives me another one-word answer. "Yes."

My stomach sours.

Betina glances to the window and elbows Niko, angling her head toward the light.

Niko looks, taking in the time of day before facing me. "I need to set out."

My face falls, and my lips quiver at his need for departure.

His amber eyes soften as he steps closer to the mirror, addressing me. "I'm sorry I am not in the best of moods today. I-I—" His head drops, and Betina pats his shoulder gently.

Deities, I wish I could wrap my arms around him.

His red hair moves with him when he faces me again. "I-I didn't think this would be so hard, but it is. Fuck, I miss you, Tee."

"I miss you too, Niko." I clutch the stem of the mirror, wishing I could touch him.

Betina coughs harshly, and I roll my eyes. "I miss you *too*, Betina."

She smirks, each of us laughing. My eyes find Niko's again, longing pulling me toward him.

"I'll see you soon," he whispers, his baritone voice soft and kind.

I smile faintly, watching him leave.

Betina's gaze tracks him before she turns on me. "He is not handling your marriage well."

I sulk deep into my bed. I figured that out myself by his shifting demeanor today.

"Y-You didn't tell him anything, right?"

Betina's eyes widen as she shakes her head. "No! Absolutely not!"

Relief swims over me at that, at least. I doubt Niko would want to know the details of my relationship with the King of Palaena, so I've kept them tucked away for both of our sakes.

Betina continues, "What happens between you and the King of Palaena while you are married is your business. Not mine or Niko's."

I crack a laugh, unable to suppress the reality of my arranged marriage. "Yeah, nothing *is* happening on that end."

Betina cocks her head, lifting a brow as she asks, "Do you *want* something to happen?"

I blanch, blurting. "No!"

Betina rests her hands on her hips as my face warms.

My defenses rise to prevent further focus on my marriage. "You said it wasn't any of your business," I scold.

Betina rolls her eyes. "That doesn't mean I won't ask."

I groan, smacking my head. From everything that happened when I first met Jerrick in Axidoria to now, I *still* couldn't shake the consuming thoughts of Jerrick touching me and kissing me on our wedding night. How he pinched my nipple so tightly I could've burst right there.

Sweet Makers, that could still happen, and I don't know what I'd do then.

Looking back to my friend, I say, "If I *were* to tell you anything, you'd have to swear not to tell Niko."

"Tove, you will always be my priority." Betina places a hand over her heart. "What you say will always be held in confidence."

The validation of our friendship warms my chest, leaving me feeling fuzzy. I can trust her, and it eases some of the tension in my shoulders, knowing that, with everything swirling in my mind, I can always count on her.

"What you say will always be held in confidence with me as well," I tell my dearest friend, hoping she knows I share the same sentiments and admire her loyalty to our friendship and my role as queen.

A knock comes at the door, and I jolt, blurting to Betina. "I have to go."

She swishes her hands with complete understanding I will never deserve. "Go, Go. Love you." Betina's tight-lipped smile matches mine.

"Love you, too," I whisper, doing a rotation around the frame of the mirror and severing the connection from home.

"Tove?" Dorit sings.

I rest my mother's mirror on the bedside, scooting up in bed as my heart races. She knocks again, and I brace myself for a quick inhale of breath.

"Come in," I say.

The door swings open, and Dorit enters holding a tunic and trousers. She holds them up with a bright grin.

"I was told you have plans with the king today, so I've brought you new clothes."

My own mortification sets in. I take in the pants and boots, terrified by the idea of wearing them.

Women in Axidoria do not wear trousers and tunics, and this is a custom often looked down upon. And I never worried about that because I love wearing gowns. *Love* them. But to have one of the last things I enjoy be taken away while I'm here is the final tear in my control.

I snarl.

This outfit, Jerrick's words, and the abrupt end of talking to Niko and Betina at home have my skull rattling. The King of Palaena married me, ignored me, and promised to answer all my questions. And Jerrick's failure to deliver has rage fueling through me.

I hurry in getting ready, stewing in my fury before seeking out the king himself to emphasize he is not the only one who is feared by others.

I am a monster, too.

Adrenaline drives me forward. Not even knowing his gifts will keep me from giving him a piece of my mind.

He *will* train me, and I *will* go home.

I stumble through the castle, wearing trousers and a simple cotton tunic for the first time. Staff members glance when I pass by, and I fight the embarrassment and stifle my anger.

My lungs search for air when I reach the bottom level, catching Jonas and Jerrick conversing.

My feet are throbbing when I approach the brothers, smiling in surprise when Jonas steps forward and wraps his arms around me. "Tove! I was told you would be with Jerrick today." He ends the embrace as Jerrick's blue eyes flick to me.

My jaw works. "Yes," I manage through gritted teeth, hatred, and pure annoyance fuming from my pores. "Your brother is *supposedly*, ready to deliver *one* of his promises."

Surprisingly, Jerrick is here and hasn't scurried off. I take that as a hopeful sign.

The adrenaline building from my fury is hard to settle, but I inhale a deep breath. I need to play nice if I am going to get answers and wield my gifts.

But that *damn* dimple makes an appearance on Jerrick's face, and fuck if it doesn't cool my temper.

Instead of saying anything, he turns and walks in the opposite direction.

My face falls. "W-Wait! Where do you think you are going?"

I can't have him leaving. I just got here.

"We'll be starting small. Now, come along," he says over his shoulder.

I try to argue and look at Jonas for help. But Jonas shakes his head in amusement, shrugging as if he, too, doesn't know what to expect from his brother.

Jerrick takes further strides down the hall, and my irritation doesn't stop me from fumbling after him.

21

BLOOD BOILS OVER

Parading through the castle after Jerrick leaves me grasping for air when we enter Palaena's royal library. My feet ache from the laced-up boots, a stark contrast to the slippers I am used to wearing. And when I catch the fluffy cushioned lounge in the far corner of the room, I groan in relief.

Floor to ceiling bookcases stretch down the vast hall, filled to the brim with books. Rows of more shelves are lined around the perimeter, and the smell of leather-bound parchment gives me a sense of peace.

I inch closer to plop into one of the many cushioned chairs, half a step away when Jerrick tugs my elbow and tosses a book at me.

I scowl. "Why are you handing me this?"

"Because..." Jerrick skims through a few texts before walking farther and gesturing to the books. "As I said earlier, we are starting small."

My mouth falls open, and I'm caught off guard. "But you said—"

"That I would train you, yes. But you don't understand everything, so we have to start from the beginning."

My anger boils over at his comment, annoyed that he thinks I have not done any research on my abilities. When I first came into my gifts, I enlisted priests to aid me in scouring Axidoria's royal library for scrolls, journals, and documents of each heir's inherited power. But none of them had magic like mine.

My response to Jerrick is on the tip of my tongue when I pause that train of thought, realizing what he says *does* make sense.

Did Palaena have a previous monarch with abilities like mine? Is that why we are here?

I remain quiet, fighting through the anger and resentment festering in my chest, hating how I need him more than he needs me.

When Jerrick adds the seventh book to the stack I carry, I stumble and catch myself.

"Any more books and I might collapse," I grumble.

"Think of it as strength training, then." Jerrick exhales and waves off my remark.

I want to fight his logic, but again, deep down, he is right. I could gain a little more muscle on my limbs.

He drags me along to ledgers and more books.

Tilting my head, I examine the titles I carry, but I trip and fall forward.

Books explode as I brace for impact, and I tumble into Jerrick. I cling to his tunic while my already sore feet tangle around each other as books drop on top of them.

"Fuck!" I yelp in pain, hopping.

Jerrick chuckles as I turn red, fumbling through my toe-piercing pain.

I tighten my grip on his tunic as I steady myself, my toes curling in my boots. Sweet Makers, that fucking hurt.

Jerrick helps me upright. "Are you alright?" He assesses me and the pile of books I dropped, then squats, picking up each one.

"Sorry, I didn't mean to drop them, I was trying to—" I stop and watch him in silence, guilt eating at me.

I bend down to help with the mess I made.

With the books gathered, we stand, and I tilt my head up to him.

His height seems worse in these damned boots, my short stature making my neck extend all the way back to meet his gaze.

My nose pinches a little at the tinge of sweat in the air, and my pulse quickens at being his sole focus.

His chest is close to mine, and the inkling I have to touch him again has me wiggling my fingers.

I turn toward the stacks of parchments, ledgers, and books, knowing the aroma of parchment will stifle Jerrick's scent.

He passes by, and I hate that my gaze tracks him.

Jerrick approaches the soft chairs, first placing the books in one and moving a short wooden table to rest between the lounge area. He separates them into various stacks, gesturing for me to sit.

I hesitate momentarily, doing as he says, loathing how I have to wait for his next move.

Jerrick smacks down the last book on its stack. "Here we have Palaena's ledgers on glamour magic and some paperwork and correspondence between your mother and my father." He points to each of the piles.

My brows furrow in confusion.

Jerrick's mention of my mother throws my intentions for the day off course. I feel underprepared and exposed, yet again, in his presence. And that pisses me off.

"Wait, why are we looking into glamour magic and letters between my mother and your father? I thought you said we were starting small for my magic?"

Jerrick sits in the other lounge chair, propping one of his boots on the corner of the short wooden table. "We will get to that. But you have to earn the right first."

I clench my fists on the armchair as I lean forward, the ability to stifle my rage fleeting the more I'm around this man.

"And *how* am I supposed to earn that right?" I demand, irritation thick in my voice.

He flicks a few strands of hair from his face before crossing his arms, his posture relaxed. "With both of us researching and finding how to break my curse first."

I roll my eyes. "You *can't* be serious."

"I am."

Jerrick glowers as I huff in amusement and disbelief.

But I can't prevent myself from laughing. I giggle and snort, each one growing more loud and more hysterical, the winding well of my thoughts finally reaching their tipping point.

I am truly fucked.

This man *never* had any intention of training me, and somehow, I find it hilarious.

"Oh, alright, *Your Majesty*. Let me see if I hear you correctly." I play along with this web of lies he has spun. "First, you come into my kingdom, threaten to kill those I care about, then kidnap me and almost cost me my life. Thankfully, I live and awake in a foreign kingdom, only to be told my mother had brokered a marriage agreement between us."

"Yes."

"But *now*, in the midst of it all, there is a curse?"

"Precisely," he confirms, not budging from his story.

I shake my head. This is unbelievable. Why am I even laughing?

Probably because you most definitely are going to Oblivion now, Tove.

I hold my stomach, my own thoughts running me into delirium.

Jerrick stands, grabbing a piece of parchment and extending it to me.

My chuckles stop when he shakes it. Suspiciously, I examine it, reluctant to reach for it. But curiosity has me grabbing it and scanning the contents. I make it past the first two sentences of the document before I stop.

Annoyance returns at the harsh reminder of our marriage arrangement. "I've already seen this," I tell him, vexed he is bringing this up *again*.

"Did you read it *all*, though?"

The decree itself is heavily detailed, lined with intricacies that were established between my mother and Jerrick's father.

I shake my head, rest the parchment on the table, and fold my arms, looking at Jerrick.

He points at the document. "That marriage decree was originally meant for your mother and my father, but when she came here to sign the agreement, our names were glamoured to replace theirs, along with a curse your mother cast to take effect after she killed herself."

Shock colder than winter prickles across my skin. A shooting pain erupts over my heart, sharper than any arrow or dagger piercing me.

Mother... killed herself? No. I refuse to believe it. She couldn't. She *wouldn't*.

"You're lying," I shake out, denying she would do that to herself—to me.

"I saw the entire thing happen."

Our gazes meet.

I can't stop the doubt in my mind from my own beliefs versus his story. This man has lied repeatedly, and as his eyes roam over me, I get the feeling he is still hiding something.

I can't stand it, and I look away. I bite the inside of my cheek, thinking over his words, unsure if this is something my mother would do.

Magic was always tricky, and abilities varied based on the skill of the user. Mother gained her powers when she was younger than Runa and me, allowing her plenty of time to learn the ups and downs of her gifts. But she didn't use it often. I *know* she didn't.

Jerrick explains, "When she signed the agreement, she broke something off of her necklace, drank it down, and collapsed in front of my father and me. It happened faster than we could react, and I held him back from going to her out of fear for his safety. But when my father ran to her—that was when my vision turned red."

I search Jerrick's expressionless face, all charm and dry wit tossed aside, replaced with something dark. His eyes are distant, glossy, as if memories of his past eat at him. Gone is the demeanor of Rick, the charming man with whom I danced, as well as King Jerrick, who dragged me into enemy territory.

Instead, the man in front of me is different.

Haunted.

Jerrick shudders and closes his eyes, releasing a long exhale before he continues, "I prowled after my father, not letting him get close to her. I tore him away from her, unable to stop my actions. The only thing running through my mind was this all-consuming need to kill him. My dagger was unsheathed faster than my father's magic, faster than the king's guard could follow. I dragged my blade across his throat without a second thought, and I did the same to my own men. As I took down the others and my father bled out, his magic was transferring to me.

"I blacked out in the aftermath of everything. And it wasn't until I awoke that I saw the decree reveal your mother's curse. My brother and I fabricated a story for the people while I fought these urges. Ever since then, I've spent the last five years unable to fully quench this thirst to kill. I've resorted to hunting and training my magic to help me with this..." He flexes and unflexes his hands, his tone void of all emotion. "*Curse.*"

The word, again, lingers between us.

I focus on his hands as the silence hangs heavy in the aftermath of his admission. I remember admitting I felt the same during our travels.

But my mother could only do glamours. And even though I knew she blamed Palaena for Father's death, Jerrick's story still did not feel complete.

I meet Jerrick's eyes. "Wh-What did you do with my mother's body?"

I try to mask the tremble in my voice.

Jerrick swallows thickly, casting his gaze downward. "We held a small funeral for her and my father and burned her body, scattering both of their ashes."

My breath hitches, surprised from his response. Emotions clog in my throat, wishing I could have been there to light the pyre or be present for her burial to offer her a final goodbye.

I turn when Jerrick lifts his head, blinking away the tears threatening to fall, trying to remain indifferent, even though I want to crumble. Grief seeks to consume me, but I steer my thoughts, needing to understand my mother's intentions with Palaena.

She drafted a trade agreement to find proof of what happened to Father, not cause destruction herself.

Did Mother lie to us all?

Why would she curse Jerrick instead of his father? Especially if she believed King Ivan to be the one behind Father's death. Why a marriage agreement with the enemy?

Maybe this is Jerrick's hunger for power and he murdered my family and his father, and somehow, the action itself is what cursed him.

Still, I ask, "Is *this* why you—"

My words trickle away, almost asking if that was why he left on our wedding night. No, I could not voice that question, even though it sits at the forefront of my mind.

"Is this why you haven't been around?"

I am still convinced his story is fabricated, but he nods silently, allowing me more time to assess what he is telling me.

The tormented look in his eyes remains.

I shake my head, nothing making sense about the mother who raised me and the man facing me. "My mother wouldn't do something like that. She didn't know how to curse. She would *never* do something like that," I say with finality.

Mother wouldn't hurt a fly.

Jerrick contorts, reaching for a book near us. It's bound in leather and worn around the edges. He opens the book, skipping through some pages, and stopping to show me.

Records of Axidoria's criminals and their crimes are in this ledger. My eyes widen, and I yank the book away, reading the names of recorded murderers, rapists, thieves, and more.

My heart stops when I read over sentences dealt.

Those captured were cursed with a variety of punishments. Each name noted their curse, the duration of their punishment, and who performed the curse. Every one was recorded as cast by my mother. The bottom of each record was signed by my parents, an Alorian priest, and my parents' advisors.

"H-How did you get this?" I rasped as I filter through the logs.

How have I never seen this before?

"I have my methods."

Meaning he stole it or paid someone to steal it.

I rub at my chest as I read on. My mother and father never showed me this side of ruling. Looking through these records, one would assume my parents were cruel and evil.

How could the royal advisors agree with this and not a battle?

I knew every kingdom had its own variety of laws and orders, but I was told any crimes were managed by sentencing them to be monitored and tracked their service to the kingdom. It's how Niko and I have handled any of the criminals since I've stepped into this role.

Nothing like *this*.

Did Mother glamour this from me? From the kingdom?

But this doesn't touch on the marriage agreement created by my mother. These documents still do not prove why Jerrick is cursed.

"Why you and not your father?" I ask and put the book back.

His story still does not make sense. I've stumped and spoiled his tale from winning me over, and I lean back in my chair, crossing my arms in victory.

Jerrick gestures to the varying stacks of paperwork and ledgers related to magic and correspondence between my mother and his father, pulling the marriage arrangement again to give to me, guiding me to a specific section.

I roll my eyes at the constant reference to it, but if there is any truth behind his claims, I would need to read this thoroughly. *Eventually.*

Rubbing the parchment in my hands, I trail a finger over lettering that looks squished in between the decree, marked in a darker ink. Dry flakes of red brush off the page, sticking to my fingertips.

Is this... *blood?*

I swallow thickly and read the text.

Ivan, oh Ivan, how you've betrayed me,
killing my love 'cause you were consumed by
jealousy.
Ruling two kingdoms filled your heart with greed,
As punishment for your actions,
I've placed a curse on your legacy.
Your kin will become the bringer of death,
turning on you first when I draw my last breath.
You'll be forced to watch from beyond the grave,
Knowing your kingdom is failing
due to the choices you've made.

Endless questions run rampant in my mind. I reread the cursed text, working through each line, seeking and hoping for an answer or an explanation. I'm only left with more confusion.

There is no proof of what happened to my father, just my mother's accusations against an *old* lover and extracting her revenge.

Mother was not in the right state of mind after Father, but she never was this cruel. She raised me with empathy, teaching me to show mercy to our people, to our neighboring kingdoms.

I can't shake the impression of something missing from all of this.

What is and isn't the trick?

Jerrick's voice chimes into my thoughts, pulling me away from falling into a deep, dark pit. "I was present at all my father's meetings, and not once were there any plans for the death of your fath—"

I flash a look, warning him he is on thin ice.

My heart and mind are being torn apart, unsure of what to believe.

"Your father could have hidden that from you," I sneer, trying to gain semblance over something.

But Jerrick shakes his head. "I've spent the last five years combing through *everything* of his investigating this. I've hunted to quench this need to kill, trained my magic to help me, and done *everything* in my power to find a way around this curse, to avoid marrying you and involving you."

I don't understand why he kept this decree to himself.

Maybe if he had come to Axidoria, the Makers wouldn't have punished me with all these years of grief. Maybe the Makers wouldn't have punished me with the inability to control my powers.

I turn on him with hatred oozing and spewing from my tongue. "*Why?*"

"Because I didn't want to associate with the daughter of the woman who put a curse on me and had me kill my own father!"

I lurch back from the booming anger in Jerrick's voice.

The rage and darkness surround him—surround us. But his words carve deep into my soul, words I have already carved for myself.

Fear mixed with sympathy is dangerous, especially when it is for a man who is my enemy—for a man who is a monster.

Just like you, Tove. Your mother made him a monster, and her death made you one.

I plunge my empathy down as Jerrick masks his own dark fury, brushing hair away from his face as his voice levels.

"And I truly don't know what happened to your father. Regardless of how obsessed my father was with your mother, I've never found any evidence of my father arranging the disappearance or death of yours."

Just because Jerrick didn't find any evidence doesn't mean there isn't any.

Did Mother do all of this for Father? Could she really cast curses?

His words halt my brewing questions. "What do you mean *obsessed?*"

"They were involved before becoming rulers, and your mother broke it off, knowing they wouldn't have a future together. And that was all I knew about your mother until she came to Palaena *after* your father had disappeared, offering my father the one thing he wanted. Marriage. She believed her husband died during his travels, and she drafted this marriage agreement, claiming it as fate for the two of them to finally be together.

"She made sure I was there as a witness to such a decree, knowing the magnitude of joining two kingdoms. My father was obsessed and infatuated with your mother *and* the idea of ruling two kingdoms. He agreed without a second thought. Jonas and I tried for weeks leading up to her arrival, begging him to reconsider, and we both were reprimanded for speaking against our king."

He gestures to the pink scar on the side of his face, and my mouth falls. One of the first questions I ever asked him finally answered.

"I promised I would answer all of your questions."

"Y-Your father did that to you?" I ask, heartbroken that a parent could do such a thing.

Jerrick shrugs, unbothered and detached from his father's cruelty. "That and more. But your mother ensured his debt came due."

I want to pity and sympathize with him, but I still can't believe everything he is saying. I'd done nothing to earn this vulnerability, and I am tired of being manipulated.

This *has* to be of his own doing.

I would not fall for another one of his tricks. I refuse to let him diminish all faith and trust I have in my mother.

"Who is to say this so-called *curse* isn't your own magic?" I challenge.

"It's not."

"You are full of shit."

My uncertainty about his abilities has drifted into my thoughts more often than I would care to admit, and this is the perfect opportunity to learn if he is a threat or a really good liar.

His eyes lock on mine, and a crooked grin appears, sending heat to blossom within my chest.

My body's internal temperature shoots up, and a bead of sweat forms along my brow. Despite the inferno in my body, I study him intently, knowing I need this information.

I will stare him down until he fesses up about his abilities.

If I know who I am up against, it will make or break the notion of returning home.

I grip the sides of my armchair, desperate to fan myself to cool down. It feels as if my blood could drain out of every pore in my body.

I plead for my gifts to surface, if only to grant me a reprieve from my veins feeling as if they were on fire. But my magic is silent, nothing flickering in my chest.

My internal battle fights on while I stare at Jerrick, his grin growing wider.

He cocks his head. "Feeling warm over there, Frostbite?"

"That's none of your concern," I grind out, ignoring his quip and that stupid, *stupid*, question.

Jerrick leans away, breaking our stare, and I slump from its state of fire, feeling weighed down from the sudden shift. He flicks his wrist around, and I watch in confusion.

He examines his fingernails. "It seems it would be my concern, being as I was the one that caused it."

My mouth slackens. I think through the stories of my ancestor's abilities. None of them matched up with the gut feeling I had about the Maker who granted Jerrick his power.

It has never happened before.

"That's impossible."

Jerrick's haunted eyes I saw mere moments ago are gone, replaced by a cunning, vicious grin.

"I can manipulate your blood, Frostbite."

22

AGAINST WILLS OR WALLS?

No heir in Axidoria had ever been blessed by Yeva or Letum. The Deities of Life and Death were the most powerful of the Makers, the cognizance and oblivion of all things. Aiyana, the Deity of Nature, created all four seasons with the presence of Leander, the Deity of Beasts, controlling all creatures. Anwir, the Deity of Illusion, constituted a government of monarchy, while Alora, the Deity of Divination, established religion and justice to allow there to be a balance.

Terror clutches my soul as I sit in front of a monarch that could lead to the destruction of us all if provoked.

I force out, shaking my head in disbelief, "Y-You can't—"

Warning bells alert every muscle in my body, and I want to run and hide. I lean back, gripping the armchair now for support as the King of Palaena leans forward, knowing I have caught on to his little game of show-and-tell.

The temperature drops around me as those blue eyes pierce my soul. Goose bumps prickle along my flesh, turning icy and frigid, sending me into a shivering frenzy.

Is this his doing?

Or is this my own doing?

My lungs inhale as he closes the gap between us, lowering to his knee. I try to scoot away, fighting the nudge of winter crawling up my chest.

The glimmer of power awakens at last, and I find myself seeking to cling onto something, *anything*, in desperation for an escape from this—from *him*.

Magic is explosive in my blood and along my skin, fear shaking through me for the unknown of what these gifts will do to me.

Will I ever see home again? Niko? Betina? My family?

Jerrick latches onto my wrists, preventing me from scooting any further, and terror threatens to escape from my throat.

I open my mouth, and my breath is visible. It does not stop Jerrick from pulling me closer. I turn away, and he leans in, terrified he is going to breathe death itself into me.

Sweet Makers, I don't want to die.

Panic and my powers fight for an escape, chills swimming through my veins as the cold stings, causing me to hiss in discomfort.

Jerrick's head tilts to my arms, my magic manifesting on my skin and slowly freezing it over.

Death itself seeks to swallow me whole, and ice cracking around me banishes all sense of instincts.

I can't get away from Jerrick, and I can't get away from my past.

This is all my fault.

I hate this, I hate myself, and I hate my magic.

I shake uncontrollably, the power threatening and all consuming.

The room, too, pulls air away from me, my chest and my heart erratic. Tremors wrack through my body, a complete and utter defeat drowning me here and now.

"You need to breathe," Jerrick says.

But tears blur my vision. "I-I can't. I can't," I stutter through gasped breaths.

My bitter cold magic travels across my arms, chilling and running down my legs. It is too powerful to contain. I can't stop the hatred I have for my misgivings and these abilities, my gift on its own journey to freeze me whole.

I hate this fucking curse of winter's kiss.

Jerrick moves, his hands gripping my face tightly. "Breathe!" he demands in a panic, only sending more tears down my cheeks.

I fight to send air into my lungs, to not think beyond the piercing pain of the frost and ice manifesting on my body.

But the terror of magic itself refuses to shake its grip.

Images of frost spill from my fingertips, turning into snow, while my feet would send more of winter outward and around me. My own frigid hand turns white as ice cracks splits my mind. The cold sting mixed with memories a blade plunging repeatedly into me.

I cower, my fears drowning me. "Please, no. Please, stop," I cry, pleading through the cold air.

Jerrick pulls away, scanning my entire body, muttering curses as he watches me lose myself to my own magic. Concern etches across his features when his eyes find mine again, and my heart breaks as I realize these could very well be my final moments.

The last thing I'll see is an enemy instead of a friend taking pity on the lack of control over my abilities.

The last heir of Axidoria, dying because she let frost and death consume her.

I deserve it.

At least my people will have Niko.

Jerrick's lips crash against mine. His kiss is rough and demanding, and my mouth meets the neediness.

One of his hands is wrapped around my head, the other gripping my neck. Heat, a shock to my body, creeps across my face when his tongue mingles with mine, pulling it into his mouth to suck and deepen our joining. The warmth in my cheeks grows, sending waves down the sides of my neck and melting away the speckles of frost rising from my pores.

His hold on my throat tightens as the kiss becomes messy.

A guttural moan comes from me, a sense of euphoria from my breath being blocked.

My blood boils, the surface of my skin no longer cold and the numbness in my hands gone. It feels as if he is suppressing the frosted air and inhaling it through our kiss.

Slowly, he releases me, both of his hands roaming down my arms, heat immediately following from his touch. The switch from ice to fire in my veins should give me more reason to panic, but Jerrick's lips remove all sense of fear.

I sweat as my body halts, realizing who it is I am kissing.

I push him away, forcefully ending the contact between us.

My own shortness of breath is evident, given my body's temperature was being thrown around. But I do not know if it is due to that or from his kiss.

He kissed me *again* to distract me from my panic.

Jerrick holds my stare, his blue eyes dark, greedy, and filled with lust, and he licks his lips as if he didn't get enough.

"Stop doing that!" I feign disgust and block out the desire burning in his eyes.

My mind imagines taking control of him and pushing him against the table and mounting him. But remembering Niko back home is the only reason I fathom over the sudden urge to really see what that lust behind Jerrick's eyes could lead up to.

I clear my thoughts away as Jerrick smirks. "Kissing you allows my magic to work faster. And besides, you liked it."

His face eases in toward me again, but this time, I see through the taunt and push him. I need to create some boundaries with this man.

"You can't go throughout your life kissing me whenever you want!"

He chuckles darkly under his breath, easing back. "I gained that advantage upon our marriage."

I stand and glare at him. "You never gained that *so-called* advantage because you left me."

A flash of surprise crosses Jerrick's features, but I've dealt with this parlor trick for long enough.

Even though I need his help, my annoyance supersedes that. At least for today, I am not giving him another chance.

Jerrick hasn't been present during the meetings Jonas and I have had, and with my shoulder healed, I need to cut my losses and find another way to learn my magic and rely on Niko.

I stew in my vexation and head for the door.

When I pull the latch, a large hand blocks me.

Warmth emits from behind as Jerrick's chest meets my back. He lowers, whispering softly, "You are not leaving this room."

I pinch my eyebrows in irritation, watching his large hand's veins twitch. "*Yes.* I. Am," I grit out, fighting against his weight pressed on the door.

A shudder rolls down my spine when Jerrick traces the length of my arm, my breath hitching.

"Are you so quick to forget what I can do?" His voice is low and guttural as his lips tickle below my ear. "I can make your blood boil, and I can make it cool down. All from a look, a touch. I can even make you need me, *want* me."

The admission has me wanting to scream and run away, yet my feet remain planted, unable to move beyond his tantalizingly sweet touch.

I arch into him as he wraps his hand around my hip.

His scent is intoxicating, and I want to rub against him and savor the desire blooming from his grip. Jerrick's throat bobs near my skin, and I move faster than my mind can follow.

My eyes widen when our bodies have switched places, his back against the door and my body pressing up on his.

"I *knew* you wanted me," he rumbles, low and sensual, as his eyes twinkle in amusement.

My lungs cease expanding while I fight against his touch, his gaze, his everything. An unquenchable need surges down to my core, arousal happening between my legs.

It latches me in place, making it hard to control my reactions. The sweat hanging between us does nothing for my rapid beating heart.

I shut my eyes in concentration, hoping to gain some traction with myself.

A moan almost escapes when Jerrick holds my sides again. It makes me feel like a starved woman, needing to cry out in ecstasy from this man.

"Stop it," I demand, desperate to have control of myself again.

I'm still holding him against the wall when something clicks, and I let go of him. I run my hands through my hair, still frantic with my body's needs. Hot, heavy, sensual, and euphoric.

I need to know how much of this is his magic and how much is purely me.

No, it doesn't matter. I just need it to stop.

"You will help me because, if you don't, I will not sign off on trade to help your kingdom, and I will not train you," Jerrick vows, sending a pulsing sensation down to my core.

A bitter sharp plunge of ice hits my system, my magic coming forward and trying to fight whatever Jerrick is doing. But Jerrick grips my shoulder, swiftly moving us again, with my back braced against the wall.

I hiss from the sizzle exploding across my frosted arms.

Heated blue eyes meet mine, and the hold on my arm tightens. "Agree to help me, Frostbite," he orders, his touch pulsing heat into my system, diminishing the frost I gained a small reprieve from.

I swallow thickly, the magnitude of the danger this man is to others, himself, and me settles in my gut.

A curse of death to pair with his gift from one of the two greater Deities? Whether his abilities are from Letum or Yeva, I still wonder if my mother knew about this. Surely not.

There is no way she could have known.

He is a walking omen to all. A monster, born or made, didn't seem to matter at this point.

He controls my fate, can manipulate my blood, and is cursed with death.

I need to carefully curate myself around him if I am going to give Niko and Axidoria a fighting chance to separate from this man.

I push through my tight breaths, knowing I need to play along in order to succeed.

"I-I'll help you," I squeak, the whoosh of magic ceasing its hold on me.

Jerrick steps back, and I slump to the floor, the toll from the temperature shift and magic used exhausting me.

I try to dodge from Jerrick's grip, but I'm easily lifted, forced to meet this cruel man's gaze, defiance of my own melting into his darkened stare.

He reaches to tuck a loose strand of hair from my face, and I recoil. Jerrick pauses.

Anger rolls through me when he leans in and kisses my cheek. I stare at his dimple on full display when he withdraws, opening the door.

"See you tomorrow morning, Frostbite," Jerrick coos.

23

LIVING IN THE LIBRARY

My head *pounds*, racing from the darkening hours to the first break of light. The light rain trickles down my bedroom window, fresh life singing in the air. I envy this flourishing weather, wishing for it to visit Axidoria.

I pray to the Makers I can fulfill my end of this arrangement with Jerrick and train fast. I need a way to remove my magic and melt away my winter.

But despite the cold filling and spreading across my home, I grew to relish and enjoy the longer winters. The darkened, cloudy skies would always match my mood, and I, somehow, found comfort. Those days would call for locking myself away, bundling up next to the fire with wine and blankets for company.

But my own preferences are irrelevant, the need for other seasons essential for new and plentiful crops.

I push through the dull ache, rising for the day and choosing to dress for comfort in anticipation of being down in the library with Jerrick. Our altercation yesterday only sent everything blowing up in my face.

He can manipulate blood.

He is cursed.

And I think he is still hiding something. I didn't have a chance to challenge him further about my father yesterday, but he better know I am not going to let that, too, be swept away.

He knows how to use his magic, and I need to do whatever I can to take advantage of his knowledge to help myself.

A greeting from Dorit is welcoming when she enters wearing her pleasant smile. She carries a tray of dried meats and cheeses.

I am not one to gorge myself on food in the mornings, and I am pleasantly surprised she has made herself aware of my habits. It makes me like her even more.

Offering my thanks, I fasten the laces binding the top of my tunic together, concealing my breasts. I hate to admit that the shirt and trousers grew on me, despite only wearing them yesterday. I couldn't help but reach for a second set today.

"Here, let me help you," Dorit offers, resting the tray down and helping me lace the string through the trousers.

"Thank you."

Dorit eases me through my minor setback, ensuring the tunic is properly tucked into the trousers with the fabric billowing away from my body.

"There," she chides. "Now, let's do something with that hair of yours."

I reach for the dried meat and cheese while she combs my hair, plaiting it into one long braid that goes down the length of my spine. A loose strand works itself free in her efforts, and I tuck it behind my ear before she notices and starts all over.

Dorit is not the only observant one, though. Bless her, but I've noticed she is a bit of a perfectionist.

As my stay has continued, her little quirks became more noticeable. The need for hair to be perfectly styled, the right amount of food on each tray she brings, the dresses and ensembles fitted and tailored flawlessly.

I chew through a slice of cheese, hiding my snicker from her as she ties off my braid.

"What?" she asks.

I chew on through my amusement quietly. She sees my laughter, and she pushes her hands against her hips, eyebrows raised in question.

I break into a fit of giggles, nostalgia flooding my senses. "You remind me of my sister, Runa, and my friend Betina."

Tears well in my eyes as I realize how much I miss Niko and Betina. And my laughs stop when I'm reminded of who I really miss. My family.

I mask the pain, blinking away my grief. "I apologize if I offended you."

Dorit slumps in relief. "Thank Yeva. I thought I had something in my teeth."

I throw my head back in laughter, and Dorit laughs as well.

She helps herself by reaching for a slice of dried meat, earning approval that she feels comfortable enough to do that.

"Meetings or library today?" she asks, her jaw working through the meat.

I swallow my food, biting my tongue. I pinch my features at the sharp, abrasive pain. "Library with Jerrick today. And probably the rest of my life, if we are being honest."

"Why do you say that?"

I shrug, building more lies. "We have a lot to work through. With my magic and his magic—"

"You mean his curse?"

My lips pop. "You know?"

She gives me a knowing look, and we both speak at the same time. "*Gossip.*"

We grin, my heart content, and she continues, "I don't know the extent of it, only that he does have a curse."

Has she felt Jerrick's powers like I have? Does she know what his magic is versus what his curse is? They knew each other before he inherited his abilities.

"What was he like before?" I ask, unable to stop the question from escaping my lips.

Her face sours slightly, growing quiet. "He is still very much the same as from when he and I—*you know*. But I can't say for certain. I don't think anyone can but Jerrick."

"Not even Jonas?"

She shakes her head. "They are close, but I don't think Jerrick lets in anyone fully. I think he believes he is alone in the world between his curse and being king."

Shoving another piece of cheese in my mouth, I nod to her in understanding. I know all too well the mantle and stigma of managing a kingdom can weigh on one's shoulders. A pang of guilt claws at my chest for Jerrick, similar situations befalling the two of us.

But he killed his father, whereas I brought doom.

Two different types of monsters.

I catch my own reflection in the vanity, the monster within filling the frame and sending ice crackling around me. I blink away my fears, grimacing at the evil shining back.

No, I was wrong.

There aren't two types of monsters, only one.

And it is staring right at me.

I flinch away from myself, darting my attention to Dorit, seeking to bury my wretchedness.

She quietly tidies up the sheets on my bed and gathers my chamber pot. My boots sit near the door she passes, a reminder of the final thing needed to get me out and into the world.

A hesitation turns my gaze toward Mother's mirror, which I haven't touched in a while. I need to warn Niko about Jerrick. I don't have all the pieces yet, but I have to give him something.

"Tove?" Dorit draws my attention from Mother's mirror, concern lacing her question. "Are you alright?"

"Yes, just reminiscing," I lie through my teeth.

She drops into a low curtsy and leaves my bedchamber as I make my way over to my boots, slipping them on with more ease than yesterday.

I descend the hall toward the library where Jerrick greets me, waiting for me, along with a new pile of books stacked on the wooden table. I grumble at his greeting, knowing I am half here against my will.

He gestures toward the other chair, and I join him, looking over each spine of the books. Jerrick hands me a book, taking away my freedom to choose what to read, and I sigh when the title tells me nothing about my magic.

I look at Jerrick, needing reassurance that I am not being strung along again. "Are you *really* going to help my people and me if I help you break your curse?"

Jerrick's eyes flash, and I expect him to yell or threaten me, like he has done since I've arrived. But instead, he surprises me with a faint glimpse of the man I met in Axidoria.

"I have signed off on the most recent trade exchange as a token of good faith in you helping me," he says with tenderness.

Food and clothing being approved and sent to my people fills me with gratitude.

But he shortens my moment of relief by adding, "Now you *really* need to earn the right."

I scowl, grinding my teeth. "How else am I supposed to do so if I am already helping you?"

A hint of amusement dances in his blue irises, a devious smirk gracing his features.

I squeeze my thighs together when his voice turns velvety and smooth.

"We could revisit what happened with a certain *wall* yesterday."

I clench the book tightly, the leather rubbing against my fingertips, when Jerrick winks.

The bastard is fucking taunting me.

I bristle through my annoyance, hating the blood rising to the surface of my skin.

Choosing to pick my battles rather than goad him on, I lean back and sever the lust building in the air. Reacting to his every touch has me wondering how often he has used his gifts on me.

Could he have used his powers on me without me knowing? Sweet Makers, how often *does* he use his gifts for his own advantage?

I avert my gaze from Jerrick, not wanting to think about him any further. Opening my book to the first page, I wipe away some collected dust.

Jerrick takes religious texts featuring priests that specialize in documentation on Anwir, the Deity of Illusion.

Leaning back, I read the title before glancing up to see Jerrick mimicking my actions. I incline my head, and he returns it in kind prior to returning to his text.

And so we read.

Betina falls back against my bed, and Niko's eyes widen when I tell them about Jerrick's curse.

But their jaws slacken at my last update. "He can also manipulate blood."

The news is disheartening, especially because it darkens the bright day Niko and Betina were having before I reached out. I pinch my features, regretful, as Niko runs a hand through his hair, his visible muscles flexing.

The chandelier is lit in my room rather than the hearth, Aiyana's spring finally peeking through winter back home. The dressing down of blankets on my old bed clue me in, as does Betina's coiled locks, which is frizzier than normal. The humidity in the air when warmer weather comes has her styling tight plaits along her scalp versus wearing her hair unbound and voluminous during the colder seasons.

Here, in Palaena, the staff have already removed blankets and stacks of firewood from the hearths in every room in the castle, as well as near Jerrick's and my claimed area of the library.

Tunics and trousers are a new constant for me, noting how much cooler it is to be in them with the temperatures rising versus stuck in a comfortable lounge chair in regal attire, pinching and tugging at the seams.

I thank the Makers Niko and Betina have still only seen me in my day gowns and dressing robes. If their reaction to the news about Jerrick is anything, I don't even want to imagine how they'd react if they saw me in a tunic and trousers.

"H-How did you come to find this out?" Betina asks.

Niko focuses on me, envy and rage replacing his shock.

I remind myself his anger is not directed at me, just the situation. But it still does not make being underneath his scornful gaze any easier.

"He told me and then proceeded to use his powers on me."

Niko steps up to the vanity, lethal calm forming his own line of questioning. "What did he make you do?"

"The king did not make me do anything," I reassure him.

His eyes soften, but I can still see the fury and violence he wants to extract on Palaena and their king. It is evident in his demeanor.

I convey as much love as possible to Niko. "All I felt him doing was awakening my powers while also dissolving them."

Betina stands and approaches. "But how do you know that was him and not you? He has already kept information from you. Who is to say this isn't just another lie?"

Niko nods in agreement, but I turn down her logic. "I have always been able to tell when my magic awakens and when it quiets. So, I know he is not lying about that, at least."

"But what about your parents? The curse?" Niko asks.

I look away from his frustrated gaze, my mind reeling over everything Jerrick and I have already read so far about glamour magic, curses, and letters exchanged between my mother and his father. They validated Jerrick's story of their past involvement. Not to mention the ledger of Axidoria's cursed criminals proved that my mother could cast a curse.

That and Jerrick's dedication to our research has me believing even more truth in his tale.

He's the first to arrive and the last to leave each day. Deities, he might actually *live* in the library.

I toss aside Niko's question, putting my trust in Jerrick's actions and the proof of what I've read so far. "There is truth and evidence behind his statements. But I still do not believe that my mother killed herself and that Palaena was not involved with my father's death. Something still feels like it is missing."

The two of them are silent in their own contemplation.

"Did the king say when he would train you?" Betina asks.

"No," I grumble. "He said I had to earn that chance by helping him first."

Niko shakes his head. "What an asshole."

I shrug, familiar with people being assholes. There have been *plenty* of occasions when I've been one, too. I am sure Niko and Betina themselves have muttered how much of an asshole I can be when my grief is unbearable.

But each day I meet Jerrick in the library, I understand his cause a little bit more, finding him not as awful as I thought.

He did not associate with me because of his mistrust of my family, a sentiment I, too, hold close to my heart. But Jerrick put his issues aside when he chose to tell me everything and even offered a small token of peace. He is facilitating trade between Palaena and Axidoria, and if I ever *earn* the right, he will help train my gifts.

Even though Jerrick went about telling me everything in a fragmented way, I find myself empathizing with him.

"He told me he did not want to associate with the daughter of the woman who cursed him, and I get it," I tell Niko and Betina.

"You get it?" Niko protests.

I don't react to the sharp bite in his tone. "Palaena views Axidoria as Axidoria views Palaena—as the enemy."

Niko grimaces, angry and annoyed that I'm living with the enemy.

I place a hand on my heart. "I only get it because it is how I feel myself."

Those amber eyes flare as Niko seethes silently. "It's not because of anything *else*, right?"

Confusion draws my eyebrows together, not understanding his question.

Betina glances between us and lightly touches Niko's elbow. "Tove knows how hard you've already been working on calling the banners and training everyone."

Emotions strain in my throat, and my eyes water.

For the first time since talking to Niko, he relaxes, and the ache in my chest tightens at the strain I have put him under.

"*Niko.*"

My voice strains.

His head drops, patting Betina's hand in thanks.

Her deep brown eyes offer me sympathy.

I mouth the words *love you* to her, and she does the same in return.

Betina peers out the window, checking the time of day.

I do the same, panicking when I realize I am running late for my standing appointment in the library with Jerrick.

She grabs Niko by the arm, ushering him out as she speaks. "Tove is running late. We need to let her go."

I hurry out of bed, carrying Mother's mirror with me as I watch Niko and Betina try to leave.

Niko's eyes find mine, and my heart springs out of my chest, hopeful to see his handsome, boyish grin. But his features remain stark as he warns, "Be careful."

My hope for him saying something else cracks my mood. I nod quickly, uttering the same to him. "You, too."

24

THE FOOD TRAY

Given my tardiness, I hurry for the kitchens to say hello to Ophelia and Cordelia in hopes of taking my breakfast on the go and even bringing some to Jerrick. I cannot recall him eating any time since we started meeting in the library, and I pray to Alora he will not reprimand me for being late.

Perhaps he'll also take the food tray as a peace offering.

Even though it crushed my mood to see Niko angry and jealous, I still stand behind my reasoning for believing Jerrick. And deep down, I pray I can save my kingdom, heal, and find my happy again with my husband by my side.

I hold on to that wish, pushing through the corridor of the kitchen, smiling when I catch not only Ophelia and Cordelia, but Dorit as well.

They work and converse in comfort, stopping short when they see me.

"Tove!" Cordelia beams, drying off her hands with a towel and rushing to embrace me.

Ophelia and Dorit carefully put down the dishes before they, too, hurry to me.

Ophelia's arms wrap around me as Cordelia still holds me. Appreciation for hearing and seeing their visible joy at my presence warms my chest, feeling as if they truly see me as a person.

Stuck in their embrace, I eye Dorit, signaling for help, but she braces her hands on her hips, shaking her head with amusement.

"You're running late," Dorit states as the two women break apart from hugging me.

"I know, I know. I should have taken you up on waking me."

The pit in my stomach deepens from my deception.

My time with these women might be enjoyable, but I don't belong here. I belong in Axidoria with Niko.

My intentions for not having Dorit wake me this morning were pure, though. I wanted to let her have some time for herself. Her assistance and company are one of the few things I value in Palaena.

She, Ophelia, and Cordelia have been my support during my dark days here. I can only thank Dorit for introducing me to the two women that one crisp morning where we all visited late into the afternoon.

"Have you eaten yet?" Ophelia asks.

I shake my head. "I was hoping I could have a food tray made so I may take it to the library for myself and the king."

Cordelia's green eyes twinkle with mischief. "A picnic for you and the king? How romantic!" She clasps her chest, twirling in a circle.

I level my gaze on Cordelia. "It is *nothing* like that."

Dorit wiggles her brows, the three of them snickering. I sigh.

The three women love to tease, and I often find myself joking alongside them. Clearly, today, I am the brunt of their antics.

I roll off the taunt, my tardiness the bigger concern.

Ophelia presses her lips to stifle another laugh as she grabs a tray. Cordelia gathers breads, cheese, dried meats, and a bottle of wine.

I smile when they extend it to me, along with their wishes of luck.

But Dorit stops me before I can go, adding a few sugared solstice pastries to the dish. Her observance of my love for sweet treats leaves me beaming.

"Thank you."

As I approach the library, my pulse quickens, and my heart hammers in my chest. It is a feeling I have experienced more recently on my way to Jerrick. The time spent in his company reminds me of the man I met in Axidoria, where talking with him felt refreshing.

But being late today might crush even that small blessing.

I square my shoulders and turn, bracing my back against the doors to push and let myself in. When I face the room, Jerrick is reclining in his chair, nose deep in a text.

My entrance pulls him away from reading, those glacial blue eyes and his scar alive with intrigue. I lick my lips, preparing for an explanation, but Jerrick scans me from head to toe, stopping back on the food tray.

His full face comes into view as he lowers his book, lips ticking up. "What do you have there, Frostbite?"

Heat punctures my skin as I try to not react to the nickname. I swallow the tightness building, counting myself lucky he is asking that rather than pointing out my lateness.

I cough before gesturing to the food tray. "I notice you do not eat while you are in here, and I thought it could help."

Jerrick's features soften.

It catches me off guard, so I add in my regret. "I *also* brought it as an apology for my lateness."

He arches a brow just as my stomach growls.

I stiffen, mortification setting in as Jerrick's and my own eyes widen at my hunger voicing its misery.

"Clearly, you *also* brought it because you were hungry," he teases, and I relax when his dimple appears through his devastatingly beautiful smile.

Jerrick breaks into a fit of genuine laughter, a deep rumble that vibrates in my bones.

It draws a blush across my face at the pureness of it, and I let my own join his. The surprise fills him with something more humanizing, making me realize I am, no doubt, one of the *very* few his mask has slipped around.

The mask of a ruler, the mask of a killer—the mask of a *monster*.

My heart aches as I realize it's me looking at myself through a mirror. The thought is laced with a sharp fracturing of ice, forcing me to pinch my eyes and shudder.

When Jerrick's laugh eases, he catches me just as I gather myself. But when he stands, he places the book on his chair, approaching me.

The thoughts I had have me arching away when he nears.

The amusement in his features dissolves quickly, and he stops midstep at my movement.

Jerrick cocks his head, confusion furrowing his brows. From his softened gaze, he looks apologetic, and that pang of guilt from earlier slams against me as I look upon the King of Palaena, the two of us having so much to apologize for.

Him for deceiving me and kidnapping me.

Me for my tardiness, when it should have been an apology for being so mean—so rude.

Both our actions are justified in our own minds, and right now, seeing Jerrick, I can't help but wish things were different.

While I have every intention of going home, I don't want to hurt anyone. And maybe if I took myself beyond my own thoughts, I could have seen his perspective earlier.

He, too, is burdened by his gifts, and I should have been more understanding.

If I had, maybe we both would be inclined to help one another. Maybe we could have made the best of our situation and worked together instead of against each other. Maybe we could have struck true peace, and there would be no need for Niko's plan.

Kindness might be something Jerrick does not experience with many, and I should have been offering that sooner. I should be offering pleasantries I already share with his brother, Dorit, Cordelia, and Ophelia.

And as I study Jerrick, the wordless thought of apology feels thick in the air.

"I'm sorry—"

We stop ourselves after speaking in unison.

I cinch my mouth shut as Jerrick's eyes widen. But it vanishes quickly, replaced by the softness from earlier. My heart stutters at this man, who's offering me more than he has with his mask lowered.

I could give him that too, at least.

I smile kindly, and he visibly relaxes.

Jerrick gestures to the food tray. "May I?"

I bite my lip and nod sheepishly. "Thank you," I say, marveling at the tenderness he is offering.

He inclines his head, returning to his seat, and I join him. He opens the bottle of wine with ease, filling the two glasses and passing me one.

I reach for it carefully, my hands shaking from this uncharted territory.

Jerrick's softened gaze studies me, and when our hands graze each other's after touching my glass, calm sweeps over my body.

I lift the cup to my lips, savoring the drink despite its harshness.

Palaena really needs to stock its castles and taverns with Axidoria's wine.

Soon, Tove. Soon.

I am surprised when Jerrick reaches for the sugared pastry first, a little hurt he will be eating one of the few on the tray.

He catches my expression and asks, "How did you know these were my favorite?"

I huff a laugh. Dorit, the little sneak, helping me smooth things over with Jerrick. Ever the protector, she is.

I grab one for myself and take a huge bite.

Jerrick arches a brow, but my eyes squeeze shut as I blush, working through the solstice pastry and swallowing it with a grin still on my face.

"I didn't," I say.

If Jerrick was showing me himself without a mask, I could at least offer him the same vulnerability—I have more in common with him than I realized.

The heavy mantle of Snow Queen and grief lay thick against my shoulders, but those lighten as the mask I wear shifts in the King of Palaena's presence, showing Jerrick my love for sweets.

"I just knew that they were mine."

Jerrick and I started the habit of discussing our reading. We took turns summarizing what we read, allowing our eyes a brief rest.

I would immediately forget everything I just finished absorbing, but information was easier for him to retain.

He was always quick to engage me in conversation, forcing my brain to turn and think.

Conversing with Jerrick during these moments was easy and enjoyable, reminding me of when we first met at the Celebration of Spirits.

And at the end of each day, I'd drag my feet up the stairs, mentally exhausted.

Dorit would occasionally find me asleep in my clothes from the day prior, and even communication with Niko and Betina was the last thing on my mind.

On nights I managed some energy, I would try to see their faces and give them updates. But the second I would see Betina asleep in the reflection, my heart would pinch with guilt and defeat, not wanting to disrupt her, no matter how badly I wanted to converse with her and Niko.

Some days, like today, Jonas joins us in the library so all three of us can be part of the meeting. Jonas is exuberant and ecstatic, our conversation fluid and natural.

"Finally, I will get to have a taste of the wine you brag about, Tove," Jonas muses after receiving letters from Axidoria confirming the transfer.

My heart lifted when I saw Niko's signature, a small glimpse of home bringing me cheer today.

I chuckle with Jonas, his teeth gleaming.

"I promise once you have it, you will need more," I tell him.

Jerrick scoffs beside his brother, and I brush off his typical behavior whenever Jonas and I go off topic during meetings. His nose is stuck in a book as he plops a cube of cheese in his mouth.

The food tray, a daily occurrence now, usually lasts a few hours, but with Jonas present and hosting a meeting, the food was scarfed down in an instant.

I linger on Jerrick's mouth as he eats the last kernel of food. His blue eyes flick to mine, a hint of a smirk tracing along his lips as heat scorches underneath my skin.

Jonas asks, "Promise we will all try it together?"

"Dorit and I already have an agreement but adding you in to the celebration would be a delight."

Jonas wiggles in his seat, earning another grumble from Jerrick. The brothers ignore the other, comfortable with their differences and similarities.

"Maybe we can have more delivered before the ball," Jonas suggests. "Which reminds me, what colors were you thinking of for decorations, Tove?"

I purse my lips at the question, contemplating the layout of Palaena's castle and decorations.

My favorite part of planning celebrations is choosing the colors to blend and complement. The majority of the castle has warm and rich tones, which can be hard to pair with other tones.

I have a few in mind that could work, but instead of choosing, I ask for Jonas's input. "What colors do you think would be good?"

Jonas opens his mouth, but Jerrick interrupts, "Black."

We turn to Jerrick, surprised he is voicing his opinion, the two of us knowing he would much rather be reading.

Jonas and I share a suspicious glance.

Jonas asks, "Just black?"

The King of Palaena shrugs, turning to the next page of his book. "Why not?"

I quirk a brow, not understanding his motives behind suggesting anything in the first place.

"We could do black and red?" I suggest, offering up the other color I had in mind.

"Oh! With touches of gold!" Jonas exclaims, shuffling a few books around on the table to grab a parchment for notes.

He scribbles down ideas quickly, muttering to himself.

I rest my hands across my lap, catching a few of his words such as *fabric, veal, musicians, masks.*

"Yes, yes," Jonas sings as he continues to write. "The vision is coming to life. We will need to send out invitations that you both will sign. We can hire extra staff from the villages, and we'll send for extra barrels of wine."

"Do not forget that extra staff means extra cooks, too," I comment, knowing Cordelia and Ophelia will need help in the days leading up to the event.

Jonas points his quill at me. "Yes!" He jots down more notes.

I am about to add another suggestion when Jerrick stops abruptly, rising from his chair.

Jonas and I look up at Jerrick, his jaw locking in steel determination.

"I should have known you two would be talking for hours," he grumbles under his breath, placing his book down and heading for the door.

Alarm has me looking at Jonas, not understanding what we did wrong. We have had meetings before in the library, and today should be no different.

Jonas calls to his brother, "Where are you going?"

Jerrick halts, his body stiffening. Concern has me studying his body language, an apology on the tip of my tongue.

Jerrick relaxes briefly, and peers over his shoulder. "*Hunting.*"

His eyes find mine. His irises are blown out, but he blinks once, a flash of softness peering through his tense body.

Through gritted teeth, he says, "Everything you need to read is there. I expect a report when I return."

As Jerrick leaves, my rebuttal dries out.

Glancing around the room, I try to think back on anything we might have done that could have caused such vexation from Jerrick. I come up short.

Jonas sits calmly, unbothered by his brother, still jotting down notes.

"Why did Jerrick just now decide to go hunting?" I ask, unable to help myself.

Jonas's brown eyes flicker with hesitation. Instead of answering, he asks, "What do you know about his curse?"

"Not much."

He hums to himself in contemplation, the quill resting on the parchment and no longer moving. Jonas places his notes to the side, bracing his forearms on his thighs as he leans toward me.

"Well, let's just say he gets especially moody when his *urges* decide to fester," Jonas quips.

I'm unable to hide my amusement from his choice of wording. "That would explain *a lot*," I reply, an understanding of Jerrick's mood swings clicking into place.

Jonas bellows. "Yes, though he does need to be better about apologizing when he is moody."

"You and I definitely align there." I grab a book from the large working pile while Jonas resumes making notes.

I barely open to the cover page of the text before Jonas adds quietly, "I am sorry you have been the target of his mood swings."

Looking up, genuine sorrow etches across his furrowed brows.

He takes a long breath, sighing deeply and explaining, "I swear Jerrick means well *most* of the time. It's this *fucking* curse that plagues him day in and day out, and I hate how others are affected by it beyond him." He reclines against his chair, our conversation clearly something that weighs heavy on him.

I rest my hand on Jonas's knee in comfort, and his brown eyes find mine. "I am sorry you, too, have been a casualty of his moods.

You handle your role in being a brother, a prince, and a royal advisor in stride. Jerrick, I am sure, is more grateful for you than he ever will admit."

Jonas waves my words off, trying to mask the stress he carries.

It is like seeing my own situation play out in front of me. Their relationship has me understanding and knowing how vital Jonas is to Jerrick, just like how important Betina and Niko are to me—how Dorit, Jonas, Cordelia, and Ophelia are becoming important to me, too.

Jonas may not get the credit he deserves from his brother, but that doesn't mean I won't voice my admiration for him. Even though I am still a little suspicious of their motives, it has been evident from the beginning that Jonas is an excellent advisor.

I tighten my grip on his knee, directing his attention back. "Jonas, do not wave this off. You deserve to know how amazing you are. You deserve to be appreciated." His brown eyes are lined with tears, and I smile softly, placing a hand over my heart. "I appreciate you *and* your company."

A tear runs down his cheek, but he whisks it away as the library door opens.

I look up, eyes widening when a man enters wrapped arm in arm with Dorit, the duo snickering quietly.

Jonas's entire mood shifts at the sight. "Viggo!" He stands quickly, hurrying toward the two with his arms wide.

The man perks up, his boyish features reddening at the sight of his partner. The red is stark against his dark-bronze skin, and it stays plastered on his cheeks when Dorit steps away, allowing the two to kiss and embrace.

I beam at the love shining between the two of them, my heart full and heavy at the sight.

A bleak chord of longing strums in my gut, wishing I could have that. To be loved by someone I love and to have that feeling never dwindle, even through the bad days.

Jonas pulls away from Viggo, holding his face before acknowledging Dorit. My brother-in-law turns to me, gesturing to his partner.

"Tove! This is Viggo," Jonas sings pridefully.

I stand, inclining my head in greeting. "A pleasure to finally meet the man Jonas talks so much about."

Viggo turns bashful as Dorit and Jonas grin. Viggo awkwardly side steps his partner, his hands fidgeting at his sides before bowing.

His unruly brown waves cover his face as he says, "An honor it is to finally meet you, Your Majesty."

Viggo's stare stays on mine, and I smile gently, understanding the shyness of meeting new people. I have an urge to befriend him as I have Dorit, Ophelia, and Cordelia.

"If you ever feel inclined to, you may call me Tove," I reply to Viggo, the same offer I extend to any staff.

But here, in Palaena, I do not know why I want to prevent others from calling me the Snow Queen. The uncertainty still has me gesturing to the table, seeking to be different from what rumors claim.

"Please, join us?" I ask.

Dorit occupies the seat next to me as Viggo follows his partner, hand in hand.

Viggo sits where Jerrick was earlier, and Jonas returns to his original spot.

Dorit glances at the heaping array of books, rolling her eyes with exhaustion.

"*Please* tell me this is the already read pile," she says, pointing to the stack Jerrick and I are working through.

"It's not," I tell her.

She sighs and leans back, crossing her arms.

Jonas and Viggo chuckle under their breaths.

Looking between them, I gesture to the books. "You three could help me, you know?"

Dorit snorts and waves me off. "No, Viggo and I have tasks to do. We only stopped by when we saw the king leaving the castle."

I flick my eyes to Jonas in hesitation, unsure how much she and Viggo know about Jerrick's curse.

But Jonas nods, a sign that they know enough.

I still choose to keep Jerrick's movements and actions to myself.

Jonas steers the conversation in a different direction. "Tove and I were just discussing plans for the celebration as well as the first of many planned deliveries of wine."

Dorit lights up at the mentioning of wine. "You did? Don't tell me I have to wait for you, too, in order to try it."

All three gazes flick to me, and I shrug, unable to help myself as I speak. "*Unfortunately*, you do."

Dorit puffs. "Dammit, I wanted to sneak extra away."

A chuckle escapes, and I stifle it with my hand. "Do not fret, Jonas and I are already working on having more for the party as well as stocking it, too. Once everyone tries it, I'm afraid you will not wish to go back."

"I'll say," Jonas remarks. "That is quite a steep promise, Tove."

I smirk. "It's a guarantee, Jonas."

Jonas and Dorit wiggle their brows with delight.

My eyes meet Viggo's, and he grins bashfully.

From what I have heard about Viggo, he is shy. I do not want to push him out of his comfort zone, so I smile in return before leaning back and reading late into the night.

25

EXTRA PASTRIES

My morning habits drew me to greet Cordelia and Ophelia, leaving them with a food tray in my hands. Even though Jerrick was gone, I kept up with the routine, enjoying the added benefit of extra pastries for myself.

I enter the library and almost drop my entire food tray at the sight of Jerrick holding an extra food tray in his hands. A startled huff of air escapes me, and when our eyes meet, we both shine before breaking into a fit of laughter.

His laughter vibrates in my soul, his mood from before he left completely vanished. Jerrick is the first to break through our amusement.

"I thought it could count toward an apology for my surly behavior."

I beam, remembering doing the same for him. "It counts." My love for food is an easy way into my good graces, after all. "And now we *each* get our own pastries."

Amusement lights up his features, a trace of relief smoothing away the concern from his brows as I join him.

"Did you find anything worthwhile?" he asks as he eases into his seat.

"No." I give him a quick report of what I read while wishing I did not have to see the disappointment on his face.

Jerrick makes a valiant effort to hide his dismay, nodding quickly to move forward with our task. And in his lighter mood and seeing everything we have read has been a bust, I debate whether or not we would find any clues.

Sparing a glance at him, I lift my lips.

He is stretched across the lounge with one hand tucked behind his head, the other holding a book.

I watch him for a few moments, his comfort bringing me an odd sense of peace, before reaching for a cube of cheese and drawing my eyes back to the ancient journals.

Jerrick and I work through the day seamlessly, having built a system of books, ledgers, and paperwork to read, switching topics between glamours, curses, and the Deities. Yet disappointment hangs heavy in the air when Jerrick and I conclude the letters exchanged between our parents would not provide any clues.

And with each new day without any clues or answers, worry grows in the back of my mind. Worry that the curse was unbreakable, worry I would never be able to fix and save Axidoria, and worry of the unknown for Jerrick.

I remain vigilant as I skim through my most recent book, a journal of a past ruler mentioning there was a recorded decree of divorce, one that happened here in Palaena between one of Jerrick's ancestors and his wife. The king had fallen for another and was only granted a divorce by every monarch agreeing and a priest from each kingdom signing the separation.

But in reading section after section of this journal, my guilt festers, and my mood sours. This past King of Palaena, who had ruled maliciously, caused much pain and distrust.

I scoff with disgust as I read his belief in the Makers *calling* him to cleanse his people.

"What did you find?"

Jerrick's voice startles me.

My eyes meet his, hope faintly shimmering in them, and I gently ease the disappointment. "It's nothing regarding your curse. It's just—" I smack the pages, irritated I read so much of it. "This king was so cruel to his people."

"Many of them are," Jerrick states calmly.

I grumble, not understanding why rulers were uncaring and callous, why they would hurt their own people. "Did coming into abilities mean they no longer held compassion and empathy for others?"

We are all the same, as the only thing separating royalty from citizens was the magic in our bloodline. One would think that being a descendant of the Deities meant following through with what our priests and the Makers themselves taught us, to be a land that strived and lived for peace.

But so many rulers had used their gifts to hurt rather than help people. As my parents had.

As I have...

I toss the book down, folding my arms and hating to see so many falter into taking lives of others. Hating how I, too, found myself falling for this spell and have Niko rallying men behind me.

Jerrick eases up, bracing his arms against his thighs. He places his book on the table, eyeing me carefully.

"You care for your people?" Jerrick asks.

"Of course I care for my people."

I may hate my powers and hate being around people on my dark days, but that doesn't mean I don't care. Their lives lie on my conscious every waking moment.

Some days, I can fight against my demons to help, and some days, I can't.

I am not a perfect queen, but I do care.

"Even though they dislike you and do not even call you by your given title?"

"Even then," I answer. "Even if they hate me, I still have a duty to them. I can be indifferent to them while still negotiating on their behalf with other kingdoms to offer them the help I myself cannot give them."

He scrunches his brows. "They scorn you."

"As they should. I did cause an unrelenting winter in their home. I let them see what they believe because feeding back into the hatred they have will only turn me into a monarch like this." I gesture to the journal.

Jerrick hums thoughtfully. "You are too merciful for your own good."

I roll my eyes. The Snow Queen of Axidoria being merciful feels like a slight. I wave off his comment, releasing a long shaky breath.

"My own parents were cruel. Cursing their citizens—cursing their neighboring kingdoms."

Jerrick bristles and clenches his fists.

Cruelty spans across all kingdoms, even to this day, between Jerrick's father and my family. And bringing up his curse is like calling forth my grief.

A dark burden neither of us wants to linger on longer than necessary.

Memories of my family draw my next question, seeking answers. "How do you *know* your father was not involved with my father's end?"

The king stares, and I hold his gaze, a rapid fire of emotions swirling behind his eyes. His features turn distraught, exhausted, as if working through his own thoughts and his curse.

But getting proof about what happened to my family takes precedence.

Jerrick breaks eye contact, fracturing this odd sensation of him holding my air supply.

Doubt taunts its suspicious melody in my mind that he used his powers on me just now, even as air fills my lungs, but his magic was nothing like this. When he used his gifts on me, I felt as if I were on fire.

Stealing my breath, however, is something new, and I don't want to believe it was my own natural reaction. I calmly regain control of myself, still watching Jerrick intently.

He rises from his chair, stepping down one of the rows of bookshelves.

It is quiet for a few beats, but the sounds of books stacking against each other have me wondering what he is doing now.

Is he ignoring me again?

I slump back against my chair, hating that the minuscule peace between us has fractured again. I try to remove the unanswered question from my mind, hating I have only dug a deeper hole for myself.

You should have stuck to reading about rulers, Tove.

My gaze falls back to the journal, reluctant to read onward. I grumble under my breath, reaching for it, when footsteps fall.

Jerrick's blue eyes find mine as he returns, resting more books on our never-ending pile to sort through. But he places these ones directly in front of me.

"This is everything of my father's dealings and financial ledgers," Jerrick says.

Confusion furrows my brows as I sit up.

He filters through them, selecting a few and opening them to specific sections. When a flurry of text is spread before us, he gestures to them.

"Here is a record of his dealings with our spy master and his team of assassins." He lifts another book up. "This is the ledger noting what each transaction was near, leading up to and after your father's disappearance." Jerrick lifts a stack of letters. "And these are all the letters exchanged between Axidoria and Palaena."

I scan each text, taking the letters first. I shuffle through a few, my surprise keeping me from reading the contents. Doubt in Jerrick not answering my questions flushes my cheeks.

"Why are you giving me these?"

My question comes out in a breathy whisper.

Jerrick eases into his seat, grabbing the text he was reading earlier, and shrugs. "Because you care. And because Palaena has nothing to hide and was not involved with whatever happened to your father."

I almost ask him again about my mother but refrain, knowing Jerrick could take these texts away if I push.

Jerrick's attention turns back to his book as I scan through each document, each letter, each financial account. But the more I peer deep into King Ivan's life, the more I see no proof of King Ivan killing my father.

No traces of my father are mentioned in these journals. No traces of assassins. No money transactions—no *nothing*.

The only accusations come from my mother in the letters they exchanged *after* my father's disappearance.

Even as I trudge up the stairs at the end of another long day of reading, I hate how the questions I sought to have answered here in Palaena feel unsolvable. My gut tells me my answers would be in Axidoria, and I will need to ask Niko for help the next time I see him.

But even as I lie awake deep into the night, waiting for sleep to take me, my beliefs and assumptions of Palaena and their intentions change before my very eyes.

The notion weighs me down, as does the hope of returning to Niko.

I scream for my mother, my father, and for Runa.

But it doesn't stop.

The pain won't stop.

A sharp icicle wedges itself over my heart, preventing me from dying with them—being with them.

I curse and yell, slamming my fists into the lake, desperate for it to melt and swallow me whole.

Mother is... *gone*. The last member of my family is dead.

I am alone...

I have no one...

And the *pain*—Sweet Makers, the pain of that knowledge is all-consuming—all-wretched—all-suffering.

"You can't take them all away from me!" I scream to the Makers above.

Frost slams outwards from my clamped fists while my own tears freeze on top of the already frozen lake.

I slump, face down against the ice, hopeful it will spread onto me and take me, too.

"Take me!" I beg to the clouds above, completely alone in this world. "Take me to my family!"

A frigid burst of wind blasts through me as I sob the words again, slamming my fists on the ground in agony.

I shriek in pain from the cold ice continuously spreading.

"Take me to them!" I toss my arms out, desperately seeking to end this torture. "Kill me and let me reunite with them!" I scream louder into the lake as darkness descends over me.

"Tove!" a feminine voice calls.

I pray it is Mother or Runa coming to reunite with me. I close my eyes in gratitude, thankful the Makers are letting me go.

"Tove!"

The voice is frantic and worried.

The surrounding void shakes me profusely.

A tightness squeezes my body, and I hiss, flinching from it, needing to see my family again.

I am going to be with them.

"Tove!"

Dorit's voice fills my consciousness, and my eyes jolt open. Her long brown hair is undone, waves a mess as she looks upon me with worry.

A bead of sweat trickles down the side of my brow as I take in my surroundings, recognizing my rooms in Palaena. My heart hammers as Dorit's arms remain tight on my shoulders, my dream crashing against the forefront of my mind, bringing tears to the surface.

A choked gasp comes out instead of words, and Dorit's face wrinkles, pulling me to her as the thick and torturous wave of grief drowns me.

Her stuffy floral scent is the only thing grounding me.

I snake my arms around her, squeezing her as I weep into the crook of her neck. Tremors rock through my body as she holds me tight, her hand running in my hair and whispering the same words over and over.

"You're alright. You're okay."

"I-I'm so sorry," I whisper, shaking my head at my shortcomings unfolding around another person.

Dorit breaks away from our embrace. "You have nothing to apologize for."

I keep my eyes downcast, my tears cold against my heated cheeks. "No one should ever see me like this."

Niko's words from the past surface, reminding me of the very few who have seen me in such a vulnerable state.

A pinching nerve surrounds my heart at his words, hating how true they really were.

Dorit tilts my chin up. "Do you want to talk about it?"

My lips quiver at her compassion, my heart unable to keep up with her kindness and awareness of me.

She reminds me so much of Runa and Betina, and I cannot stop myself from confiding in her.

"The deaths of my family follow me in my dreams."

"It is never fun to relive that," Dorit says carefully, squeezing my upper arm.

I wipe my eyes and look away, biting my lip before confessing more she should know. "Most are nightmares I can work through, but others can lead to sleepwalking."

"I am sorry you experienced one of these tonight, and thank you for letting me know it could be worse," Dorit says, voice tender, wobbling through her choked words.

I nod to myself quietly, tears still fighting to escape.

"I will ensure to check on you more often."

My shoulders cave in, feeling unworthy of her kindness. "Y-You don't have to do that." I rub my sides with regret, wishing to not burden another person with my problems.

"Pfft," she remarks.

But my gaze averts from her, peering out to the window, trying to solve everything on my own.

Dorit takes my hand, the cold and brittle touch soothing my heated skin. I stare at our hands as she pats mine gently.

"Grief is a part of you, Tove, as is your trauma, your past, your everything."

I remain quiet. They aren't just a part of me. They're all I know about me.

But it catches me off guard when Dorit speaks again.

"But healing, learning, and growing will also be a part of you." I meet her gaze, and she smiles sweetly. "And I am honored to witness it all."

Remorse mixed with grief flows around me, my eyes tearing up again at her compassion. I do not know what I did to deserve this, but I cast my regret aside and pull her back into my arms.

I send my thanks to the Makers, grateful and honored that my time here is not a prison. It's been pleasant and completely different from what I thought.

The space in my heart that used to be for my family expanded for Niko and Betina. But during my time here, I have carved out more for Dorit, Jonas, Cordelia, and Ophelia.

I squeeze Dorit tighter when her arms wrap around me again, her kindness soothing my aching heart.

26

INTRUSIVE AND IMPULSIVE THOUGHTS

Sweat beads across my brow as the convulsing grants me a reprieve.

I groan after dry heaving for the third time this morning, clutching the chamber pot tighter, knowing Jerrick expects me in the library. Yet I can't seem to care about the reprimand for not showing up, my cycle finally arriving.

I was sorer than usual yesterday, and I did not think anything of it. But I should have known. I should have tracked my days to prepare for it and taken medicine the night prior.

Instead, my mind was preoccupied with thoughts I shouldn't even be thinking, *especially* now as my insides clench.

Sweet Makers, why does every day my cycle starts have to consist of pain, nausea, and fatigue? Why can't I just bleed and be done with it?

My intrusive thoughts have me comparing this pain to when I was shot in the back, which was far more tolerable.

Only because you fainted and don't remember much about it, Tove.

Easing my grip from the chamber pot, I hold my stomach and pray to the Makers I can make it back to bed.

I will crawl if that means preventing further embarrassment here.

Dorit has already seen me cry and has witnessed my nightmares. There is no telling what she will do if she sees me like this.

A burst of pain radiates above my center, my nerves pinching and seizing.

Tears line my eyes as I bite down hard on my lip, trying to fight through it while finding my bearings as I stand.

I brace my body on the wall, the interior stones of the castle cold and a relief against my hot, clammy skin. Trudging through each step, I stagger while maintaining pressure on my abdomen.

But bile shoots up my throat, and I collapse to the floor, hand covering my mouth to stop it from escaping. It doesn't force its way out, just triggers the heaving again, and this time, I am too far away from my chamber pot, so I keel over into the bathing tub, clutching the cool sides of the metal as pain erupts through me.

It could be worse, Tove.

I press my forehead against the tub, counting my breaths and building up energy. When I want to move again, the door to my chambers opens, and I call for Dorit.

"Tove?" she answers, hurrying in.

Her sentence is inaudible, my heartbeats thrumming in my ears as my breaths begin to increase faster than I can handle.

My groans and heaves fill the chamber, and a cold hand touches the small of my back, rubbing in soft circles. I cannot even savor it because my vision turns spotty.

I gasp to Dorit. "*Cycle.*"

I pant. "*Medicine.*"

Another pant. "*Please.*"

I hang my head, exhaustion tugging in my chest. The soreness from yesterday has increased, the tension tight and weighing down my arms and legs.

I blink slowly, feeling as if I am drifting in and out of consciousness.

Time slows without Dorit.

The cramping remains, gnawing and gnashing its way through me.

I lose my grip on the lip of the tub, and I slink back to the floor, curling myself into a ball. Darkness and light take turns as I lie here, waiting, pleading for medicine.

Once I have medicine, I will be fine. The pain will dull enough for me to function, and then I can dress for the day and maybe ask Cordelia and Ophelia for extra pastries.

Jerrick won't be happy with my absence.

In the back of my mind, I fear he will withhold training for a longer period.

The thought adds to my stress and brings forth more tears.

I tuck my head into my chest, squeezing myself tightly. Sobs escape me as I tremble and lose control over my body.

An aching song wraps itself around me, unsure why each step toward redemption, toward saving, toward healing, is stripped and ripped away.

Darkness sings and calls to my pain, the abyss of grief creeping to the surface of my mind, knowing my misery will be joined with good company.

My breaths turn ragged, a figurative idea of Oblivion not only dragging me from my family, but torturing me for deceiving those I've come to care for here in Palaena. The harsh reminder of guilt persecutes me, my efforts to rectify my assumptions and misgivings gone.

I wish there was something *real*—something tangible to bring me back from the disarray of my mind.

Warmth prickles against my arm, and I whimper at the small prayer being answered.

But even through my agony, I cannot manage to face Dorit and thank her. I'm too wrapped in myself, body and mind, to break free of this torment.

I burrow deeper into myself, hating the feeling of helplessness that always seeks me out.

Helplessness is a wound which opens any time a glimpse of hope shimmers in my life, festering and infecting its way through my body and soul to keep me from helping myself, my people, and my kingdom.

But now it's also keeping me from helping Palaena, from my friends, from—

The warmth trickles down my arm again, and it only makes me bawl harder, believing this small mercy will be taken away soon, too.

"Tove," a feminine voice says. "Tove, we are here. I've brought medicine."

The soft sound touches my heart, but it's the second familiar, beautiful, rich tone that touches my very soul.

"Come here, Frostbite," the man murmurs in my mind.

I scrunch my face tight, the nickname Jerrick gave me sounding endearing and beckoning. Deities, if he were here, he would probably scold me for not bringing our food tray to the library.

I would take being scolded by him rather than the throes of misery right now.

At least if I were around him, rather than dealing with this, I could offer him extra pastries from the kitchens, only to gorge on them myself when he wasn't looking.

A gentle hand touches me, gripping tight and tugging me away from the shell I've hidden in.

My face is damp from crying, light salt in the air, but when I am dragged out from under myself, cologne hits me like a boulder.

I whimper as Jerrick's smell and touch guides me from the pit of darkness in my mind, drawing my eyes open to see him.

My turmoil and suffering dissipate as I take him in, my heart hammering.

And when that *damn* dimple appears through his worried gaze, relief overcomes me. I don't know if I am crying because he has seen me in worse conditions or because he is here and helped drag me away from my despair.

I can barely stutter an apology through my pained sobs. "I-I'm sorry I am running late this morning."

Jerrick's brows pinch in confusion before he shakes his head. "Do not apologize for things beyond your control," he says softly, scooting closer to me.

He snakes his hand around the back of my head, bracing it as I rest on his knee. It's *much* more comfortable than the floor.

He tilts his head up to Dorit. "Are cycle's always like this?"

Dorit shrugs, unsure. "It varies based on the woman."

"M-My first day is always the hardest. I just need medicine to dull the pain," I bite out, still holding myself together.

Jerrick combs his fingers through my head, gently massaging my scalp and—fucking Deities, I might die right here and now from how amazing it feels.

"Leave the medicine with me," he says. "Go get food and have a few staff members assist you in bringing up the books on our table in the library."

Dorit hesitates, checking to see if I will be okay.

I offer her the best smile I can, nodding once to her. As long as I have medicine, I will be fine. Maybe I can even rest for a bit.

Jerrick darkens his tone once more to my lady-in-waiting. "*Dorit.*"

Her eyes turn on him, placing medicine in his upturned hand. "King or not, *Jerrick*, I will beat you senseless if you make her feel any worse right now."

My eyes widen at her threat, and Jerrick rolls his eyes.

Dorit rests her hands on her hips and lifts a brow at him. Her features are scornful, but Jerrick is unaffected.

"You have nothing to worry about, Dorit. I've got her."

Dorit holds his gaze for a few seconds before she glances back down, and I don't know what I did to have earned such loyalty and devotion from her. She nods once to Jerrick, leaving my rooms in a hurry.

Jerrick's attention remains on her departure before he glances at the pack of medicine, then to me. His brows pinch tightly, perplexed.

"You promise this will help you feel better?" Jerrick asks cautiously.

I eye the medicine, wishing I had the energy to take it before he can hold it against me. "It will dull the pain." I sigh.

His blue eyes hold mine, sincerity lacing his next statement. "There has to be something else to help you."

A twist in my stomach has me scrunching my features, and I apply more pressure.

"Frostbite?"

Worry heightens Jerrick's tone.

The sensation abates, and I relax a little, opening my eyes and meeting his gaze. "I-I'm here. Just cramps."

His features remain bundled tight, scanning me over. He moves to open the medicine pack.

"Here." He offers me the herbs.

I move my hand away from my stomach to take it, but another twinge of pain ruptures, and my thighs clench and muscles flex. I wince inwardly, returning my hold on my abdomen.

"Here, let me," Jerrick says, slowly and tentatively extending the medicine to me.

I lift my head as his fingers brush along my lips.

A tremor unrelated to my cycle rocks through me. Dark desires pulse, wanting to draw my tongue around other areas of his skin.

I gulp down the medicine, shaking away yet *another* intrusive thought of Jerrick, praying to the Makers the herbs will take effect soon. "Th-Thank you." I smile softly.

But Jerrick's jaw works for a few beats before he asks another question. "How long do we have to wait?"

"It's hard to say. I am usually better about taking medicine proactively, but I've been preoccupied."

His entire face falls at my admission, his dimple vanishing and eyes turning distant. "I am to blame for that."

"No, well—yes and no," I amend.

Jerrick's head drops, his warmth retreating.

I rush to explain, "I don't blame you for my stress. It's everything we are trying to do and accomplish for your curse, for the ball, for the kingdoms, and for my powers. I know we have not tackled everything, but managing it all can be a lot."

Our eyes meet, and he offers me a solemn nod.

It feels like he is withdrawing more, despite me still resting on his knee. I push through my pain and grab his hand.

His gaze flicks to it, and I squeeze it once, rubbing small circles as he has done for me. "I don't blame you," I repeat in reassurance.

His stern and distraught features lighten, his thumb rubbing my hand gently. "You should," he says, low and quiet.

I shake my head adamantly. "*I don't.*"

I try to voice that I don't blame him for my family, for my trauma, but the rest of my words run dry in my aching throat, the only two that really matter lingering between us.

He looks me over, our hands still rubbing against each other. Being the object of his attention has always made me flush, but now I am molten.

I swallow carefully, and his eyes track the movement.

"May I try something?" Jerrick asks.

Caution prickles up the length of my spine, unknowing where he is going with this.

I *really* hope he isn't trying to pick me up. I don't even want to think about how mortified I was when Niko did that during my last cycle.

But at least Jerrick is asking.

"Wh-What do you mean?" I ask.

"May I use my gifts on you?"

I tense, the past occurrences of him using his abilities on me flashing in my mind. But he wants to help me, and he is asking for permission.

Hesitation ebbs the longer he stares, waiting for my response.

"H-How do you intend to—"

"You said you have cramps. If I heat your blood, it will increase your blood flow, and I could—" He stops when my face falls. "You don't have to say yes. I'm only offering a suggestion that could help."

"I wish you did that the last time this happened," I blurt.

Recollection draws a chuckle from him as he quirks a brow. "Who is to say I didn't?"

Surprise widens my eyes. I drift to the last time I was on my cycle, remembering the pain—the fainting.

"Did you use your power on me when I fainted?" I ask. "At the ball in Axidoria?"

Jerrick's teasing shifts into regret. "Yes," he admits quietly.

I fidget with my other hand, seeking more answers. "Have you—have you used them without my knowledge beyond that?"

Jerrick's eyes fall to the floor before repeating himself. "Yes."

"If you can manipulate blood, why didn't you heal me when I was shot?" I ask curiously, feeling a phantom prick where the arrow punctured me.

Jerrick slumps, as if it pains him to revisit our past. It is evident he is trying to avoid replying, his features mask away the pain as if I cannot read him.

His demeanor shifts, and I ache seeing the transformation.

Jerrick smirks, rubbing my hand. "Why can't you just tell me yes or no to my question?" he asks, half annoyed, half amused.

But the haunted, kind Jerrick is beneath this mask, just as the tortured mess I am lies underneath my own.

Even with his question hanging between us, I don't let him get away with not answering mine. I've seen different sides of this man, and I want to understand him. The need to differentiate the man from the king and the king from the curse grows the more I am around him.

I remind him. "You promised you would answer all my questions. Do not make me ask you why you are avoiding answering me, too."

The smirk vanishes, and he withdraws. Jerrick averts his gaze, but I remain focused on him, studying the rise and fall of his chest to see if I have angered him.

But then he closes his eyes and slowly inhales.

He confesses, "My gifts are that of Letum. They are not meant to heal, only to take."

A spasm rolls through my gut, and I wince, moving from the twisting happening internally.

Jerrick acts quickly, helping brace my body seizing.

I am beyond grateful for his quiet support. When it settles, I give myself a few moments before trying to communicate again.

"Well, maybe in this situation, taking will make me feel better," I concede.

The anguish in Jerrick dissipates when our gazes meet once more, a soft smile drawing back his dimple.

But the knowledge of feeling his powers again brings unease to the surface. I harness my courage and brace myself. "H-How do we do this?"

He touches my chin, tilting me up to him as he leans in close. "Well, I could always just kiss—"

"No!" I blurt, sending him back in surprise.

But he doesn't let that stop him from saying, "Last I remember, you liked it."

"Last I remember, you did it without asking."

"Hmmm," he muses, feigning he is not affected by my remark.

Jerrick shrugs, his decision made. His hold on my chin lessens as he asks, "Can you move at all?"

"Why?" I groan, not wanting to move but willing to if it means faster relief.

"If you want immediate relief, the best course is to place my hands wherever the most pain is."

The thought of his hands warming me so close to my sex lures desire to the surface.

But the potential immediate relief has me mentally preparing for the energy to move, but Jerrick halts me.

"Here, I have a better idea." Jerrick carefully helps move me off his knee.

I relax, grateful to not have to move more than necessary, but confusion furrows my brow when he stands.

Jerrick moves behind me, his legs stretch around my body before he touches my side.

"I'm going to ease you upward. Is that alright?" he asks.

Gratitude hums in my chest. It is reassuring and comforting despite the daunting thought of moving. But I brace myself and muster my strength, nodding quickly to Jerrick.

The movement is swift and over before my next heartbeat, Jerrick pulling my back to him.

I keep pressure on my stomach, my chin dipping as another ricochet of cramps explodes. I tense, wincing, and I immediately regret moving too fast.

Jerrick trails his hand around my neck, guiding my head up to rest against him. His heartbeat is erratic in my ear, my own drowned out by the sound of his.

A need surges forth when more than his hard chest presses against me.

My nipples harden as his hands snake above my breasts, a teasing caress before removing my hands from my stomach.

I close my eyes from his touch so close to my center as he leans in, whispering softly, "I'm here, I've got you, Frostbite."

His soothing voice uncoils the tension from my neck and down my spine. His words and hands envelop me in a blanket of safety.

I release a breath, giving him permission.

Jerrick remains close as his magic flares to life. His power is recognizable, the essence of power reminding me of my own.

Heat radiates through his palms as they hold a light pressure against my abdomen. The balm his abilities offer uncoils my muscles one at a time, and my entire body submerges in warmth and relaxation.

"Mmmm," I moan my gratitude.

Jerrick's lips kiss my hair. "Is it working?"

"Mm-hmm," I respond, too lazy to offer any answer beyond that.

Jerrick exhales behind me, easing us backward as he rests against a wall. "Good." He chuckles, hands still warm and holding my stomach.

I hold them as waves of relief cocoon me and my entire body now. "How do you manifest your gifts?" I ask, envious of how he can control his gifts and wishing for the chance to do that myself.

Jerrick is quiet, the moment spreading as his lips graze my hair. "Meditation," he answers.

"Deities, I wish I could do that," I reply, knowing I get too far gone in my own mind that meditating seems impossible.

"You can, though."

I shake my head, not wanting to admit aloud another flaw about myself.

"Let me show you," he says, drawing our hands forth.

I almost beg him not to, but with his pressure removed from my stomach, my blood thrums and the comfort in my body remains. I lift my head in astonishment.

"H-How are you—"

"Meditation, Frostbite," Jerrick repeats, sitting straighter against me as he turns my palms upright. "When you feel your magic, where does it stem from?"

"Mostly in my chest or stomach."

"Okay, good, you already know that." He holds my waist. "Now, close your eyes and count your breaths."

I do as he says, remembering times when counting my breaths had helped, but I never managed to do much beyond that with my abilities.

I remain focused on each breath, one right after the other.

The fortitude of Jerrick behind me mixed with tension leaving my body is comforting.

But the fear of the past, fear of the pain, fear of my magic call forth—

A cracking shakes through my skull, and my eyes burst open.

"Why did you stop?" Jerrick asks.

I cover my face with my hands, shaking my head. "I-I can't." Shame and fear dig into my skin.

Jerrick eases my hands from my face. "Try again, but this time, when your mind wanders away from counting your breaths, give yourself grace. Then return to focusing on the rise and fall of your chest."

I close my eyes. The dread of returning to those same thoughts has me hesitating.

Jerrick holds my palms steady, never letting go, and kisses the top of my head once more. "Relax your eyes," he murmurs against my scalp, drifting his thumbs back and forth across my skin.

I listen to his guidance.

"Good girl," he purrs, and my heart stutters at the smooth drawl behind his approval. "Now, breathe with me."

I focus on the rise and fall of Jerrick's chest, concentrating on moving past his praise and having my breathing align with his. The heat in my stomach remains strong, granting me more relief from my cycle and a chance to try again.

With Jerrick's power surrounding me, it's easier to match his breathing, especially as he repeats the same words. "Inhale. Exhale."

Eventually, he stops speaking, letting our bodies breathe in tandem. His calloused thumb taunts me, and my thoughts wander again.

Jerrick's voice keeps me at bay, as if knowing the second my mind wandered.

"Now, feel," he breathes.

Memories, distant and far between, twinkle along the edges of my mind. Faint feelings beyond grief and despair drift back to me, causing my lip to quiver.

The caress of love and happiness of my family is light, drifting away faster than I can follow. The pit of my own Oblivion crawls forward, snuffing out the glimpse of emotions I long felt forgotten, and the reality of my situation thrashes.

I instinctively move my hands, but Jerrick holds them firm.

"Grace, Frostbite," he reminds me gently.

A weight builds in my chest, and I try to resist accepting the monster that I am. I squirm adamantly.

"I-I—"

"Say you are doing your best," Jerrick instructs.

Warmth spreads over me as I struggle through repeating him. "I-I'm doing my best..."

"Say it is okay not to be okay."

I hesitate at his words, tempted to peer up at him and ask why he wants me to say that.

He nudges me with his body, reminding me to do as he says. "It's okay not to be okay."

"Good, now focus on those words and come back to your breathing," Jerrick says. "I'm here with you every step. I've got you."

He resumes his own meditation, keeping hold of my hands and twiddling lazy circles.

Concentration should be hard, yet his touch and magic ground me and help me find my own center as I chant. The conscious thoughts of matching Jerrick's evened breaths pull me away from the phrases, even as Jerrick's uplifted voice instructs me to open my eyes.

I hesitate, my mind too preoccupied with breathing. But a beacon of cold kisses the center of my palm, drawing my attention to it.

A startled gasp escapes at the small snowflake hovering a few inches above my hand, with no sign of frost or ice along my skin and no sign of it expanding beyond what it is.

I cannot help but laugh at the sight, a flurry of snow twirling around in response.

Tears blur my line of vision.

"Beautiful," Jerrick hums from behind.

Words can't escape me, so I nod, shocked to see my magic manifest like this.

The weight of Jerrick's chin rests on my head as we both study my gift. "Now, close your palm," he encourages gently.

I do as he asks, the familiar heat of his magic closing over my hand.

The surge of power lingers in the air, Jerrick's hold lingering as if he doesn't want to let go. But even as he does, I still keep my palm closed, debating on opening it.

Drawing a long inhale, I hold it for a few seconds, expelling my lungs and opening my hand to see the snowflake completely dissolved. "I-I-I made my magic not appear on my arms."

A breathless sob of joy escapes.

"With my help, of course," Jerrick teases from behind.

I deflate. "You just have to go and ruin all my fun now, don't you?"

Jerrick's chuckle is light as he says, "Manifest your magic without my help and then we can train."

He—he offered to train me...

I peer up at Jerrick, my teeth flashing with excitement and his wide grin matching my own.

His head tilts toward mine as the air surrounding us shifts.

Jerrick's intoxicating cologne has me licking my lips, my hungry gaze lingering on his mouth inching closer to mine.

The sound of staff entering my chambers, with Dorit in tow, reminds me of myself.

"Thank you," I spill out, averting my gaze from Jerrick and saving myself from acting on impulse.

27

WAVERING

Jerrick refused to let me roam beyond my chambers, claiming he did not want to witness me fainting again from my cycle. He brought me food trays every morning, stacked high with pastries, courtesy of Ophelia and Cordelia. He also ensured Dorit and Jonas checked on us periodically, visiting while helping bring and take books Jerrick requested while I rested.

And as annoying and embarrassing as his teasing was, I could not complain.

But when I fell asleep while reading on the second day, Jerrick tossed a pastry at my face. It startled me awake, and his laughter roared throughout the room.

I couldn't even stay mad at him, my heart thawing at the sight and sound of him.

The richness and elegance of his laughter while tracking my breath is a tingling taunt.

I pinch my features tight, concentrating on understanding the magic begging to escape. Crackling and air drift in a flurry around my mind, wanting to drag me away.

I twitch from the sound, seeking mercy for myself only to struggle.

Hands hold mine, and Jerrick's breath hovers near me. "Kindness, Frostbite."

My gift flickers in response to Jerrick's voice, soothing and sweet. I bite back my smile, fighting against the surge of desire spreading in my stomach from his touch.

I square my shoulders, coaxing and caressing the ice in my body to nurture it and harness the blizzard into a morsel of snow. The depth of power pulses around me, and creaks and cracks swirl.

I push through the disarray clouding my mind, which wishes to accept myself.

The magic eases as I drift back into my breathing.

My faith in succeeding today draws my eyes open, but when he pulls away, there is nothing. Disappointment lines my brows as I lower my hand in defeat.

Jerrick touches my upper arm. "*Almost*," he chimes.

Almost is not good enough.

Jerrick offered me this small lesson, and I have made no improvements without his assistance.

I fold into myself, frustrated with the lack of progress.

Jerrick gathers a few books from a pile we have not touched this week, and when he turns to me, he shifts around uncomfortably. He seems beside himself, even as he approaches my bed, placing them on my table. He angles them toward me, and I read the titles.

The texts catch me off guard. Looking up at him in question, I am thrown off when he squats next to me.

Jerrick peels my hand from my torso, his comforting circles grazing over my knuckles as he inclines his head to the books. "These are what Palaena has on Aiyana. There are some of my ancestor's journals as well that aided me when I was learning my gifts. I thought they would help you."

"Wh-Why are you giving me these? We have not found anything regarding your curse."

"You've been earning your right." He smirks.

I don't understand what I did to warrant this change of mind. "What, with all the food trays?" I joke, knowing he originally said I had to help break his curse in order to train.

Jerrick chuckles lightly. "It *could* have been that."

I roll my eyes, absentmindedly running my thumb along his hand.

Jerrick tracks the movement, the rise and fall of his chest easy and relaxed. "I am setting out today, so I thought pairing some exciting reads with the curse reads could lighten your spirits," he says lightly.

Maybe in reading these texts, I can find something useful to practice while Jerrick is away. Strengthening my resolve is vital if I want to save my kingdom, and a fluttering in my chest responds to the challenge.

But a pang of sadness at his absence suddenly dampens my mood.

"Y-You're going hunting?" He silently bobs his head, avoiding my gaze but still holding my hand. "You'll read more than the Aiyana texts I gave you, right?"

"Yes."

The lie slips easily from my mouth, the need to read these texts more important than another boring book.

He smiles with gratitude, lifting my hand to kiss it, and instant regret forms a tight pain in the back of my throat.

I cough, masking away my own grimace and smile gently.

Lacing my fingers together tightly, I remain steadfast in my goals. If I can master the smallest of magic, I can *finally* train.

Jerrick releases my hand and stands, debating whether he should leave.

Knowing he needs to hunt just as I need to read these texts, I reassure him, the corners of my lips lifting. "I will do my best to give you a report when you return."

His blue eyes lined with amusement meet mine. "I'll return soon."

Jerrick takes a long breath into his formal goodbye, an unnecessary gesture, given we are both royalty, but it is chivalrous and sweet, something I linger on longer than I expect.

And in the days following Jerrick's departure, I couldn't stop thinking about him. Guilt at lying to him and the knowledge of reading from Aiyana's texts took turns with his noticeable distance.

With being on the mend from my cycle, I returned to the library.

Dorit accompanies me each day, but the days drag by, disappointment slackening my body every time I enter the library and Jerrick has still not returned. Dorit and Jonas provide excellent company, but I crave the routine Jerrick and I share more.

I read my preferred texts over his other stacks of books, practicing each time I am left alone for brief durations throughout the day. And each night ticks, sleepless and filled with meditation.

But joy has me jumping out of bed at the manifestation of a snowflake in the center of my palm.

I bounce around my room, almost hurrying down the hall to find Jerrick.

But I am reminded he still has not returned, and my triumph dies a little bit, knowing he isn't here to witness it. I want to shove it in his face and brag that I can do it on my own, just to see if he would tease or praise me.

But in his absence, I turn to my mother's mirror.

I impatiently wait for Betina and Niko's presence, the vision of my rooms barely visible when my squeal escapes. "Betina! Look!" I beam with pride at my magic, my palm still cupping the snow.

Betina flicks up from the bed, shock and sleep swept away as she rushes toward the vanity. "Tove!" She breathes in awe.

I grin, giggling in bliss. I've mastered this!

I lock gazes with Betina, and the two of us are teary eyed. Missing home hits like a wave as I take her in, disbelieving that I did this.

"You're training. Does that mean the king's curse is broken?" Betina asks.

"No," I admit, my gaze trickling back down to my palm.

Magic radiates toward my hand, a steady stream of frost seeping under the surface of my skin. It is breathtaking the longer I gaze at it, my heart leaping out of my chest when Niko bursts through the door.

"Betina, you'll never believe it!" he rejoices, running toward her and embracing her tightly.

The wonderment and joy drains from my face at the sight. A void of betrayal stings and tightens my stomach.

The frost in my hand vanishes, the flow of power obliterated without a second thought.

Longing to be the one Niko holds turns my blood cold and my heart heavy.

Niko opens his eyes, finding me across the mirror with surprise. "Tove!" he exclaims, releasing Betina and hurrying toward me.

I dismiss the pleasantries, and Niko's demeanor shifts.

He gazes back at Betina, who tugs her arm. Niko's amber eyes find mine.

"It isn't what it looks like, Tee," Niko explains. "I've just received news, is all."

Betina raises her hands in surrender when I dart to her. My trust wavers as I study the two of them, unsure of my own feelings about what I witnessed. Betina's brows pinch with concern as I direct my attention back to Niko.

"What news did you receive so late into the night?" I ask, hiding my hands.

His fear remains in the back of my mind from the last time he saw my powers manifest, and part of me believes he would shrink away again should I show him.

"I received word of extra shipments of clothing and weaponry," Niko says.

I nod silently, and Niko arches a brow. "Tee, don't you get it? We are so close!"

A small tug of my lip lifts at that, the plan still happening in Niko's mind. I do not want to dampen his spirits now, seeing as this is one of the few occurrences he's not mad or jealous.

"We are, Niko," I reply.

Betina scowls at Niko as she steps up, directing her question to me. "We have not heard from you in a while. What news do you bring?"

She tilts her head at Niko, a signal for me to share my news.

The longing to show him is squished, and my only intention is to explain everything else. "I've been away due to my cycle, but there have been developments regarding my father's disappearance and the upcoming celebrations."

Shock flashes in Niko's eyes, and curiosity draws his next question. "What have you found out?"

"Well, that's the thing. I haven't found any proof of Palaena's involvement with my father."

Betina moves to speak, but Niko interrupts her. "No, not that Tove. What has developed with the ball? Is there a day set yet? When will invitations be sent out? We need to discuss the next steps for battle. I think the following morning will be the best plan for attack."

The next steps...

Sweet Makers, has my time already run out?

Panic laces around my body, and I try to grant myself more time. "I don't have that information yet," I lie, my fears drawing forth my cowardice.

I am not ready for the next step; I have barely navigated meditation. My progress is moving slower than I can afford.

Worry over the inability to save my kingdom after all this pinches in the back of my throat as nausea churns deep in the pit of my stomach.

I scrub my hand over my face as regret grows.

"Tove," Betina starts, concern lacing her voice, "are you well?"

What a loaded question.

Still, I stumble over my words. "I-I need to go. I-I'm—"

My gaze finds Niko's, his eyes so full of hope and love. It kills me to leave them like this, but I run my hand over the mirror.

Niko yells, "Tov—"

My old bedroom vanishes from the mirror.

My reflection, sad and distraught as it may be, stares right back. I've avoided myself for so long, yet inspecting myself, I see a liar, a failure, and a monster.

Tears fall onto the mirror. I hunch over, gripping it tightly.

The intention to fight has been Niko's motivation, whereas mine has been for so much more.

I haven't even scratched the surface of my gifts.

My entire time here has been to save my kingdom and find answers, yet I could not bear to see the disappointment on Niko's face when I denied him news of our plan and future reunion.

Am I being selfish in wanting to find answers and controlling my abilities first?

Anguish wracks through my body, and I close my eyes, clutching Mother's mirror tight to my chest as tears seep down my cheeks. It strains against my muscles, even as I roll to my side and draw my knees to my chest.

I *need* to do better.

I need to *be* better.

Moments of my past, my present, and the possible future weave together in a mixed melody. Some of the chords are seamless and complementing, while others are brittle and searing to hear.

I hone in on the rise and fall of my chest, tracking my breaths and slowly relaxing my body.

And when my mind wanders again, it goes back to Jerrick.

His lush laugh, his flirtatious taunts, and the knowledge he has of his kingdom and his magic.

I nuzzle into my pillow, disappointed it's not his hard chest I mistook for a cushion so long ago. Sleep pulls me away from wondering what Jerrick would have done at seeing my snow manifested on my own today.

28

WINE AND CONFESSIONS

The memory of Jerrick's low laugh strums again in my mind, bringing me faint joy as the sound of liquid pouring into a cup drags me from the book I've barely focused on for the last hour.

Dorit regards me with concern. "I hope that face is for the wine I poured you. It is one of the first we received from your kingdom."

I sit up, gently placing my current book to the side. "Oh, Sweet Makers, I love you."

I reach for the glass, and a small burn hits the back of my throat as I drain the dark-red wine from the goblet. When its contents are empty, I place it on the wooden table with a huge grin.

"I've missed our wine."

Dorit rolls her eyes but fills my cup again. "Rude you couldn't wait for me."

Before I can bring the cup to my lips, she grabs it, wiggling her eyebrows mischievously as she takes a long gulp.

She lowers the glass and says, "I see why you couldn't wait." Her voice drops to a hushed whisper. "Don't tell Jonas we tried it without him."

We snicker through each glass, taking a break from the books I read today and catching up on the castle and village news.

Dorit is mid-sentence in telling me the run-in she had with a friend of hers when she loses her balance and falls a fraction away from one of the lounge chairs. Her eyes widen when her ass lands hard on the floor, and I can't help the burst of laughter escaping me.

Tears of joy line my vision as she joins in.

I move to help her up. "I think we may have had too much to drink." I giggle like a young child.

A small hiccup escapes Dorit, and that's how I know she is a goner. If my head is swimming, surely, hers is as well.

There *is* a reason Axidoria's wine is so coveted in each kingdom. We make it stronger than others, reducing the need to drink much to have a good time.

She sways as I hold on to her sides, making sure she doesn't collapse again. "Come on, let's get you to my room," I say as her weight shifts on me.

"Shh!" She slurs slightly. "We can't tell anyone."

A hiccupped giggle escapes as I reach for the empty cup in her hand, holding her tighter as I place it on the table. She stumbles over herself, causing me to lose my balance.

We both fall to the floor, unable to keep the laughter at bay.

A cough from behind gives me pause.

I turn to meet Jonas and Jerrick's gazes, and my heart stops.

Jerrick's tall frame is relaxed as he leans against one of the bookshelves, looking at me. His hair is tied half-back, his light tunic bright in contrast to the dark vest matching his leather trousers with his sword and dagger strapped in place.

Jonas has his arms crossed, shaking his head in disappointment.

Dorit laughs hysterically.

I suppress my laugh and stand, Jerrick's eyes tracing up and down my body. I mimic his movements, scanning him head to toe for any changes, any injuries, and find relief in seeing him whole.

"We were supposed to wait and try the wine *together*, Dorit!" Jonas scolds, stepping in to help.

I break my stare from Jerrick to help Jonas.

Dorit lifts an arm around his shoulder as he pulls her upright and gives me a knowing look.

"You *just* couldn't wait, could you?" He clicks his tongue. "I've got her from here. Try to get some sleep tonight, Tove."

I extend my thanks to Jonas as the two of them lurch out of the library. My attention remains on the door for a few moments before braving another glance at Jerrick.

When I meet his eyes again, his softened expression makes my heart swell and return it in kind.

"Hello there, Frostbite," he purrs.

I swallow down the lump in my throat at the nickname reserved for me.

Taking a tentative step forward, I offer a small wave through my squeaky reply.

"*Hi.*"

He gestures to the door Jonas and Dorit left mere seconds ago. "Are you returning to your chambers for the night?"

I offer him a tight smile, afraid the wine has loosened my tongue.

"Would you like an escort?" he asks, extending his elbow.

I shuffle to him without a response, and I wrap my arm around his as we leave the library.

We maintain our companionable silence as we walk through the castle.

Staff members close the windows, light the lanterns, and tidy the rooms. Each of them acknowledges us, a kind smile offered to me and a curt dip of the head toward their king.

Our steps are slow and quiet while we take in the night blanketing itself over our residence.

But with Jerrick's hair freshly washed, his soap lingers in the air along with the smell of leather and whiskey. And it's... *distracting*.

"How about that report?"

Jerrick's smooth voice fills the dimmed corridor.

The playfulness in his tone buzzes in my ears.

We approach a set of stairs as I recall the last few books I scoured through. "I read on Aiyana, comparing a lot of the ancestors that inherited nature gifts, better understanding the connection you made regarding meditation, magic, and emotion."

Jerrick hums in approval of my findings, his elbow tightening a little more as we step into a narrow stairway, our bodies inching closer.

I'm eager to share my improvements with my magic with him, but nerves ravage my body, worried at what he might think. I squeeze his arm after the first couple sets of stairs, using him for support to push through the climb up. As I toss the idea of showing him my progress again, his tall frame looms over me, reminding me he could be farther up without me and dragging me along.

Yet his steps choose to match mine.

The notion sends heat to my cheeks and other places.

"Did you research anything else?" he asks, hopeful of a breakthrough.

I want to pause on the stairs to hold his stare and assure him I made a breakthrough regarding his curse. But I keep stepping up each stair in tandem with Jerrick's.

The guilt of letting him down and not reading much about it while he was hunting gnaws at me. And yet I still strum up another lie.

"I did," I start.

He finishes my thought. "Still nothing?"

I nod quietly, his disappointment seeping into my bones.

There are *hundreds* of texts to still scan through about the Deity of Illusion and curses. Even through my lies and everything we've read, the lack of any information, any breadcrumbs, tells me something is missing.

I've been muddling with that knowledge for a while, tempted to suggest we return to Axidoria and visit my kingdom's archives for research on his curse. I have been wanting answers about my family and practicing my magic at home, but I also considered how going to Axidoria could be beneficial for Jerrick, too.

Thoughts of home remind me of the guilt keeping me awake most nights, hating how I left things with Niko and Betina along with the lies I have built here.

My guilty conscience pushes me to make the suggestion. "We could go to Axidoria."

He gives me a suspicious glance when we reach the top of the stairs. Even as we stroll down the wing leading to my bedchamber, Jerrick remains silent.

I blurt, "We can review the texts there, and maybe something of my mother's might help us. And we could try to search for clues about what happened to my father. Or if not, I could send word requesting to have some texts sent over with the next transfer of resources. I am sure if I asked, Niko would grant us that."

From the corner of my eye, Jerrick's jaw works while he stiffens at the mention of Niko. Cooling his features, he relaxes into the cocky mantle of king he wears before he offers me a response.

"I'll take it into consideration."

I nod in understanding. Deep down, I hoped he would have jumped at the offer, but I find myself disappointed and feel as if he does not trust me.

He has every right to not trust you, Tove.

The thought stings against my soul, and I remain quiet the rest of the walk. I stop first, and my arm slowly releases from Jerrick's as I turn for my chambers.

He folds his hand over mine, giving me pause. Our eyes lock, and he smiles softly.

"I think this is the first time I've walked you to your chambers."

I'm surprised at the comment, and smile in return. "It is."

Thinking back to the times we have walked around the castle together, the only time I can recall walking to a bedchamber was on our wedding night. Although that was to his rooms and not mine.

The memory of that night fades my smile. As if he, too, has the same thought, his expression dims, releasing my hand and lowering in a small bow.

"Good night, Frostbite."

His voice is flat as he pivots and hurries back down the hall.

I whisper after him into the night, "Good night, Jerrick."

I fidget through fastening the latch, pressing my forehead against the door and inhaling deeply. The light scent of oak issues from the wood as I savor each breath.

The flicker of frost within me perks at my increased heartbeat. I try to simmer it into idleness with positive thoughts and even breathing. My heart rate slows as I harness everything I'm feeling.

Balancing emotions is key.

I remove my boots, digging into the heel of one to push it out and repeating the same action with the other. I still feel the light effects of the wine Dorit and I drank earlier, but it isn't going to keep me from trying to contact Betina and Niko.

I need them both to help me through my torment.

The kernel of power quiets as I undress, and I opt for a lighter nightgown and a blue silk robe.

My hair stays fastened in the plaited crown as I sit on my bed, reaching for my mother's mirror.

I pause momentarily, taking in my reflection and noting a brightness in my eyes. For once, I linger on my features, admiring the glow in my blue irises. I take in every inch, not looking to peel myself apart.

But I break away from the distraction, rubbing the mirror three times and opening the line to Axidoria, hoping and praying I can have them both on my side.

Tears surface when Betina's youthful features come into blurry view. Her rich skin is tanned, and my heart leaps that she is not locked away in my chambers all day and is absorbing the spring sun's rays as often as she can.

I was upset the last time I saw her, but my heart still fractures knowing I left them without any explanation.

She runs to the mirror on her end, gasping in joy. "Tove!"

Through my blurry vision, I laugh with relief at my dearest friend's reaction. "Betina."

Her joy is infectious, and I imagine her arms wrapping around me, encasing me with her scent of nutmeg and cloves.

My cheeks hurt from grinning at the scent that is home.

"I don't know whether to scream at you or hear you out," she starts, readying to scold me.

Her lips fold into themselves, and I know she wants to refrain from lecturing me, her queen, but also reprimanding her friend.

My glee is gone, replaced with a grimace as pain etches in her features. "I know. I know."

Her eyes peer into mine, and I can't stop wiping away the dampness on my cheeks.

"Tove," Betina starts with a long sigh, drawing my attention to her softened gaze, "we were so worried the last time you reached out. And you did not get to show Niko your magic."

I turn away, glancing out the window. "I was upset and scared," I admit.

"Why?" Betina tilts her head with worry. "You were so happy when you said my name, but you changed before my very eyes the more you spoke to us."

I give her a knowing look, and her mouth falls in surprise.

"Don't even think that. You have no idea how badly Niko fell apart when you severed the connection. He is worried about you. He misses you. And he wants you to be here with him."

A hint of frustration is etched in her tone. The doubt from her words does nothing to make me feel better.

"He broke down?"

"Yes, Tove. *Of course* he broke down. Niko has been coming in every day, trying to count down how many days he has left until he gets to see you again."

My stomach flips, and my heart surges. I rub my chest as my lip wobbles, still unsure what to believe.

"He—he does?"

"Yes, Tove. *Every day*," Betina says again. "He has had no one to confide in with while you've been gone. Niko rants and complains every time he receives letters from Palaena. And even though he is happy to see your name on those, most days, his determination and jealousy get the better of him. It is tearing him apart to be separated from you."

I resign at Betina's words, a pain in my throat making it hard to even speak.

I know Niko is determined and jealous—I've seen bits of it when we have spoken. And to take away his brief glimpse of happiness the other day builds regret in my bones.

"Oh Deities, I am awful." I cover my face.

"No, you are not awful. What is awful is that he complains to me. Every day," she says. "Do you know how annoying that is?"

I half laugh, lowering my hands to look back.

A half smile forms through her pain-stricken eyes.

"He misses you so much. It's physically painful to see. Niko has been throwing himself into training every man as well as himself from sunrise to sunset. He loves you so much."

Her voice turns grave, and tears sting my eyes.

"He is so excited to see you, but he was stricken with anxiety last time. I told him I would smooth things over with you the next time we heard from you and give you two a chance to speak alone next time. And don't think I do not know how much you are missing him, too. I know you are as stressed as he is."

I crumple underneath her gaze, my resolve to keep everything together breaking apart at the seams.

"I'm sorry, Betina," I cry out. "It hurt to see him so happy and not be there for him. But what really hurts is that I am not getting the answers I need or improving fast enough with my gifts. I want to return home, but I also don't want there to be a battle. I just want to help everyone."

Her gaze softens. "I know, Tove. You've said that from the beginning."

"But I don't want to leave without knowing what happened to my family and how to break Jerrick's curse. Everything feels as if it is my fault, and I want to fix everything, but I keep coming up short."

Silence fills the air as my chest rattles from my confession.

I care about the well-being of Palaena as much as I do for Axidoria. The addition of duty and responsibility grows the more I seek to make amends and find closure.

"I want to ask for help and show Niko my progress," I rasp. "But I am so terrified of failing everyone and not removing this winter that I will regress deeper into the monster that I am."

I brush the tears away as they cascade my cheeks.

She holds my gaze through her own remorse as I sniff through my congestion, gathering myself.

"I miss you both so much. And I am sorry I withdrew from you two. You both are important to me. I don't want to let either of you down," I finish.

"You are *not* a monster, Tove."

I am quick to dismiss her words, no one understanding my true torment. "I'm at least a monster for complaining to you."

Betina chuckles under her breath. I lift at her amusement even as her seriousness returns, her lips tightening before she speaks.

"I have *never*—nor will I ever—view you as a monster. You are my best friend, and I will always prefer to hear your complaints over anyone else's. *Always.*"

Her empathy and friendship leave my lip quivering, I truly am undeserving of her. "Even complaints that leave me feeling confused and frustrated?"

"Even then," Betina promises. "I will always stand behind you." Betina dips into a low curtsy.

The gratitude and love I have for her makes the tears more difficult to fight. I bite my lip as she remains lowered, sniveling through my emotions for the purest of souls the Makers have blessed to keep in my life.

Betina takes everything I am in stride, even when I make her angry. Her loyalty to me not only as her queen but as a friend is overwhelming and powerful in its own way.

Braving through myself, Betina rises, and her chestnut-brown eyes find me once more, and a small dose of life behind them gives me hope.

We smile at each other.

Betina leans close to the mirror. "Now, tell me *everything*."

29

A CHANGE IN THE ROUTINE

Sleep didn't take me until the early hours of the morning. Fear of my thoughts blurring into night terrors kept me pacing long after Betina and I conversed. Seeing her last night had me realizing I've been slacking off, reading the winter and spring away by learning about my magic, yes, but not pushing for training.

Betina agreed to help investigate my family's dealings to see if there were any answers back home. She was grateful to have something to do aside from helping manage my correspondence with Niko while working.

Even with that relief and comfort, I can't stop worrying I am behind—that I am doing something wrong.

A dull ache pulsates down my neck anytime I maneuver my head while roaming through my wardrobe. With my mind feeling frazzled, wearing a dress rather than the set of trousers lying across the chaise by my bed could lift my spirits.

Swiping backward through each gown, indecisiveness weighs in over the colors and fabrics. I settle for a pale blue cotton dress. It is loosely fitted and perfect for my morning trip to the kitchens to see Cordelia and Ophelia.

The thought of seeing their loving faces makes me smile, knowing they will provide anything my heart desires. The excitement of food has me rushing to dress, quickly finger combing my hair into a long plait drifting down the side of my head.

Barefooted, I pounce around my chambers, searching for slippers that will match my gown instead of the boots I've worn. I give my appearance a once-over in the vanity as I slip on my shoes, making sure the gown is loose around my waist to conceal all the food I've consumed that goes straight to my stomach and hips.

Ascending the stairs, I salivate with each step that guides me toward the kitchen. My excitement is short-lived as the doorway of the kitchens comes into view when I hear footsteps. The scent of cologne and leather fills the hallway, and the hair on the nape of my neck rises.

I hurry toward my friends, hopeful I can avoid a one-on-one with Jerrick.

As I enter the kitchen, I am met with silence as the two cooks I've come to know enjoy their peaceful work of preparing well-seasoned dishes for the castle.

"Your Majesty!" Cordelia beams when she sees me, lowering into a small curtsy. I am surprised by her sudden formality but bristle when she adds, "My king."

A knife clatters against Ophelia's workstation as she turns faster than I think she anticipated, almost losing her balance as she slumps into a curtsy.

I don't move to look behind me, aware of Jerrick's body heat surrounding me. I hate being caught off guard, especially in the mornings when I've had little sleep.

Jerrick's footsteps inch closer to me, and I ignore his advancing presence by walking farther into the kitchen, past the two stone hearths to the small table at the far right side of the room.

The dark oak table sits low to the ground with matching benches pushed in to keep the space tidy.

Pulling out a bench to sit quietly, I try to follow the routine I've adopted during my time here in Palaena, hopeful to ease some of the anxiety for Ophelia and Cordelia about Jerrick's presence.

Reaching for food on the table, I take in the various types of bread, cheeses, and wines, putting most of my efforts into sifting through the loaves closest to me, wanting to find the freshest slice first.

Ophelia stands closer to Cordelia, brushing Cordelia's long curly blonde locks away from her face, protectively wrapping an arm around her.

Cordelia looks up at Ophelia with mystery playing along her lips, her hands fidgeting with nervousness.

But Jerrick joins me, pulling out the bench and folding his hands, his stare melting into the top of my head. His inhalation has me scrambling for words to keep calm under his gaze.

I am not late in meeting him in the library, so I cannot understand why he is joining me in the kitchen. Still, I keep my shoulders squared, wondering if he wanted extra food.

Yet I'm too shy to ask, opting to speak to my friends instead.

"What are you planning for supper tonight, Ophelia?" I pick up loaves and rolls, testing each one for warmth to choose the freshest for myself to enjoy.

There is a brief pause between the four of us when a low grunt comes from the two women followed shortly after by a stammering Ophelia. "R-Roasted venison and onion soup."

I toss a few rolls between my hands that have similar heat levels, and I decide to eat both.

"Y-Your Majesty," Ophelia's light voice chimes again.

I tense as my title drops from a friend's lips, and I can't stop the scowl forming along my features, wishing they were not intimidated by Jerrick.

He wears his mask as king around most staff and people, letting their own horrendous gossip scare them and keep them in line. But I wish there could be a day when we both didn't have to feel the need to do that.

I reach for a butter knife and cut a sliver of cheese from the block.

"Would you like us to set some food in the main dining room, Your Majesty?"

Cordelia's frail voice fills the void.

Again, the mention of my title.

I stop midway through my routine to look at Cordelia and Ophelia, hoping I can ease their trepidation. "No, I only want to indulge first before making a tray for the library."

I grab a roll and add the slice of cheese. Bringing the food to my mouth, the smells surround my nose. I moan contentedly and close my eyes as I chew the soft bread paired with cheese.

The tastes explode in my mouth, the yeast, spices, and cheese all blending together to send my taste buds into a frenzy.

When my eyes do open, Jerrick's now-heated glare meets them.

I swallow. "Exceptional as always, my friends," I say brightly, taking another bite of my food.

They clasp their hands in a small cheer before Jerrick whirls on them, ceasing their joy. The women lower into another curtsy and return to their workstations.

My jaw slows from their reactions to Jerrick, worried I've altered their mood and working conditions. Rising from the table, I brush the wrinkles from my dress and push in the bench, tidying any messes I created.

Jerrick mirrors my movements, slow but sure to follow me.

I know we will be conversing, but my anxiety about him surprising me this morning in the middle of my routine throws me off balance to the point where I leave for the library without a food tray.

I beam to the women behind me, losing the scent of food as I step farther into the castle's hallway. "Thank you again!"

I take the final bites of my roll to keep my anxiety at bay and allow my thoughts to catch up for when Jerrick and I are alone.

The windows to the right of me have the curtains tied off to the sides, allowing the sun's rays to lighten the halls. Every other one I pass shows the varying amounts of ivy growing up the exterior walls, joined with climbing roses in blues, pinks, reds, and violets.

I make a mental note to visit the courtyards soon to pick a few flowers to enjoy prior to the summer heat creeping in and forcing the outdoors to be unbearable.

I continue through the castle, heading toward the library.

A few staff members pass, carrying bed sheets, candles, and buckets to various levels of the castle. I greet each of them with kindness, regardless of the man lurking behind me, preventing the staff from lingering too long.

I glance to Jerrick matching my strides, observing his strong jawline with a light scruff. Jerrick's black hair is tied back, with a few strands escaping his knotted bun, framing his high cheekbones. He remains silent as we turn down a final well-lit hallway.

I miss the floor's transition from stone to carpeted rug, and my balance shifts.

Jerrick grabs me, pulling me to his hard, leather-clad chest. The hand around my side draws me closer, and our bodies touching as Jerrick's low huff sends shivers down the length of my back.

"Are you alright?" he asks softly.

His proximity unsettles my nerves even as I reply, "Yes, sorry about that. I'm just tired, but I know we have a lot to read today."

He squeezes my side as a handsome grin graces his features. "Well, I actually canceled our plans for today."

I connect the dots for his presence so early in the morning. My throat bobs as I try to understand the motive behind the changed plans.

"But Jonas and I were supposed to hash out ideas for the celebration while you and I were reading. He practically begged me days ago for another meeting."

Jerrick loosens his grip around my waist, dropping his hands to his sides. "As he is my royal advisor, it was easy to give him a reason for the plans I made today."

I cross my arms, skeptical of change. "What plans did you make for us today?"

He mimics my stance, as if he is gearing up for my rebuttal, but I have yet to hear this so-called plan. That damned dimple appears, and my attention darts to it.

Jerrick notices, and it lingers. "You and I are going to head into town to meet the people and some vendors we are hiring for the celebrations," he says, face remaining bright as if our conversation is something he enjoys.

A flicker of excitement raises my curiosity at the prospect of going to the village, but—

Realization has me looking down at my dress.

They, too, will view me as the Snow Queen. The indifferent mask I wear around townsfolk requires preparation, and the drastic change of my day unsettles me.

Spontaneous trips like this don't end well. For anyone.

If I'm going to be scrutinized, the least I can do is look presentable. I swallow thickly while tugging my dress into proper placement. Maybe I should change.

I unfold my arms, smoothing the fabric of my dress and touching my hair, only to have Jerrick cover my hand.

"You don't need a fancy dress to meet them," he assures.

Heat floods my cheeks as his hand runs through the ends of my plait, moving it behind my shoulders.

But he doesn't let go when it is along my spine. Instead, his hold tightens, tugging my hair.

My scalp aches, and the shimmer of warmth twinkling in his gaze has me clenching my thighs.

"You are beautiful as you are," he whispers softly along the bridge of my nose, withdrawing to offer me his hand.

My breath stutters, the man I met in Axidoria making an appearance. This is the first compliment he's given me since my arrival in Palaena, and it sparks heat in my stomach.

I take his hand, craving the luxurious cologne and whiskey to surround me a little while longer.

His hand encompasses mine, squeezing it once and leading me through our home to meet our people as a united front. Jerrick's touch sets my skin ablaze, the heat of him buzzing up and down my arm as he guides me to the stables.

I look for a carriage. Instead, the stable boys bring two horses, strap saddles around them, and fasten the buckles, giving each a small tug as a final check.

I recognize the steed to the right, its black coat different from the spotted coat of the creature adjacent to it.

"Um..." I pause, a phantom pain in my shoulder sending memories flooding to the surface of the last time I was around horses.

Jerrick releases my hand as he approaches the steed, combing its mane and patting it gently. I watch the interaction, completely different from when Jerrick and I rode through Biala Forest with me inching toward death.

"I-I-I don't know how to ride a horse," I stutter, admitting a weakness versus the trauma from my injury.

Yet the memory swirls and thrashes against me as I fight to keep my true hesitation from being voiced.

I turn back to the castle, its stone walls and the solid structure providing me more safety than sitting atop a steed. Lifting my skirt, I allow my feet the freedom to escape into the courtyard, deciding today is the day I should go enjoy the roses.

"Wait!" Jerrick calls back, but I am already increasing my pace.

Crossing through shrubbery, various shades of green foliage surround the courtyard, and I release a breath when a bench comes into view.

I sit against its cold, solid surface, trusting it is indeed a seat I can rest on without the fear of falling. Brushing a hand across my forehead, I wipe the tinge of sweat along the side of my brow before I hunch forward.

My magic ignites in a flurry, winter's kiss caressing my blood and making my breath visible.

Footsteps approach, and the easily recognizable stained boots come into view. The soil sinks in from the weight of the man lowering to a knee in front of me.

"Remember your breathing," Jerrick gently instructs as frost swirls along my skin.

But the possibilities of falling, being scolded, and reliving what happened in Biala Forest make focusing on only my breathing unbearable.

My pulse quickens as I grip the bench, shaking my head, knowing there is too much happening at once.

"I-I can't," I pant, unable to focus. "Please, just go."

I want to prevent him from being harmed and also save myself from showing more vulnerabilities around him. Those wants strum a chord against my rib cage, my powers flaring in response to the idea of my fears coming to pass.

The reminder of damnation I bring to everything and everyone thrums thick in my blood, and eternal loneliness dances in the back of my mind at Niko's past words.

You aren't going to find a husband if you keep acting like this!

I'm not going to have anyone if they truly saw the monster underneath.

Dread holds my lungs in a tight grip, keeping air out of reach.

My disarraying thoughts drift farther from my past injury and fear of falling, pulling every fear I've tucked deep in the back of my mind to the surface, twirling and taunting it and drawing me further into myself.

Jerrick rests a hand on my knee, his steady voice soothing my panic. "I've got you, I'm here."

His touch alerts my magic. The frosted chill creeps across my skin, my power meeting his warmth to help lower my temperature and slow down my heartbeat.

"Breathe," he says softly, his hand rubbing small circles.

I close my eyes, focusing on his touch.

I'm not upset about Jerrick using his magic on me. In fact, I find a small bit of gratitude through my panic, embarrassment weighing heavily over how close I was to an anxiety attack in front of Jerrick and the stable boys.

Jerrick's magic courses through me, quieting my own and granting me a chance to even my breathing without the stress of calming my gifts. When his power pulls away, I can't help but find relief in his aid.

"Th-Thank you. I just—I need a few minutes," I force out through shallow breaths, addressing the boots touching the hem of my dress.

The boots move from my vision, Jerrick's pant leg brushing along my dress as he sits next to me. He cups my chin, pulling it to meet his gaze.

"Would riding with me be better?"

I bite my lip, nodding quietly and knowing that helps solve part of my fear.

He relaxes, smiling softly and releasing my chin to stand. Jerrick eases me up from the bench, and I quickly lace my fingers through his. He rubs the same numbing circles as we walk back to the stables.

I keep my head down, studying my own feet. Other footsteps recede as we approach the saddled horses.

"May I?" Jerrick asks, offering to help me on to the black steed.

I look to the familiar horse, a tremor rushing through me. "Not that one," I blurt, averting my gaze.

Jerrick glances back and forth, a silent understanding shared between us before he guides me to the other horse.

The weight in my chest lightens, and I squeeze his hand in gratitude.

He places his hands on my hips, carefully lifting me into the saddle. When he mounts, his warmth cocoons me, and his arms flex when one wraps around my stomach.

I grab the pommel and rest my other hand atop his, the thought of his fingers trailing downward sends a wave of arousal down to my core.

Jerrick's lingering whisper prickles my skin. "I've got you. Just hang on."

His lips tickle my earlobe, more desire feeding my thoughts and settling between my legs.

30

THE SIGHTS, THE SOUNDS, THE SMELLS

The air is humid, and the summer heat has sweat dripping down the sides of my dress, only soothed by the swift wind.

Our horse trots toward the northeastern village, Yadir. It is small and quaint, with cobblestones lining a few streets and others only having dirt and grimy mud.

Homes of the citizens are built with stone and metal, their roofs varying with metal, stone, and thatch. Each wooden door is accented differently, and some have intricate carvings, metalwork, or colorful wreaths.

Nearing the center of the village, it is easy to see the merchant sections of town versus the market side. The voices of the merchants boom down the street, selling fabrics, metals, tools, spices, and more, as they try to barter and negotiate the right price for every customer.

The market area teems with citizens, traders, and children, and I can't help following the path each child takes, noting how some are laughing, playing, or hurrying toward their families.

Jerrick tightens his hold around my waist as families lower into bows or curtsies as we pass and providing a steady comfort.

Internally, I am pleading to the Makers I am well received, but the churning in my stomach only amplifies.

Many observe us, but I keep my head forward, smiling politely at those making eye contact and glancing away from others who are grimacing.

I acknowledge them, unsure of the relations Jerrick has toward his people as we reach a hitching post.

Jerrick dismounts and ties off the reins around the post. When he offers to help me down, I drift to meet his touch.

I land hard in the mud, my slippers sinking into it, ruining the hem of my gown. A grimace instantly appears as I fight the thick grime, hoping to push through the mud's resistance.

Jerrick holds my waist, providing support as I pull my feet from the sludge.

With my slippers free, I turn to Jerrick in appreciation, wiping the sides of my gown and eying the market. A soft brush of his hand has me reaching to interlock it, earning a small chuckle.

"Nervous there, Frostbite?" he teases as we walk toward the busy streets.

I shrink inwardly, not wishing to draw any more attention, especially when I already was on the brink of a breakdown before arriving.

We make our break into the sunlit street. The cobblestones are smooth and different from some of the villages in Axidoria.

But as we walk down the street where more townspeople stop and greet us, I remain tense and alert, bracing for the whispers and the scorn when others think I am out of earshot.

Through it all, Jerrick's hand remains fastened to mine, squeezing as we pass each person.

We stroll through the vendors and merchants, and I remain silent, waiting for Jerrick to approach and interact with each vendor helping with the upcoming masquerade ball.

I introduce myself and greet the people of Palaena as I would my own, understanding they probably know of the marriage by now, although I do not wish to feed them gossip regarding the events surrounding it. However, I am shocked that many I have conversed with are kind and responsive.

Jerrick addresses everyone with a quiet stoicism while still showing gratitude. And each person we speak with is engaged, lively, and excited to be talking to us.

Our conversations ease the tension in my jaw and shoulders. I even smile brighter with each person, hopeful somehow that my Snow Queen nickname and the cursed winter will not ruin their lives, too.

But my luck runs out when we approach an elderly merchant, a vendor with baskets full of crafted metals which might decorate the ballroom in the castle.

The hunched-over man is sun kissed with grayed hair. He is finalizing a trade when his brown eyes catch mine, recognition hardening his expression.

Fear locks up my spine as his gaze shifts into pure hatred. As much as I want to shy away, I brace myself for an unhappy resident of Palaena.

The man spits at my feet, disgusted, before Jerrick or I can even greet him. "I know who you are, *Snow Queen*."

I bristle at the nickname, my failures evident and exposed amongst the hushed silence transitioning throughout the market.

Eyes all around us burn into me, the back of my skull, drawing my magic forth. I have a death grip on Jerrick's hand now, hoping he can sense my power awakening.

"Have you so tired of freezing your kingdom you sought to come here and ruin our lives as well?" the merchant challenges.

The glimmer of hope for these people seeing beyond my powers dies with his question.

Unsure of the customs, the dynamic of the people, I don't know how to act. I am too petrified and caught off guard to do or say anything, terrified my magic could come out to play and hurt others. I remain silent and try to meditate away my powers, but the decision whether to let him finish his insults or react strains my concentration.

I cannot show frost and snow manifesting on my skin. It'll only prove his accusations true.

Lips graze my cheek, a crackling jolt of heat descending from my face straight to my core.

It seeps over the winter threatening to climb up my chest, guiding my breathing into a steady calm.

I glance at Jerrick to extend my gratitude for the distraction, but his menacing glare is focused on the elderly merchant.

"That is my wife you spit at," Jerrick says darkly, stalking toward the man till they are almost chest to chest.

The merchant steels his stance, a muscle ticking in his jaw, but it is nothing compared to Jerrick's tall frame hovering over him.

"The Snow Queen will ruin us." The merchant points at me. "Everyone should stay away from her. She is a merciless temptress! Fooling even you, Your Majesty, with her wretchedness!"

The villagers watch in silence, and the unfolding scene cracks my heart open, the joy of thriving snuffed away from the entire square.

All because of me.

I never thought hearing it spoken would hurt so much. Maybe it was because it was coming from a stranger and not my own people.

But when the man opens his mouth again, Jerrick grabs him. "You know *nothing* of that which you speak. You will apologize to My Queen this instant."

The merchant fights Jerrick's hold as if even saying those words would condemn him to Oblivion. The hatred remains in his eyes as he lashes out at Jerrick.

"She has doomed Axidoria, and she has come to bring doom upon Palaena as well. And when that day comes, it'll be all your fault."

Jerrick's entire demeanor shifts, altering into a darkened persona of the King of Palaena. He chuckles darkly, a smirk emphasizing his lone dimple.

"Well, if a little colder weather brings doom, I would *hate* for you to learn what I bring." The King of Palaena leans away, showmanship and awe drawing everyone in.

"Do you want to know what I bring?" Jerrick asks the elderly merchant curiously.

The air thickens as my face pales, knowing what Jerrick intends to do.

The merchant's brown eyes widen, realizing the king is waiting for his response. "Wh-What?" he stutters wearily.

Jerrick leans into the man's face, smiling viciously as his face turns cold and lethal.

"Your death."

The merchant's mouth falls, abruptly collapsing to the floor.

My own heart stops at the man lying on the cobblestones.

Lifeless, unmoving—*dead*.

There are no screams, no reactions. Only silence thick enough to send goose bumps up my spine.

Jerrick addresses the crowd. "You will *all* show the same respect you have for me to my wife. She is your queen as I am your king." He pauses, pointing at me. "She is here to help our kingdoms achieve peace."

His passionate voice embosoms my heart, and Niko's plan to attack Jerrick's home weighs me down. This is not the first time Jerrick has defended me in public, but it is the first time I don't feel scared.

Instead, I'm relieved someone did what I never could do for myself.

When he lowers his hand, the crowd still hangs on by a thread, including me, unsure of his next move. He straightens his shoulders as he turns to the crowd, making eye contact with everyone.

"Be wise to remember this day that between the two of us, she is merciful." Jerrick lowers his voice with a promise. "I am not. Now go."

His eyes rest on me at the finality of his words, and voices boom to life. Citizens weave around us, a few village guards approaching to attend to the elderly man who was alive mere minutes ago.

The dark aura surrounding Jerrick remains as I approach. The darkness of his mask and his curse ebbs away when our blue eyes lock.

I take his hand and interlace our fingers, squeezing. I should be terrified this same hand ended someone's life seconds ago, but I can't stop myself from running circles over it, his defense of me shocking and comforting.

Jerrick escorts us from the scene, and it isn't until we leave the crowded section of the market that I want to understand his motivations.

"Why did you do that?" I ask.

We pace a few steps quietly, our hands still linked, and ignore those who pass.

Only when there is a break between people does Jerrick respond. "He disrespected you, and to disrespect you is to disrespect the crown."

I nod, understanding the finality in his tone, and don't try to push him. When we turn down an alley that leads toward more shops and homes, I can't help but voice another thought.

"Can your magic always do that?"

Jerrick chuckles lightly as if he knew that would be my next question.

I half expect him to sweep it under the rug with a deflection but am surprised when he says, "It depends on whether I've hunted or not, but the majority of the time, I have to be touching someone."

I gulp a silent nod, the small admission revealing more about his powers and sending doubt rippling through my mind over mine and Niko's plans. I try to remember how often he has used his gifts on me, worried there are more instances than we have discussed.

"I don't use my magic as often as you think," he comments, as if knowing my thoughts.

"*Sure* you don't," I blurt, my mind reeling over every interaction I've had with this man, questioning my own feelings and bodily reactions.

He has used his abilities on me, and I know what it felt like in the moment, but what if there were other times I haven't?

We come to the end of the alley, I flick my eyes left and right, waiting for Jerrick to guide us in the next direction. But when he doesn't move, I tilt my head up.

The pale blue eyes I've grown used to seeing most days are not visible. Instead, his head is lowered, and he is avoiding my gaze.

He removes his hand from mine as if it was burned.

"I know what it's like to have something control you. I-I just killed a man."

His voice is solemn in the quiet.

The admission and lack of Jerrick's warmth cleaves at my heart. But I stand there, finding myself waiting for something within me to change. To have my questions answered and feel disdain or dislike for the quiet king in front of me.

But nothing happens...

Instead, there is a tug of understanding settling that his curse, and our powers connect us in more ways than I had considered. Not only that, but this man before me has offered me answers, given me everything he could regarding my mother and father, and has given me more knowledge about my gifts.

We have made no progress on his curse, and, yet he still has done this without any reward.

For me.

A quiet whisper resonates in my rib cage, my gut flipping, shaking my entire core as my trust and understanding for this king—this man—in front of me grows.

I exhale shakily, my stomach still reeling as I take another leap.

Reaching for his hand, I force his long fingers to latch onto mine once more. When our hands are linked, I wait, trying to sense the shift in my emotions and in my blood with him now touching me. Relief floods me as my emotions and feelings remain intact.

I run my fingertips in circles along his hand in our mutual silence, a comfort I hope will let him know I understand that small vulnerability. "I know," I whisper.

It isn't until his eyes meet mine that my heart skips.

"I-I try not to—you know, *kill* people," he confesses.

"I know," I repeat.

His curse controls him, and his magic and his feelings about it match my own for my abilities.

"Do you, though?" he asks worriedly, as if I cannot relate.

I tuck a loose wisp of black hair away from his eyes, his scar shining for me to admire as I smile softly. "I do."

Jerrick takes a long breath as my favorite smile of his illuminates his entire face. His dimple scrunches his scar in all the right places, and my own lips tug up into a wide grin at the sight.

We turn to venture on, and children run across the new street, playing with sticks, touching each other, and running in circles. Nostalgia waves through me at the interaction, remembering games from my childhood that Runa and I would play together.

I shudder at the thought of ruining children's lives with my cursed winter.

Manifesting my gifts beyond myself is like starting back at the beginning, and I can't help but wonder if drawing a large amount of magic will drain me.

If what I am already doing is exhausting, will there be a way to melt it rather than remove winter from Axidoria?

I've not made enough progress in learning about my abilities, and if I am going to avoid that elderly man's prediction, I need to push myself and find my limits. I halt my steps, looking at Jerrick with another question playing on my lips, hoping it will keep me focused on the present.

"Have you ever been able to give rather than take with your abilities?"

Confusion etches across his features as he turns to me, biting his lip in contemplation. He offers me a small shrug. "I've never tried."

I dip my head and lower it in contemplation, trying to puzzle together how to stop my winter.

Jerrick tilts my chin up to him, and his eyes scan mine.

"You okay?" he asks softly, leather and cologne thickening in the air.

I blink, seizing the courage to practice more of my gifts. "I'd like to start training."

A hint of skepticism graces his features, and I take it as a challenge. I close my eyes with excitement in my veins to finally show him what I have been meaning to since he last went hunting.

His hold on my chin disappears as I tap into my breathing, my thoughts directing me to my powers. I harness my strength and show Jerrick what I can do, what I need to do, and breathe through my own beliefs, my own encouragement, and Jerrick's supportive guidance.

Lifting the palm of my hand, I see my breathing turns cold, and the glimpse of ice prickling across me ripples down my arms in stride. I channel that energy, focusing on targeting all magic toward my hand.

My eyes open to a beautiful snowflake twisting in the center of my palm. Pride shines through as I nurture this gift, gently coaxing it back into slumber. When the sensation of magic in my core has ebbed, Jerrick's eyes shimmer.

"We can start our first lesson tomorrow," Jerrick says.

His hasty reply earns me a moment of success, the relief of something finally working out for me, and I can't help wrapping my arms around him in an embrace.

I've caught him off guard, but I still whisper softly into his chest, "Thank you."

Only then do large arms encompass me, pulling me in tighter and planting a kiss on my forehead.

"Always," he whispers into my hair, my head buzzing when we resume walking.

Jerrick's movements cease upon our arrival at a shop with wide windows surrounded by rose bushes.

My eyes widen at the displays of gowns in varying colors. Each gown is decadent and vibrant, details visible even from far away.

"This is the best seamstress in our kingdom, and I thought it would be good to save best for last by picking up a gift for you," Jerrick says, continuing toward the shop's entrance, holding the door for me.

"You—You got a gift for me?" Guilt swirls from his thoughtfulness, unsure of what I did to warrant this. "But I don't need any gifts, Jerrick."

"Don't worry, it's a surprise."

He winks mischievously as we both enter the shop. Jerrick releases my hand to close the door behind us, leaving my heart to somersault at his words.

I follow his movements, uncomfortable at the thought of a surprise. A surprise is a change in routine, and I live off my routine. Anytime it's different, my entire day needs adjusting.

When he faces me, I swear he notices my train of thought. I evade him by glancing at the shop, a small gasp escaping.

Varying fabrics hang across the sides of the shop, organized by hue and material. I am obsessed by the rainbow of color. Every tone is separated by little ladders with patterns, line work, and accessories that can be added into a gown's ensemble.

Even though I could stare at the interior prism of color, the gowns are what have me stepping further, examining each one with envy. They are all so intricate and original, nothing like the day dress I currently wear or the outfits back home.

The thought has me inspecting my outfit, making sure the dirtied hem does nothing to touch these stunning gowns.

A large wooden table built into the foundation of the store sits at the back. Packages big and small are being wrapped by an elderly woman.

She looks fragile, but each task she does is accompanied by a soft hum, which lingers in the shop. Her short pixie hair is light brown, with mixed sections of white around her face. She is short and petite, and there are wrinkles visible from where I stand.

The more I observe her, the more I admire the tenderness of each fold she makes on the emerald gown she fits into a medium-sized box.

She lifts her head, warm skin complementing her own ensemble as her brown eyes meet mine. Her upturned eyes flash over toward Jerrick as a grimace covers her features.

Why does she look so familiar?

Confused we've done something, I look at Jerrick to see his demeanor shift. He runs a hand through his hair, offering her a wave in greeting.

My brow remains raised while the woman maneuvers around the table to approach us.

Her stomps creak on each wooden plank of her shop. When she comes face-to-face with us, I lean away from her as she rises to her tiptoes to swat Jerrick on the side of his head, leaving my jaw on the floor.

She *swatted* the King of Palaena.

Jerrick winces as she crosses her arms and shakes her head.

Looking between them, I try to answer questions no one seems to be addressing. Who is this woman? Why isn't Jerrick doing anything?

I grip the sides of my dress, ready to lift my skirts to flee if this woman tries to swat me. Sweet Makers, I don't think I would risk coming to the best seamstress if getting a swat was her form of payment.

"*Months* without paying a visit to your grandmother and *then* you show up without warning and with a wife no one has seemed to have met?" she scolds, her tight voice heightening at the mention of wife.

The anger laced toward Jerrick delays me briefly while he rubs the spot she smacked.

Realization dawns, and my heart constricts at the thought of having a grandmother as part of this new family.

"You're—You're his grandmother?" I ask, my own grandparents flooding through my mind.

My ancestors all died when Runa and I were very young, only flitting memories of them watching us when Mother and Father traveled.

Her hooded brown eyes give me a once-over, scanning slowly down my frame. They lingered at the dirty hem of my dress, sending self-consciousness to the forefront, and I lift my skirts above her shop's floor. With one brow raised, she judges Jerrick's bride.

I shift uncomfortably.

"Yes, and I suppose that makes you my new granddaughter," she declares, drawing my attention.

Jerrick clears his throat. "Gran, this is Queen Tove of Axidoria and Palaena."

The woman humphs in acknowledgment.

"This is Frida Johannesen, my mother's mother," he says to me.

Paintings of Jerrick's mother are few and far between in the castle, but her features match that of her mother's, answering my question from when I first laid eyes on the seamstress.

Unsure of whether to speak first or not, I wait for her to meet my gaze. When she does, I rush to break the silence.

"A pleasure to meet you, Frida."

She tosses her hand as she huffs again, turning for the rear of her shop as if she isn't meeting a monarch.

I flick my eyes to Jerrick while her back is turned to us, only to see him gesture for us to follow her. Following his lead, I allow his tall frame to shield me, knowing he has had years of dealing with this woman.

Her steps on the wooden slats of her shop creak quietly, but mine and Jerrick's are louder, making this visit more uncomfortable than I would have liked.

I keep a firm hold of my dress, preventing it from touching her displays of fabrics and gowns.

"Short or long?" Frida asks Jerrick as we meet her opposite of her workstation.

Jerrick braces his hands against the table, and I follow, careful to avoid her bubble.

A sigh escapes Jerrick as he responds, "Short."

I stand and observe their interaction, unsure of what to do. My thoughts swirl as I try to piece together the meaning behind the words as Frida inclines her head, rotating to her shelves of boxed orders, grabbing one from the very bottom and putting it between the three of us.

She goes to open the box, but Jerrick shoots out a hand to stop her.

"It's a surprise, Gran." Jerrick earns an even deeper scowl from Frida, but he tries to win her over by adding, "Besides, I trust your work. It's going to be your best creation."

What surprises me is Frida's instant grin. Her face wrinkles in pure joy at Jerrick's words, and she pats his hand, holding his cheek with her other palm.

Frida pecks both of Jerrick's cheeks affectionately, and Jerrick returns kisses to his grandmother.

"I knew my sweet Liva raised you right," she chides, bringing a hint of color to Jerrick's cheeks.

I almost question her statement, still unsure of the man next to me.

The hint of pink remains on his face as he pulls away, withdrawing a large sack of coins and dropping it on top of the workstation.

Frida's eyes bulge, and she reaches for the sack as Jerrick takes the boxed package. She wiggles it, the sound of coins smacking against each other as she smirks. It's uncanny how similar it is to Jerrick's.

"Always treating your Gran Gran right."

Completely lost to the conversation, I'm surprised when Frida acknowledges me again with another once-over before adding, "You better be doing the same for your wife."

The warning in her tone takes me by surprise, and I can't stop myself from attempting to save Jerrick from another smack on the head.

I tell her, "Jerrick has been very kind to me, ma'am." I maintain eye contact with Frida, Jerrick's bewilderment burning into the side of my head.

My cheeks heat.

Frida beams in approval, and I immediately fiddle with my gown, desperate to distract myself from speaking again.

"We should be going now. Thank you again, Gran," Jerrick says.

His footsteps turn toward the exit, creaking on each wooden panel, and I meet Frida's gaze again. "It was a pleasure, ma'am."

I dart off after Jerrick.

31

CATACLYSM

The clink and clatter of each dish Ophelia washes is the only reminder that I am delaying the inevitable. Her tall frame hunches over the basin, scrubbing with a different amount of strength as Cordelia dries each one, placing them into a stack on the opposite workstation.

Their silent workflow and loving touches mesmerize my attention as I sit and help myself to a few of the hot rolls Cordelia pulled from the hearth.

"If you avoid it any longer, he is going to show up and drag you to the training arena himself," Ophelia chides, accidentally dropping a clean dish into the filled sink.

Cordelia inclines her head in agreement.

I *hate* being rushed.

"I need to eat first," I lie while taking another bite of the fifth fresh buttery roll I've treated myself to this morning.

"Sure." Cordelia faces me with a stack full of plates.

Placing them on the counter, she wipes her hands on her apron, giving me the look. "I know our cooking and company is great, but we know who you'd much rather be spending your time with." Cordelia puckers her lips in a kissing motion, breaking into a wicked smirk.

I pause at the jab when Ophelia snorts. Without thinking, I aim two rolls at their foreheads.

Cordelia sees it coming and ducks, and shockingly, the roll strikes true and smacks Ophelia on the back of her head.

A dish falls, splattering water all over her as she turns to face me, rubbing her sore spot. "Hey!" Ophelia exclaims, but I point at them.

"I said one nice thing about him, and now the two of you are jumping to conclusions thinking that I—"

"Thinking what?"

Cordelia and Ophelia's eyes go wide at the low voice filling the room.

I lower my hand as my friends drop into a curtsy before flashing me a sneaky grin as they resume their tasks. I roll my eyes at the low snickers they give when they return to their duties.

Intrusive thoughts have me stuffing the bread I was eating in my mouth, seeking for something, *anything*, to get me out of answering his question.

Footsteps indicate he's moved closer, the usual leather and cologne scent lighter, replaced by something crisp as Jerrick meets me at my side.

Jerrick's command echoes in the void. "Clear the area, please, ladies."

While I chew through the roll, I plead for them to stay, only to watch them leave without a second thought. I shake my head, realizing too late I could have commanded them to stay, forcing confusion between the four of us and keeping me in the kitchens versus the training arena.

Not that I am scared of training. I'm scared of each day inching us closer to the ball.

Betina and I spoke last night, confirming Niko and I will be able to talk alone soon. While I should rejoice in seeing his face, I can't shake the feeling of calling his plan off.

I don't want to hurt anyone, yet I can't stop thinking if the plan works, the ones hurt the most would be me and Jerrick.

Jerrick guides the chair out next to me, sitting down and folding his hands. "You were supposed to meet me for training this morning."

I swallow the remainder of my food, reaching for another roll to delay my response, only to have him snatch my hand, halting my efforts. I hiss at the light shove and glare at him.

He glares right back.

"Let's go." He pushes from the bench.

Sighing in defeat, I rise as Jerrick turns to leave the kitchens, expecting me to follow.

He leads, and I chase after him, his long strides making it difficult to keep up. I wish he would match my stride, remembering the countless times he's done it before, only to wipe away the thought.

This brisk walk is a form of reprimand for not being on time.

The doors into the training arena are opened by the guards standing nearby. They offer a silent nod as Jerrick dismisses them. I thank them as we pass through.

Jerrick walks straight into the center circle as he removes his tightened vest, sword belt, and dagger. He gestures to everything surrounding us.

Stone rises along the walls and pillars, holding most of the architecture of the training area. A few of the columns are shadowed and hidden away, with some benches and equipment holding weapons. The overhang bordering the domain is less shaded than I remember when I toured the castle.

The center of the grounds is roped off into a circle lined with sand. Buckets and towels are on the outer edge near stacks of hay. A sweltering breeze drifts throughout, causing the sand in the circle to rise and fall.

I forwent a dress today, opting for the tunic and trousers I have grown comfortable wearing, knowing pants would grant me more of a reprieve from falling flat on my face.

I trudge through the piles of sand and join Jerrick in the center as he rests his sword against a stack of hay.

His hair is fully tied back instead of his normal half-back look, displaying his scar fully with no shame. The ruggedness is harsh but handsome, his features still sending my stomach into a nervous frenzy of lust.

The fire within me is extinguished when he commands sternly, "Now, show me."

I swallow down the fear, doubt, and failure, trying to remember the readings and meditation I've combed through. The muscle memory kicks in, the small flickers of magic growing more from the little practice I've done at the end of a long day.

I remind myself that this is for Axidoria, no matter how overwhelming my stress has grown as of late. My eyes drift closed, combatting my emotions. If I am not in tune with myself, my magic won't call to me.

My breathing is easy to track, the beginning of this process easier each time. My thoughts wander. I coax the thrall of power to life and tap into it, feeding and nurturing it while denying the darkness of my heart.

Liar, betrayer, monster.

My magic flares, pulsing in my body, and I wince.

I mask my deceit, needing the ice and frost to listen, to obey, to manifest. I settle back on breathing when my gift tries to seep out beyond my intentions.

A shift in the sand breaks my concentration. Anger curls in my gut at the distraction, needing this training to work now more than ever.

I open my eyes to Jerrick nearing, and I can't stop my venom. "Keep away from me," I demand, wanting and needing to make vast progress.

Jerrick's surprise at my anger restrains him from ignoring my request.

My small victory dies when I glance down, a gasp of shock escaping me. I jump back from the frost shooting outward, ice blooming above the sand.

I peer over to Jerrick, whose eyes widen as he inspects my power.

Shit, I wasn't expecting that.

Power still courses deep in my chest, my concern at the mess and Jerrick taking more precedence.

"Brilliant," he commends, taking a step toward the ice. "This is the perfect way to test your idea from yesterday."

Panic grips my heart as he advances.

I shake my head, my power twinkling with delight at my fear surfacing and its winter flourishing on the ground. My emotions coax more magic to flood from me.

I can't focus on that right now; he is still approaching.

I stretch my hand out in warning. "No, don't!"

Frost bursts from my fingertips directly for him.

He lunges out of harm's way, following where the swirls of snow flurries lead, on a pile of hay that has ice expanding in all directions.

I gape in horror. I've done it again.

Jerrick glances back and forth as I stare at the hay, and my hand in distress. Now, instead of magic coming from my core, it's stemming from the ends of my hands and feet, cold air sizzling as small snowflakes bloom down my palm.

"No, please stop," I plea to the Makers.

This is too much. This is what happened when my powers first manifested.

Cracking and the bitter plunge of disaster excite my cursed winter even more.

I want to focus on meditating, but memories come crashing in.

"Frostbite."

Caution laces Jerrick's voice.

My heart breaks because this day is not going as he had planned, and he will become another person to fear me.

"I-I can't stop it!"

Everything I've learned and read about is tossed to the side, replaced with the past. My heart hammers in my throat, my pulse quickening with terror.

"I know you can," Jerrick says softly, stepping closer.

My past relives itself before my very eyes, and I take yet another step away from him. "*Please*, don't come any closer, Jer."

Guilt claws underneath my skin as tears line my eyes.

I... I can't control myself. I will *never* be able to control myself.

I can't blink my tears away fast enough as Jerrick ignores my plea, coming closer and closer, my heart breaking more and more, forcing me further and further.

"Just try."

His voice breaks softly, and I contort from the visible pain etched on his features.

Just try.

Those two words cut deeper than any I've ever heard from Jerrick. The repeated words haunt me and plague me. He isn't affected by the frost yet, and regret and horror of the past replaying itself again in front of me is the only hope I hold.

My heart breaks as I give him a final look in apology before closing my eyes to try the impossible.

A tear escapes, and it warms my cold cheeks slightly, drying slowly, as I turn all my attention to it.

No worries, no fears, no feelings.

Just the focus and awareness of my body.

From my head to my toes, I figuratively run through every nerve, every tendon, every muscle of my body. Searching and scouring for that fleck of abnormality that is and isn't a part of me.

My magic has always come from my core, the sensation of it being a somersault of kisses coasting up and around me. Yet this time, my power darted forth without any notice, and I'll be damned if I let it happen again.

"That's it, good girl," Jerrick encourages.

The enticement of pleasing him and not failing him increases my drive as a long-inhaled breath leads me to where that flicker of power stems from.

My heart.

My lips quiver as air leaves my lungs, and more tears fall down my cheeks.

I paint the image of my heart, bitter and frozen from the power rippling from it. A figurative hand reaches to hold and cradle it close, and I want to turn away from the cold and the frost, but it is a part of me.

It is a part of me I need to harness and live with.

With effort, I try to pull from past and present, moments that are with and without my magic. I fight to keep my emotions in check, knowing many of my happy memories are now connected with sadness and grief.

But I push through the darkness, allowing myself to feel.

The first ballad I composed, Runa's talented voice paired up in the accompaniment, Mother and Father's loving faces and hugs. Betina's laugh and taunts like ones I would get from Niko.

The first time I manifested snow...

The wonderment, the awe.

I push beyond, recollecting the brief times I've felt comforted by my gift, Jerrick's presence integral to a lot of those moments.

I imagine his dimple, his spontaneous sincerity, and his kiss. Our entire history replays itself in my mind, lingering most on his teachings and understanding him.

Contorting my face, I sniff deeply through the brighter moments of life I've experienced, and finally choosing to wrap them around my heart with love instead of mourning, hoping my magic will listen, will understand.

Dorit's kind words about my grief being a part of me as well as healing becoming a part of me drift in the back of my mind.

I am not happy nor am I sad. I am both. I am all and so my magic should be.

The overwhelming acknowledgment repeats in my mind. I replay and relive each memory as if they were each a prayer, over and over, beginning to lose track of how many times I've repeated it.

The endless pit of regret grows with each passing day, and I finally find my breath easy to track.

Inhale.

You're doing the best you can, Tove.

Exhale.

It is okay not to be okay.

Inhale.

Frostbite.

Exhale.

Just try.

Hands land on me, and a yelp escapes at the pale blue eyes so close, so near, to mine.

Jerrick's features are glowing from the wide grin he wears, dimple on full display and teeth shining brightly.

"You did it." He points at the impacted stack of hay behind him, showing all signs of frost and ice gone.

I stopped it from expanding and drew it back into myself, but the toll of doing that small amount was crippling.

I am nowhere near ready for the magnitude of drawing in Axidoria's winter.

I can't even melt ice.

I don't think I'll ever be able to—

Concern laces his question, noticing the lack of joy on my end. "Wh-What's wrong?"

The respite of Jerrick unharmed floods my thoughts. His words, my exhaustion, and the realization of how far I still have to go pull me back into the void of despair.

I clamp down to suppress the well of emotions stirring, but I slump and my lips tremble.

I can't do this here.

The need to escape, his proximity, and the breakthrough I made buckles me down. I drop my head, arms folding around me as I recoil from his touch.

I kick off against the unfrozen sand as I make a run for it, tears running down my cheeks as I break apart more and more. The sharp sting of unworthiness and guilt push me faster toward the exit.

I almost make it to the threshold of the training arena before something hard yanks my arm, whipping me against a wall. I hide my face, pushing through my exhaustion to escape Jerrick's hold.

He responds by pushing his hips into mine.

I'm unable to think with how right it feels to have him close, the haunted unknown of hurting him sending tremors throughout my body as I fall apart. I avert my gaze, trying to escape, but Jerrick shakes me, halting my fight.

"Look at me, Frostbite," he orders, his voice oozing with power as he towers over me, the nickname making everything worse.

If I hurt him, I never will hear him call me that again.

A choked whimper escapes, and I cover my mouth.

Jerrick holds my chin, looking down the bridge of his nose. My tear-filled eyes meet his, the anger diminishing from his gaze and softening.

"Tell me what is wrong." This time, the order comes with more of a plea, tenderness filling the dip in his voice. "Don't hide your pain from me."

I shake my head as the well of emotions burst, and I break.

He relaxes his hold on me as I burrow into him. I clutch his tunic, crying harder in this small space he has engulfed me in, knowing I don't deserve this.

I don't deserve any of this.

The guilt of my deception joins in with the rest of the memories eating at me when his cologne floods my senses. My magic is spent from the breakthrough, my body is spent from the lies I've told and the memories that won't shut off.

He pulls me from the wall, arms wrapping me tightly, trying to anchor me to the present. Even the kindness of his touch forces my cries to turn into hyperventilating.

"I'm here, Frostbite. Let me help you," he whispers delicately, cradling my head.

I weep, tremors rocking through me and refusing to abate. "Y-Y-You can't h-h-help me."

He tugs on my braid, forcing my neck back. The concern in his expression breaks my heart even more.

To think, if I didn't control myself, I would have lost him.

"*Please*, let me?"

His voice cracks from the smallest of movements of his mouth, carrying the softest of pleas I've ever heard.

My tears fall as I reach to hold his face for the first time, my heart swelling when he doesn't react, grateful he is someone who doesn't flinch or cower away from the monster I am.

I pull his forehead to mine, sobbing through each strenuous syllable. "I-I almost lost *you* how I lost her."

"Lost who?" Jerrick asks between my shaky inhaled breaths.

I confess through a choked sob, "*Runa*."

The memory of her death and what I'd done hit me full force, a part of my life I will never escape.

I cling tightly to Jerrick, clutching him close and squeezing, as my demons voice my greatest loss. "I almost killed you how I killed my sister."

32

MY BED IS THE
ONLY SAFE PLACE

I twist and curl my fingers in Jerrick's cotton tunic. Remorse, exhaustion, and grief thrash through me at the admission that has tormented me for years.

The guilt over what I'd done has been hidden, the knowledge of it shared only with Niko. And the secret we keep remains concealed from the world, surfacing in my sleep, never letting me forget the aftermath of what happened the fateful day my mother and sister died.

I've become too familiar with how my magic affects me inwardly versus the terrorizing trauma when my abilities expel through my fingertips and feet.

The darkened thoughts add to Jerrick's earlier surprised expression, suggesting that if his life, too, were taken by me, his face would join in haunting my nights.

I squeeze him harder, my fingers now running through his hair, fearful I'd never be able to see him again.

What would his death do to Jonas? To *Palaena*?

The sheer possibility of it unsettles my nerves, making it hard to breathe as the arena closes in around me, plunging my shame and regret deeper into my soul.

If Niko and I follow through with his plan, I won't be able to live with myself for condemning an entire kingdom.

The merchant's words of warning echo in my mind, making the guilt unbearable.

Jerrick keeps me close, rubbing my back and holding my head. He threads his fingers through the plait along my scalp.

The silence is only broken up by each shuttered breath I release.

He leans me against the wall, holding my upper arms.

The cold, solid stone mixed with the wood of the threshold anchors me as he whispers, "Frostbite."

I slouch, exhausted, as Jerrick grips the sides of my face, angling it up to his while his thumbs seek to dry away each tear on my soaked cheeks.

Blinking away the tears, I focus on his softened expression, and when our eyes meet, the tenderness he offers cripples me more.

There is a temptation to ask him to use his gifts to make me feel something, *anything* other than this guilt and grief, but the courage never comes.

Instead, he curves his body over mine, the pale blue irises scanning my face.

"I am a *monster*."

I am a liar, a murderer, a betrayer—and a wicked, *wretched* Snow Queen.

Jerrick's features furrow. "No, you are not a monster."

I shake my head, denying his claims. "I've hurt so many people. Isn't that what monsters do?"

Jerrick's lips thin, and he blinks slowly.

He sees the truth in my statement, though he does not know just how much Niko and I intended to hurt people—to hurt him.

I don't want to be tied to the name Snow Queen, yet I have been preparing this entire time for Niko's fight, which I never wanted and need to stop.

"Monsters do hurt people," Jerrick says, confirming my thoughts. "But monsters do not care, Frostbite. You do." He rests his head against mine.

I pinch my eyes closed at his statement.

I've never wanted to hurt anyone and am desperate to ensure it will not happen here in Palaena.

My lips tremble, and disbelief squeezes my chest that I thought this man to be a monster.

More tears fall as I shake my head, unworthy of Jerrick's kind words.

"I know how this grief feels. I've been where you are," he says, voice quiet.

My stomach hollows out, realizing the depth of his words.

The same day he killed his father was... the same day my mother died...

The same day I killed my sister.

I stare deeply into his eyes, seeing the vulnerable admission for what it is.

We both inherited these gifts—these *curses* simultaneously. And yet here he is, well-trained in his power, knowledgeable, and aware.

He does not show any signs of his grief like I do. Instead, he has spent his entire time trying to manage himself, his kingdom, his magic, and his curse.

How does it not swallow him whole? How did he get past doing what he did?

"H-How do you do it? How did you find your happy again?"

My voice strains as the one thing I have wished for these last five years is laid bare to someone who has everything together.

"I have not found my happy," Jerrick admits.

My hopeful heart is crushed, but my soul calls to Jerrick again. "How did you heal?"

Jerrick sees me—has *always* seen me—and has never once backed down.

A flicker of life gleams in his gaze. His features relax as his thumbs caress my cheeks.

He leans in, and the comfort of that should scare me, but it feels so right—so perfect.

"Accept yourself, Frostbite. Flaws and all. Only then will healing and controlling your magic get easier. And maybe then you'll find your happy again."

I don't hesitate with my response. "I don't know if I'll ever be able to do that."

He kisses my forehead, sending a twinge of warmth to spread from tenderness I don't deserve.

Selfishly, I indulge in the heat of it, and when our eyes lock again, determination and hope shimmers in the depths of his blue eyes.

"If anyone can, it's you."

Jerrick's kiss lingers as he leaves me to my thoughts in the training arena, but really, he granted me the freedom to run through the castle.

I push my strides hard, taking the brunt of my exhaustion and emotions, stomping into the varying surfaces of stone, rug, and stairs, inching me closer to my chambers in hopes of an escape or a reprieve—anything to prevent me from feeling anymore.

If anyone can, it's you.

I want to banish the sentence from my mind. Anything to remove the image of his eyes, his kindness, his touch. My deepest secret confessed to a man who I believed to be my enemy yet never was.

The guilt of lying to Jerrick has been eating me alive this entire time. I've been pretending to help break his curse, using it for my own personal gain to learn about my magic and to stall him while preparing Axidoria for battle.

What have I done?

I want to slap myself in reprimand, hating how my mind and body are at war with one another when it comes to this man. My heart skips from the heat on my brow, forcing me to count the stairs below me.

Don't trip, Tove.

I bite my lip in concentration, almost tripping on the final step, grabbing the wall for balance. I hunch into myself, exhaustion taking over. But I fight through it, catching my breath to push on.

Someone coughs at the end of the hallway, and I shoot upright when the shadows reveal Jonas coming from my chambers. "Are you alright?" he asks, concern raising his brow.

I don't know how to answer, and the words I try to formulate into a full sentence won't make any sense. Heaving, I throw my hands and head up in defeat. It's pointless anyway.

I sulk down the hall to him and to my chambers, and he follows as I open the door, gesturing for him to enter.

"What is it?" he asks again.

"Just get inside," I command, my voice harsher than I intended.

He doesn't react, and I trail him, pausing to close the door.

Spinning to my bed, I wave toward the lounge chair for Jonas to sit and make himself comfortable as I flop onto the bed. I have not a care for the world as I roll, grab a pillow to hold over my face, and scream.

My screams are loud but muffled, and I continue until the scratchiness of my throat forces them to halt. Even then, I take my time before removing the pillow, throwing it off to the side and staring up into the canopy of my bed.

"Training bad, huh?" Jonas asks.

I humph a reply, exaggerating the sigh to convey more than what I can vocalize right now.

Jonas hums as we sit in the silence while I try to get over the ringing in my ears caused by my screams. One thing I have come to admire about Jonas is his patience.

Every time I've met with him, he has been observant and attentive, offering me a chance to voice my concerns and always finding a compromise. He's been like that outside of the meetings, too, recognizing everyone's body language and moods, while navigating a way to ease any tension in a room.

But the silence he offers now...

I am not sure if it is helping or making me feel worse.

Jonas clears his throat, breaking the silence. "I know magic can be tricky and difficult, but from what Jer told me—"

"*Don't* bring him up right now," I groan.

Jerrick's words and features are still strong in my mind. I am in a knot of feelings toward him, the biggest being my attraction, along with the regret for believing a fight was the best way to go home.

I need another option.

It is Jonas's turn to sigh, and the squeaking sound of him standing from the lounge chair grabs my attention. He approaches my bed, perching a knee up to climb on and join me in the middle.

The bed sinks down with the added weight, and he lies on his back to join me in staring at the ceiling. I rest one of my hands on my chest, and the other Jonas takes and locks with his.

The comfort is calming and reassuring, and I take what I can get as my mind roams on how to fix everything.

"When we were kids, I remember Jer always wearing the mantle of big brother, taking it seriously by taunting me, bullying me. You know, the whole shebang. It used to annoy the shit out of me," he says.

A light chuckle escapes at the thought of Jerrick and Jonas getting into it as kids, seeing glimpses of that whenever the two are in the library with me. And yet I don't know why he is offering me this information.

Jonas is closed off when it comes to his brother, but I remain quiet as my gaze turns from the ceiling to Jonas, the waves of his dark hair hiding his ears while he works his jaw.

"When our mother died, we were only teenagers, and my father took her death hard and blamed it on us. Jer did everything he could to keep it from affecting me. Sometimes, he would succeed, and other times... not so much," he forces out.

The thought of a parent doing such a thing to their children hollows out my stomach. I clutch my chest, hurting for Jonas and Jerrick.

I shiver at the memory of Jerrick mentioning his father reprimanding them for speaking out against his wishes.

"He told me about how he got his scar," I confide, earning a soft exhale from Jonas.

"Good. I am glad he told you. He doesn't let anyone in. Not even me that much anymore."

"Why?"

He shrugs. "Responsibility? Guilt? I'm not sure. But when *it* happened, something shifted in him. And I just—" Jonas breaks off and palms his head in defeat.

A long breath escapes from him, and I squeeze his hand.

"I can't help him. I try to, but I've let him down," he confesses, turning to me with tears in his eyes.

His confession is something Runa would confide to someone about me. A hopeful grin comes from the thought as I meet Jonas's gaze, understanding he needs comfort right now more than I do.

I lean in, pecking him on the cheek, relating to Jerrick and Jonas so much. It makes my heart swell when I see a small blush form.

"You haven't let him down, and you are a good brother. Deities, you're the best brother I could have ever asked for."

A sweet chuckle escapes from him, warmth spreading as I know I spoke true. I am undeserving of them both.

"What I mean to tell you, Tove, is I know he can be a cocky asshole. I know he can be mean and cruel. I've seen all sides of him. And while I don't know what happened between the two of you earlier, we *both* need to help him. Underneath all that hardness, underneath his magic, his curse, there is a light within him."

"I know there is."

I remember Jerrick's charm when we first met in Axidoria, the amusing faces he'd crack when waking me up in the library, the gifts he's given me, and the tenderness he offers the more I am around him.

The riddling guilt of not helping break his curse constricts around my heart. Maybe if I cancel the plan to invade and dedicate my time to helping Jerrick, he will grant me freedom and safe passage home.

A thought crosses my mind, and it is too tempting to not voice.

I tread into slippery territory. "Do you think if we broke the curse, Jerrick would divorce me and let me return home?"

Jonas shifts uncomfortably.

It is law to follow a monarch's binding decree, yes, but my readings have shown divorce is possible. The downside to making it happen is that it is a long process, which is why it is so rare.

But I can't help but think if Jerrick's curse was lifted, there would no longer be a reason to be together, and I could return home.

A change in a monarch's decree is not taken lightly and has to involve all the rulers and a priest from each kingdom. It requires the revised version to be as close to the original as possible but with a few changes. Then it has to be read and approved and signed by each one.

My heart is banking on the hope that breaking the curse means breaking the marriage, and it means going home.

Jonas shrugs in uncertainty. "That is between you and Jerrick."

I hold his gaze, begging for the new plan I have in mind to work. "But do you think he would?"

He looks between my eyes, releasing a long sigh. "I think when it comes to your happiness, Jerrick would grant you anything."

I scoot across the mattress, wrapping half of myself around Jonas. I sigh as he rests his head against mine.

The solid comfort and support of Jonas weighs me down as this overwhelming, yet familiar feeling overtakes me. I've felt this before.

With my parents, with Runa, and now with him.

My love for Jonas blurs my vision.

This could all work. It *has* to.

Faith and hope tighten in my chest, knowing I will not hurt any of the people I have come to care for here.

A tear slips on Jonas's skin, and his eyes meet mine as he asks, "What's the matter?"

I pull away, wiping my eyes, my own liberation warming my heart enough to tell him how much he means to me. "It's just— you *really* are an amazing brother, Jonas. Not only to Jerrick but to me. I thank you for your constant stream of kindness and company. They are something I don't deserve."

He faces me, pulling me in tightly. "Oh, Tove."

Something wet touches my cheek, and I joke, "I thought men weren't supposed to cry?"

Jonas half sobs, half laughs. "Yeah, well, I wasn't expecting such a heartfelt moment."

We break into a laugh, comforting each other for a few minutes as my tears dry.

When Jonas pulls away, he holds my cheek, forcing me to look at him. "I am honored to know you, honored to be your family, and I can only hope Jerrick will realize how much of a light you are to us and our kingdom." He kisses me on my forehead, and emotions I stupidly thought were done coat my cheeks yet again.

I whisper, "Thank you, Jonas."

"Anytime, sis." He winks as he peels up off the bed to make his way out of my chambers.

I call after him before he leaves. "Wait, why did you come to my chambers?"

He waves it off. "Nothing too important, only letting you know preparations are being finalized for the party in a fortnight."

I think quietly to myself, and Jonas departs. Warmth and a fuzzy feeling seep deep into my bones as I lie down, the exhaustion and events of the afternoon come full circle.

I grab a second pillow, drawing it close as my chest rises and falls. The bed sinks me into a comfortable place, relaxation finding me and creeping up my body.

Hope clutches my heart in a firm grip, believing that if I truly did help Jerrick, he would let me go. I muster confidence and form a prayer to the Makers above.

Taking my time, I recite each of their names and abilities, expressing gratitude and admiration for them, unsure if pleasantries will gain me anything.

Struggling to reach the end of my prayer, I whisper the final words repeatedly, "Please. Please, help me, and please help Jerrick."

33

A FIGHTING CHANCE

I wake the next day earlier than anticipated, a sign from the Makers that, for this new plan to work, I needed to dedicate every waking second to finding answers. Trusting Jonas has a handle on the final preparations for the masquerade ball, I am eager to spend the day in the library, regardless of if Jerrick planned more training or not.

I opted for the cotton tunic and leather trousers Dorit laid out in the night while I was sleeping. Fastening my hair in a loose plait, I slip on my boots quickly, pausing on the threshold and looking into my room. I land on my mother's mirror on the nightstand, reminding me to speak with Niko tonight and propose the new plan.

Squaring my shoulders, I find my resolve and leave my chambers, hurrying down to the kitchens for a quick bite. The thought of food drew me faster through the castle, sending my saliva to drip from the side of my mouth.

Sweet Makers, I must be famished.

I push harder into the stone floor, my muscle memory kicking in, taking me through my usual path. A smile forms when I reach the second level of the castle, noting the light smell of yeast in the air.

I turn the last corner for the kitchens and bump face-first into someone.

Stumbling backward, I lose my footing.

I anticipate the sharp impact of my ass, but it is worse than I thought. Unable to evade the inevitable, I crash against the floor, teeth smacking, and sending a searing pain through my jaw. Even my wrists strained when I tried to help cushion my fall.

Heat blooms around my cheeks as I check my hands, flicking my wrists and noting the small cut from my fall.

A hand shoots in my line of vision, causing me to jump, lifting my head to see whom it belonged to.

Wildfire flows throughout my body as Jerrick stands above me with an undone shirt.

We scan each other for any noticeable injuries, and I use this to my advantage, peeking through his clothing. His chest is chiseled and muscular, and the hardened muscles drift downward to his stomach.

I inch forward as I take his hand, finding myself trying to look further. But the pulling of my arm forces me to break my stare as I stumble into him.

I right my footing, but Jerrick doesn't release my hand. Instead, he holds it closer, inspecting the small cut.

"You're bleeding."

"It's just a cut. It'll be fine," I say, unconcerned.

Jerrick pulls my hand closer and scowls as if it is the villain in this altercation. And maybe it is. Deities, my magic *does* come from there.

But when he drops his gaze, he propels us forward. "Come, let's go get you bandaged up," he says, dragging me down the hall.

"What? Don't want to use your magic to help me instead?"

"I've already told you my powers don't work like that."

My memory jogs, and I want to ask another question but refrain when we enter the kitchens.

The yeast is thick as we inch closer, and my stomach releases a low growl, earning me a side glance from Jerrick. All I offer is a shrug, hopeful he doesn't catch the hint of embarrassment on my end.

Ophelia and Cordelia hum the same song in harmony, seamlessly working together and around each other as they prepare meals for the castle. Their eyes meet mine and Jerrick's, and I wave to them as Jerrick guides us over to the table.

"Where are the bandages?" he asks.

Ophelia's head whips up to us with worry etched on her features. "What happened? Are you alright?"

Cordelia simultaneously says, "I'll fetch them."

Cordelia hurries to the opposite side of the kitchen near a vast variety of cabinets, withdrawing a small pouch and swiveling to us. By the time she reaches us, Ophelia has sat across from us, examining the cut on my hand.

"It's nothing, really," I assure them as Cordelia hands Jerrick the small pouch of bandages.

Only then does he release my hand, taking the pouch and revealing an assortment of cloths varying in length and size. "It is when it is my fault," Jerrick mutters loud enough for us all to hear.

Both women's eyes meet mine in a flash of curiosity, so I fill them in, "I bumped into him and fell on my ass."

Cordelia stifles a laugh, and Ophelia looks between us, a discernible grin lining her face.

I roll my eyes, knowing they will not let me forget this.

Thank the Makers Jerrick was paying close attention to my hand, or else he would have seen the wink Ophelia gave me before elbowing Cordelia. He cleans my cut and ties a small cloth around it, forming a knot on the outer part of my hand instead of my palm, allowing me to open and close it with ease.

"Thank you," I tell him while inspecting the bandaging, catching his small smirk.

I ask my friends, "Any quick bites Jerrick and I can take to the library?"

Both nod eagerly, standing to assemble a tray of food as Jerrick's gaze burns into the side of my face. When I meet it, his stare is unsure, unsteady.

The women bring me a tray, and I rise to take it, a smile of gratitude extended to each of them. Without waiting for Jerrick, I leave the kitchen with the library in my sights.

I don't make it very far when a soft touch caresses my elbow. I am half tempted to ignore it and keep walking, but I plant my feet.

Jerrick stands in front of me. "I thought you might want to try to train again today?"

Holding his stare, I try to convey my eagerness to break his curse.

This new plan could be the only chance to avoid a fight.

"My magic is something that can wait. Your curse, on the other hand? Not as much," I tell him, psyching myself up to not be deterred from my goals.

Surprised lifts his brows when I sidestep him.

I succeed a few feet before he tugs me back once again. The tray, thankfully, remains between us, keeping a sinful desire within me at bay.

"Is this you trying to avoid what we discussed yesterday?" he asks, his voice rising in concern.

I am quick to debunk his worry. "I am not avoiding it."

Well, you sort *of are, Tove.*

"Only delaying the inevitable?"

I tilt my chin at his quip. "Precisely."

I have grown to understand the *basics* of my magic, yes, but delaying my progress to prevent the fight from happening takes precedence.

Break the curse.

Achieve peace in each kingdom.

Practice my magic more and return home safely.

Then deal with everything else after that.

I can do that.

Jerrick scans me, worry and suspicion abandoning his features as he takes the tray.

Grinning appreciatively, I try to thank him, but he interrupts, "I appreciate your efforts in aiding me, Frostbite. But don't forget, I am here to help you, too."

My stomach flips.

We are both here to help the other, and I truly feel it now more than ever since I've been arrived.

The sincerity behind his voice pulls me closer as we walk in a peaceful tandem toward the library, continuing our efforts in search of a breakthrough on his curse.

Wavy auburn hair is the first thing I see after running my palm on my mother's mirror for the third circle. Dark eyebrows lift in glee, and the golden light in Niko's eyes shine through the reflection.

He beams from ear to ear, lips as luscious as I remember, and his grin as genuine as my dreams depict. His happiness brings tears to my eyes, the love and adoration from him shining like Yeva herself.

I squeeze my mother's mirror for dear life. Somehow, the small crack makes him appear more real. For once, my tears are of relief to see the person I care about the most.

When his entire frame fills the reflection my heart leaps out of my body. His broad shoulders, his sexy shadow of stubble, and his eyes.

I clench my thighs, knowing I am going to have a hard time sleeping tonight.

It is quiet, and the silence is tender. I don't want to ruin it. I want to take him in. Every crevice, every detail of him that I haven't seen in person. Niko is here, and I am completely utterly speechless.

"I am so happy to see your smile," he says with the utmost tenderness, and it sends my heart skittering across the floor.

I nod eagerly, wiping a tear from my eye. "I'm happy to see *your* smile."

He leans closer to the reflection, observing me. Heat rises to my cheeks when he smiles.

I must look like a lovesick child because he says, "I wish I was holding you, kissing you."

I tuck a strand of hair behind my ear, glancing down at my nightgown, wishing he could be removing it with his hands. "I wish the same."

"Soon, Tove. *So soon*. We have everything we need to fight after the masquerade ball," he says pridefully.

My stomach sours, remembering the serious discussion I want to have.

Niko catches the fall of my expression. "What is it?"

I drop my head as my shoulders fall, my lungs expanding as I concentrate on keeping my emotions in check. A small inkling of power ripples within me, alert and aware of my conflict and festering guilt.

I close my eyes, eliminating the negative reflex of my magic awakening and breathing through it to quiet it down.

Scuffles come from the other end of the connection, and I ignore it, slowly letting the magic calm. The snowstorm in my heart and mind silence, and as my eyes open, relief floods my system.

I wish Jerrick were here to see it.

I imagine home, winter still creeping across the kingdom despite the warmer weather. If I keep making progress with my magic, Axidoria could see real seasons once more at some point. But I need to ensure the home I return to is going to be the same as when I left.

Determination and trust in my own judgment have me rising to meet Niko's gaze.

I offer him a tightened expression. "I want to call off the attack after the masquerade ball."

Niko's jaw falls, and his eyes widen in disbelief.

I wait quietly, allowing him the chance to recover as he granted the same mere moments ago.

His head tilts as he closes his mouth, biting his lip. He goes to speak, but nothing comes out. Instead, he pushes from the vanity and paces, completely forgetting my presence.

He rakes his hands through his messy hair.

I can't tell if he is worried, shocked, or mad. I try to improve my view to no success.

He finally turns, feet planted, and arms crossed as resentment grows in his gaze.

I immediately want to take back what I said.

The anger he has been reserving for Jerrick blazes. It stings again to see it being directed at me.

A lump forms in my throat. He is not going to like anything I have to say, but he needs to know everything as my advisor and as my partner.

I speak up, hopeful the new offering will bring back the smiling man from moments ago, "I have a new plan. One with no bloodshed and the chance for me to come home."

"What is this *new* plan?" he grits out, anger lacing each word.

I tell him the new plan.

His demeanor is something I monitor with each new tidbit of information, each memory, and recollection I think would be beneficial in winning him over to the new plan. He remains unmoving and angry but listens to everything I say.

I don't know what side is logging the information, but I hope it is the man who is my partner and not my royal advisor.

"I don't want to hurt anyone, Niko. I never have. This is the best way for that to not happen, not upset the Makers, not break the peace, *and* have us keep a political relationship with Palaena for trade," I finish, reaching my hand up to dry a few wet spots on my cheeks.

The guilt I have been feeling is finally exposed, and it should be a weight lifted from my shoulders. But the more I speak and try to explain myself, the worse it feels as Niko's gaze doesn't change.

The tender silence that had my heart skipping earlier has been snuffed out by the wrath festering from Niko. I scan him head to toe, trying to find something that tells me he understands.

He finally moves and his hands smack down on the vanity so hard the bang echoes in my bedchamber.

I jolt back from the pure rage blurring in his eyes.

"Why are you *really* doing this?"

He darkens, voice lethal and venomous.

I break from the drastic shift of longing to frustration. "I already told you! I don't want to hurt anyone!"

He continues to seethe, disbelieving everything I've said.

I pray the plea is enough for him to understand where I am coming from. "I've been here for *months*, Niko. I've been watching, learning, and growing. And, yes, I know you had every intention of going to battle to bring me home. But now? After everything I've learned?" I shake my head, refusing to budge on this.

Palaena is not the enemy we once thought they were. The answers I am looking for about my family could be in Axidoria or in another kingdom.

I square my shoulders. "I've made my decision. We can't fight. Ready or not, Palaena doesn't deserve that. Jerrick doesn't deserve that."

I meet Niko's features, tears running down my cheeks, my powers alert and ready to unleash. My thoughts drift to Jerrick, remembering our day in the library and hoping the image of his smile will quiet my magic from surging across my skin.

My voice is exhausted.

"Battle is going to make matters worse for everyone. My new plan is our only option."

He stares me down in silence.

I want to apologize, knowing this was all time wasted. I want to applaud him for everything he has done for Axidoria in my absence. I want to let him know that I see him, I love him, it's all going to be okay and that we'll be together again soon. But I don't know if saying any of that will bring his smile back.

Seeing him so quiet—so *angry*—breaks my heart.

When he breaks our stare, a visible tear runs down the side of his cheek.

I didn't mean to upset him.

"Niko, I—"

"Are you in love with him?"

34

TRIGGERED

"Wh-What?" I stutter in disbelief.

Fury and jealousy flare in Niko's eyes as tears coat both our cheeks.

"It's a simple question, Tove," he snarls.

I blanch from his toneless reaction. I haven't seen Niko this mad.

Ever.

I hesitate underneath his scornful rage, barely able to stutter out, "N-No. Absolutely not."

"So, I am supposed to believe you've changed your mind about everything because you feel *sorry* for him?"

"Yes," I tell him sharply, hating that he is making this about Jerrick more than about me not wanting to hurt anyone.

Niko's laugh is bitter, still doubting me. His body fills the frame of my mother's mirror, the rage inside of him escalating.

"You're quick to forgive a man who lied to you, kidnapped you, and forced you into a marriage?"

"I forgave a man who shot me with an arrow!"

I clamp my mouth shut.

Hurt flashes across Niko's features as he flinches. Niko masks the pain while he tosses his arms into the air, growling in frustration.

"Don't you get it, Tove? That man *isn't* going to let you return home. There is a marriage decree that binds you to him, and he is not going to agree to a divorce. Calling the banners and killing him is the only way you will get to leave that place. It's the only way for us to be together." Niko curses in disgust, refusing to stand down.

"You aren't going to kill him," I command, desperate for him to listen.

Niko wants to fight, but I can't watch another confrontation between him and Jerrick.

My new plan will work. It must.

I keep my anger caged, containing my fearful thoughts at bay as Niko's cold, menacing gaze meets mine.

His jaw tics as he leans in close to the mirror, showing no hint of any other emotion aside from pure unfiltered rage.

"Yes, I am," he states, stepping back.

Panic explodes when he disappears from the reflection. I don't hear the door opening, so I raise my voice.

"As your queen, I command you to stand down!"

The door slams hard from the opposite end of the reflection, and a few things on my old vanity in Axidoria shake from the abrasiveness of Niko's exit.

Terrors sets in.

Niko is too far down this path of revenge.

Fear creeps in.

I've ruined my relationship with Niko before I even had a chance to experience it.

A door opening again startles me, Dorit entering in greeting. I clutch my mother's mirror to my chest, my lip quivering from heartbreak and stress sinking deep into my bones. Fighting the tears away is no use because Dorit notices and rushes to my side.

"What's wrong?"

Her sweet, perfectionist heart is desperate to fix everything.

Wiping away the tears, I sniff twice, careful to keep my mirror close so the connection to Axidoria is not visible.

"It's nothing, just—just nightmares," I lie, the half truth I rely on easing everything consuming me.

Her sympathetic touch is a blade plunging into my heart. "Would you like me to stay?" she asks, knowing company helps me immensely when my nightmares are bad.

I haven't had many night terrors haunting me lately, but they certainly are following me while I am awake. The soft circle she runs around my shoulder is comforting, but I dismiss it.

I don't deserve it.

"I'll be alright. I'm just stressed. Thank you, though," I say.

She regards me warily, skepticism etched in her features as she stands. "If you say so. I'm going to empty your chamber pot, then. Let me know if you need anything though, alright?"

"I will," I sigh, watching her go into my privy to take the chamber pot and replace it with a fresh one.

She reaches the door and pauses before turning to me. "I hope your dreams are sweeter."

"I hope yours are, too, Dorit."

Her brown eyes light up as she closes the door.

Moments pass before I collapse onto my mattress, embraced in the soft linen sheets. They are light and weightless, designed to accommodate the hot summer nights.

I still clutch my mother's mirror, holding it as I stare into the blank ceiling of my chambers, a hole burning in my chest. The burn is not comforting or filled with lust or desire.

It is frigid, abrasive, and harsh—meant to swallow me whole.

It even snuffs out my magic, smothering it away and forcing me to feel this sting of pain.

My vision blurs as tears trickle down my cheeks. The panic, the fear, the loss, and the guilt send me spiraling.

When I lift the mirror, no one is on the opposite end.

No Niko. No Betina.

I run my hand in a circle to sever the connection, and I am met with my own reflection. The monster I am stares back, thrashing against the hopelessness in my features. A mask patiently molds itself to my entire being.

Placing the mirror on the nightstand, I look into the darkened night. The lack of stars shining in the sky brings a void to this evening.

Once again, I am reminded of not having a family, and I've ruined any relationship with anyone who has offered me kindness.

I wrap my arms around my pillow, holding it close to my heart and cheeks. It is barely enough to dry my face as I heave and tremor through each sob. I muffle my exhausted screams with the cushion, but it does nothing to reduce the sting.

I clutch my pillow tighter as the grief, terror, and failure I can never seem to escape grows larger, dragging me into darkness worse than Oblivion.

35

RELIVING THE PAST

The spring grass is freshly sprinkled with a light rain, but Runa insisted we take a walk outside the castle's walls.

Peering over my shoulder, Nikolaj is a few feet behind us.

Runa snickers at my lingering stare, and I elbow her, which only makes her laugh harder.

"Stop doing that!" I demand.

She snickers more, swinging our arms together. Her brown hair blows in the wind, a strand getting caught in my vision, and I fight to remove it. Our steps sync into the same rhythm, and her head rests on my upper arm, fingers removing loose strands from my face.

The sweet scent of flowers usually calms my senses, but it does nothing for my worry over Mother being gone this long.

Father used to travel on business alone, and when Mother was required to venture outside of Axidoria, she always had one of us with her. But I can't stop thinking about what she told me before she left.

My sweet daughter, you will do a great many things while I am away.

Her silky, sweet voice echoes in my mind, hating that I've done nothing while she's been away. I'm normally good at dedicating my time to the tasks she does, helping her more since Father passed.

The memory of Father before his last trip seeps into my bones. I swallow the thought down, focusing on the scenery.

Runa rubs soft circles in my palm to calm me and reassure me. It brings joy as I return the circles in kind. She is sweetness and joy, appeased to be a part of everything.

The sunshine to my rain cloud.

Always.

My lip ticks upward, amused by her teasing me about ogling Nikolaj. I probably deserve it and should keep my longing stares at a minimum.

"I'm enjoying the view same as you," she teases, the two of us always commenting on men as handsome as Nikolaj.

"We don't need him to catch us staring," I tell her as my slippers catch on a thick pile of mud.

The mud-stuck shoe stops both Runa and me. I lift my skirts to my other foot closely tied with being stuck like the other.

Runa braces herself on the ground to help pull me and my shoes out, but Nikolaj lifts me with ease, placing me next to my sister. His auburn hair is damp, but a sweet smile graces his cheeks as he swipes away the sweat along his brow.

"Easy there, Princess," Nikolaj says.

Runa gives me a side-eye, hinting she is up to no good. I dismiss her intent, gazing at Nikolaj while forcing the butterflies in my gut to settle.

"Thank y—"

A searing chill prickles to life inside me.

What the—

I clench my stomach as something fierce and painful forces me to topple over.

Niko catches me and holds me tight. "Whoa. Easy there, are you alright?"

The chill in my abdomen sinks deeper into the pit of my stomach while goose bumps prickle along my skin. The sensation creeps up the length of my spine as a frigid kiss shoots my posture upright and away from Niko's warm, tender touch.

Runa arches a brow, echoing Niko's concern. "Tove, are you—" she starts, but I can't stop my dreadful, looming thought from voicing itself out loud.

"M-M-Mother is—th-this is—"

Horror settles into my bones at this feeling waking within me. Magic.

No.

"I can't... I can't—"

I croak, covering my mouth as tears cascade down my cheeks. My body convulses, my heartbeat hammering and blurring my vision.

No, no, no. This isn't real.

Mother is not dead. She *can't* be dead. This is just anxiety.

I am okay. I am okay.

Just breathe.

I pinch my eyes shut, focusing on my breathing to calm the panic. But a soft touch lands on my shoulder, my sister's serene voice seeking to soothe me.

"Tove, I am here. What's wrong?"

I recoil from her, scowling. "Don't touch me! I-I don't—"

A sharp chill rumbles in my gut again, controlling my movements. A whimper escapes as my knees hit the muddied plains beneath me.

I fold my arms over my stomach as I heave choked sobs as reality sinks in.

Mother is... *gone.*

I scream, panic and grief crash against my already weeping heart. "No! Please. I am not ready!"

Runa moves, kneeling and taking my hands into hers. I look up at my sister, her jade-green eyes tearing up as she takes in my own tears.

Our parents are dead.

"Tove?" she whimpers through her quivering lip, the question lingering in the air between us.

I wrap my arms around my sister, the two of us hugging each other tight, as if the Makers will condemn and break us apart. We cling to one another as the grief seizes full control.

Nikolaj wraps his arms around us, cradling us close. His tall, broad-shouldered form seeks to protect us from further harm. His messy red hair and light stubble rubs against the side of my face.

"I am so sorry," Niko whispers softly, his voice cracking.

Runa wails.

Darkness sinks over my life, and the urgency to go into a frozen slumber claws at me. Something kisses my breath away as the three of us hold each other, a bitter cold still plunging me deep into the unknown.

I turn to prepare for my new reality, but a small inkling of frost appears around me. My eyes widen in horror at what this chill is doing.

I break free of their hold. *"Oh no."*

I stand and sprint for the castle.

Runa and Nikolaj simultaneously say something, but it is muted by my command to them. "Run! Get far away from me!"

I scream at this frost to stop. Yet the more I cry, the more magic releases from within as if it is trying to defend me. But the chill won't abate. And I can't help myself with my emotions.

Breathe. Run. Breathe.

Just breathe.

The thought of breathing dies as swirls of snowflakes escape from my fingertips, my mouth falling agape. But I refuse to stop sprinting, not until I can figure this out alone. I keep going, hurrying for the trees beyond our home.

Exhilaration plants itself in my core, blossoming into more frost from each step that touches the semi frozen grass.

When I make it to the plains outside of our home, I veer right, passing the Queen's Road, hoping to reach the lake near the border of our lands.

If I can get far enough and put distance between myself and the others—I'll try to think of what comes after that.

An ache pulses against my chest as I pound my feet hard into the ground. A whoosh of relief courses through me as water comes into view.

My feet throb when I stop running, and I hunch over, bracing myself against my knees. I watch my boots in a stupor as snowflakes trickle out from where I stand, bleeding into the grass, drowning it in frost.

Blinking again in disbelief, I swallow and attempt to even my breathing.

I can't help but marvel in awe of this—this power.

I've never seen anything like this.

The magic from earlier repeats itself. The ice stretches and manifests toward the lake. I follow it, watching it solidify. Curiosity has me stepping on the frozen land, testing its structure, and chuckling with wonderment. I ease one foot after the other, inching closer to the center.

The chill seeps into my bones, and I sense its power wanting to console me. The familiarity of peace forms, tugging at my heart as a cold hug envelops me.

My eyes close at the feeling, my arms wrapping around myself in response. I absorb and latch on to this magic as it pulls memories of heartbreak and grief away.

It is cold and dreary, yes, but somehow, these abilities seek to soothe me. The thought of quieting the magic gives me an idea to try to calm the ice storming within me.

I extend my hands, a pulling tug of power emanating outward—

CRACK!

I jolt, magic exploding from me in response, frost surrounding and turning everything in the vicinity into ice. When it relaxes, I marvel at the vast power of winter filling and clouding away this spring filled day.

But the faintest of voices stops my heart.

"T-T-Tove." Runa shivers.

I whip my head to my sister.

She breathes heavily, crying and shaking furiously.

Before I can even scold her for her actions, I stop dead in my tracks when I notice her feet are frozen to the bottom of the lake. Terror turns my blood cold as I am unable to hide my fear from lashing out.

"Runa, I told you to run away from me!" I hurry to her, hesitant to touch her.

A small line of frost trails up one side of her dress as she hugs herself to stay warm. "I-I didn't want you to be a... alone," she struggles.

That line of frost stops and stays steady before I turn my panic on her.

"I was trying to protect you!" I shout, worried at the sight of her clattering teeth and upset that I can't touch her.

I could make it worse.

"I... I am... am su-supposed to protect youuu, too," she says.

Another line of frost crawls up the other side of her dress. I glance around for Nikolaj, knowing he wouldn't let her run after me alone.

She knows my own thoughts, and she admits, "I... I... commanded Nikolaj... to... to... to stay put."

Of course she did. She didn't want him to become mortified by me and hate me. It breaks my heart to watch her dwindling.

"Runa... I'm... I'm not sure I can get you free." I stare down at myself, opening my palms. "I think this is my magic." I show her the flicker of snow hovering over my hand.

"J... jus... just try," she encourages through rattling teeth.

The frost slowly turns to ice along her body, drifting up to her knees.

Lowering to the ground, I eye her frozen feet, still hesitant to touch her. But if I do, I might reabsorb the magic.

I tremble as I extend my hands, resting them along the most frozen parts of her body, careful not to touch anything else. I pause and close my eyes, imagining ice melting.

But when I open my eyes, I am met with nothing.

I touch another area of her body, trying to not think of the frost growing. The magic around us even expands. I try to picture ice stopping and melting in my mind. But again, when I open my eyes, there is no improvement.

Ice now covers her waist.

Runa's arms are half stuck in place, her shivering getting worse. The breath she releases between each chatter is visible, landing on me and drying the wetness on my cheeks briefly, only to be soaked again with my own tears. Her doe eyes watch me encouragingly, the blue and purple hues lining her lips twist and knot my heart.

I can't help but plea internally. *"Please."*

Ice shoots up and over her arms, faster than the frost did, and she wails in response.

I jerk up, frantically touching her frozen hands in hopes I can cease the ice's movements. But when I look back, the fear settles into her panicked state.

She... she is *afraid* of me.

"I-I don't know what to do, Runa," I sob in complete defeat.

"P-P-P-Please h-h-help me, y-y-you must kn-know how to st-st-st-st-stop this," Runa pleads.

"I don't know what to do!" I scream, tears running down my face.

The ice moves again, and I flinch at the sound of her screams.

I can't stop myself from crying.

She is frozen up to her neck now as I shake uncontrollably, losing all faith in whatever this dark and evil magic is.

Why are the Makers punishing me?

Please, help me. Please. I don't know how to fix this.

Runa watches through her own tears, her drenched features stark with grief, fear, and panic. Her skin is losing all warmth that enlightened her.

My heart fractures at the pain I've caused. If I can't stop this—

"Tove, please!" she whimpers, the effort of speaking hurting.

The desperation in her plea fractures my soul, unlocking the gates of determination within me. The ice creeps up and around her head as I wipe dampness from my cheeks.

I find even footing and hug her waist, pinching my eyes shut.

Please. Please work.

I try to calm my emotions, placing thoughts of Runa at the forefront of my mind instead of the frozen ice surrounding her. I try to imagine only the happiest of memories.

But then I remember I am not happy.

I don't have my father and now my mother. Yet I still try to think of Runa, knowing I still have her. I think about her sunlight, her happiness, and her love—

"T-T-T-Tove—"

I lift my head, and my jaw drops. Frost surrounds Runa's face.

No. No. No!

"Runa!" I gasp, my hands moving to her cheeks.

My eyes scan every detail of her, trying to find some improvement.

But it's not stopping.

I made it worse.

I'm so weak and so stupid.

Stupid! Stupid! Stupid!

I cry, frantically touching her head, her shoulders, her arms, begging for this torture to end.

Magic can't kill her. It *can't*.

Why is it even doing this!?

"T-T-T-Tove, you h-have to let me g-g-go."

Runa's voice cracks with defeat.

I blanch, disbelieving, refusing to stop. "What!? No. Runa—"

"I-It's o-okay. The M-M-Makers have sp-spoken. This n-n-n-needs to h-h-h-happen."

"What!? No! Fuck the Makers. They *just* took our parents. I am not letting them take you, too!" I search again for that kernel of power within me to do something.

Runa takes a shaky breath, her wheezing voice cutting me deeper than a knife. "T-T-T-Tove, our kingdom n-n-needs you."

"*I* need you!" I sob.

I hold her again, internally chanting the words please and stop over and over, begging for this nightmare to end.

Her features pale more with each second, her blue lips form a tightening smile.

Why is she smiling?

Desperation and turmoil thrash against my panic and terror as the magic refuses to relent. The ice grows around her hair, her forehead, her face.

Straining to help her, I hug her as tight as I can, pinching my eyes shut in concentration. I steer my focus to silencing and snuffing out this stupid magic, needing it to listen and to stop doing this and stop hurting the people I love.

Runa clears her throat as my eyes remain closed, my full attention driven into stopping the ice—stopping it all.

"T-Tove, I l-l-love—"

Silence...

My heartbeat is all I hear through my ragged breaths as foreboding prickles up my spine.

Goose bumps ripple across my skin, the tension coiling tight in my chest, air itself incapable of filling my lungs.

Slowly, I open my eyes...

And I stare in silent horror at my completely frozen sister.

My heart stops.

I shake my head as tears drench my cheeks, the enormity and dread of what I've done ceasing time.

I shudder away from her body, the cold chill returning and running a blizzard within me, refusing to stop its own demise. Air clamps down as I struggle to breathe, tremors rocking through me as a defeated wail sends snow shooting out and around me.

"RUNAAAA!"

I *scream* in my defeated rage, collapsing onto the frozen lake at my dead sister's feet.

Through every harrowing gasp, I roar her name over and over and *over*—*screaming* and *pleading* for this torture to end, for this not to be real.

I lament for my mother, my father, for Runa.

But it doesn't stop.

The *pain* won't stop.

A sharp icicle wedges itself over my heart, preventing me from dying with them—being with them. I curse and shriek more, slamming my fists into the lake, desperate for this ice to melt and swallow me whole.

Even when my voice is hoarse and aching—I *still* scream.

"YOU CAN'T TAKE THEM ALL AWAY FROM ME!"

Frost slams outward from my fists, my own tears freezing on top of the lake.

I crawl to my sister, wrapping my arms around her legs and burrowing into the cold, frozen statue, hoping it will spread and take me, too.

"Take me," I plea to the clouds above, only to be met with silence.

"Take me to my family! You can't leave me alone here!" I shriek.

A frigid burst of wind blasts through me as I plea the words, slamming a fist on the ground again. "TAKE ME!"

My voice breaks from the pain, the ice evolving around me yet not doing what I desperately seek for it to do.

I toss my hands, insistent on escaping this nightmare.

"*KILL ME*!" I roar as darkness surrounds me.

I cling to Runa's body, the void creeping and igniting a small hope within.

Praises and gratitude to the Makers are on the tip of my tongue when a rush of heat plasters itself against my back.

It latches onto me, warmth cascading through my blood. The searing inferno tries to separate me from Runa, but I fight it, unwilling to be parted from the last piece of my family.

The last piece of my heart.

"No! You can't stop me from being with them!"

I wrestle against the heat attempting to smother and silence me and my grief. My hold on Runa tightens despite the flames burning me from the inside out.

Maybe this is Letum coming to drag me into Oblivion.

I shrivel at the thought, refusing to be apart from my family.

A deep voice echoes in the wind, *"Please, come back to me."*

I pause, and my heart skips. My fight lessens as I sniff and wipe the tears with the sleeve of my shirt.

Into the darkened, frozen void, I question, "Father?"

Has he come to take me? Is this real?

Come find me, Father. Please.

I cannot live without you all. I want to see your face again. I want to see Mother's face again. I need to see Runa's jade-green eyes and tell her I did try, and I am so sorry.

Yet something strong and abrasive weighs down on my entire body, as if it is trying to steal the light from me. It coaxes my grip off Runa, yanking me away and toward my family. I weep with relief knowing I am reuniting with them and will not be alone in this world.

I welcome the deep voice into my mind, even as the unrecognizable pleading turns my vision black.

"Come back to me."

36

THE LEDGE

A blast of wind hits me, forcing my eyes open. Scanning my surroundings, I hover on the ledge of my balcony. Warm hands are wrapped around my torso, pulling me in the opposite direction. My movements are sluggish, my nightmare still hitting me through the repeated whispers against my hair.

"Please, please come back to me, Frostbite. *Please* wake up," the deep voice pleads once more.

I am dragged backward and swept away from my balcony, my backside making contact with a hard chest. That voice, the heat—

"Jer?"

Jerrick's breath hitches, and he stops and rotates me. The heat running through my body is swiftly removed, replaced with his cold hands on my shoulder and my cheek.

"Frostbite?" Jerrick asks, scanning me from head to toe.

His eyes are red, his hair messy, his clothing disheveled. By the time his blue gaze meets mine again, the shock of what *almost* happened sinks in.

My own breath catches at the temperature shift along with the terror in his eyes. And I can't believe he is here, in my chambers, right now.

Tears well in my eyes as I reach for him, my arms snaking around his waist and gripping his tunic. The side of my face meets his chest as I burrow into the rich cologne and leather, honing in on the scent as I struggle to ground myself after my nightmare.

A shuddering cry leaves me as Jerrick embraces me.

He laces his fingers through my hair and squeezes me. But the tighter he holds me, the harder it is to stop the choked sobs from escaping at the relief of being awake and in his presence.

"I've got you. I'm here." He rubs soft circles along my back as my tears soak through his tunic.

"Wh-What happened?"

He hesitates. "I-I came to check on you. Dorit told Jonas and me you had a nightmare earlier, and when we finished our meeting, I had to make sure you were alright." He breaks our embrace to hold my cheeks, wiping away my tears. "When I came up here, you were shouting, and the next thing I know, I was knocking down the door and seeing you standing outside on... on the ledge."

I try to look to where I could have met my death, but he tugs my attention back. "I tried to wake you, but you kept fighting me. And—I used my magic to try to wake you, to get you to stop what I thought you were going to do."

A lump forms in my throat, still unable to process how close I truly was, remembering in my dream the heat and the voice.

Jerrick's voice.

His features are distraught and pained.

It scratches underneath my skin, my chest aching and hating I am the cause.

"I know I used my magic on you, and for that, I apologize, but I *needed* you off that ledge." Jerrick takes a long sigh, lowering his head and avoiding my gaze as if he is in the wrong here.

But I am. I am the one hurting him every day.

My soul tears, a festering mournful song plaguing me from the pain I am inflicting on Jerrick. My efforts to help him and ensurE the fighting does not happen need to be more earnest and intentional. I will never be able to live with myself if anyone in Palaena were to get hurt.

I feel that even more with Jerrick here.

The complexity of our meeting was jagged and splintered, but the time we've spent together has sealed those cracks, smoothing them over with a deeper, more meaningful understanding of one another.

I blink away my tears, taking a deep breath before reaching for his cheek and guiding him to me.

The bright and cocky king is gone, the moody and cursed man has vanished—but the broken and tortured soul of Jerrick stares back.

I release a long breath, taking in this man and knowing so much of our lives has been dictated and planned by our parents and by our bloodlines. But our experiences have brought us together for a reason, and I believe we are meant to bring healing to the two of us and our kingdoms.

That thought deepens my need to call off the fight and help break his curse.

I smile softly, my expression softening as I admire the beautifully complex person he is, inside and out. "Thank you, Jer."

Relief blossoms across his face and relaxes his body.

He returns a kind smile as I add, "I haven't had that happen in a long time."

Jerrick's eyes widen. "T-This has happened before?"

I nod sheepishly. "A few times since my family passed."

He regards me, brows pinched together as if he is restraining himself from something. But he takes my hand, rubbing it softly as I lower my own from his face.

I watch his fingers run circles along my hand, the repetitive motion soft, comforting, and distracting.

Knowing he might be one of the few people to understand my grief, I confess, "I relive my sister's death in my dreams, and sometimes, I think my subconscious tries to win over and take me back to her and my parents."

His hold on my hand tightens briefly before he recovers, returning to the soft circles. "That must be pretty awful."

I peek up through my eyelashes to offer him a tight-lipped smile. "It can be."

My attempt at lessening the gravity of my sleepwalking is caught, Jerrick meeting my eyes and lifting his lips. Warmth spreads across my chest at him being here and the little glimpse of his dimple.

But it vanishes as Jerrick takes a small step back. "Now that I have checked on you, I'll leave you to your slumber." He bows, turning for the door.

"Wait," I call.

Jerrick freezes midstep, meeting my gaze.

"Could—could you stay with me for a bit?" I ask, my bravery immediately leaving my body.

I brace for rejection and hold my arm, rubbing up and down to comfort myself.

Instead of speaking, Jerrick walks to the bed, lowering onto the mattress and patting the opposite end.

I hum and join him as he settles himself above the bedding. Pushing up on my toes, I climb into my side of the bed and pull the sheets over my torso. I lean on my side to face him, and he follows suit.

A chill drifts up my body as we stare at one another, and I shiver, trying to rub my arm as Jerrick reaches across. "Are you cold?"

I dip my head.

He adjusts his position, scooting closer and guiding my hands to his mouth, blowing on them to warm them.

Heat blooms in my core from his lips touching my fingertips, the cold within me melting away.

I bite my lip as he looks up through his eyelashes. "Feeling warmer, Frostbite?"

I nod, breathless at the sight of him.

He releases my hand, allowing me to grab the covers and pull them up higher to shield myself. I fidget underneath the blankets at our closeness, my blood heating my cheeks the more he stares.

He gestures to the covers. "May I?"

Words still won't form, so I nod again.

He stands, and I hide under the sheets, my blush worsening. Boots clank on the stone floor, and a belt is unfastened.

I sneak a peek but have to return to normal because he faces me, peeling the blankets back and sending a gust of air around as he climbs in. My eyebrows rise a little in curiosity as he takes a long breath.

Jerrick lies close as he rests on his back, lifting an arm above him and tilting his head over. He then rolls and faces me, tucking a hand under his pillow and mirroring my movements.

We stare into each other's eyes.

"I—" We catch the other one wanting to speak and say in unison, "You go first."

I laugh out loud, and Jerrick smirks. Sweet Makers, his smile is devastating. My laugh quiets, and this peace over him being so close soothes me.

"I have to admit something," he says.

Alarm has me wondering what else he could possibly disclose to me. I remain silent, unsure of what to expect, and he takes my silence as a chance to speak.

"This isn't the first time I have checked on you."

Guilt forms a tight knot in my chest, worry churning into nausea. "Oh?" I ask curiously, part of me wondering if he has overheard anything of me reaching home.

"I try to check on you most nights before I go to my own chambers, to make sure you're alright."

My heart lurches in my throat at the confession. "Y-You do?"

Sweet Makers, does he know?

"It's just... I just—" He breaks off, looking down. "I remember the one nightmare you had on the road. I felt awful about it, knowing you had shit you were going through, and I felt terrible having added to that mess."

The rapid increase of my heart slows, relieved it was not what I thought it was, yet still skips a beat from his kindness. I fidget my feet under the covers, unsure of what I did to deserve this.

"Th-Thank you," I squeak, my skin heating when his eyes find mine.

Shame and embarrassment make me feel like an inferno. *Especially* when Jerrick's dimple appears. I wish my magic had been invisibility so I could hide from everything and everyone and not deal with any of this.

My thoughts drift to earlier in the night.

The way Niko and I ended our conversation, the nightmare, and Jerrick.

I bury my face into my pillow, ashamed of this mess I've made. I need to fix this—and fast.

"Frostbite," Jerrick begins.

I lift my head and pinch my features into something that hopefully conveys I am okay and not being tortured by this festering guilt.

He reaches and combs through my hair, moving it away from my face. "I am here, and I've always got you. You need only ask." His forehead rests on mine, and I close my eyes, my heart sputtering again.

I keep my eyes shut, hoping this moment will stop time, and I can remain here forever.

Everything between Jerrick and me has been chaos, yet we've worked together and have attempted to help each other. I want to let him in more. I want to help him and myself.

I care about everyone here. They all pushed and tugged their way into my fractured heart, having found and sewn pieces together that Niko and Betina have struggled to find for years.

Everyone here in Palaena has peeled away the tight mask I have become so used to wearing, making me feel seen more as a person beyond my abilities and beyond my role as a queen. They have each brought out a part of me I forgot existed, as if my heart and mind themselves had lost them.

But something about my time with Jerrick has gone deeper than that.

It's as if he has exposed every flaw, every issue, and every problem I've ever had with myself, that others have had with me, and doesn't back away. It was not something I imagined anyone doing because I thought I had to do that myself.

And yet here they all are, making me not feel like a monster.

And here is Jerrick, reaching and coaxing my soul to make me feel like... *me*.

"Please," he whispers, catching my attention as his breath warms my nose. "Will you consider that?"

I breathe in his scent, pulling away to gaze at him. Adoration and gratitude press against me as I touch his face, tracing the portion of his scar on his eyebrow.

He closes his eyes at the contact, leaning into my touch.

Guilt, stress, and responsibility feel lighter with Jerrick near, and it makes me *want* to help him beyond my own ends. Beyond learning my magic and saving my kingdom, I want to help him find the chance to find happy again as I have wished for myself.

With that feeling blooming in my heart, I incline my head earnestly, seeking to befriend him even more and build a better working relationship with a kingdom and a king I once thought to hate.

"Only if you allow me to do the same for you," I answer, lying on my pillow, a peace settling in my heart and making my eyes heavy.

Jerrick scooches closer, drawing me tight against his chest. "Deal."

I can't contain my giggle.

Our breaths steady and even out, comfort and safety drawing my arm to snake under his hold of me so that I might keep him close, too.

As we lie there, my mind focuses on Jerrick.

How his eyes twinkle each time he smirks, his scar wrinkles with his eyebrows when they furrow, and how he has one dimple instead of two.

I drift to the sound of his laughs when he threw food at me, how his hands hold mine and run circles, calming everything inside of me. But I focus most on his heartbeat matching mine as we lie intertwined, agreeing to help each other and to tackle problems together instead of alone.

"I want us both to find our happy again," I murmur into the quiet.

With his lips pressed against my forehead, a balm of protection washes over me.

"Me too," Jerrick utters in a hushed breath.

The comforting words are a soothing melody I repeat as I snuggle closer into my husband's arms, drifting into a peaceful slumber.

And for the first time since I lost my family, I feel safe from my nightmares.

37

ALONE TOGETHER

My own smile appears more often as Jerrick and I work in the library, searching for answers. It still plagues and muddles my mind that there are no traces of evidence about the curse and no one present at home in Axidoria.

I remain vigilant despite that fact, knowing Betina is working hard and looking into my mother and father and confident Niko believes and trusts my judgment. I reflect often on his angry departure, wishing I could have done better about acknowledging him and his diligence, telling him how much I love him, and also wishing I trusted my gut when he first suggested battle.

I am putting all my faith in the Makers that Niko will come around and listen.

Jerrick suggested training today, and I found myself open to the change of scenery. There has not been any discomfort when donning the breeches or braiding my hair alone, simply spending another day with my husband.

When I looked back at my reflection this morning, I brightened, being around people I care about and feeling as if I have purpose for being better. That tug of joy is evident in the arena, my magic easier to manifest and control.

Frost, ice, and snow appear along my arms as well as expand outwardly now.

It is surprisingly comforting to see the progress I've made with little direction on Jerrick's part. Reading texts about meditation and magic manipulation while practicing in my downtime has done wonders. My progress is still minuscule in the wide depth of removing my ice. The effort behind withdrawing the amount I can expel exhausts me.

But I keep diligently praying to the Makers, hopeful I can build my stamina to remove more.

I *need* to do more.

Melting away my winter, however, feels impossible.

Jerrick and I have tried different methods of meditation, and each one leaves me more frustrated and exhausted. I might already be reaching the limits of my abilities, but I've only touched on calling my magic back to me...

It's hopeless, Tove. Just admit it.

No.

This is all part of my new plan. If I can manifest my magic and break Jerrick's curse, I can return home and *hopefully* remove or melt away my winter by then.

I try not to let the guilt of keeping secrets from Jerrick and Jonas eat at me as we research and practice, but I snuff the feelings away, trusting Niko will understand and arrive at the ball with peace in his heart.

Pulling away from my thoughts, I focus on an archery target, practicing blasting frost from my hands to a specific mark.

Jerrick is to my right, arms crossed and that damned dimple on full display.

It is hard to pry my thoughts away from him, but when I do, small pebbles of frost cascade out from my hand, but don't make it too far toward the target. Disappointment rocks through me, the consequence showing along my arms that my magic can work against me if I don't keep myself in check.

Jerrick advances in concern as I lift my hand to stop him. When he stops, I smirk and close my eyes, and I focus on leveling my emotions.

The frigidness of my magic tingles along my skin, quieting down toward a place of solace in my core. By the time I open my eyes, Jerrick stands in front of me, grinning wide as I jump in glee.

"That was amazing! I've never been able to do that so quickly!" I cheer as he studies me, his grin turning into a small smirk.

"All you need to remember now is to watch the control in your wrist. Using your magic is just like using knives," he says, removing a dagger from his belt.

He holds the blade, resting the hilt on his shoulder. Flicking his wrist lightly, Jerrick launches the blade across the room, landing a bullseye on the target.

I whip my head back to him, and a cocky grin appears as he finishes his thoughts. "The smallest effort can make or break where your target lands."

I nod in understanding, making a mental note to try again the next time we practice. I walk toward the washbasin at the edge of the arena, then wet a washcloth to wipe along my brow before leaving for one of my last meetings with Jonas for the masquerade ball next week.

"I better get going," I tell Jerrick politely, hating to end our training session. "Jonas and I need to wrap up some of the last details for the party."

Jerrick approaches the wash basin, dipping a second cloth and wiping his brow and neck and dumping it into the bucket, causing water to splash on me.

He crosses his arms.

"I won't keep you any longer then, but I have cleared our schedule for the next few days, so be sure to wrap up all last-minute details because you'll be indisposed," he says nonchalantly.

The meaning behind his words has me biting my lip, tempted to imagine what they mean. Maybe something lustful and full of desire. The picture painted in my mind seeps into my core.

I swallow thickly, trying my best to remove the filthy image from my mind.

When he stayed in my chambers, I woke the next morning with him still there. And Sweet Makers, I swelled at the bliss of it.

Jerrick nuzzled into me as he slept, his light snore and little mumbles initially what roused me.

But I still cannot remove the feeling of his hard length pressed into my lower back. The feel of him set my skin on fire, the desire to grind against him, to wake him and lose myself in him ran through my mind and surfaces in moments like this when he is so close.

Fucking Deities, getting along with him is making my attraction to him worse.

You are *married to him, Tove.*

I cower away from my tempting thoughts and ask Jerrick for clarification. "Indisposed?"

His eyes twinkle as he fastens his belt along his trousers. "I'm taking you on a hunt."

My mouth slackens as panic sends out excuses. "I can't go on a hunt. I've never been on one. Jonas might need my help with the party. We still haven't made progress on your curse. I have to—"

Jerrick rests a finger on my lips, my mouth closing at the contact. He steps in, his intoxicating cologne clouding my sense of judgment.

Deities, I want to taste that scent along his skin.

Stop that, Tove!

"Never mind all that," he says, waving off my excuses and trying to entice me into his plans. "I want to give you a chance to try your magic outside of the training arena as well as see what I can do."

I swallow thickly, unsure still and nervous from the last time I went into a forest. I was bleeding and dying last time. It would be nice to not face that again.

His eyes gaze into mine with reassurance, as if he knows where my mind went. "I promise we will be safe."

I try to find a way out of this, but he lowers his hand when I sigh in vexation. "Will we have a hunting party?"

His crooked smirk appears and somehow finds a way to crowd me even more in this space, his being consuming me as his head shakes softly. Jerrick lowers his head, his upper body hunching over mine and making my breath catch.

He tilts my face up to meet his.

Jerrick leans in closer—*closer.*

I secretly wonder if he is going to kiss me. Anxiety refuses to settle, my body and nerves wrung tight as I lick my lips in anticipation.

"Just you and me." He steps away, stealing my thought with him and smiling deviously. "Be sure to pack accordingly."

He winks, pivoting away from the training arena.

I distract myself with my plait as I hurry to my meeting.

Viggo leaves Jonas's study when I make it down the hallway, his wavy brown hair disheveled and sweat along his brow. He scratches the light beard that sculpts his features handsomely. Viggo is quieter than most staff members here, but he has always been kind whenever we interact.

I smile pleasantly, hopeful he doesn't feel any hint of embarrassment around me. Yet of course, his warm tanned cheeks turn pink as he hunches, trying to hide and run away.

He bows in greeting. "Queen Tove, a blessed afternoon."

"Yes, it is, Viggo. Is Jonas well?" I ask, waiting for the day he will forgo pleasantries and open up more.

Dorit has told me everything there was about Viggo, including the part where she befriended him for a year before he gained the courage to speak with her.

I thought I was beating those odds on the occasions he would stay after meetings or conversations with Jonas, but the way he nods while politely skirting away hints I still have a ways to go.

One of these days.

I open the door and step onto the plush rug spread across Jonas's study. Jonas is hunched over his desk, shuffling a few stacks of paper as I enter, masking my breathing to prevent further questions. But he catches it as I flop into one of his comfortable chaises, lifting my feet up as I fan my cottoned tunic around me.

"Training going well?" Jonas asks without lifting his head.

Still breathless from my encounter with Jerrick and the brisk walk that brought me here, all I can give in a response is a "mmm-hmm."

His face wrinkles as his brown eyes meet mine, fondness glowing across his features.

A little thorn stabs my chest, envious of the happiness radiating from him and praying one day I, too, will have that. I shake it away before he can tell, eager to discuss our plans.

"Did you hear from any of the guests we invited from Axidoria and the other kingdoms?" I ask, hopeful I haven't ruined everything for my people.

He reaches toward a stack of letters on his right, sweeping them to the center of his desk as he beams.

"Yes," Jonas starts. "Our worries were valid, but I think with the three of us stating we have no intention of invading other kingdoms, they have taken the news better than we all expected. They want to plan a meeting for all six kingdoms at a later time.

King Beauvais and King Bernard, with his daughters, will be the only ones in attendance at the masquerade ball, though."

I lower my head at the news, relieved other kingdoms received the marriage announcement well.

I am excited to reunite with King Bernard and meet King Beauvais for the first time. Northtry and Unterkirch are farther away, so it is understandable that the journey might be too long for them solely to attend a party.

My heart thunders to ask the next question, but I push through it, voicing my trepidation. "Any news from Axidoria?"

I adjust my position, inching closer to see if any of those letters might have Niko's or Betina's handwriting. *Something.* Too obvious with my efforts, Jonas aids me, pulling two letters from the pile and offering them to me. I dart my hand out, crinkling the paper from snatching them to read.

> *We humbly accept this invitation to celebrate the union of King Jerrick of Palaena and Queen Tove of Axidoria. As we have made strides in uniting our kingdoms, it is our highest honor to attend to meet and converse with our king and queen and staff members that serve our monarchs in Palaena.*
>
> *Lord Nikolaj Drost,*
> *Royal Advisor of Axidoria*

His baritone voice reads each line in my mind, and I linger on his signature. Fear gnaws at me even as I run my fingers over his name. Is he coming as my advisor? As my friend? Or the man I want to marry?

The questions repeat as I read Betina's acceptance letter, hoping I will hear good news from her soon.

My heart somersaults at the thought of embracing the two of them, regardless of Niko being upset with me about calling off his plan.

I yearn to see him and hold him. I yearn for his smile and his attentive ear.

I blink away the tears lining my vision. "Thank you for this." I sniff, folding the letters and returning them to the pile of accepted invitations.

Jonas takes them while helping himself into his high-backed armchair. A sigh escapes as he lifts his legs to rest along the edge of his desk, earning a smile from me.

As if we both know of the stress the other carries, we sit in silence and stare at the ceiling. A few stones are different in coloration, and I count them to calm my mind from other additive stresses of ruling.

"I am told you are going on a hunt with Jerrick," Jonas says into the quiet drifting between us.

His statement forces my own lungs to heave a long exhale, a new problem rising to the top of the pile of problems I'm already juggling. Luckily, Jonas finds my sigh is answer enough because he chuckles, easing his body and stretching.

He says, "While I've enjoyed planning a ball these last few months with you, a hunt sounds much more peaceful to me."

I scoff. "If you mean hiding in the woods, bodily odors in the air, and sweat caking every inch of your body, *sure*. A hunt sounds *much* more peaceful," I tell him, tilting my head back toward the ceiling.

"It could be fun," he suggests, as if he knows it will only be Jerrick and me.

Alone.

I drag my stare to him, skeptical this is somehow his and Jerrick's doing. I am met with a smirk, *eerily* like when his brother is up to something.

The small features of Jerrick in Jonas have me flicking my eyes away, fearful of my own thoughts betraying me again.

"It will be hot and boring."

I am *not* looking forward to revisiting Biala Forest.

A sharp phantom twinge drags along the right side of my shoulder blade. The memory of my injury is still fresh, even though I am fully healed.

My insides twist with every negative emotion swarming and seeking to drown me.

"You haven't been outside the castle walls very much. Maybe fresh air will do you well," Jonas suggests, standing up. "Besides, it's not like you must be here for any more arrangements for the celebration. I have it all sorted."

I rub my head across the soft armchair, my unease with everything coming to the surface. I don't want to leave because I want to find out more about Jerrick's curse. I don't want to leave and go into unfamiliar territory. My work here isn't finished.

"I could help you with—"

Jonas waves me off, approaching with happiness in his eyes. "I've got it, Tove. I always will." He rests a hand on my shoulder, lightly squeezing in reassurance.

I look at it before gazing up at my brother-in-law, my royal advisor, who has delivered everything time and again with little to no word of complaint.

"Go have some fun in the sun," he encourages, brotherly love pouring from him as he squeezes my shoulder again. "Just promise me I'll get my own time away when this is all over."

I snort, throwing him off guard before he joins in with his own laughter. "I'll be sure to tell Jerrick to grant you and Viggo time away after the ball."

His eyes shine at my mention of Viggo, a blush glimmering across his cheekbones.

I take his hand. "A holiday is long overdue for the two of you." I beam.

He huffs a laugh. "You're telling me."

I pat his hand as I sit up from my chair, dragging him into an embrace.

He stumbles and grunts his surprise, but he halts all movement when I squeeze him.

A familiar leather scent drowns my senses, followed by the scent of a forest. Oak and grass pair with leather, transporting me oddly to a comforting peace as my bond grows more with my time spent with Jonas.

I do not know if I will ever be able to stop showing my gratitude for everything he has done, everything he has counseled me on.

I wish I did this more for Niko when I first stepped into my role as queen.

I wish I did it more, even now.

But I can be better at showing my appreciation, starting with Jonas. I can't help but try to prove to him how much I care about him, too.

"You've done wonders on everything, Jonas. And I mean *everything*. You are the royal advisor every monarch needs. You deserve the world and more."

My brother-in-law returns the tightening hug, holding me closer as if protecting me from the world.

When we pull away, I stand and cup his face. Lifting on my tiptoes, I peck him on the cheek.

A memory from my past crashes against me, stealing my breath. When Runa and I were younger, we had always wished for another sibling, and I had prayed to the Makers for a brother. I remember giving up when it never came to pass.

But it *finally* did. I've finally gained the brother I've always prayed for.

My lip quivers at the finality of that revelation, and I pull Jonas in once more, tears drawing to my eyes for my brother-in-law—*my family*.

The words whisper in my mind as I try to swallow the emotions feuding within me.

"Thank you, Jonas, for *everything*."

My voice strains at the last word, my face scrunching up and burrowing into his embrace.

Jonas holds me close, simply existing and rubbing my back as my tears dampen his shirt. "Anytime, sis."

His response is tender and sweet.

Everything he is and everything he does is exactly what I had always wished for my brother to be.

38

A Gift for the Bride

As I lace up my boots, thoughts about what is going to happen on this hunt scatter through my mind. Excitement and fear are taking turns in my stomach at the thought of spending time with Jerrick, riding a horse, and practicing my magic in the open.

While I can admire my own improvements, I still struggle to rein in enough focus to mind my emotions and concentrate on my magic.

My thoughts drift to when I first came to Palaena, how frost would prickle along my skin and refuse to settle. I struggled to be aware of the flicker of power within me and would question everything, but I couldn't stop it.

And then Jerrick kissed me, using his magic and blending it with mine.

It warmed me—and utterly consumed me.

I clench my thighs at the thought of spending time alone with him.

He hasn't stayed in my room since my nightmare, but every night he has escorted me back to my chambers, his presence remaining outside as if in waiting. And each time, I almost invite him in, only to cower away in fear... fear of ruining everything with him.

But I can't dwell on that.

Not with everything I am trying to fix and prevent.

I look up from my boots and adjust my tunic in the vanity, and then plait my hair.

Dorit loads up my satchel for the next few days. When she finishes, she turns to the wardrobe, pulling out a belt Jerrick had made for me, armed with the knives he had forged.

The knives were so beautiful I didn't want to take them on our trip, but Dorit suggested I should because we are hunting.

Tying off my plait, I stand from the vanity as Dorit reaches around, securing my belt into place.

"The daggers are beautiful," she says as she admires the handles.

"They are," I agree, humming at the memory of him delivering them last night.

Touching the silver beaded hilt sprinkled with blue sapphires in swirls, my heart tugs at the comment he made when delivering them.

They match your eyes, he told me.

Our eyes, I wanted to say back to him in that moment.

Fuck, I *really* almost lost my resolve then. I can't stop the blush from gracing my cheeks.

Dorit's smirks.

I cross my arms, arching a brow. "What's that face for?"

She tightens her lip, stifling her chuckles.

I roll my eyes. "It's not what you think."

"I never said anything," she teases through her giggles.

"They were a nice gift."

"Mm-hmm."

I exhale and glance around the room once more, savoring the comforts of being indoors versus hunting in the woods. "Alright, well, thank you for your help."

I walk to my bed, my hands running over the sheets I'll be without for the next few days. Tension coils in my back, a phantom pain pinching near my shoulder blade.

It's a few days in the woods, Tove. You've survived once, you'll survive again.

I remind myself that Jerrick will be with me. Knowing I won't be venturing into the forest injured like last time is most reassuring. I pick up my satchel and give Dorit a hug.

She whispers, "Be safe and good luck."

I sigh into our embrace, half disbelieving I am *willingly* going on a hunting trip. I break away before I lose my courage.

When I reach the stables, Jerrick has one horse saddled, and a sense of relief rises, grateful he isn't pushing to teach me how to ride on top of hunting. Yet my stomach churns because we'll be sitting together on one horse.

Jerrick's hair is tied into a low bun, small waves too short to be held cover his features.

My mouth runs dry at the sight of him, and I bite my lip, preparing to not say or do anything stupid. Approaching, I notice the two knives, a sword, and a bow draped over his chest.

"Well, don't you look dressed for a battle?" I tease.

I internally cringe at my poor wording, hating the immediate thoughts of what a battle would look like here. Sweet Makers, what is wrong with me?

I walk up to the horse and offer my hand for him to sniff, anything to distract and drown out my never-ending thoughts.

The steed huffs quickly, moving his head to me. I stumble, and Jerrick jerks toward me.

He helps steady me as I laugh breathlessly, the animal relenting enough to huff again into my palm. I run my hands over the beast's black coat, the mind-numbing movement and steady presence of Jerrick reassuring and quietening my thoughts.

I peer up at Jerrick, and he answers my question with a half-smile. "You never know what you might run into."

My features slacken, and I grab my satchel tighter for support.

Jerrick smiles as he dips down and kisses my forehead. I close my eyes at the contact of his lips for a moment, slowly opening them only to stare back into his softened blue irises.

"Don't worry," he reassures teasingly, letting go of my hips and lifting my satchel over my head, strapping it to the horse.

He mounts up on the horse, and I cannot help but worry of getting hurt again. When Jerrick extends his hand, I stare at it, licking my lips in contemplation.

Do I really want to do this?

I look back at the castle, trying to ease the thoughts of being mauled by a bear or attacked by a mountain lion.

Could there be anything worse than that?

Fiddling with my hair, I exhale and raise a brow at Jerrick. "I'm not going to get shot again, am I?"

His laugh catches me off guard, and my apprehension deflates a little. Jerrick stretches his hand further. "I won't let anything happen to you. That, I guarantee, wife."

Wife.

His words ease my discomfort, and I gulp down air, bracing for a change of scenery.

I take Jerrick's hand and lift to mount.

His lips tickle near my ear when I rest in front of him, heat warming my back and pulling me to the night we spent together. His hands reach around my stomach, easing me further into him.

I rest my head in the crook of his neck as the softest of breezes kisses my skin.

I clench my thighs in protest, relaxing them only for his breath to warm the entire side of my neck as he says, "I've got you." Jerrick motions for our steed to take off.

As we leave the castle, I am surprised when we change our direction from Yadir and Biala Forest into venturing north toward Thresborn Forest. With the Velkan Mountains coming more into view, the dread of returning to the woods didn't taunt me as we trekked into a new environment, allowing me a different perspective and appreciation for nature.

A breath of fresh air, as Jonas would call it.

The fresh smell of pine and moss linger near my nose, the mix of fallen leaves and Jerrick's scent has me smiling softly. We ride much of the trip in comfortable silence.

Every so often, he adjusts himself on the saddle, and I miss the seconds of his touch on my abdomen. And whenever we slow, he rubs my stomach in soft circles.

The worry and anxiety diminish the further we venture. I sway, taking in each tree we pass and listening to the chittering of all creatures. Even as nightfall spreads across the pinkened lavender sky above, I fall deeper into tranquility.

Jerrick eases the horse into a slower pace, scouting for a place to camp. He tugs on the reins lightly, guiding us to a space in between trees. When Jerrick dismounts and steals the warmth, a chill that should not be present in warmer months crashes against me.

My teeth chatter as Jerrick offers his hands, helping me dismount. When I touch the ground and I look up to thank him, I can't hide my tremors.

Jerrick takes my hands and blows into them. His lips touch the inside of my palms, sending a fire scorching down to my core. He watches me and my mouth runs dry as he sends more heat into my hands, checking to see the shakes cease.

Memories surface of the last time he touched me and set my body ablaze.

"Feeling warmer yet, Frostbite?"

The same question he asked me all those months ago, changing each time he's voiced it. Yet instead of anger I felt from that first time, there is something else.

His thoughtfulness and efforts warm me a little, so I nod slowly.

He smiles, only to pull away and remove all warmth again.

Jerrick scans our surroundings. "Stay with the horse. I'm going to make a fire."

He looks for dry branches as tremors greet me again. Feeling too awkward to speak, I hug myself in hopes of giving myself the same warmth Jerrick did. Trying to be helpful, I take the horse's reins, bringing him near the campsite.

As Jerrick feeds the fire, I wrap the reins around a tree, attempting to tie it off before rubbing the horse's neck and fiddling with his mane. His coat is shiny, and the mane hair is as soft as mine.

Deciding we should have matching hair, I plait the mane, heat building as the fire grows. I sigh when the horse brushes against me while I finger comb the mane into multiple plaits. By the time I finish the third plait, I spare a glance back at Jerrick.

He cocks his head and crosses his arms, the well-lit fire behind him and his amused face warming my entire body. He smirks and approaches.

The steed huffs beside me, and I run my fingers through its mane as Jerrick removes our packs and inspects my handiwork. He hoists the satchels over his shoulder before meeting my gaze.

"I have enough food for tonight, but tomorrow, we will need to work. It'll be beneficial for my curse to hunt before the ball and find provisions for the rest of our trip. In our downtime, we can practice your magic," he says.

I incline my head while Jerrick strolls back to the fire, putting the packs down and unpacking them. He stops suddenly.

"Where is your blanket?"

Confusion crosses my features, and I face him. The weather is so warm in Palaena, and I will only sweat more in the night.

"What blanket?" I ask.

Jerrick slaps the front flap of my satchel closed and pinches the center of his nose as a sigh escapes. "You're supposed to pack a blanket because it gets cold during the night. We are at a higher altitude near the mountains."

Dorit.

"Dorit helped me pack my bag." I try to defend myself while also throwing her under the rug.

Maybe she forgot? Regardless, I don't need a blanket. It'll be fine.

Jerrick tosses my sack aside, pulling his own thin blue blanket, woven in yarn instead of a luxurious fabric. "You'll have to sleep next to me." He fluffs the blanket out, layering it on top of a section he swept down to have even leveling for his sleeping space.

The blanket is small, barely big enough for him to sit on and wrap himself in. Looking at it, I gulp down a nervous tremor at the implication of sharing.

My blood races to my cheeks, and I swirl back to the horse, fiddling with the plaits I made.

Even as I crave his touch with the idea of sharing a close space again, my mind thankfully keeps my heart in check and prevents me from voicing my lustful thoughts—for the most part.

"It's warm, and we have a fire. I am sure I will be plenty fine without a blanket," I say to reassure myself.

Jerrick adjusts the branches in the fire. "As you wish, Frostbite." He winks.

That damn sultry voice of his.

If I could slap myself now, I would. But it would only raise questions I do *not* want to answer.

Jerrick sets out some food, and I decide I should not make anything more awkward than it needs to be. I approach the fire and stretch out my hands, smelling the burnt leaves. The embers flare and drift upward, reaching the limits of the night sky before disintegrating. The faintest of stars glint as I observe the pale moon compared to the little flickers of light from the fire.

I close my eyes to the serene peace surrounding me. The wind brushes through the forest, the softest of insects chirping, and I open my eyes at the hoot of an owl.

"You probably don't remember much from our last expedition through the woods," Jerrick says, offering me a napkin of food.

I shake my head and move away from the fire, grabbing the napkin and adjusting into a sitting position. Opening it, there is some dried fruit, bread, and a pastry.

My stomach flips as a smile spreads wide across my face. I lift my gaze to Jerrick, met with a bashful grin.

"Thank you," I breathe.

Jerrick scratches the back of his head in response, both of us going for the solstice pastry first. We each study the other, chewing and swallowing the treat before the rest of our dinner.

Jerrick tends to the fire every so often as I finish my food. He takes my napkin, brushing the crumbs off past a fallen tree, and folds it into the satchel.

"Go ahead and rest. I'm going to tend to the horse," Jerrick says.

I glance around our campsite, a cold breeze blowing in the air. Not being close enough to the fire, it sends a tremor through my body.

I look at the flames, the blanket, and Jerrick, deciding against my better judgment to scoot over to a small section of the blanket. Knowing I am falling for this trap, I hug myself and face the fire, hopeful it'll keep me warm all night and that I won't do anything stupid should Jerrick lie beside me.

I make myself comfortable and ease down on my side, darting my eyes between the embers in front and Jerrick. He catches me staring, and I avert my attention back to the fire, grateful he did not say anything.

Jerrick's footsteps crunch on the fallen leaves, making their way to me.

My heartbeat hammers in my ears as he settles beside me, keeping as much distance as he can while attempting to make himself comfortable. I watch the base of the fire, listening to the crackle and smelling the smoke permeating the air, trying to focus on the heat warming me rather than the man behind me.

He is so close—*so* close that if I moved a muscle, we would be touching.

I push down the thought, needing to suppress my desires while we are away.

I need to stay focused on breaking the curse.

I need to stay focused on training my magic.

I need to *not* focus on the man next to me.

Even though I say nothing to Jerrick, I try to push past my conflicts and the phantom touch of his hands on my stomach. But I imagine them drifting lower—low enough to have my insides flex with need. The temptation furthers my arousal, repeating itself through my mind.

I bite my lip, desperately fighting the urge to roll over and ride my pleasure into release.

I watch the embers as a distraction. They dance and spin, the wind blowing as each one floats into the sky. Counting them clears my mind, sleep dragging me into a deep slumber when the fire dies out.

39

PREDATOR AND PREY

A slight tug on my shirt wakes me. I ignore it, adjusting my sleeping position. But the tugging of my clothes starts again like I am being nudged. Finally annoyed by the poking sensation, I move to tell Jerrick to let me sleep, only to stop when a hand clasps over my mouth.

"Shh. Don't move," Jerrick whispers in a hushed tone.

I barely register what is happening as Jerrick guides my backside to him, his hard length pressing into me as he wraps a protective arm around me. Groaning inwardly, I bite my lip to refrain from moaning.

This is not the time or the place to be thinking about that, Tove.

It doesn't help when Jerrick pats my body. "Where are your knives?"

I finally open my eyes.

"Fuck," he says, sounding distraught.

I clench my thighs at the guttural tone, sinful thoughts distracting me, and my nipples tighten in response.

Fuck, fuck, fuck.

Are we about to—

"I only have one knife on me." Jerrick hovers over my ear, lips kissing it slightly, making everything much more heightened.

He slips the knife into my hand and my eyebrows knit together.

I peer up at him, only for my blood to run cold at the sound of leaves crunching somewhere nearby. My heart stops as the horse, too, perks its head up from its sleeping position, aware of the sudden shift in the air.

Goose bumps prickle up the length of my spine as I scan the surroundings, terror gripping my heart at the tall mahogany-brown bear meandering near our campsite.

My eyes flick from the beast to the horse and the gear and weapons resting next to it.

Shit.

I look back at the bear carefully. The sunlight reflects against its thick—probably extremely soft—fur, and the red hues draw in the creature's natural magnificence.

"Use your magic or throw the knife at it," Jerrick whispers.

"Are you insane? I can't do that!" I hiss.

I don't want to harm anything or anyone.

Jerrick's mouth lingers near my ear again, his body warming mine, holding my hip. "You can. You have the closer shot. Besides, we came here to hunt and train. Think of this as a surprise lesson."

I fucking hate surprises.

The horse's ears dip backward, aware of the threatening presence. The steed shakes its head, unable to move much from being tied to the tree stump.

I freeze in place, panic on the verge of escaping me as the bear sniffs the ground, coming more into view with its head crowned with a tree-branch halo. It is as if Leander, the Maker of Beasts himself, is walking amongst us. His god-like powers are contained in this behemoth of a creature that reigns over the forests of Draymenk.

Fucking Deities, I am going to die today.

"Wh-What about your magic?" I mumble quietly, still gaping at the bear.

"My magic doesn't kill animals. They have to be severely wounded before I can do anything."

Every step the bear takes is inches closer to me—its *meal.* "Y-You can't expect me to do this when a predator is mere feet away from *EATING* me!

He lowers his mouth to my nape, kissing it softly as his hand rests on my hip and squeezes. *Hard.* "You need to practice all aspects of your training in stressful situations, and this is the perfect opportunity. Just try."

I tighten my fingers around the hilt, shaking my head in silent objection. "What if I miss?"

My motion rustles the leaves underneath the blanket, and Jerrick's grip moves from my hip to my head, stopping me from making more noise.

I stop when his whisper is low, dark, and demanding. "Don't doubt yourself. Now, do it."

Jerrick gives me some space, careful to minimize the amount of noise he makes to prevent the horse and bear from reacting.

I look back to the steed still unable to see the predator approaching behind it.

My magic could have more consequences for the surrounding area. I could start another ongoing winter in Thresborn Forest if I use my gifts. Without the guarantee of removing the ice, I choose to use the dagger.

Jerrick squeezes my thigh as I glance at my target, waiting for him to stop before throwing the knife.

"A flick of the wrist. Just like I showed you," he mouths.

But my aim is terrible.

I know it, and the Makers know it.

I send a prayer to Alora, pleading for this to work and that the bear I am about to attack is not Leander himself.

All I have to do is injure it enough for Jerrick to take over.

I... I can do that.

As the knife touches my shoulder, the bear slows to a stop.

But the horse grunts its unease, and a low grumble responds. The steed staggers, its neighs drawing the beast's full attention to us.

I go rigid, my lungs and heart stopping when the bear makes eye contact.

A force shifts the dagger from my hand into Jerrick's, and he uses all his strength in the release of the knife over a longer distance. It launches toward the bear, and my prayer is answered as it inches close enough to strike true.

But the bear shifts, and the knife slashes across its arm.

The beast's loud roars are deafening as the knife meets the tree beside it, the horse neighing once more, earning another bellow from the beast in challenge and fury.

All I can do is gape in fear, frozen in place.

"Freeze him!" Jerrick screams, needing a distraction to get to his bow.

But I can't sense my magic.

I'm going to die. I'm going to die.

Rustling behind drums in my ear as Jerrick jumps up, his movements rapid as he unties the animal from the tree, smacking it on its ass to run.

Jerrick looks between his weapons and me.

The horse neighs again, jumping up on its hind legs and standing taller than the bear.

Jerrick staggers as the steed rotates its front legs in defense when the beast meets the threat. He rushes to my side, pulling me upright as the black horse lands on all fours, running away from the scene.

The world stops as the bear turns on us, growling and ready to devour me.

Jerrick grabs my face, pulling my attention away from the massive predator. "RUN!"

He pushes me ahead, I finally remember to move, running away from the bear with no end goal in mind. All our gear, weapons, and horse abandoned and forgotten.

Darting through trees and branches, I avoid fallen logs, praying to the Makers we don't run into another creature.

Jerrick's pace passes mine, and exhaustion tugs at my body as I run. My heart thumps as I scan my surroundings in fear.

Jerrick takes my hand, steering me to the left.

"This way!" he yells, dragging me with him.

I bump into him, almost causing us both to fall. I struggle to keep up with his pace, and like an idiot, I glance behind me to see the bear following closely.

"Jer!" I shout in warning, my feet stumbling underneath me.

We jump over a fallen tree stump as Jerrick drags me along. His hold yanks every few steps, tugging me to keep up with his pace.

"There's a river up ahead, and we can let the current take us away."

My heart falls out of my chest.

I cry through ragged gasps. "I can't swim!"

But the bear's movements still echo behind us, and I know the lesser of evils will be the river.

The ground beneath us hardens under crumpled dead leaves, dirt, and soot as we near a cliff.

I smell the river before I see it, and the fear of drowning shifts my balance unexpectedly, sending me and Jerrick down.

I hit the rocks, and I hiss in pain with barely any recovery time.

Jerrick bounces up like it is nothing, tugging at my clothes to aid me up.

But I can hardly breathe—let alone move—with fear and exhaustion gripping me.

My tunic loosens from my trousers, the fabric ripping from Jerrick's strength.

He stops to look behind him, seeing the bear hurrying toward us—*fast*.

"Come on, Frostbite, we're almost there." He pulls me, and I slump, muscles fatigued and pinching in pain.

"I *can't*, Jer. The water," I pant, my voice hoarse and inaudible.

"Hold on to me, and remember to take a deep breath," Jerrick orders, scooping me into his arms and running to the edge of the cliff.

I scream, my heart flipping as I grip Jerrick in my panic when his footing leaves the ground, and we plummet.

Being airborne is nothing as my lungs inhale of their own accord, knowing what is to come.

Water attacks my skin, and the force of the element takes us by surprise. It pulls us down, and the lower we sink, the colder it gets.

I am pushed and pulled in all directions, and the only hold I have on Jerrick is his hand.

I strain to hold my breath, even when another current crashes against us, the impact forcing us apart.

No.

My movements turn frantic as I flail underwater, seeking the surface or Jerrick. The world weighs down as the push and pull of the river gnaws at me.

It gets colder the more I panic.

My chest aches from exertion and lack of oxygen. A tightness latches onto my sternum, my ribs, and my lungs, caving in as my arms and legs can't do anything.

A kernel of my magic sways against the pain, trying to be useful, but I am so cold—*so tired.*

Images of someone's face dance through my vision as they call my name.

My name. My—*nickname.* Not Snow Queen but... *Frostbite.*

I try to speak, but something gurgles, ceasing the action. I feel heavy, almost double my own weight, and I can't sense a lick of air. No air.

I can't breathe.

A force pounds down on me. *Hard.*

Bile rises and caves my chest inward. The pressure from my abdomen lurches my eyes open, and I have no time to stop from rolling over to empty the contents of my stomach.

I heave and sob, still not enough air passing into my lungs. My senses are muddled, the heavy scent of pine makes me need to vomit even more.

A warm sensation touches my back, the soothing heat the only thing I can focus on.

With my stomach emptied, my vision adjusts. Black rims the sides, slowly turning into a blur and then clear images. Solid ground is beneath me, trees line the river in front of me, and summer's heat blazes against my exhausted body.

My clothing is soaked against my skin, goose bumps prickling in one spot. I turn to my exposed shoulder and the man completely frozen and gazing at me with disbelief.

Jerrick.

We stare dumbstruck at each other.

He scoots closer, touching my arm gently, as if I am not real.

Grief-stricken, my husband sinks to his knees and scoops me into his lap, cradling me close.

"I thought I lost you," he gasps, his voice thick with emotion.

Jerrick dips his head into the crook of my neck, inhaling long and slow. A shuddered exhale escapes him, and I feel capable of moving.

I hold his neck and close my eyes, fighting the choked sob that builds when his arms flex, hugging me tight. Nuzzling into him, I'm desperate to bury myself in his skin, his bones—*anything* to have him closer.

Adrenaline, exhaustion, and emotions wrack through me as I shake uncontrollably. Tears fall down my cheeks, soaking Jerrick's skin.

"Jer," I croak out.

He threads a hand through my damp hair. "I'm here, Frostbite. I'm here."

I try to apologize for losing my grip on him. "The water—"

"Shh, I know, I know. I've got you now. I am here. It's all my fault."

His voice is low and somber.

I hold him, still adamant on apologizing. "It's mine, though. I didn't use my magic. I could have—*we* could have—" I break off, the what-if questions coursing through my mind.

We *both* almost died, and it's my fault.

Jerrick pulls away and holds my face in his hands. He brings my forehead to his, the warmth of his body pouring over me. His lips touch my brow before he tilts my gaze to meet his.

The haunted look and pain in his eyes carve a haunting melody in my soul.

"I am *so* sorry," he whispers.

I break, unable to stop the unknown from consuming me.

He guides me back to him, and I grip his tunic as I cry.

"I'm sorry, too. For not packing a blanket, for not using my magic, for tripping, for letting go under water, for—"

Each word strains against my vocal chords, my throat dry and scratchy. Even when I want to be dry and warm, I know I won't be able to with tears flowing and the regret of all my wrongs festering.

"I'm sorry for *everything*," I sob, pleading for him to forgive me for that which I cannot voice—that which I desperately seek to fix.

He remains silent as I hyperventilate, caressing the top of my hair as he holds me. With everything coming to a head, I am unable to stop the overwhelming shame from tearing me apart.

My husband sways us as I struggle to control myself.

"You have nothing—and I mean *nothing*—to be sorry for. Everything is my fault. I am the one that needs to apologize. And

I am. I am *so* sorry, Frostbite. For *everything*," he murmurs against my ear and kisses my head.

"I should not have pushed you when we were in danger. I should have listened to you rather than use it as an opportunity to teach. My aim should have been better. I should have been faster, should have grabbed a weapon and protected you. I should have listened when you said you couldn't swim. Fuck!"

He breaks, and his hold on me tightens.

Jerrick goes quiet, his fingers threading through my hair as he takes another deep, shuddering breath.

My heart sinks to my stomach at his apology, knowing everything he means. I wish I could do the same and confide in him. About Niko, my mother's mirror—

But if Jerrick knew *everything*, I don't know what he would do. He could kill me or help me. If I told him now, he might not see past my initial intent in coming here. And then my efforts to prevent a fight would crumple.

But what if he heard me? Truly heard everything I had to say? He would listen, right?

Hope flutters through my tremors when I break apart from our embrace, his blue eyes holding me captive once more. They flick back and forth between mine, and I am at a loss for words.

I'm too overcome by relief that he is here, that I am here, and that we are alive.

The moment sinks in deeper as I absorb every crevice of his features, constantly admiring him. A fire swelters in my chest, an ache of gratitude and longing for the man in front of me.

I cup his cheek, refusing to remove my gaze as he melts into my palm.

His eyes close slowly, lips grazing the inside of my hand. Heat prickles from his touch, and I can't stop myself from leaning and drawing our faces near.

Unable to stop the need running through me to thank him, to convey my appreciation, I kiss him.

The warmth of his lips spreads over mine and expands, drifting down and heating my body. I hold his face between my hands as I kiss him softly, tenderly. Sorrow and gratitude pour from me as the kiss deepens, hoping he can sense it—understand it.

Jerrick shifts, gripping my hips tightly.

I mimic the action on his face before ending the kiss and slowly pulling away. When I open my eyes, his are twinkling with mischief.

"Did you just fucking kiss me?"

I snort so loud I cover my mouth, my head rocking up to the sky. Laughter sings between us, remembering when I said the same thing to Jerrick the first time he kissed me.

I play on old memories, teasing him as he had. "It worked, didn't it?"

A playful smirk graces Jerrick's lips as he purrs, "I might need you to try it again in case it didn't."

I am tempted to do just that as a shiver runs up my spine. My body contorts, and I hate the tension in my limbs.

Jerrick rubs my back, trying to warm me, perking up and scanning the surroundings. "We need to return home. Can you walk?"

I nod and move off him.

He stands and takes my hand, tugging me up as I ask, "Don't you still need to hunt, though?"

"Yes," he sighs heavily. "And find my horse and retrieve our weapons. But I think it would be safer if you were back on the castle grounds, especially as the current dragged us closer to home than our campsite."

"But—" I pause when he lets go of me, immediately losing my balance.

His reflexes save me from slumping onto the dried leaves. "Easy there, I've got you."

I blush.

He always has a way to say he is here for me. He holds my waist, hunching slightly, and I bring my arm around his upper torso to lean on him as we walk.

The thought of not finding our steed tugs at my heart. "I can help find our horse."

I *just* plaited its mane.

"I—" Jerrick's boots crunch against the leaves as he huffs a breath. "I-I can't have you help me."

"Why?"

He cringes, and it has me worried I overstepped moments ago. Heat floods my cheeks in embarrassment that I misread his actions and response earlier.

"I can't risk that," he admits.

I drop my head in shame. "Oh."

The burden I am twists and churns in my stomach. I've ruined his hunting trip, sent his horse running, and can't even protect myself enough to help fix my mistake.

He is right. It's too much of a risk for me to be in the forest with him. If we encounter another predator, who's to say I won't freeze up again?

I sink in defeat. I'm a hazard to bring along, and my options are limited to within the castle walls. I can't believe he is going back out here. Alone.

There are only a few more days left before the masquerade ball, and I know this hunt is important for him. For his curse and for his magic. Guilt eats at me and the lack of progress we've made in breaking his curse. I need to be in the library while he is away.

It's my only hope.

My only chance of doing something right for once.

We stop at a small clearing away from the river, a space surrounded by more trees. I look at Jerrick for him to guide us onward, but he stops, scanning the area before turning to face me.

He takes my face, tilting it to meet his. Wisps of his black hair blow in the breeze, sweat on his brow, and his scar still beautifully sculpting and illuminating his features, making him more striking than I remember from the first time I saw him.

His blue eyes behold mine as he says fervently, "I failed to protect you here. You've almost died twice in my company, and I... I can't risk losing you." He draws me close for a quick peck faster than I can process.

I blink in surprise when he pulls away with a smirk.

But when he winks, *Sweet Makers*, I soar.

Jerrick has saved my life twice. Gratitude warms my heart immensely, sending it skipping. Holding his gaze, I can't stop my own bashful smile.

"Would it be alright if I used my gifts to help warm the two of us?" he asks.

I am soaked to the bone and have water in my boots that slush and sway with each step. I huff a breath of relief.

"Thank Yeva. I thought you'd never ask."

Jerrick chuckles low, drawing me in.

"Stay close," he murmurs into my hair, guiding us in a new direction.

The sun rises as we hold each other, our clothes going from soaked to damp as heat lifts from the ground. We scan the surroundings often, aware of any new noises. Whether we are looking out for a bear, our horse, or a break in the forest's tree line, we remain close.

Jerrick's power warms my entire body, mind, and soul. His magic no longer feels foreign to me, rather, it is comforting and calls to my own. The dynamic is balanced, peaceful, and harmonious.

We pass occasional glances, catching and bashfully darting our stares away while leaning closer as each step we take leads us home.

40

SEEING IT IS ONE THING

Jerrick and I make it home as the sun sets. I remain leaning on my husband as we step past the threshold, guards dispersing quickly, fetching Jonas and Dorit.

Staff members pace through the halls. Some carry vases, fabrics, linen, candlesticks, sacks of food, and I barely track where each one is hurrying to.

An exhaled grunt beside me is startling and when I look up at Jerrick, his entire demeanor has turned dark and lethal. His features harden, jaw clenching, with a vein pulsing in his throat.

Tentatively, I touch his chest, drawing his focus away from others.

I still.

Jerrick regards me with darkness painted with pure rage, hatred, and loathing. It's a side of him I have never seen. His pupils are dilated, the black taking over the icy blue of his irises.

Hunger flickers in his eyes as I mouth his name softly. Jerrick's movements are slow, and I hiss when he digs his fingers into my arm, clutching it tight.

The entire hall is quiet, and I swear time has stopped. Footsteps come from the right of me, but I refuse to move under Jerrick's studied stare.

A gasp escapes, and those footfalls, too, halt.

Dorit rasps, "Tove—"

Jerrick growls—actually *growls*—at me before moving his stare to her.

I turn to not only Dorit, but to Jonas and Viggo coming into view with more staff and royal guards walking through the entryway.

All eyes are transfixed on Jerrick altering in front of us.

Jonas and Viggo raise their hands to calm Jerrick. When Jonas reaches Dorit, he elbows her to do the same.

She hisses, earning me a tighter squeeze from Jerrick.

I stiffen in response to Jerrick's hold, trying to be unaffected. When I meet his gaze again, I understand what this is.

I glance at Jonas once more, noting the subtle bow of his head.

Jonas guides Dorit back a slow, tentative step.

I can't do much for the others, so I force my attention on my cursed husband. I call my magic forth, hoping I can control it.

Jerrick notices the flicker of power from me as it sends his own forth in defense.

"Don't even think about it," I warn him when his magic tries to crawl up my frost-covered arms.

His eyes flash. "And what if I *do* think about it?"

Each syllable is gravelly as frost manifests on my hand, remaining on my skin but not touching his.

Whatever his magic or curse is doing builds a wall over his chest.

I focus, trying to harness my emotions and all thought into not hurting him but bringing him out of this rage, trying to distract him as he has done for me so many times.

His jaw clenches, arm tightening around me, and the pushback sends my magic outward from my hand, frost appearing on him.

I inhale a sharp breath. "No!" I yank my hand away as Jerrick watches the frost on his skin.

He lets go of me as the frost on his tunic turns into ice, growing.

I clutch my chest as staff members around us gasp.

No, no, no.

It's happening all over again.

The thought and panic are short-lived as Jerrick closes his eyes in concentration, his hand holding the impacted area.

The ice *disintegrates*.

A breath escapes Jerrick from the effort, and when he meets my gaze, the blue in his irises take over. He blinks a few times, regret furrowing his brows as he takes a few steps away, his eyes conveying a wordless apology.

Turning to all staff members, he commands, "Nothing to see here. Move out!"

The staff jump to attention and resume their tasks.

The scene around me changes as Jonas rushes to Jerrick and Dorit runs to me.

She holds my shoulders, checking every angle as my stare and Jerrick's remain fixed on each other.

Jonas and Jerrick speak, and although I am unable to hear, I can tell the conversation is not important because Jerrick waves off his brother, stepping back toward me.

He leans in and kisses my cheek.

Dorit's protective grip tightens around my wrist as Jerrick drags his lips to my ear.

He whispers softly, "*Please* forgive me. I have to go. I'll return as soon as I can."

My husband leaves without any more explanation, leaving me breathless despite everything that just unfolded.

Frost thrums down my arms, and I look to see a light chill expanding from my hand. I concentrate on eliminating the sensation, hoping since the danger is gone, my magic will recede.

The ice numbs my fingertips momentarily before my power drains, sucking itself back into my body, pouring into each vein as heat returns.

My frost is silent again, and all I can think about is Jerrick.

"I have to get to the library," I say.

Jonas and Dorit share a glance with each other before turning back to me.

"H-How did you do that?" Dorit asks.

Looking back to where Jerrick left the three of us, I feel a pang of longing to go after him and help him as he has helped me so many times.

I shrug, understanding he needs time alone.

"I have no idea."

Dorit steps closer to me, voicing a reasonable suggestion. "Let's get you changed first, though."

The scent of the forest hits me, the slight dampness of fabric mixing with pine needles and a small tinge of bodily odor. I scrunch my nose.

"Right."

My mind races as I bathe. I replay the day's events, my muscles aching and exhausted. At first, I thought the trek back home from the forest was what tugged at my tired body, but it was more than that. It was how Jerrick had only been gone for a few hours, and I couldn't stop worrying about him.

Missing him.

I let out a long drawn-out breath before standing to wrap myself in linen and exit the bath. I enter my chambers and rest against the soft plush mattress as Dorit fiddles with my hair.

I remain quiet and still, unable to banish my concern over how to help Jerrick while also wanting to give up and sink into this bed and sleep these next few nights away.

More time without Jerrick means fewer eyes helping me break his curse.

I have an idea to ask Dorit about, but when a glimmer comes from my mother's mirror, I turn and watch it carefully, seeking to reach Axidoria.

Maybe Niko and Betina have not left yet.

When Dorit grabs a brush from my vanity, I take the opportunity to pick up the mirror and hold it close. A ripple runs through the reflection, a secondary one coming from the crack that happened when I first came to Palaena all those months ago.

I say, "I can finish dressing myself, Dorit."

"Are you sure? I can—"

"I'm fine."

She flinches a little at my higher pitch, but I soften it in reassurance. "Sorry, I just—I need some time alone, please."

She slackens her shoulders and bows. "Call for me should you need anything," she says, turning away.

I incline my head, watching her close the door to leave me alone. I don't move, focusing intently on Dorit's footsteps walking down the hall, allowing no one to listen in on my room.

Once it is quiet, I hurry and pull clothes on from my wardrobe. I rummage through each item of clothing, opting for a day dress instead of my now preferred cotton tunics and leather trousers.

If Betina or Niko saw me in this... Sweet Makers.

I need no distractions from them if I am going to get help.

I tremble as I move, suppressing it when I grab the mirror, circling its frame three times to channel a connection. It blurs momentarily, my old chambers in Axidoria coming into view with no one on the other end.

I slide against my mattress in defeat, sinking down on the rug beneath me. Gazing into my rooms, books are stacked and papers are scattered across both nightstands near my old bed. I have the urge to speak, but my throat runs dry.

"Betina?" I ask, jolting when something crashes in the background. "Hello? Are you okay?"

A feminine voice grumbles. The shuffling of papers mutes her words, making it hard to hear.

"Betina?" I call out, pleading to see her.

"I'm here," she shouts through the slamming of books stacking against each other.

I angle my head, trying for a possible glimpse of my friend, but I'm too impatient. "Betina, please, I need to see you."

She stumbles into view, looking exhausted. Her undereye is darkened, and her natural aura feels missing.

My heart splits at her hardened scowl, but when it softens, my hope remains.

"Tove," she whimpers, the crack in her voice tightening the guilt in my chest.

"I'm *so* sorry," I say.

Tears form when she gasps a smile. I pant my own relief, the two of us breaking into a sad laugh. But mine dies knowing everything I've put her through.

"Hey, hey, hey, now," Betina consoles.

It does nothing to help the wave of stress crashing against me. I catch myself as I regard my closest friend, grateful she is there but confused as to why she is not already traveling.

"Is Niko with you? Why aren't you on the way? You—you sent your invite acceptance?"

Her head tilts as she gazes upon me with sympathy. "No, Niko isn't here. And I couldn't go. Not after—"

"Not after what?"

She watches me warily. "Not after what I found."

The hair on the back of my neck rises as foreboding sinks deep into my bones. I clear my throat.

"What did you find?"

She pivots, walking toward a stack of books. She grabs one and faces me.

"Remember how you wanted me to investigate?"

"Yes," I tell her, eager at the possibility of her finding answers about my father and mother.

"Well, when I went to ask our priests about past criminal archives, I spent a while researching, trying to find any assassination attempts or any traces of evidence your mother may have gotten wind of. But I came up short, finding nothing correlating to your father. I only found logs of what criminals were arrested and prosecuted for."

I frown and my shoulders slump. "Oh." I avert my gaze, trying to not show my disappointment with her investigation.

"However," Betina says, drawing my attention, "I kept combing through the criminals, hoping there could be a connection, and I found a few names that were very familiar."

I sit up, leaning into the mirror. "What family names?"

Betina's throat bobs. "Albertsen."

I *knew* it.

She adds, "And Drost."

My heart stops, my own doubt voicing itself. "Just because they are an ancestor doesn't mean Niko is a criminal."

"I know, but that didn't stop me from asking him about it," Betina admits.

"You *what*?"

She wears a scowl in defense. "I'm not the one he is mad at, Tove. It wasn't hard for him to admit his uncle was convicted of murdering someone, and your mother had him cursed."

Shame creeps in.

My mother and father hurt his family, and he still showed loyalty to the kingdom and enlisted in the guard. My heart aches, knowing how much I've taken advantage of his kindness and love for Axidoria.

"He never told me," I whisper.

"Nikolaj only told me he looked for a way to break his uncle's curse when he was investigating your father's disappearance after you stepped into your role."

I massage my forehead at that confession, hurt Niko kept what happened to his family from me. Maybe that is why Niko encouraged community servitude rather than execution, like many of the other kingdoms. But Niko keeping Mother's cursing ability secret twists in my gut. He, the priests, and the retired royal advisors all kept that from me.

But I remember how cut off I was when I dismissed everyone. Even if Niko told me, I doubt I would have even been receptive to it.

Each revelation is heavy and weighs down on my body. I shake my head, wishing Niko was here to talk to.

He was trying to look out for me, even when I didn't know it.

"Nikolaj told me he couldn't find anything, but I asked him what he researched, and that led me to investigate your mother. I thought if it was something you could know, it might help him not be as angry at you."

"He told you?"

She nods, stepping closer and clutching the books to her chest. "I thought, since I wasn't making progress on your father, I could help you help Nikolaj with his uncle. If we found a way to lift the curse, maybe he'd be willing to hear you out about your plan."

"But Niko is already on the way, Betina. I can't help him now!" I drop my head and release a long exhale.

My plan was never going to work.

"But you can. And you can help the king, too," she says.

I blanch. "Wait. Why would you want me to help Jerrick?"

"Because Nikolaj convinced my father to go with him, to fight."

The stinging news draws the air away from me, horror gripping my heart. "*What?*"

The walls close in as I rub the ache in my chest, my mind racing and heartbeat thumping loud in my ears.

Niko is not standing down. *Thump.*

He is still mad. *Thump.*

He is too far down this path of revenge. *Thump.*

Betina says, "Nikolaj still plans to ambush the king the day after the ball. But I know you can convince him otherwise."

There is determination in her eyes, but I don't know what she means. If he didn't listen in the past, I don't know what else I can do.

"I already told him to stand down. How else am I going to stop him?"

Betina opens the book, turning a few pages, then stops to read aloud. "All curses cast by Queen Asta of Axidoria were created and recorded as punishment for criminals instead of execution. Each criminal was promised a chance for the curse to be lifted but only through the queen, herself. Queen Asta left instructions for future heirs to lift curses cast on criminals if she dies before a criminal redeems themself."

She stops and looks up. "It goes on to say, 'For a monarch to know how to break a curse, they must read it alone. Then and only then will the rest of the curse be revealed.'"

I blink in disbelief as my mouth falls. "Did Niko ever hear about this?"

Betina shakes her head. "No. No one has checked out this book since your mother. It is prohibited from being read by anyone other than royalty."

I arch a brow. "How did *you* get your hands on it?"

Her cheeks deepen as she shrinks inward, pressing her lips tight and using the book to conceal herself.

"Betina?" I press, and she blurts her explanation.

"I may have spent a few nights with one of the keepers to learn where it was located, and I *may* have borrowed it."

"Betina!"

"I know, I know!" She waves it off. "But how could I *not* look into it? If it is only readable by royalty, it has to have something! And I was right!"

Blinking in astonishment, I'm baffled she wasn't caught. I press my head against the mattress in relief of one thing but not the other.

Betina, no doubt is expecting me to scold her more, yet I can't be mad if she has answers that could help me not only with Niko but, *finally*, with Jerrick.

The thought sends my heart sputtering at the prospect of seeing Jerrick no longer burdened by his curse.

"I have to read a curse alone to see the end of it?" I ask.

She inclines her head. "And then it should tell you what the person needs to do for the curse to lift."

I huff a startled laugh. "This *entire* time, he really did need me." I rake a hand through my hair, stunned by my mother's choices and intellect. "We've been missing a piece of the puzzle."

"Tove, you need to tell Nikolaj about his uncle when he arrives at the ball. You need to break Jerrick's curse, come home, and help his uncle."

I bite my lip, our argument still sore and heavy on my heart. A thickness builds in my throat, fearful of ruining my relationship with Niko all before I even had a chance to experience it.

"I don't know if he will even listen to me. You didn't see him, Betina. He was so angry."

"He loves you," she tells me as tears form and slip down my cheek.

I glance away, licking my lips as I try to think of a response and hate my own hesitation.

How will we win each other's trust back?

"Don't you still love him?" she asks.

I care about Niko. He has always been there for me. I have pined after him for years, yet when I needed him to listen, he let me down.

We have let each other down.

"I-I—"

"It's okay if you don't."

"No, it's not that." I hesitate for the right words but draw up short because I think of Jerrick instead of Niko, comparing the two as I did when I was trying to find a suitor in Axidoria.

"Then, what do you mean?" she asks.

"It's just... he's so different from—"

"From the king?"

I dip my head, looking down at the floor, ashamed to even admit it.

Betina will not judge me for my feelings. She has always been unfazed whenever I find myself offering deeper and more intense emotions. It is one of her greatest qualities that I miss being around every day.

"I don't want either of them hurting the other, even more so now that I have realized Palaena is not an enemy," I confess, pulling my knees up.

"I built so much resentment for Palaena and everyone here for years. But even when I was kidnapped, I still did not want to hurt anyone. I never wanted a fight, but Niko convinced me it was my only option. It wasn't until I could find no evidence of their involvement with my father that I knew I needed to call off the fighting. And when I did, Niko lost it, believing I was doing it for Jerrick. I care about both of them and just want there to be peace."

"Maybe they can fall in love with each other." Betina wiggles her brows.

I laugh. "Wanting to fall in love yourself?"

But when I look at my friend, a blush blooms along her cheeks.

My eyes widen with questions.

"Have you *met* someone?" My own smile grows at the possibility.

She looks around before shushing me.

I squeal in delight as realization dawns. "Is it the keeper?" I ask, delighted and grateful for a change in conversation.

She bites her lip, and I grin.

"Tell me *everything*!" I demand as I pull the mirror close to my face, as if to intimidate the story out of her.

Betina quirks her brow and braces her hands on her hips. She pauses to peer out the window, the moonlight highlighting her features before she faces me once more.

"Go save *our* kingdoms. And when you do, I will tell you everything when you come visit."

I exaggerate a groan of disapproval. "You are such a tease."

"Don't need you to go chasing after them." She winks.

I roll my eyes in amusement, her love and aura peeking through her exhaustion. A twinge of pain clatters against my heart, knowing I've done this to her, and she has delivered, giving me a chance to help everyone.

The miracle I have prayed for.

"Betina, I don't even know how to thank you for this and for everything. Love you."

"Love you too, Tee." She waves a farewell, her grin bright and genuine. "Now, go. I'll be here when you come back."

A tear falls down my cheek, and I close my eyes, nodding. I have to wait a little longer to see her in person, but when I do, I will tackle her to the ground.

I swipe my hand once over the frame, severing the connection, and the image of Betina's smile fades away.

The moon shines into my room as I put my mirror on my nightstand. I study the night momentarily, taking in a moment of peace before hurrying down to the library, determined to set my sights on my marriage arrangement.

Running down the staircases, I debate visiting the kitchens but decide not to once realizing Cordelia and Ophelia have turned in for the night.

When my steps lead me into the library, I stride over to our designated spot, moving books and ledgers around in hopes of finding the marriage agreement. I'm berating myself for never considering reading it all the way through.

When none of the scrolls look familiar to me, I flop against the cushioned chair as footsteps creep in behind me. Turning with the hope of seeing Jerrick, I am surprised when Jonas comes into view.

I lift a brow in question, and he shrugs.

"Jerrick asked me to check on you while he was gone. Since you weren't in your rooms, I figured you might be here," he says.

I stand and rush to him. "Do you have the marriage agreement?"

Concern etches his features. "It's in Jerrick's study. Why?"

I hesitate, choosing a half-truth that could work in my favor. "I never read it thoroughly. I was hoping if I did so and revisited the curse, it might help," I admit bashfully.

Jonas's eyebrows shoot up as he huffs a laugh. "Come on, sis"—he gestures toward the door—"I'll take you to his study."

"Thank you." I grin, even though the guilt gnaws at my gut as we leave the library.

Jerrick's study is on the second level of the castle, and as Jonas opens the door, my breath catches at the essence of Jerrick in this room.

I walk in, my hands brushing against the chair I sat in the first time I was here, realizing I hadn't been in this room since that day. Hints of his cologne are in the air, and heat builds in my chest at the memory of him holding me earlier this afternoon.

Not once was I afraid. I only wanted to help. Even though my magic could have killed him, it was enough to catch his curse off guard, allowing me the chance to get the Jerrick I know back.

The door closes behind me, and my posture shoots up.

I remove the thought of Jerrick as Jonas approaches the desk, moving around piles of paperwork.

He grabs a scroll-like parchment that looks to be my marriage agreement.

Jonas extends it toward me, and I open it, looking upon the cursive handwriting at the top before skimming to the bottom.

I mutter, "This is going to take a while."

Jonas comes around the desk and pats my shoulder. "I'll leave you to it, then."

Looking at him, I smile before turning my attention to the document. I use my finger to hover over the top of the page for good measure, where I really need to read will have to wait until Jonas leaves.

And as soon as the door to Jerrick's study closes, ink drops of blood manifest on the sides of the paper. I stare in awe as the blood inks itself into letters, scrambling down the parchment and forming words underneath those etched in the curse.

I scan over the remnants of the spell, drifting to the beginning, reading it thoroughly and finding the final piece to break Jerrick's curse.

> *Ivan, oh Ivan how you've betrayed me,*
> *killing my love 'cause you were consumed by*
> *jealousy.*
> *Ruling two kingdoms filled your heart with greed,*
> *as punishment for your actions,*
> *I've placed a curse on your legacy.*
> *Your kin will become the bringer of death,*
> *turning on you first when I draw my last breath.*
> *You'll be forced to watch from beyond the grave,*
> *Knowing your kingdom is failing*
> *due to the choices you've made.*
> *But if your son so chooses to learn from your*
> *mistakes,*
> *Only in faithful consummation with love*
> *will then the curse break.*

I slouch against the chair, pinching the bridge of my nose. Tension and exhaustion take over my body as my thoughts run.

Mother had *every* intention of ruining Palaena. She signed not only King Ivan's death sentence, but Jerrick's as well.

He never would have had a chance to break his curse because she orchestrated us to marry.

Arranged marriages hardly ever turn into love, especially when it is with an enemy kingdom. And there is not even the possibility that he loves me, especially when he finds out everything I have kept from him.

Love is built with trust and respect, and I've done nothing but withhold information from him. But Jerrick doesn't strike me as someone who *loves*.

He cares about others, yes, but love? I've seen how he keeps everyone at a safe distance. I try to do the same, but he excels at it.

My heart breaks at the revelation.

He has to be in a faithful relationship *and* in love.

Maybe this new information will convince Jerrick to divorce me so he may give himself a chance to break the curse. It would be a strenuous process, but it gives him the freedom to remove the need to kill.

He would divorce me happily then, right?

We have good relations with all the kingdoms, and they all would authorize it because the world would shift back to what it once was. And if we divorce, I return to Axidoria, keep the peace and trade routes, and get to be with Niko.

If he still even wants you, Tove.

My thoughts do nothing to ease my heavy heart.

"Deities, Mother!" I shout up to the ceiling in frustration at everything she has done.

If she had told me and allowed me to help, maybe we could have researched our home for clues about my father's disappearance. Instead, she put blame on Palaena and set herself on a path of vengeance without any concrete proof.

She left me an entire kingdom to take, but I don't want it.

I don't want it when there is a perfectly capable king already here.

I run my fingers along my hair in guilt and pity for the trials Palaena has been through, all because of my mother. My insides twist in guilt, frustration, and worry as the burden of everything sinks in.

Not only do I have to convince Niko to stand down but also inform Jerrick of his only chance to break his curse. Both conversations are tied to feelings and emotions, and I have a strong sense that neither of them will take the news well.

41

WORDS ARE HARD

I search frantically for pins to secure some loose strands of my hair. My hands shake in anticipation of the ball tonight. I had hoped it would be excited nerves, but it is only dread.

Dorit arrived to help me about an hour ago, and I almost broke down. Even now, as she helps with my hairstyle, I still can't seem to gather myself.

Dorit takes my hand. "There is no need to be nervous," she says, rubbing my hand.

I shrink inwardly, trying to keep my distress at bay.

Jerrick greeted me this morning with that damned dimple of his, and instead of telling him everything right then, I ran in the opposite direction.

I don't know how to even tell him everything I discovered the other night. Plus, he is going to arrive here any minute to escort me, and my hair isn't ready.

Dorit pins small plaits to the back of my scalp, pulling most of my face-framing strands away while still leaving some space for my crown to rest on my head.

I distract my thoughts and focus on lining my eyes with smashed kohl. I don't want it heavy but enough to make my eyes stand out more than normal.

Deities, I wish Betina was here to help me.

When I finish, a long breath of air escapes at the success of not looking like a forest creature. A miracle from the Makers themselves.

Dorit's excitement is visible in the reflection. "Are you ready to change?" she calls back as she takes a box from a staff member at the door.

Dorit places the box on the bed and my stomach flips. I recognize the packaging from his grandmother's shop, and as Dorit removes the lining, we both gasp.

A magnificent, tight-bodiced gown is surrounded by its full skirt. I run my hands over the smooth fabric, marveling at the intricate designs, unable to fathom the amount of time Jerrick's grandmother put into this.

Black and red are woven and sewn together, sheer fabrics layered over one another.

I take the dress out of the box, and my heart lifts at the ruffled layers of the skirt, a thigh-high slit on one side, and off-the-shoulder sleeves dripping with delicate gold chains.

My lip quivers as I clutch the gown to my chest at the realization.

Jerrick had this made *so* long ago. Back when we first discussed the festivities and he suggested black, while I suggested red, and Jonas, gold.

If my mouth could fall to the floor at this moment, I am sure it would have.

Dorit's brows furrow. "Tove, you're crying," she says, taking the gown and placing it on the bed.

She helps dry my damp cheeks, but I can't stop the emotions.

This is too much.

The unbearable feeling strikes my heart. I cover my mouth and sob harder at the magnitude of Jerrick's quiet, observing thoughtfulness. Everything Jerrick has done and still does drives my shame deeper. I am truly undeserving of such kindness.

Dorit's arms wrap around me, and even that makes me feel awful.

"This is too much, Dorit. I don't deserve anything," I sob as guilt takes over.

"Oh," she murmurs into my ear, hugging me tighter.

Clutching Dorit tightly, I try to brave through my weakness and push on past the storm of talking to Niko and Jerrick. I haven't done anything helpful for Jerrick, and he goes and does this selfless thing for me.

I hate how he snuck up on me.

Every glance, smirk, retort, and touch thawed my heart into caring about him and understanding him. He isn't even in the room with me, and my heart is soaring, trying to reason my feelings.

Why is he affecting me so much?

"Jerrick has done terrible things, yet here he is, doing kind things for me? I don't understand it," I mutter.

"He has saved my life twice and has helped me with my magic while my mother has cursed his family line. He has been stuck with his enemy, trying to break a curse he doesn't even deserve to have. I can't tell if he is using me for some greater purpose. Does he feel bad for me? Is he just being kind to me? I don't know."

I groan in frustration as guilt eats away at me.

He never deserved any of this to happen to him. And it's my mother's fault.

I hug Dorit tighter. Another person who has been kind to me, while I've been sneaking around and biding my time, while Niko plans to attack her home, all so I can return to my kingdom.

Someone else I don't deserve.

Dorit pulls away and holds my sides. "He does these things for you, Tove, because he cares about you."

Shame strikes through me, sinking deep into my bones and permanently joining itself with the gloom and sorrow I always carry.

"He shouldn't care," I tell her.

She rubs my sides as if to reassure me, but everything in me wants to deny her statement. I can't even consider the thought because feelings make everything messier.

A cough comes from beyond my bedchamber, and our heads whip to the door. We both look at each other as mortification sets in.

Fuck.

I mouth, *It's Jerrick!*

I freeze in place as Dorit tilts her head to the door.

"Her Majesty is using the bathing chamber and still needs to get dressed. Come back in a few minutes!" she hollers.

"I'll wait for my wife out here."

Jerrick's low response is rich and makes my stomach somersault.

I bite the inside of my cheek as my grip on Dorit tightens.

She whispers softly, "It's going to be okay. Let's fix your liner, and we'll get the dress on quickly."

She nudges me to the vanity and sits me down. Dorit goes into the bathing chamber and returns with a damp cloth to rub over my eyes and clean up the kohl.

I tremble with worry of everything happening tonight and reach for her hand, forcing her to stop her actions. "*Dorit.*"

She halts her movements, glancing to my hold on her arm before meeting my gaze with understanding.

Magic flares awake within my core, sensing the fear and danger I am bringing upon myself. I release her immediately, my power cascading my arms in rapid succession.

Breathe, Tove.

Just relax.

The success of this ball tonight is extremely important, as is talking to Niko and Jerrick. Sweet Makers, how do I keep ending up in this position where everything relies on my ability to throw a good party while I struggle to remain calm?

Everyone from both kingdoms was invited, meaning noblemen and citizens that view me as a monster will murmur my nickname.

And Niko is supposed to be here. How will I face him?

Deities, Jerrick is in the hall waiting for me, and fuck if that doesn't make me even more sick to my stomach.

What if there is another duel between them right in the middle of the ball?

What am I going to do if someone calls me Snow Queen?

Fuck.

I close my eyes and grip the vanity, attempting to calm the swirl of emotions. I focus on my breathing, focus on my training, balancing my emotions at least to a point where I can keep my own magic from using them against me. I struggle to find graceful words for myself, the process longer than normal for me.

But the frost mercifully disintegrates from my veins, and when I look to Dorit, she is smiling.

Tears line my eyes at her confidence in me and her close presence when my magic manifested. I blink the tears away quickly, allowing her to proceed.

Dorit resumes putting kohl over my eyes as if she has no care in the world.

One thought sinks my heart, refusing to leave my brain. "What will everyone think?"

"What everyone thinks doesn't matter. You are a queen in your own right, *and* you are married to a king. They are here to celebrate you. They will be wise not to challenge you or Jerrick," she says.

"And if they do?" I panic, not wanting to wear indifference around people anymore.

I want to be myself and find my happy. I don't want to be this Snow Queen, and I don't want there to be a battle.

"Then, I will step in and knock them down a few pegs." Dorit smiles brightly, resting her hands on my upper arms. "Now, let's get that dress on you."

Dorit pulls out the dress, and I try not to admire it more, or else I might cry again.

I close my eyes and avoid the mirror over my vanity as Dorit laces up the back of the gown.

"Now for the best part." She retrieves my mask and my crown.

The crown is different from the one I wore on my wedding day and coronation. This one is simple and sleek, black metal adorned with small rubies coordinated to complement the rest of my ensemble.

Dorit places the crown on my head and secures it with pins and finishes with draping the mask over my face. "Tove, you are a vision!" She claps and lowers to a curtsy.

I grab her by the arm, hoisting her up as her arms fly around me. "Dorit, you're going to make me cry again," I try to joke as tears line my eyes.

Stupid tears.

"Tove, it truly is an honor to serve you. Your friendship has been momentous. I'm so glad you gave me a chance," she mutters into my ear.

We break apart, and I grab her hand, squeezing it tight. "You are a friend I never knew I needed."

Her features squish together, and it is her turn to cry. I cradle her again in my arms as a sense of pride and love courses through me, and I wish it was Dorit and me taking on the world.

Remembering Jerrick on the other side of my bedchambers, I harness my strength before ending the embrace.

Dorit asks, "Are you ready?"

I nod slowly and fidget with the sides of my dress as my heartbeat lurches from my chest. Heat floods my cheeks with embarrassment that he might not like what I am wearing, given we have not seen each other dressed up since our time in Axidoria.

I try not to let my heart speak for me, biting my tongue in hopes of not saying anything stupid.

Dorit steps away and opens the door slightly, whispering something on the other side before she vanishes down the hall.

Inch by inch, the doorway fills with Jerrick's frame.

I shouldn't have looked because—*fuck*.

He is immaculate.

I scan him head to toe, noticing a new pair of boots, dark hues of red woven into his vest and trousers, drawing my gaze to his mask and black crown. His crown is like mine, simple and coordinated for tonight's event.

But his mask, Deities, I wish it wasn't hiding his scar. It is one of my favorite features.

When our blue eyes meet, I beam, my worries and concerns dissipating.

His jaw slackens, no words spoken between us. He relaxes as a tender smile lights up his entire face, emphasizing his dimple and making my knees weak.

Jerrick gracefully lowers into a formal bow, extending his hand.

I stare before taking it, and I am caught off guard when he leans in.

His lips hover inches from mine, but then they drift to the side. He kisses my cheek, and I shiver. Jerrick takes my hand and pulls it to his lips.

"There are no words, My Queen," he purrs against my skin.

Knots form in my stomach from the lull of his utterance and his kiss blooming heat along my skin.

He stares intently, and I gulp. "No words?"

"There are no words to describe you. None will ever suffice for your divinity."

The compliment sends my heart skipping as he loops my hand over his arm. I'm not sure there are any words I could offer him, either. He himself is a deity and exalting to behold.

Jerrick runs his hand in those small circles around mine, immediately calming and soothing me. I smile, and he breathes again, shaking his head and brushing a strand away from his face.

"I wish there was a word that could define everything I see and admire in you, Frostbite."

I shy away from his words, hiding the heat of my cheeks and the desire blooming in my core. "Th-Thank you, Jer," I say.

His compliments are more than I deserve. He leans in flirtatiously, turning my gaze back to his, and winks.

"Don't worry, I know I look great, too."

I scoff at his ego.

He chuckles, and I can't help but join in as he guides us from my chambers, well on our way to attending our first festivity together as husband and wife.

42

Faces on Parade

Floral arrangements rest delicately in vases, and lanterns glow and illuminate the hallway as we reach the main level of the castle. Beneath us is a long maroon velvet carpet centered in all areas where the party is taking place.

We pass and acknowledge the staff on duty tonight, approaching the doors to the ballroom.

Jonas appears from the corner of my eye, coming to greet us with a familiar elderly woman who brings a smile to my face. He wears all black to match his combed-back hair, standing out with a red mask held in place by his permanent grin.

Frida is dressed in a deep red gown, silk draped to hug her small body and yet make her presence big enough to fill the entire room. Gold stitching matches the half mask she carries. With an arched eyebrow, she analyzes Jerrick and me before we even reach each other.

Jerrick embraces Jonas before the prince looks upon me and kisses my cheek. I reach up to hide my blush from the gesture.

Jerrick grunts, "That's *my* wife."

Jonas rolls his eyes, waving his brother off. "She is *my* sister-in-law and my queen."

Frida scowls, tilting her head and then swatting his arm. "She is everyone's queen. Now, stop talking as if we ladies are not here."

I try to hide my snicker, Jerrick chuckling as Jonas winces but nods at his grandmother.

Frida holds the prince's gaze before turning to me. She lowers her head to Jerrick and me, a complete contrast from when we were in her shop.

"I must say, you wear the gown better than I expected, granddaughter," Frida says, eyes meeting mine.

Remembering her interactions with the two men, I try to appease her with a compliment in return. "Not as well as you wear beauty, ma'am."

Frida flicks her attention to Jerrick, her jaw working. "She learns fast."

Jerrick huffs a laugh. "That, she does, Gran Gran."

Frida turns to Jonas. "You, on the other hand, *don't*."

I stifle my snort as Jonas's mouth falls and as Jerrick cracks a loud laugh.

Frida smirks. "Be sure to show off that gown for me. I need more customers."

"You already have enough customers," Jerrick says.

Frida looks at him with challenge, and to save each of us her discipline, I chime in. "I will do my best to show off your work."

Her teeth shine brightly, and it takes me by surprise. "That's my granddaughter," she says with praise, turning into the hall without her grandchildren.

The belonging she gives is overwhelming as I try not to let it affect my emotions.

Jerrick asks his brother, "How is the party going so far?"

Jonas's lips tighten, and my concern rises.

"Oh, no. What is it?" I ask.

We planned this ball and thought through every intricate detail to make sure everyone invited would be comfortable. I would hate for something to go wrong before I got to interact with anyone.

Jonas shrugs, smiling as he says, "It's going well."

I exhale in relief, elbowing my brother-in-law for giving me a fright. An oomph escapes Jonas and Jerrick winks at me in approval.

It does nothing to chase away the heat from my cheeks.

I look at the guests entering the throne room we turned into a dance hall. The memory of the last time I was in a tight space with people unsettles my gut.

Jerrick observes my movements before settling on Jonas. "Is *he* here?" Jerrick asks with lethal calm.

Jonas lifts his hands up, unsure.

I cringe at the thought of Niko, worrying he will not want to hear me out.

Jerrick catches the fall of my shoulders and rubs a circle around my hand.

"Let's get through tonight and then we can plan accordingly," Jerrick says.

I lean into Jerrick for moral support as he gives the guard the okay to announce us at the entrance.

Music floods my senses as performers and nobles dance in merriment to the rhythm of the song. My eyes widen in awe at the clash of beauty in the black and maroon decorations adorning everything from the walls to the people themselves.

The musicians finish the piece of music, pausing for the guards to announce us, but I am too distracted with taking in everything as we walk into the ballroom. The performers, staff, and nobles all turn to us and lower to a bow.

Jerrick raises a hand to stop them. "Welcome! Thank you so much for joining my wife and I this evening! Your king and queen are working hard to help unite the kingdoms, and we are indebted to everyone attending to celebrate our efforts and our marriage." He turns and smiles brightly before returning to the crowd. "Enjoy the party!"

The entire ballroom breaks into thunderous applause, forcing me to grin as the music picks up where it left off. Everyone returns to their conversations when a tall burly man rushes into view, adorned in a golden crown and followed by two beautiful women I recognize.

King Bernard and his daughters, Princess Vivienne and Princess Marian. Bernie's friendly aura shines through his mask as he opens his hands for an embrace.

Jerrick releases me in time for the King of Belmur to wrap his arms around me, lifting me off the ground and spinning me.

I squeal in delight.

Returning the embrace, I am grateful he and his kingdom have always been a strong supporter of me—and now Jerrick.

"Oh, my sweet Tove! You are glowing!" Bernie chuckles, setting me down.

The straps of my gown shift slightly, and I adjust them as I beam back. "As are you and your daughters. It's an honor that the three of you were able to leave your kingdom under safeguard with your advisors so you could attend our celebration," I say.

I clasp his upper arm, and I can't contain the water lining my eyes. "It *really* is wonderful to see you, Bernie."

He pulls me in for another hug, and I welcome it but go rigid when he mumbles, "Are you alright? Say the word, and I will take you away from here myself."

I close my eyes with fondness. He treats me as if I am his own.

Despite everything I've gone through and have to do, my response feels honest as I whisper back, "I am well, promise."

He nods. "Good." His arms relax as his daughters step forward and curtsy.

"Princesses, welcome," I say. "Thank you for traveling to join my husband and me in celebration."

Jerrick's eyes find mine, and his handsome grin lights up his features at my choice of words. I fight against rolling my eyes at his taunting, lifted brow, needing to keep up appearances.

Vivienne and Marian rise, looking at their father.

He waves at them to speak or say something, and I almost laugh at how much these ladies are rule followers. Near my age, they are beautiful and regal, keeping up with royal protocol and appearances. Eying the two of them, I wonder if they too wear a mask, as so many monarchs do.

Princess Marian says with her alto tone ringing through, "A beautiful work of art you and King Jerrick are, Your Majesty. We are so very grateful to be here to partake in the festivities."

Glancing at Vivienne, I go to greet her, stopping on the bandage wrapped around her arm. I lift a brow in curiosity as she sees my line of vision and bashfully covers it.

Maybe something embarrassing happened.

My husband loops his arm in mine and gestures to the three of them. "It's a pleasure to have you—" Jerrick pauses, looking beyond our group.

I, too, look beyond Bernie and the princesses, seeing another man with a crown coming toward us. It must be King Beauvais Rosselot of Torgem. We've written in correspondence but have never met in person.

King Beauvais is tall and broad, his demeanor making him seem a little older than Jerrick. He holds the stem of a golden mask that matches his blond hair and honey-colored irises shining through.

Jerrick smiles at the man, and I incline my head. But Bernie goes rigid, as do his daughters.

King Beauvais's eyes dart between Bernie and his daughters, his gaze lingering longer than normal on Princess Vivienne, who hides her face in a lowered curtsy with her sister.

When he turns and gives us his full attention, he lowers his mask, smiling brightly. Every feature on this man is illuminated by gold, yellow, and pure sunlight. He is striking and stunning to take in.

I can't deny the heat blooming across my cheeks underneath my own mask.

"King Jerrick, King Bernard, Queen Tove, and—" King Beauvais pauses.

Princess Vivienne's green eyes meet the king's, and he says, "And princesses, a pleasure to see you all."

Jerrick grasps King Beauvais's arm in greeting, and they nod before releasing each other.

Bernie leans in, whispering, "We'll leave you to converse. Save me a dance?"

I incline my head as Bernie escorts his daughters into the swarm of guests.

King Beauvais watches them leave before returning to the conversation. "Believe me when I say I was shocked to hear about the union," King Beauvais admits.

I bite my lip with unease, worried this conversation will turn political before I even have a chance to dance.

"But seeing the two of you now, it seems it was a meant-to-be match." He clutches our sides, pushing us together, and grinning brightly. "My congratulations. And should you need anything, the Kingdom of Torgem is happy to continue our relations with Palaena and Axidoria."

Jerrick smirks. "Much thanks, Beau. We will need to coordinate a hunting trip soon. I could always use more of those tricks you keep to yourself."

Beau?

"Ah," King Beauvais says. "Agreed. It has been too long. Maybe even prior to you taking on your new role."

Jerrick flexes his jaw, and I bristle.

King Beauvais doesn't know about Jerrick's curse, right? No, he couldn't.

"You're right. It has," Jerrick recovers. "Stay here for a few days, and we shall plan an outing."

King Beauvais nods. "I can afford an extra day or two."

"Excellent."

"Wonderful." King Beauvais pivots to me.

I lower my head slightly but not enough to appear lesser than him.

King Beauvais takes my hand and lifts it to his lips to kiss. "It's a pleasure to meet you in person, Queen Tove. I've always been pleased with your efforts at communicating with Torgem, and I must extend my thanks to you and your advisor for always negotiating and seeking trade with us."

"The honor is mine, King Beauvais. Thank you for having resources to trade with us."

Deities, I did not expect him to be so *genuine*. He seems so happy and cheery. My cheeks would be aching if I smiled that much.

King Beauvais steps back, looking between Jerrick and me. "I best go find some food and refreshment. Thank you for having me." He lifts his mask over his face and leaves.

Jerrick reaches for me, and we remain linked arm in arm as we make the rounds to greet everyone. The fear of murmurs and dark whispers have me gripping my husband tight, and I am surprised when I do not hear anyone call me the Snow Queen.

A new hope twists inside me as I look into each face meeting mine, pleading Niko's features will be recognizable. After a group of nobles leave us, Jerrick and I are alone, yet I remain distracted, scanning the entire vicinity for Niko.

Jerrick leans in to whisper, "Would you like a drink?"

My mouth waters at the thought of wine touching each of my taste buds. "Please."

He kisses my cheek again, my heart hammering as I watch him leave.

Jonas approaches, and I face my brother-in-law, seeking to distract my thoughts. "Where is Viggo?"

Jonas sips his goblet of wine lightly. "I had him on duty tonight so that we can plan for our holiday once everyone leaves."

I grin. "Where are you planning to go?"

I only get a shrug when a staff member approaches my brother-in-law, and he turns to assist them.

Jonas glances back at me. "Duty calls."

I smile as he strides off to ensure the festivities remain without error, glancing through the crowd for Jerrick.

Someone coughs behind me, and my heart leaps at the thought of it being him. But I turn, and my heart plummets when amber eyes I've known for so long stare back.

Red hair, slight stubble, tall. Deities, I forgot how tall he is.

"*Niko*," I breathe.

A boyish grin, one I know so well, forms, and I am transported home and to the moments I've shared with him. My heart leaps at seeing him here, my lungs unable to function. I've longed to see him, have been nervous to see him, and it all vanished.

I am only happy and filled with excitement that he is here. But I lose the chance to jump into his arms when he lowers into a bow, rising and scanning me from head to toe.

"Queen Tove, it brings us joy to see you in such great health," Niko says politely.

Us?

I peer behind him, recognizing a few men. One is Betina's father, and another is Ulrik Albertsen. My mood sours when Ulrik's eyes meet mine, and he averts his gaze. That's *odd*.

I flick my attention back to Niko, not letting it keep away the joy of seeing him.

He extends his hand, his smile deepening. "May I have this dance?" he asks calmly and lovingly.

My words run dry, but I immediately seek his hand, his entire demeanor lifting as he escorts me to the dance floor. I have no fear of our steps faltering as he pulls me closer, chest to chest.

Heels and shoes click to the rhythm of the song as Niko and I jump into the current waltz, joining all the others who are masked and dressed luxuriously.

"You look good," he says with kindness, all anger and resentment I last saw completely vanished.

"I've missed you, Niko."

He hums at my confession, squeezing me and admitting, "And I you. I hate that we fought, Tee."

"I hate that, too, and I am sorry, but I still don't want there to be a fight," I tell him, reaffirming my decision.

The dance pulls me in a spin. He circles around as I do before returning to the swaying embrace. When our bodies collide again, he speaks low and lethal, the hatred bleeding through.

"I'm sorry, Tee. Just because you don't want a fight doesn't mean there shouldn't be one. I told you I was coming to get you."

Anger rises to the surface, and I am furious at his unrelenting sentiment. "As your queen, I—"

"You stopped being queen when you left, Tee," he blurts, and my eyebrows shoot up.

"I am queen of *both* Axidoria and Palaena, Niko. *Just* because my location changed doesn't mean I ever stopped being queen. I've had to reconfigure how to rule from afar, and I trusted you to help me. I have undergone training to try to stop my winter. So, don't tell me I stopped being queen. Just because I'm not there doesn't mean I haven't been doing *everything* I can to help my kingdom. Now, I have found a way to avoid hurting anyone during this process, and you *will* listen to everything I have to say because it's valuable to the kingdom, to you, and to your uncle," I snap right back.

He goes rigid.

I use it to my advantage and press on, "I know my mother cursed your uncle, and I know how to lift his curse, just as I know how to lift Jerrick's. I will bargain for a divorce and tell Jerrick what he must do for his, and this will allow me to return home to *you*, Niko. You *must* call off the attack."

His jaw works, and the anger still refuses to leave him.

I cup his cheek, earnestly begging him to listen. "I don't want to see you get hurt. I cannot bear the thought of it. I cannot even fathom it for my own people, Niko. I don't want to wage a battle with a kingdom we have made trade alliances with when there is a more civil and peaceful solution."

He looks perplexed by this tidbit of information. "Y-You found a way to help my uncle?"

"Yes, and that is not all I found," I tell him as the crescendo of the music builds, pushing and pulling us apart.

Our chests touch again, and he holds me tightly. "Tee, what else—"

A hand lands on his upper arm.

My breath catches at the black crown pointing to the chandelier ceiling coming into view. The small wisps of onyx hair escape down Jerrick's face as he looks between Niko and me.

"Hello, wife," Jerrick coos softly, sending my heart skipping.

Niko's features harden, and his posture lifts, squaring his shoulders and puffing his chest. The music ends, but everyone continues into the next song as the three of us remain still.

Niko's hold on me tightens as he stares at Jerrick, while Jerrick remains focused on me.

I swallow down the knot forming in my throat at this arrangement, praying for a miracle to keep a fight from exploding right now. "Hello, husband. Allow me to introduce the current proxy and royal advisor of Axidoria. King Jerrick, Lord Nikolaj. Lord Nikolaj—King Jerrick."

Niko releases me as I extend my free hand between them and they stare at each other, unmoving.

Jerrick says, "A pleasure, Lord Nikolaj. I appreciate the correspondence you've coordinated between my brother and me these last few months. My wife and I plan on visiting Axidoria after this evening's festivities, so we may better assess Axidoria's and Palaena's need as we join our kingdoms."

Niko remains quiet.

Fear quickens my pulse as I wait for him to say *something*.

Jerrick glances at me, and I shrug as Niko turns to me.

"Are you *sure*?" Niko asks.

I nod faster than I can reply, needing him to listen and stand down. "I am." I beam up at Niko, hope filling my chest.

Even though I haven't spoken to Jerrick yet about bargaining for divorce, my gut tells me I am right and this will work.

It has to.

Niko drags his teeth against his bottom lip, and his amber eyes peek through his mask. He bows. I reach to squeeze Niko's hand in thanks, wishing I could do more beyond that.

Soon, Tove. This will all be over with soon.

Niko moves to Jerrick, tilting his head slightly. "The pleasure is mine, King Jerrick. Thank you for taking care of our queen during this time. I will be sure to make arrangements for your arrival into *our* kingdom after the festivities."

The smirk Jerrick gives doesn't reach his eyes, and I can tell he is fighting something internally. But Jerrick claps his hands, a feigned delight in his tone as he addresses Niko.

"Wonderful! Now, if you don't mind, I'd like to steal my wife from you."

Niko stiffens, catching the intended jab that even takes me by surprise. But he tilts his head low, remaining silent.

Jerrick grins wickedly as Niko steps back, taking a piece of me with him. My husband guides me into the next dancing position. I look past Jerrick to Niko, his longing stare cracking my heart.

I mouth, *Thank you.*

Niko only turns and leaves.

I am quiet for a few dance steps. When there is room for a spin, Jerrick pulls me away, and I fall into the rhythm of the light, jolly tune. He spins me again, and when he touches my waist, I focus on the sensation.

Goose bumps trail down my exposed leg.

Jerrick leans in and whispers, "I know you enjoy dancing, but since we don't have a lot of obligations now, I wanted to show you something."

Anxiety claws under my skin, and I shake uncontrollably. I tighten my grip on Jerrick.

"That's all you have to say after that?"

He shrugs nonchalantly. "He danced with you before I got to. So, I made sure he knew what is mine."

Mine.

Like I could ever be his. He only says those things because we have to show a united front amongst our guests. It's not like that is how he really feels.

His amusement is sure to die out when I tell him everything. Stress further dampens my mood, and I hate I cannot even savor dancing with Jerrick for the first time since Axidoria.

"D-Don't you want to see?" Jerrick asks with a hint of worry.

It distracts me from reflecting on what happened, unsure of what else he would want to show me.

"See what? We have a party and guests to attend to," I say as the song comes to an abrupt end.

Jerrick keeps me close as his brother comes to his side. "It's ready."

Jerrick and Jonas both smile mischievously, and suspicion crawls up my spine.

"What are you two up to?" I ask.

They chuckle to themselves, and it does nothing to make me feel better. But Jerrick wraps my hand around his elbow as my brother-in-law pecks my cheek.

"Trust me, Tove, you'll like it," Jonas whispers as he pulls away.

My chest turns into a sudden inferno. Even though I have no desire for whatever he means to show me, hope blooms at my chance to speak to Jerrick alone and tell him everything. I need to be brave and trust he will hear me out.

As Jerrick leads us out of the ballroom, I peer back at Jonas, hoping I am not in over my head. My brother-in-law gives the same smile his brother gave me, making my unease worse.

I ask Jerrick, "Where are we going?"

"It's a surprise," he says softly, caressing my brow.

"Sweet Makers, I do not enjoy surprises." They only unsettle my stomach even more.

Jerrick responds with a light chuckle, guiding me down a hallway guarded by soldiers.

We walk for a while, guests and staff members we pass dwindling the farther we venture away from the party. When we veer left and stroll down a hall with more guards, I arch a brow in concern. Jerrick acknowledges them with a nod, and they salute.

My heart thunders in my chest, worried this is a section of the castle I am not familiar with.

What if Jerrick knows? What if he is taking me to the dungeons? Shit... I have never toured any dungeons.

I am such an idiot.

What if he is taking me somewhere to kill me? But this hallway is decorated like part of the ball.

I try to stop the never-ending thoughts from coming to a head as Jerrick and I remain linked. We pass by rooms I peek into, each of them empty. It is just *us*.

We approach the end of the hall, met with a tall black marble door. Varying tints of blue flicker in the light from the lanterns illuminating the area.

Jerrick turns to me, taking my hands in his. "I have a gift for you. It's beyond this door."

"Jer, please. You don't have to get me anything." I try to walk away, but Jerrick grabs my elbow, tugging me back to him.

The sincerity behind his gentleness physically hurts, making me wish and pray that, no matter what happens when I tell him, he won't hate me. I don't think I could live with that, knowing how much I care for him.

Jerrick rubs the back of his neck, his own nerves betraying him. "I-I wanted to get this for you." He reaches for my hands again, drawing circles, and I drop my head to watch Jerrick's hands envelop mine.

"After everything," he whispers, drawing a few circles around my opened palm.

He releases a long sigh, and I peer up at him to see sadness. Arching a brow, I open my mouth to speak, but his eyes meet mine.

"After everything," Jerrick repeats, "I wanted to get this for you. As a token of gratitude for everything you've done for me. And as an apology."

I reassure him, "Jer, you have helped in more ways than I have. You didn't need to get me anythi—"

"I needed to," he whispers, looking at my lips.

I bite my lip as I stare at his, too.

His features soften, his dimple appearing beneath his mask.

I can't help the involuntary lift of my cheeks at the sight. Swallowing thickly, I incline my head, allowing him to proceed.

"Close your eyes," he says.

My joy stays glued on my face as I close my eyes. Jerrick releases my hands, the creak of a door opening. He guides me forward, commanding, "No looking."

"No looking," I repeat, aware of the quiet in the air.

Our feet lightly scuffle against the floor and faint music trickles in from the ballroom. Jerrick's scent surrounds my senses, and he tugs me forward.

I follow him cautiously until he stops and grabs my shoulders to turn me. "Ready?"

Both his touch and the anticipation send shivers up my spine, and I nod with trepidation.

Hands cup the sides of my face, and lips meet mine. Jerrick's kiss thrums in my heart as he unties my mask. I let him peel it away, too busy savoring the buzz from his mouth on mine.

A cold touch of air kisses the portion of my face that was masked, but I keep my eyes closed, not wanting to open until Jerrick says so.

I smile stupidly when his lips meet my forehead.

His kisses make me want to drag his mouth back to mine.

He withdraws, speaking words so softly I can barely hear them. "Open your eyes."

I do as he instructs, my breath catching.

43

A Wicked Thing to Do

I cover my mouth in shock. Candles adorn the marble floor, and the same patterned stone blends from the ground to ceiling, a beautiful light-blue mixed with black.

Jerrick stands a few steps away, his mask removed, and his features illuminating the room more than the hundreds of candles scattered around us. He steps to the side, and my knees almost buckle.

At the center of the room is a grand piano.

Music echoes in my mind at the beautiful notes this stunning instrument will chime. Compositions I haven't had time to think on rush to the surface of my mind. Harmonies and melodies sprinkle together as I imagine my fingertips touching the piano keys, reveling in the acoustics of this room that will highlight each note, each song played.

I remain breathless as I approach the onyx piano, Jerrick leaning against it with his arms crossed, analyzing my every move with his gentle smile. Touching the instrument, I confirm this is not a dream.

I meet his gaze. "How? How did you—"

My husband steps close, his cologne drowning my senses as it always has. Power oozes from his stance as I take him in and all I can feel is this overwhelming confoundment.

Jerrick takes my hand, holding it to his chest as he smiles. "When you had agreed to help me, even against your will, you were kind to me. When you came down to the library every day with a scowl on your face, furious with how I left you with no options, you still showed up and were nice when I gave you no reason to be."

My eyes dart back and forth to his as he hesitates.

"I was mean and cruel to you. And when you came down with that food tray?" He huffs a laugh.

"I knew." He pauses. "I knew I didn't deserve you or your kindness."

Heat presses against my chest at the memories, reflecting on how far he and I have come. I cup his cheek, and he leans into it, kissing it.

His eyes hold mine captive as he says, "The day you did that, I knew I needed to pay you back. But then the more time I spent with you, the greater the list became."

I smirk, understanding and feeling the same with him.

He gestures to the piano. "So, I thought this was a fair compromise."

I look from him to the piano and my face crinkles, the kindness overwhelming and swallowing me whole. My heart is so full, but it is breaking at the same time.

I don't deserve this man.

I don't deserve any of this.

I've lied to him all these months, and now that I have the key to freeing him from his curse, he goes and does this for me?

The beauty and magnitude of the piano is one thing but Jerrick?

He is the exponential gift I never expected to receive.

The festering guilt and stress reaches its breaking point, reminding me of how wrong I was when coming here and how desperate I am to not ruin everything I have built with this man.

I can't stop the tears from forming.

I cover my face, sinking to the floor, everything too much to bear.

The man I knew in Axidoria and the King of Palaena are masks Jerrick wears to protect himself. But here he is now, fully unmasked, and it is absolutely breathtaking.

It is inspiring to witness, to see there is more to life than grief and being everyone's monster. I've barely missed my family since arriving in Palaena because I've found a new one with Dorit, Ophelia, Cordelia, Jonas, and—*him*.

There is more to my life than fear and trauma.

There is more to my life with Jerrick in it.

My gratitude and awe of him is unfathomable.

It reverberates through me, plummeting down to my core as my lungs deflate of all air. A smoldering inferno erupts, dousing every morsel of frost and ice inside of me. The heavy and abounding adoration I have for the man before me dominates everything.

I gasp, struggling to breathe as my feelings for Jerrick boil over.

My affection for Niko is minuscule compared to this all-consuming force.

It encircles me, sadness and sorrow distancing themselves, letting me feel a deeper, more meaningful, and more intense emotion.

A composition ignites in my soul, enduring and thrilling, and the symphony of chords ring everlasting and true.

The tears free-fall as the unyielding, magnifying emotion clutches the center of my chest, permanently finding its home by ingraining itself deep into my heart.

I—*love* Jerrick.

You don't deserve him, Tove.

I have to tell him how to break his curse. I have to tell him we need to divorce to allow him to fall in love with someone worthy of him and send me home.

Home to Niko, the man I am supposed to be with.

My heart breaks because I've wasted everyone's time.

Guilt, shame, and stupidity attack every positive memory I try to replay in my mind, a reminder of how stupid I am for believing no one would get hurt.

Stupid, stupid, stupid.

The weight of my crown is heavy, tipping forward, as if to remind me how close I am to losing everything and everyone when I confess my sins to Jerrick. I've wanted to tell him for so long. And when I do, he will demand proof and then I'll have to tell him about Betina, about my mother's mirror, and about Niko.

I reach up to unpin my crown, placing it next to me as I cry harder, hating how it feels like the only person who ever gets hurt in situations is me.

I can't do this.

Jerrick lowers to the ground beside me, removing his own crown and placing it next to mine. Through my blurry vision, our crowns lay next to each other. How perfect they are.

My lip trembles.

Jerrick tugs my chin toward him. A question lingers in his gaze, and I find myself not ready to tell him, not ready to ruin everything.

If I am going to be the one ruined from this, I am going to do what I want for once, selfishly and recklessly.

All the consequences can be damned.

I need him more than I need life itself.

Before Jerrick can speak, I finally make my move, yanking him close to lock his lips with mine. I cling to him, but he pushes away, bewilderment flashing across his features.

I study him through my own panting breaths.

Jerrick rebounds with hunger in his wake.

Holding the sides of his face, I deepen the kiss, a low rumble escaping Jerrick's mouth. I moan in response, letting him in more.

Our bodies shift, needing to be closer.

Jerrick pulls me onto his lap as I rake a hand through his hair and bite his lip as if I am starving for him. His hard length presses against my center, and I whimper.

Jerrick slips his hand up the side of my slit skirt to grip my backside.

I shudder at his warmth on my cold ass. It thrums my magic awake, and cold air drifts.

He breaks our kiss slightly, watching the air between us before he tugs me closer, his hot breath and power pouring life into me and warming away the sensation.

I tremble at the hot and cold of our joining, arousal growing in my core. I tug his hair, keeping him centered with my mouth, and nip at him senselessly.

Jerrick props me up on his lap. Our tongues thrash in the other's mouths, taking moments to nibble, pinch, and suck, earning collective moans and shudders that send my hips rolling.

My first roll earns a light graze on my ass, and I hiss in luxurious pleasure. Between our mouths and Jerrick's hand cupping my backside, his hips grind back in approval.

A low moan comes from the base of his throat as he spanks my ass again, harder. My hips move of their own accord, my hands frantically touching his body, seeking his skin.

I need to *feel* him.

My gown shifts, exposing my breasts. I don't care about my own body, only his.

Deities, I need him so much it hurts.

I rub my hands up and down the front of his tunic, fumbling with the buttons. When it is free, I rip it off with no regret for the damage I cause, moving to unfasten his silken shirt from his pants and unlace the section around his chest.

Jerrick's hands drift with mine, his fingertips tracing lines up and down my ass.

A dark thought has me wanting to explore everywhere. But when his chest is exposed, I run my cold hands over his body, shifting closer to have the skin-to-skin contact.

My hand finds shelter once again on the base of his throat, and I yank his head back, leaving a trail of kisses down the side of his face and neck.

He moans so low and guttural when my lips suck on the skin at the base of his neck.

Frenzied lust has my eyes rolling to the back of my head.

"Fuuuck," he grunts softly.

He grabs my face, guiding it back to him. He kisses me deeply before pulling away and stopping.

My gaze meets his, the two of us scanning the other half undressed. I lick my lips in anticipation as his eyes flare at my exposed breasts.

But he doesn't move. Instead, Jerrick clicks his tongue as we gasp for air.

"Don't start something you can't finish," he pants, a teasing smirk etched across his features.

My eyes darken with lust and desire. I shamelessly reach between us, grabbing his hardened cock through his pants, stroking it, giving him just enough friction to earn a groaned response.

His eyes roll as his head falls back.

I take advantage and kiss his exposed neck, needing to know every place he likes to be touched. Moving my hand from his cock, I seek my own wetness running down my thighs. I swipe a small amount, bringing it up to his lips for him to taste.

He sucks on my fingers, the two of us moaning from the act. His eyes are hooded, filled with need.

I pull my fingers out of his mouth. "I can finish this. Can you?" I challenge, committing myself to him for one night before losing him forever.

One night of everything I want and then damage control.

I peel away from his lap to stand, silently pleading he will give me what I want.

Jerrick watches me pull my dress to cover my breasts, and my upper thighs are exposed from the slit in my skirt.

I take my time adjusting, wanting him to see—*needing* him to see how much I want this.

How much I want him and what he does to me.

Jerrick reaches for me. "Tove."

My chest swells as he uses my given name. It is so foreign yet so perfect. It only expands my love and need for him more.

I rock my head back to the ceiling, grinning.

I release a long breath before gazing at him, my soul calling to his. "Say my name again," I beg.

Jerrick breathes, a small smirk gracing his features as he stands. He comes up to me, craning my neck up to meet him.

"*Tove*," he murmurs, pulling me in for another kiss.

I melt into Jerrick, holding him tight. He picks me up, and I lock my legs around his waist and fasten my arms around his neck, our mouths clashing against each other.

He kisses me deeply and he carries me away from the piano room.

I can't hide the cheeky grin plastered along my face as he takes me up a set of stairs. "Where are you taking me?" I try to ask seductively.

"Somewhere private where only I can enjoy the sound of you," he purrs, and cold sweat trickles down my spine as I bite my lip at the thrill of that promise.

44

EVERY TOUCH

We reach Jerrick's bedchamber, and he kicks the door open with his leg, entering the room without breaking our kisses.

He sets me down on his bed. "Don't move."

I nod sheepishly as he turns to close the door. It creaks closed, and we are alone in his room for the second time. Memories on our wedding night come to mind, and the phantom touch of his hands on me has me scooting my ass closer toward the edge of the bed with anticipation.

I lean back as Jerrick twists, slipping off his boots. I bite my lip as my heart hammers against my chest, and my nipples tighten.

He takes a step toward me.

I move to rise, eager to have him touching me. "Jer—"

But he halts my efforts. "Wait," he commands.

I obey.

He removes his belt, draping it on the chair next to the bed. He crosses his arms, lifting his tunic over his head.

My mouth falls.

His pecs and abs are sculpted and crafted to perfection. I love watching his arms work as he squishes his tunic into a ball, tossing it to the side without a care of where it lands.

He steps closer as I scan every inch of him, desperate to remember this. I drift over his scar, the small bead of sweat running down the side of his ribs, stopping last on the hard length pleading for freedom underneath his pants.

I want to peel the remainder of his clothes away and touch him everywhere. But when I reach for him, he catches my greedy hands, leaning down and kissing me softly.

"May I?" he asks.

"May you what?" I whisper in a tease.

Jerrick grins so big it leaves my soul aching.

My startled laugh replaces the ache as he scoops me up to move me farther onto the bed.

He crawls over me, hovering slightly before joining our lips together and resting all his weight on me. His weight should be heavy, but instead, it is a blanket of protection. Safety and love wrapping itself around me.

All I want to do is cocoon myself in it even more. I revel in the security of him being here with me. I am lost in the desire, the comfort, and the need for everything that he is.

Jerrick's hands drift up the sides of my gown as he kisses me, and I can't help myself as I touch his biceps and give them a light squeeze. His tongue mingles with mine as he unlaces my dress. We break our kiss as he pays attention to the fastening.

"I can't tell you how long I've wanted to do this," he murmurs as my gown loosens, giving Jerrick access to me.

He cups my breasts, massaging them, and kissing them.

I bite back a moan and cradle him close, loving the touch of his lips on my body. But when he pinches my nipple, I hiss and grind out a groan at the touch.

Jerrick chuckles darkly, meeting my gaze. "I love every sound you make."

When his tongue flicks my nipple, it pebbles even more.

Kisses trail up the side of my face as the fullness of his weight sinks on me. His lips drift across my skin, warmth expanding around me while a chill seeps into my blood. And when his kisses meet the tender place in the crook of my neck, *fuck*, I cannot stop my hips from grinding in response.

"That's my favorite," he whispers along my lips as I run my hands up his body, pulling him closer to kiss me deeper.

Jerrick's hips grind in rhythm with mine, and we moan at the contact of our bodies. My husband explores my body, irritation pouring into his kisses as he struggles to find my skin underneath my gown.

"Get this fucking dress off *now*," he growls, sitting on his knees as we frantically remove pieces of my gown.

I shimmy my arms out, my body rocking as Jerrick leans on his side, yanking the entirety of it off with a firm tug. I almost go with it, but Jerrick catches me, tugging me back to him.

He holds my neck and my hip, my backside against him.

I tilt up to kiss him, and I sway my ass around his cock. I try to reach between us, eager to touch him, but stop when his tongue flicks my ear.

"Not yet," he says, cupping my center.

I gasp as he nibbles my earlobe.

Jerrick snakes his other hand down my breast, and I moan as he trails further and finds my arousal. I bring my hand behind his head as we remain close, his fingers teasingly rubbing my clit.

"Fuck, your touch is better than mine." I gasp and rub my ass against his cock.

He kisses the nape of my neck. "Have you thought about my touch?"

I moan my response, knowing the countless times I've thought back to when he touched me on our wedding night, not wanting to think of him, but I still did.

The dark, impulsive thoughts festered every time he was close to me. I pleasured myself with the memory of him coaxing me and praising me, always wishing for more—wishing for *him*.

I buck when he pinches my clit.

"Answer me."

I shudder at his mercy, the pleasure better than I imagined. "Y-Yes."

"Tell me what you thought about," Jerrick demands, full of desire and hunger.

As my breasts turn taut in his hand, my response is breathy as I whisper, "I-I thought about your touch. How I wanted to see your cock. I wanted to know the length of it, the girth of it—I wanted to commit it to memory so every time I touched myself, I had an image to chase me into coming."

He rewards my confession, his fingers returning to rubbing circles at my sensitive center. I rock back against him as my hips move of their own volition.

Jerrick commands another request. "Tell me what you want."

I ride his hand, tapping into those deep thoughts and the passion of having him all to myself tonight. My heart hammers against my chest. My wants are easy to verbalize, wanting to please him as much as he is pleasing me.

"I want to relish and savor every last bit of you on my hand, in my mouth, and in my pussy."

Jerrick hums his approval, moving his lips to meet the crook of my neck and sucking my soft skin.

I moan. Sweet Makers, I want more. I *need* more.

Heat grazes my ear, his breath so intoxicating and delicious.

"Now tell me what you need, Tove," he purrs, words full of promise and seduction, coaxing me on.

My name on his lips is a beautiful melody, one I want to hear over and over again. I bite my lip, my breaths uneven and panting.

His trousers are the only thing keeping his cock from rubbing up and down against my ass. I can't tell if the friction of his clothing between us is helping or not, but it doesn't stop me from blurting what my heart and my body need now more than ever.

"I need more. I need everything—I need you, Jerrick. Only *you*."

Jerrick bites down on my neck, and I gasp at the pleasure of it when he rubs my clit in the right spot. He drags his teeth up my throat, his fingers working me as he nibbles and kisses me.

Jerrick's reply is dark, laced with promise and pleasure. "Not until I have you first."

I shudder at his words, moaning as I glance up at him. When our eyes meet, the air shifts, a new heavy vulnerability lingering from my admission. Jerrick's heated gaze tightens my chest, and I marvel at his beauty.

The love I have for him is so raw— so bare—so *freeing*.

It's infinite.

It makes me want him more.

Jerrick reaches for my chin, angling it to kiss me deeply. He grinds into me from behind, and I ride his hand in response.

The tightness builds in my body, yet I want his pace to slow down so I can savor every minute and come apart.

I moan, begging him, "Slow down, please. Right there."

I am grateful when he slows his rhythm enough to bring me down but keep the pleasure going.

"Don't want the fun spoiled too fast, Frostbite?" he teases, moving his hand from my face to pinch my nipple while the other pinches my clit in unison.

I gasp, my body jerking, and my thighs tightening. My ass rubs more into his dick.

"You're drenched," Jerrick says into my ear. "I love how fucking wet you are for me."

I move my free hand between us to touch Jerrick. When I make contact, a dampness comes through his trousers, the length of him making my mouth water.

"Let me touch you, *please*," I beg.

We kiss as he moves his hands from my center, pulling down his trousers. I fumble around to help or grip his cock, whichever comes first.

His cock springs out, brushing against my ass. As tempted as I am to see it, touching it is better. I take my opportunity and fasten my hand around his length, awkwardly contorting my arm between us to stroke him from tip to the base.

Jerrick shudders in my ear and fuck if that doesn't coax me on more. "Fuuuck," he hisses darkly.

Goose bumps prickle up my spine as we savor the moments of slow and faster rhythms. Jerrick's hold on me tightens as I use my hand, his audible pleasure encouraging my own.

I lower my voice into a breathy whisper. "Let me have you, Jer. Let me have all of you." I twist my wrist, feeling his muscles flex again.

His efforts at my own pleasure halt briefly. Jerrick's features scrunch together as he releases a moan, and fuck if it isn't a melody I want to hear for the rest of my life.

His eyes are intense when they meet mine. He surges forth to close our lips together, the two of us biting and pulling the other closer. But when Jerrick slips a finger in my center, I gasp into his mouth when the strokes gain momentum.

I almost lose all sense of him and his pleasure, fighting through the building heat and cold in my core, trying to please him as he is pleasing me.

But he splays his hand out across my center, thrusting one finger inside while his thumb circles my clit, the heaviness too tight, too rough—too good.

My breathing hitches, and my insides clench.

Our kisses break as I rest my head against his, unable to focus on more than my own pleasure. I can't stop but hold on to him as I rock with the movement of his hands.

He withdraws, lightly slapping my pussy.

I gasp in pleasure, and he does it again, my body bucking as I mewl in response.

He silences me with his mouth, returning to the steady, sure rhythm as our kiss deepens.

My chest and core clench, my insides flexing tighter with anticipation. When I think I am on the edge of climax, Jerrick breaks our kiss, his head resting against mine as his blue eyes stare into my soul.

"Come on my hands, Tove. Come on my hands so I can lick each finger and savor the essence of you as an appetizer before using my tongue for the rest of my feast."

With the pleasure at his demand, and the perfect angle of his thumb and finger, I combust, falling into euphoria as he watches me climax.

"That's My Queen," he coos, leaning in and kissing me.

His praise such a gift as my body comes down.

As promised, Jerrick removes his hand from my sex, bringing it in front of us.

My mouth waters as he licks and sucks each finger.

When he pulls the last finger out of his mouth, he smirks deviously, his dimple on full display. Jerrick guides my face to his, while a slow, sloppy kiss of tongues has me tasting the remnants of my essence.

I roll over, finally seeing him bare. His face is flushed and red, sweat along his brow and against his toned body. But his dick, Sweet Makers, is bigger than I imagined.

Wrapping my hand around him was amazing. But my thoughts are already imagining how good it will feel to have his length hit the back of my throat or to be fully seated and ride out my own pleasure.

Deities, my mouth waters, and I instantly want more.

I don't neglect the fact that Jerrick, too, takes me in from head to toe, licking his lips when he lands on my entrance. My skin heats when his gaze flicks to mine, another promise pouring from him.

"I'm going to treasure every inch of you if it's the last thing I do." Jerrick pulls down the remainder of his trousers, peeling them off before resting on his back. His cock points upward, and I admire every inch of him.

I crawl to his cock, needing to touch it, to taste it.

But he wraps his hand around my hair, pulling me up toward him. He kisses me selfishly, thoroughly.

I'm desperately ready for him again as he holds me captive.

He stops, his lips hovering over mine. "I am going to devour you."

I moan, seeking that promise as if it is one of my own and sealing it with a kiss while touching his cock.

He breaks the kiss, loosening his hold on my hair and smirking. "Take everything you want."

I eagerly comply, turning to his dick. But Jerrick stops me and shakes his head.

I arch a brow in confusion.

He chuckles, patting his chest. "Plant your pretty cunt on my face so I can revel in your taste."

Oh, *fuck.*

He sits up, kissing me once before moving me on top of him, aligning my center with his face as his cock hovers inches from my mouth.

I tremble with pleasure as his tongue licks at the wetness running down my thighs.

Jerrick squeezes my hips, and I grind against him.

I hold the top of his thighs as I lower my mouth and lick the tip of his cock. A groan of approval from behind drives me forward, my hand moving to wrap around the base of him as I slowly, tentatively, wet his cock, spreading my saliva over his dick.

Jerrick licks me, kisses me, and sucks me.

My own pleasure is a distraction, and I can't silence the moans escaping from my lips. I twist my hand up and down as my mouth surrounds his cock.

His hips buck, and I hum my own praise, knowing my touch makes Jerrick just as wild.

Our rhythms sync with our hips, tongues, and mouths. The guttural moans coming from behind me match my own as Jerrick's cock pulses in my mouth.

I inch toward another orgasm, and it takes everything in me to push through it, seeking to hear his own pleasure over mine. But when he spreads my ass cheeks, it grants him room to run his tongue everywhere from my center to my ass.

I choke out a breath, breaking away from his cock.

"Jer—" I pant, my insides clenching at the tempting thought of him lingering near new territory.

"That's it, Frostbite. Shatter for me." Jerrick runs a thumb over my clit, and his tongue joins in.

I gasp when he inserts one finger, another trailing near my back entrance.

He hums in approval as he teases me, my head falling forward in a deep moan.

I grind against him, savoring its warmth prior to returning to shoving his entire cock into my mouth. The sucking sound of his mouth pulling away from my center comes before a long, drawn-out moan escapes Jerrick.

I suck his cock, and he pants, "Fuuuuuck."

He reaches forward, his body beneath me shifting to hold my neck. "*Deeper.*"

I comply without a second thought.

I breathe through my nose as I take him deeper, deeper, and cup his balls as his cock hits the back of my throat. A pleasured groan comes from behind me, and I don't stop. I keep going, fast and slow, savoring my meal as promised.

Jerrick pushes down on my head slightly, a small gag escaping. He recovers by releasing his hold, caressing my skin in an apology.

Jerrick shifts once more, his tongue and fingers working my insides and my clit as our hips rock to the motion. It's messy and frantic, but I refuse to relent, even as another release convulses through my body.

I whimper, riding out my pleasure as I lick and suck his dick.

Jerrick's mouth leaves from my core, and he spanks my ass so hard it echoes in the chamber.

I gasp, muffling it when he soothes the ache away, rubbing my ass and kissing it. I continue stroking him, dizzy and hungry for more.

When I peer over my shoulder, I am surprised he is already watching me silently. I drag my teeth across my bottom lip, worried at the lack of words from him.

"What is it?" I ask.

Jerrick smiles lazily and squeezes my hips, kissing my ass once more and then rolling me onto my back.

My breath leaves me, and I barely register what is happening before he is on top of me, the familiar overwhelming weight resting above me.

"Now, I have you right where I want you," he smirks.

His loose hair falls forward, and he shakes it away, and I giggle. When it doesn't budge out of his line of sight, I reach up to help tuck each strand behind his ears.

Jerrick grins as he leans in, tenderly kissing me. I welcome it.

He puts more weight on me, balancing his body on his forearms and covering me entirely.

I *love* it.

He trails kisses down one side of my face, and I return the effort on his exposed throat.

I hold Jerrick's head in the crook of my neck, and I suck on the nape of his neck as his lips nip, our hips rolling into each other.

The wetness between my legs coats his cock as he teases me each time our hips link up. Panted breaths mingle as my needy hands hold him tighter.

The friction grows, my need for him turning me ravenous.

"*More*," I plea, angling his cock to rub near my entrance. "I need more."

Jerrick's face nears mine as he whispers, "You like that, don't you?"

I hum my approval.

His dick is *so* close.

"Sweet Makers, that feels—" I break off when his hips buck, and his length almost enters.

I whimper, reaching for his hips and squeezing.

Jerrick's forehead presses against mine. "No. No Makers, Deities, or anything beyond what is happening between you and me. *Just* you and me, understand?"

The gruff rasp sends a wave of pleasure down my spine in anticipation. He moves away slightly, as if to punish me for my delayed response.

I nod eagerly, trying to cling to every movement of him.

"Good girl." He cradles me close and kisses me passionately.

Then he eases inside of me.

I inhale sharply, my head falling back as I dig my nails into Jerrick's skin.

Jerrick pauses to make sure I am okay. I nod, kissing him as his hips thrust in response, easing himself deeper.

I can't stop my eyes from rolling to the back of my head. My vision blurs at the fullness of him greedily filling me.

I bite my lip in pleasure, only resorting to biting the inside of my cheek in an attempt to muffle my moans.

"Jer," I pant, reaching for him as if he is on the opposite side of the room.

Our eyes find each other, and our breathing is ragged as he kisses my forehead. He combs loose hair from my face, wiping the sweat from my brow.

"You are taking me so well," he says, lips meeting mine as he fully sheaths himself inside.

I gasp.

"I'm here, wife. I've got you," he coos sweetly, cupping my face in his hands.

Wife.

I pour myself further into him as our bodies remain intertwined together, chanting in my mind the words I don't have enough courage to say aloud.

I love you, Jer.

Our rhythm builds slowly, and my body adjusts to Jerrick's size as he thrusts harder. When I lift my head back, our bodies meld, fitting perfectly. I shudder, feeling heavy and light, a perfectly balanced moment. I am unsure if the sensation is due to my body or my heart.

Jerrick's low groans match my moans, and my hands roam along his back, pushing him down on me to have as much skin touching me as possible. Even though we are close, it isn't enough.

It will *never* be enough.

I wrap my arms around him, hugging him and letting his weight ease me farther into the mattress. Deities, he *still* isn't close enough.

I claw at his skin.

"I need more of you. I need all of you, *please*," I beg between kisses.

Jerrick's gaze meets mine as my hips buck in more need. He reaches between us, cupping my breast as he kisses life into me.

"Eyes on me, love."

I halt at his words.

Love.

I cup his cheek as he holds my gaze, my thumb running across his scar. He grunts softly with each new thrust.

I breathe in the same air as him as our tongues clash.

I tremble from exertion as Jerrick drifts his hand down to rub tantalizing circles around my clit. The tension inside me builds like a bow nocking an arrow. I'm teetering so close to the edge.

"I'm—I'm *so* close," I tell him as my entire body vibrates.

"I know. I can feel you tightening around my cock," Jerrick whispers appreciatively.

His angle shifts slightly.

My mouth falls open as my walls close in on him. "Don't stop."

I hold him as I inch toward release, and Jerrick doesn't desist from pleasing me.

He thrusts with the same rhythm but increases the movement of his thumb, teasing my clit as he kisses my neck.

I pant, a breathless moan, drawing his gaze to mine.

"Your walls are so tight around my cock, Tove. I love it. I love—"

My vision turns spotty as the pressure builds harder than before, and my mind cannot keep up with my body's pace. I pant as my nails dig deeper and deeper into Jerrick's skin.

More. I need *more.*

My body moves of its own volition, meeting each of Jerrick's trembling thrusts.

"Yes, that's it, My Queen. Give me more of you," he orders in his husky, low voice.

My pleasure and euphoria increase, still lingering and on the verge of shattering into a million pieces. Our eyes lock as Jerrick leans in, ferally kissing me as he pinches my clit eagerly, then proceeding to rub it at an increasingly fast pace.

"Take it from me. I know you can," he beckons, and greedily, I indulge myself.

Jerrick's thrusts are deep, grazing that precious point inside me, and we hum in approval.

I grab the back of his head and force him into another feverish kiss. My hips meet his, bucking upward and hard, needing him to hit the right spot a few more times.

He switches from rubbing with his fingers to using his knuckles to apply pressure above my clit, right where his dick is grazing me.

"Now come, Tove," he orders as the pulsing of his cock grows frantic inside of me.

The ballad glissandos, a rushed, brilliant pinnacle from Jerrick's words swelling my heart, body, and soul. This beautiful, tantalizing melody is one I will compose and relive for the rest of my life. The harsh, wonderful pressure mixed in with Jerrick's thrusts sends me over the edge.

"Jerrick!" I scream.

My vision turns fuzzy as I come apart at the seams, shuddering over the sound of Jerrick's long, drawn-out moan as my insides shake, his cock pulsing inside of me. Every nerve, every muscle in my body crashes from the adrenaline and the pleasure.

Jerrick remains inside of me, slowing his movements and leaning in and kissing me gently. The two of us stay close as we both try to savor our pleasures.

My entire body sags with exhaustion, while I'm still seeing stars dancing along the lines of my blackened vision. The only thing keeping me intact right now is the man I love hovering above me.

He adjusts his position, moving away from my entrance, arms bracing himself as he carefully withdraws.

Jerrick shifts off me, but I reach out to stop him, not wanting him to go.

"Stay."

His eyes twinkle, and he leans in, caressing my forehead. "Let me clean us up first."

The sensation leaves me dizzy, my hold on him slackening. I frown when he uses it to his advantage, the heat and weight of his body gone.

But he tenderly moves me, peeling away while pulling the sheets back to stand. I watch his beautifully toned body and ass as he drifts into his bathing chamber.

A few moments pass before he comes back with a wet cloth, and I smile at the magnitude of every inch of Jerrick, everything about this man only furthering my love for him.

"May I?" He gestures between my legs.

I'm too tired to move, but his soft question warms my chest. I smile bashfully, nodding and burrowing into my pillow.

Jerrick's cheeks redden as he sits, caressing my legs and wiping away my essence with the warm cloth. Jerrick leans in when he finishes and kisses me.

He tries to leave again, but I hold him in place, kissing him keenly, not letting him go. He obliges and drops the cloth on the floor, lips never leaving mine as he joins me, pulling the covers over us.

Jerrick draws me close, our legs twisting together.

We hold one another, Jerrick kissing my forehead, and I hum happily in exhaustion. Our lips meet again and again, the two of us grinning between each one.

"I promise I'm not going anywhere, Tove." Jerrick's soft promise hangs in my mind as sleep takes me.

45

RAMIFICATIONS

The air is stale around me as warmth pushes against my bosom. The heat of summer reminds me I will need a cooler bath today. But as my eyes flutter open to soak in the sunlight, I am met with a hardened chest.

Jerrick envelops me, and I can't stop the smile pinching my cheeks.

The sheets are messy, slightly dampened from the weather and our activities last night. Our chests rise and fall in blissful tandem.

As the grogginess abates, I nuzzle into Jerrick and wrap my arms around him, earning a groaned sigh before he tugs me in closer.

I snicker, unable to stop my giddiness.

Jerrick's eyes are closed, his breathing even and calm. Wisps of his dark hair escaped through the night.

I tuck each loose strand behind his ear, smoothing the furrow forming along his brow.

He hums at my touch. "Good morning."

I scoot up and peck him on the cheek, his eyes opening and focusing on me. That damned dimple appears, and I do not stop smiling.

I greet him with a slow, languid kiss. "Good morning."

Jerrick moves, arms lifting to stretch. A long yawn escapes him before he returns to his previous position. He envelops me as I, too, yawn, refusing to move from this perfect position. He tilts his chin down, kissing my forehead.

I close my eyes, savoring this peaceful rapture.

"Are you well?"

I incline my head. "And you?"

He nods slowly, and my heart thumps against my chest as if it needs to crawl out of my body and mold itself on to Jerrick. Memories of last night surface, and my insides clench as I remember his fingers, his tongue, his cock.

I draw him in, seeking his skin to touch mine and satiate the need growing within. I'm not surprised by how fast Jerrick catches the shift in my thoughts as he willingly allows me closer to him, his hardening cock teasing me.

We trail our hands around each other, desire blooming.

His movements drag up my forearm, intertwining our hands. They link and unlink, each of us taking turns tracing the other's skin, goose bumps prickling everywhere from his touch.

Deities, how could I *not* fall for this man?

You have to let him go, Tove.

I can feel his stare, watching me, watching our hands.

"I have an idea for next time," he says, promising seduction.

I raise my brow. "Oh?"

He plays more with my hand as he leans into my collarbone and drags his lips up the line of my neck. "Next time, I want to use our magic."

I lean back, eyeing him warily. I've only used magic when pleasuring myself because I could manifest the tiniest of molecules of frost. While it is insanely pleasurable, I don't know how that would work with me and Jerrick.

Without a doubt, his magic would completely unravel me faster than I could ever imagine. The suggestion is one I selfishly focus on, clinging to the idea of never leaving this room—never leaving him.

"And when is next time?"

A sinfully delicious smirk appears as he cups my backside, stealing my breath.

I startle at the proximity of his cock, inches from my entrance.

"*Now*," he says, drawing me in for a kiss.

I moan as Jerrick's mouth meets mine, savoring him, loving him. Our kiss deepens, and I tighten my hold on him, keeping him close as if he is the only air in the room.

An abrupt pounding comes from Jerrick's door, startling us, and we break away from our bliss.

"Jerrick!" Jonas shouts with alarm.

"Yes?" Jerrick calls back to the door, pulling the bedsheet up to cover us with barely a second to spare as Jonas rushes in.

"The castle is under attack," Jonas says, panting and out of breath. "Bannermen arrived moments ago, trying to break in, and there are noblemen attacking the guests inside the castle walls." He points down the hall.

"What?" Jerrick asks, stunned and unprepared.

He jumps out of the bed, neglecting his nakedness as he scrounges around for the closest articles of clothing. Jerrick grabs the pair of pants he wore last night, giving Jonas and me a full view of ass as he pulls them on, then laces the front and reaches for his sword.

"I heard some of the noblemen chanting to bring forth you and Tove," Jonas adds.

Jerrick fastens his belt and weapons with quick efficiency. "Any idea who is attacking us?"

"Niko," I whisper as realization sinks in.

Jerrick and Jonas stop their movements, pivoting to me.

I meet their stunned faces, as a knot of dread forms in my gut. Niko did not listen to me, and I did not have a chance to tell Jerrick everything.

Fucking consequences.

Jonas asks, heavy with trepidation, "Wh-What did you just say?"

I clutch the sheets, glancing at Jerrick, who is already piecing together a story before I can force words out.

Malice drips from Jerrick's words. "You *knew* he was going to do this, didn't you?"

My tongue ties, refusing to compute words as my mind runs rampant. No, no. This wasn't supposed to happen. Shaking my head rapidly, I try to explain myself, to explain everything.

Niko was supposed to stand down, was *supposed* to listen to me. I told him I knew how to help his uncle. I was going to tell Jerrick everything this morning.

No one but me was supposed to get hurt.

But the words refuse to come. I stutter, my gaze flicking to Jonas.

His face is lined with hurt and betrayal and my heart cracks with remorse.

"I-I," I fight out, reaching for Jonas, for him of all people to hear me out, to allow me a moment to explain.

"Jonas, give me a moment with my *wife*," Jerrick orders.

Jonas glances at me once before looking to his brother, his king, with another question filling the room and adding to Jerrick's anger. "What about—"

"Gather all the men and women who can fight. I will be down shortly," Jerrick seethes so viciously that Jonas flinches, stepping back toward the door.

Jonas stops to brave one more look at me. Betrayal or goodbye, I can't tell, but he takes a piece of my heart with him.

As Jonas leaves, Jerrick rushes to the door, slamming it. He scans the room for the tunic he wore last night.

Fear surfaces as I push down my emotions, rising from Jerrick's bed and wrapping the entire blanket around me. I swallow down the bile rising.

"Jer," I plea for him to hear me out.

But when he pulls the tunic over his head and looks at me, anger and something else blazing behind his eyes. "Was this all just a silly political game for you? Was this—" He gestures between us.

The walls close in on me as my skin turns cold, Jerrick's hurt pinches and tightens his features in anguish and despair.

"Was this all a *distraction*?" he demands.

My stomach folds into itself as my lips quiver from the pain etched in his words. I hold the bedsheet tight to myself for safety as he glowers.

I can't bear him looking at me like this, like he hates me.

I don't even know where to start with explaining everything.

No matter what I tell him, he could kill me, and he could kill Niko. But if I am gone, Jerrick would be left alone with his curse unbroken.

Should I lie about my true feelings?

I doubt they even matter to him now. But I could lie to save him and give him more reason to keep me alive long enough to divorce me.

I close my eyes, knowing what I have to do.

To help Jerrick be free from his curse, I have to let him go.

A deep breath fills my lungs as I square my shoulders, telling myself how much I love him before I lie once more to save him.

He studies me as I reach for the small sprinkle of frost in my chest. It is the one constant I can hold on to as I return the gift that Jerrick is for someone more worthy than me to love.

A bitter plunge of grief beckons to life with my magic, my mournful soul weeping as I fracture it again to save the man I love. My heart is in a chasm of despair, my love for Jerrick thrashing against my chest, begging to escape to tell him.

But as I open my eyes, all sense of myself is void—only the mask of the Snow Queen remains.

"I agreed to the terms of the marriage contract, as well as the agreement, to help break your curse," I tell him, not wanting to even touch on the response to his original question.

I can't lie to him about my feelings.

He shakes his head in disbelief, faltering a step.

I want to rush to him and tell him it was all real—*is* all real. I want to confess how I've never felt so cared for, so happy, and so real around anyone but him.

But when Jerrick's pained disbelief shifts to anger, I blink through the tears lining my eyes.

No emotions, Tove. You can do this. You hold the key to his freedom.

"And I did learn how to break your curse," I tell him, calling my magic forth.

Jerrick's eyes dart to my hands as the frost creeps along the surface of my skin, the chill wrapping around and numbing me as my mind, body, and soul wither and truly seek to die. His eyes flash in surprise, but the King of Palaena blinks it away, taunting me with an angry response.

"I suppose you want me to spare you?"

I nod slowly, surprised he is not reacting to anything I've said.

He folds his arms and quirks a brow. "And how *did* you find the answer?"

I level my stance, committing to the mask I wear and pleading the lack of emotion means he will listen as I speak the truth.

"My mother designed her curses to outlive her," I say, taking a small step toward Jerrick. "She designed them so that, even upon her death, the portion needed to lift each curse would appear and be visible to the next heir, to me."

Jerrick remains silent, no doubt plotting and scheming all the ways he wishes to kill me.

But I need him to understand. I sigh a prayer to the Makers that the light inside Jerrick I've come to know and love will shine through and see reason.

I switch tactics, focusing on putting more of the puzzle together for him and reserve the one bargaining chip I have. The one that will let me see tomorrow and the one that will save Jerrick.

"When you kidnapped me, I had my mother's mirror. Not only is it one of the few things I have left of hers, but it is also glamoured to be a channel of communication," I say, tempted to avert my gaze when his jaw tics at another reveal he was not expecting.

His silence is more painful than when he ignored me after we were married. This man in front of me is an entirely different person, and I don't know what to do.

Deities, what I wouldn't give to be back to when I first came here to change all this.

My mask slips underneath the King of Palaena's betrayed features as I offer him more information. "Niko told me to call our banners while I remained here, wanting to disprove your stories about my mother and father and train my magic. *Please* believe me when I tell you, I asked him to stand down, and I never wanted a fight to begin with. I ordered him to stand down, and he exploded into a rage. I hoped he would listen and obey my order because I told him everything I discovered, and I told him how I hope—" I cover my mouth to suppress my collapse.

My emotions are getting the better of me, making my voice tremble.

Jerrick finally speaks. "Hope what?"

"I hoped you would divorce me and send me home to Axidoria so you could have a chance to break your curse." The mask Jerrick wears fractures, and I seize the moment. "I found out what was needed to break your curse when you were hunting before the ball. I was planning to tell you last night but—"

I glance at the bed, pressing the sheet to my chest. Last night and how perfect and right it was plucks my heart.

When I look back, I step closer to Jerrick, wanting his touch and begging for his forgiveness.

But Jerrick averts his gaze, and everything monumental and rapturous from last night burns to ash. A tear escapes, and I wipe it away, fighting to keep myself together when he flicks his eyes back at me, clapping slowly.

A low laugh escapes him before he unleashes his wrath on me. "Bravo, Frostbite. That is some tale you've spun."

"It's true!"

"Then, how do I break my curse?" he challenges.

I hold my tongue, unable to tell him. Not until I know he believes me.

I remain tight-lipped, refusing to budge. I can't tell him anything without some understanding—some sort of negotiation of walking away from this. I don't care about saving myself, but I need to save others.

And I can only do that if I let Jerrick go and he does the same.

The silence in the air is thick, dry, and filled to the brim with angry power oozing from Jerrick. The King of Palaena, cursed with bloodlust and gifted to take others into death.

A walking omen, he should be feared, and I, too, remember seeing it and believing it.

Death has followed me before, and assuming I was used to it was a fallacy, especially as Jerrick's features darken into a lethal predator seeking to end its prey.

Fuck, he doesn't believe me.

It's my turn to take a step back.

Jerrick stalks toward me, his features shifting into the man who kidnapped me, killed a man without so much of a second thought, and used his magic against me.

I've lost my privilege of seeing the light inside of him.

I call more magic to the surface, praying I can combat the power Jerrick will release at any moment. Fear prickles up my spine as he chuckles darkly when I am stopped by the bed.

I fall against it, allowing him to get closer.

My lungs cease working as he leans in. I have half a thought to use my gifts on him, but I can't control it. I could kill him.

But when Jerrick's lips crash on mine, my eyes widen as his remains fixed on me, watching me. There is pressure against my skin, my veins, and I break apart from his kiss, trying hard not to touch him for fear of my own magic.

But it is too late. The room is spinning.

A weight blooms across my body. My heartbeat increases, blood warms beyond the summer's heat. Sweat beads along my brow, under my breasts, and between my legs.

I fall backward onto the bed, still reaching and seeking the frigid power to fight against Jerrick's abilities.

I refuse to use my powers on him, knowing I wouldn't be able to live with myself if I hurt him. I hold on to the kernel of frost fighting to not be snuffed out by the rush of Jerrick's magic, trusting it to be enough to keep me alive.

But I slacken as Jerrick observes me, tilting his head as the grip I have on the bedsheets loosens.

He guides me further on the bed.

"I am going to hunt down *Lord Nikolaj*, and when I catch him..." He pauses as a whoosh of his magic overcomes me, threatening to make my world go dark.

The use of Jerrick's magic is different this time, as if I can feel his own torment as it ripples through me. My heart fractures even more because I have done this and have failed him.

"I'm going to kill him," he vows.

Jerrick kisses me once more in a promise.

A tear falls down my cheek when his lips pull away from mine, my time running out. My blood rapidly shifts from hot to cold, dark spots lining my vision. My magic is extinguished, quiet, and I know this is death coming to take me.

"*Love*," I utter, my voice hardening and wanting to cease.

These final precious moments of my life will be here with Jerrick, and even though I've fucked everything up, I can't help but feel grateful.

When his full face comes into view, I reach for him, throwing every last ounce of strength I have, hopeful his light can come forth even after I'm gone.

There is no point in a divorce if I am dead, and maybe this is how it should be. Maybe this is how I return to my family and save my kingdom because Jerrick will have a rightful claim to the lands.

Jerrick killing me is a mercy. It is a beautiful mercy that echoes once more how he is not a monster. But I will not leave this world being the monster everyone claims me to be. I will not keep him from true love and finding his own happy again.

"On-Only in f-f-f-faithful consummation with l-l-l-love will then the curse br-br-break," I pant.

Shadows take over my vision, and I sink deeper and deeper into the mattress beneath me.

I release my hold on my husband, my heartbeat slowing, and my breaths become shallower. I slump as I fight to keep Jerrick in my mind, and I am granted one final blessing of seeing his features soften, glimpsing the man I am in love with in my final moments.

Darkness drags me deep into Letum's Oblivion.

46

LETUM'S OBLIVION

A slap reverberates through my skull, and the sting lingers on my right cheek as I open my eyes. My vision is blurry and dizzy, the warm tingling remaining on my face.

I apply a light pressure, massaging the area as the figure looming above me comes into focus.

Beautiful olive skin, kissed by the summer's sun, is highlighted and sculpted to perfection aside from the voluminous waves of dark chocolate hair billowing over Dorit's hardened brown eyes.

"Ouch," I groan, still groggy.

Dorit's eyebrows furrow at my remark. She disappears momentarily, and suddenly, I am ambushed with finger food.

From the smell of it, it's a solstice pastry followed by rosemary bread and a small cube of cheese. The cheese hits me in the center of my eyes, and I flinch, rolling to the side to prevent more food from landing on my face.

Unfortunately, three women stare at me incredulously.

Dorit, Ophelia, and Cordelia wear deep scowls, each of them crossing their arms, remaining silent, but hollering and yelling come from the halls.

I recognize my surroundings—I am still in Jerrick's room. It is fitting to wake up in Letum's realm, only to be tortured for eternity in my husband's rooms.

But looking around, I am puzzled.

No instant torture. No impending doom burrowing itself in my gut.

I imagined death to be more painful, and I can't help but ask, "Am I in Oblivion?"

Dorit shakes her head.

I slump back, almost wishing I was dead rather than dealing with the three women who are, by the anger on their faces, clearly no longer my friends.

Dorit steps toward the bedside table, pouring something into a goblet and rudely shoving the glass to me. "Drink," she orders.

I nervously reach for the glass, bringing it to my lips, and am pleased when I taste water. I gulp it down, the liquid coating my throat and soothing the scratchiness that lingers through each breath.

Once the contents are empty, Dorit snatches it away and then shoves a roll at me.

I study her angered movements, glancing briefly to Ophelia and Cordelia, unsure who to watch, who might try to throttle me or slap me.

My jaw works, savoring the bread before deciding to speak first. As soon as I swallow, though, each of us interrupts the others.

"Explain."

"How could you!?"

"I-I can't believe you!"

"How long have I been out?"

We all pause.

I cough lightly and hold the bedsheet still wrapped around me as I sit up. I take them in, relieved to find them uninjured. A blessing from the Makers.

If only the same can be said for Jerrick, Jonas, and even Niko.

Sweet Makers, I need to stop Jerrick. Even if he thinks Niko deserves it, Niko is a royal advisor to Axidoria and was my proxy while I was here.

I am furious with Niko, but I don't want him killed.

Jerrick won't listen to me, but maybe I can still save Niko. Maybe with my own life forfeit at the hands of Jerrick, he will leave Axidoria to Niko.

Sweet Makers, I need to get Niko out of here.

I brace my fatigued body up, ignoring the three women as I hurry to Jerrick's wardrobe, finding clothing to change into. Screw trying to run down the stairs in a gown I could trip over. I reach for a black tunic and trousers, wanting to smell them, but immediately dress, tightening the laces around them so they won't fall.

"What do you think you are doing?" Dorit asks, placing her arms on her hips.

I look around for shoes to wear, stopping on each of them wearing boots and not slippers. I point to their feet, and their heads drop to their footwear.

"What size are each of you?" I demand.

Dorit meets my gaze with fury in her eyes. "If you think we are going to let you out of here, you are crazy, Tove."

A defensive reflex snaps into place, knowing the longer I am here, the less time I have to stop all of this. I drop my hand.

I square off with her. "You know what, Dorit? I don't fucking care what you think of me. I don't fucking care because, when I realized how much I care about all of you, I ordered an end to this to prevent anything from even happening in the first place. And since Jerrick didn't kill me, I am going out there and finding a way to stop this. With or without your help. Now, one of you is going to give me a pair of boots or not, but as your queen, I order you to let me out of here so I can save my husband and prevent anyone else from getting hurt."

Dorit's anger simmers into shock as Cordelia and Ophelia look at each other.

Dorit is about to say something when Ophelia steps forward. "Here, take my boots." She bends over, unlacing her boots and sliding them across the floor, skipping of their own accord to me.

I offer her a tight smile, hurriedly lacing up each shoe.

"Do you love us?" Dorit asks.

I meet her stare, responding without any hesitation. "Yes."

"Do you love Jerrick?" she presses.

"*Yes*," I grit out, my heart aching at the memory of hurt in his eyes.

Cordelia and Ophelia's eyebrows lift at my declaration, a silent exchange forming between the two of them.

Dorit's brown irises remain fixed on me. But when her eyes close, she exhales before she, too, offers me her own smirk.

"Told you," Dorit jests.

The shift of her demeanor catches me off guard, and I startle.

She turns to open the door, eying me once more. "Just because I told you so doesn't mean I'll forgive you that easy for stringing us all along. Now, get out of here and put an end to the fighting. If you do that, I *might* be willing to hear an explanation later."

Tears well in my eyes.

I rush to Cordelia and Ophelia to embrace them and then join Dorit at the threshold. She arches back, trying to avoid my arms wrapping around her, but I still latch onto her for dear life for an instant before pulling away.

"I never thought family could be beyond my own blood, but it is. And it is with each of you, Jonas, and Jerrick. I love you all so much," I whisper to them.

I take a long breath and wipe the tears from my eyes. I break into a run down the hallway, with no location in mind, only wanting to stop the people I love from getting hurt.

Screams, yelling, and the clatter of swords echo down the staircase. Every instinct has me wanting to turn away and return to the safety of Jerrick's room.

But I trust I can stop this.

I can prevent bloodshed and two people I dearly care about from killing each other.

My boots smack against the stone but are quiet compared to the noises coming from other levels of my home.

When I reach the lowest floor, some guests are fighting, while others and staff members run in different directions, looking for safety or shelter.

My thoughts drift beyond those in the castle, to those in the villages, to Frida.

I pray to the Makers that they will all be safe.

I stand on my tiptoes, trying to find a familiar face, a glimmer catching my attention.

My eyes widen as Bernie and King Beauvais armed with swords, protect a group of guests. Bernie's daughters hold them together in line, threatening anyone looking to attack them.

Princess Vivienne holds a small dagger, and Princess Marian is armed with a bow and pack of arrows on her back.

Deities, I should have a weapon on me.

I look at my hands briefly, remembering I am a weapon.

I peer up, trying to get one of their attentions. "Bernie!" I shout into the chaos.

His head whips up and in my direction. "Tove!"

An armored man enters the hall with a bloodied sword, hurrying toward a nobleman fighting a bannerman.

Women scream as Bernie pivots for the swordsman, not moving fast enough.

My heart lurches as the enemy lifts his sword to strike. Panic grips me in place just as King Beauvais catches the man off guard, lunging in front of Bernie, striking the man down in one swift blow.

I gape, stunned, as does Bernie.

A weird silent exchange streams between the two of them while the princesses hurry the guests down the cleared path.

When the crowds clear, I rush to them, my breath struggling to keep up.

"Have either of you seen Lord Nikolaj or my husband?"

"I saw King Jerrick and Prince Jonas hurry outside a while ago. They ordered King Beauvais and me over here to help get the guests in here to safety," Bernie says.

He sees something over my shoulder and pushes me aside.

My back clashes against the wall as another swordsman sprints toward the King of Belmur. This time, Bernie is prepared. He holds his sword with both hands, waiting for the man to strike.

The man inches closer, but Bernie does not move.

I cover my mouth, stunned when the swordsman lifts his sword in an outward and downward swing.

Bernie dodges, unsheathing a hidden dagger and stabbing the man in his side repeatedly until he goes down. Bernie kicks the sword from the dead man's hands before meeting my stare.

"I last saw Lord Nikolaj with Lord Ulrik in the throne room," he pants through his hardened green gaze, eyes softening into sorrow. "They ordered everyone to round up the guests and meet in the throne room. They said they were going to have everyone watch them kill a king."

I need to put a stop to this.

I swallow thickly, as Bernie places a hand on my upper arm, comforting me. "I won't try to persuade you one way or the other, Tove, but—"

I take his hand. "I *need* one of you to find Jonas and Jerrick for me. Tell them I'm sorry. I'm going to the throne room to order my men to stand down. There is no need for this bloodshed, and... I want to discuss the terms of surrender."

Bernie's mouth falls. "Tov—"

"I can find them." King Beauvais steps forward.

I nod my thanks, turning back to Bernie, whose features tighten. "I'd rather have you get out of here," he declares.

I shake my head when he tries to tug me along. "You know I can't. This is my fault and I'm the only one that can talk down my men. I'm the only one Niko will listen to. It's my call. I *have* to do this."

I will talk Niko down. I will keep my kingdoms safe. I will stop the fighting.

Even if that means my life is forfeit.

He grimaces, his own hesitation evident. I am about to reassure him I will be fine, but he finally nods once. "Be careful."

I nod back, smiling and knowing he means well.

"I will," I tell Bernie.

I turn to thank King Beauvais, but he is too occupied watching Princess Vivienne and Princess Marian. All of them seem awkward around each other.

Bernie ushers his daughters away from King Beauvais, guiding them and guests down the hall.

King Beauvais inclines his head to me, heading off in the opposite direction. The tall man's blond hair gleams against the light of the sun as he hurries out of the castle, vanishing from sight before I head for the throne room.

47

THE THRONE AWAITS

The curtains are still drawn over the windows the farther I pass through the castle, a good sign no one has ventured this far. The tall wooden doors of the throne room curve into a pointed arch and are wide enough to fit groups of people at once.

I send a prayer up to the Makers as I reach for the latch.

Decorations from last night's ball still adorn the lanterns, curtains, floors, and walls. The luscious colors of black and red are bold and pull all eyes away from the beige stone.

To my relief, there is no one in here.

My footsteps echo against the stone as I step closer to the dais, the two black marble thrones bringing in the entire room. I look around once more, stepping up to touch the seat I was meant to sit and govern in. But I recede my hand when someone approaches.

For some reason, my heart thinks it is Jerrick and lifts, but when I turn, I am reminded I came here for Niko.

I shrivel with disappointment and anger.

Niko's steps falter when he sees me. He scans my ensemble from head to toe. His stare makes me want to look away, but instead, I step down as he meets me at the foot of the dais.

"Niko—"

"Thank the Makers you're alright, Tove," Niko sighs in relief.

He sheaths his sword and rushes to me, holding my arms in place before pulling in and squeezing hard. "I was so worried he killed you," he whispers.

I ignore his worry, furious he disobeyed a direct order, even when I tried to tell him about helping his uncle. I wiggle to free myself from his embrace.

He catches on and slowly releases me, pain etched in his features. His amber eyes are cool, his hair matted and disheveled from the sweat dripping down the side of his brow.

From running or fighting, I am not sure, but it breaks my heart that I don't even know the man standing before me anymore.

I raise my voice. "Niko, I told you to stand down. Why didn't you listen?"

"I did. But Ulrik, *he* was the one that—" He stops as my eyes widen in disbelief.

He is *lying*.

My steps move backward of their own accord, and I shake my head as he watches me. "How *could* you? How could you do this to *me*? To *us*? To Axidoria?"

Niko's features darken, filling with malice as he clicks his tongue. "I told you, Tove. I didn't do this. Ulrik—"

"Stop fucking lying!" I scream.

Niko's face falls.

"King Bernard told me you ordered them to join you and Ulrik in the throne room. But I don't even see Ulrik. So, I know this is you. You need to stand down and get out of here while I try to fix this. I am not going to watch more people die. I am not going to watch you and Jer try to kill each other."

"Oh, so it's *Jer* now? Not *King Jerrick*? Or *Rick*? Or the man who *kidnapped* you?" he barks back, anger still etched on his features as he folds his arms.

"At least he didn't shoot me with an arrow!"

My accusation is met with a swift laugh.

"Oh, we are back to this again," Niko says, rolling his eyes. "*Lovely.*"

My brows furrow, baffled by this... this stranger in front of me.

"I missed my target by a few feet, and you survived. Can't you get over that how you got over *him* kidnapping you?" he asks.

"I can't get over it when the man who shot me is a man who is supposed to love me!" I yell, my magic drawing itself to attention at my pain and truths coming out.

"I've *never* loved you," he spits, pure wrath burning in his gaze.

My power snuffs out, and my entire world caves in.

Niko's hardened steel features turn dark and menacing. *Lethal.*

Trepidation creeps up the length of my spine, my knees almost buckling as the hair on my neck stands with deep foreboding. "Wh-What?" I choke out.

He is lying.

I take a step backward and clench my chest.

Niko chuckles ominously, watching me struggle to find words.

My vision shifts slightly, and I stumble a step, disbelief coursing through my veins. I reach for my magic, the only defense I have, but I can't summon it.

Niko prowls closer. "Do you *honestly* think I could ever love someone who killed the only person I've ever loved?"

My heart stills.

Runa?

He continues with indignation despite my hesitation. "I loved Runa from the moment I first saw her. It didn't matter that your mother cursed my father, *not* my uncle, as you believe, for a crime he didn't commit. I pleaded with your mother and father, yet they refused to change their ruling. Your mother's curses were cruel. The lot of you always are. And when my father ended his life to end his own torment, I sought justice for the wrongs the monarchy had done to me, to my father, to so many people. He was my *only* family. And even my love for Runa didn't stop me from killing your father. And then, well—your mother planned her own demise."

I fight to hold myself together, despite the tears filling my vision from the person in front of me.

He lied about his family.

H-He killed...

Father.

I shudder through the confirmation. My gut sinks, and I cover my mouth in horror as the pieces click into place.

His voice drops an octave, low and lethal as he says, "Freeing Axidoria from a wicked monarchy and avenging my father drew a greater purpose when I met Runa. I planned for her to fall for me so I could marry her and kill the whole lot of you and rule alongside her."

Tears soak my cheeks from Nikolaj's admission, and I yelp in pain when he closes the gap between us, gripping my hair and yanking it back. It forces me to meet the furious storm brewing in his amber eyes.

"But *you* had to go and kill the love of my life and *derail* and *ruin* my plan with your stupid fucking magic," he seethes, his hold on my hair tightening beyond the point of pain.

I squeeze my eyes shut, grieving for the man I thought I knew. But he did... *everything*.

I harden my features, scorn and fury bearing into him as I strike him with the only venom I can find. "Runa would *never* be with you if she knew you did this."

Nikolaj explodes in a rage of fury, throwing me down on the ground.

My chin meets the stone hard, the brunt force sending a pulse of agony through my jaw.

"You don't *deserve* to breathe her name," Nikolaj spits.

I reach for my magic, desperately hoping it is there. But the pain is too distracting and keeps my powers just out of my grasp.

I falter, my heart crushing even more as I struggle to meditate, my thoughts drifting to the memory of Jerrick's anguished features.

I should have told him it was real.

Nikolaj's grip returns tight on my scalp, laughing at the whimpering mess I am, shoving me to the ground and kicking me in the stomach. *Hard*. His boot makes contact with my ribs, the sound of it screeching against my ears.

I scream out from the weighted force of his strength seeking to break me.

He does it again and again.

And again.

And *again*.

By the fifth time, his foot hits my lower stomach, my diaphragm shifts up my core as small amounts of blood drip from my mouth.

"Where's your stupid magic now, *Snow Queen*?" Nikolaj challenges.

He extends his arms, taunting and mocking me to strike him. Nikolaj drops them quickly when he sees I don't move, squatting to my eye level.

His entire face shifts, puckering his lips and blinking his eyes rapidly. *"Oh, Niko, I don't want to kill anyone!"*

He mocks my grief, my pain, throwing everything I confided to him in these last five years against me. Nikolaj chuckles darkly before standing, kicking his foot again toward me.

I grunt and yelp out in pain when my bones crack. My ribs are breaking, a stabbing and fracturing pain multiplying in my body, air difficult to find and breathe.

I wish I had enough strength to brace for more pain.

Boots scurry across the floor beyond, mercifully drawing Nikolaj's foot away.

My eyes flutter through pain and tears, peering over to the throne room's entrance, Jerrick and Jonas coming into view. I know they want to kill me, but I can't help my whimpered cries of relief at the two of them, even if they feel so far.

Their swords are unsheathed and bloodied, and gore is splattered across both of their bodies.

More echoes come from the hall, and my heart leaps when an armed Viggo with King Beauvais and others appear. They join Jerrick and Jonas a few steps back, a group of castle guards and bannermen behind them with swords drawn and bows nocked.

Jerrick halts everyone as they take in the scene unfurling in the throne room, and when his eyes find mine, my heart breaks.

I tried to fix everything, and I've fucked it all up.

I can't tell if it is anger or concern in his beautiful stare, but it doesn't stop me from letting out another choked sob to reach for him, for Jonas, for *my family*.

Nikolaj growls in irritation, his hands wrapping around my hair again, forcing a yelp from my lips.

I scream in pain, struggling against his hold. My prayers and pleas for my magic to manifest are ignored.

Nikolaj jerks me up, using me as a shield as he draws a dagger to my throat.

Jerrick, Jonas, King Beauvais, and even Viggo, sweet and bashful Viggo, step forward, but they are too far away to do anything.

Nikolaj laughs, clicking his tongue as he holds me hostage. "I see you've gathered quite the audience. *Finally.*"

The fighting beyond the throne room feels distant, the silence surrounding us thick and wary, everyone hesitant to make another step.

Nikolaj works his jaw, craning my neck more.

He whispers so only I can hear. "How fitting it is that the man who loves you gets to watch you die?"

Nikolaj applies light pressure to the blade at the side of my throat, the sharp jab forcing me to hiss.

"H-He doesn't love me," I gasp in shallow breaths.

Nikolaj chuckles darkly. "We shall see about that."

He returns his attention to the men at the threshold, removing the blade from my neck to point at Jerrick. "I know I gathered everyone here today to watch me kill you, but it is much more fitting to kill *her*."

Nikolaj moves the blade directly over my heart.

I wrestle against him, but with his hand fastened around my hair pulling me upward, I only give myself more pain. It erupts everywhere in my torso, my movements unbearable when Nikolaj stretches me a few inches off the floor, making a spectacle of me.

"Don't make another move," Jerrick orders Nikolaj, his sword pointed in challenge.

Nikolaj laughs wickedly, completely unfazed. "Don't you get it? *She* is the source of everyone's problems. I am doing everyone here a favor."

Everyone remains unmoving and silent as Nikolaj keeps me prisoner.

"Surrender. *Now*," Jerrick demands.

Nikolaj feigns fear at Jerrick's statement. "I will have my vengeance," Nikolaj vows, shoving his dagger into my injured side.

I yelp.

I do not know if the audible gasp is my own because, miserably, I am still reaching and pleading for my magic, if only to numb the pain of my own injuries. It could take away the pinching between my ribs, the tearing in my gut, and the shattering of my heart.

Jerrick moves, too far from stopping Nikolaj as he drags the dagger to my chest, slicing downward and cutting my shirt open.

A small steady stream of blood trickles down my body, and I hiss, pinching my eyes shut as I fight against the blade, biting my lip through the pain.

A chilling kiss blossoms in my core.

My magic.

I shudder in relief as the familiar kernel of power unfurls, seeking to console me.

Frost traces its way along my arms, forming swirls and flurries of snow and ice and numbing me as Niko's shining blade punctures my chest.

The cold steel in my body is unfamiliar, stinging more and more as Nikolaj spitefully laughs, gradually and torturously sending the blade deeper and deeper, seeking to enjoy and prolong my demise.

"NO!" Jerrick bellows, sprinting toward me.

I barely grasp anything beyond the blade and my magic manifesting in my hands.

I hiss through the searing sensation, inhaling once, and realize I am not going to make it out of this.

Jerrick and I are still married, which makes him King of Axidoria.

At least my people will have Jerrick and Jonas.

And maybe my death will end my cursed winter. Maybe finding the tools to break Jerrick's curse will allow him the chance to end the one I have placed on my own people. If anyone could figure it out, it would be my husband.

I wish I had more time to explain myself to him.

I wish I didn't lie to him.

I wish I could tell Jerrick how much I love him.

With what could be my last words, I persevere, finally and fully accepting myself. Everything I've worked toward fixing, toward healing, toward saving, will be righted once I am gone. And that is enough.

I am enough.

If I am going to die, so will Nikolaj.

I am doing this for me, for my kingdom, and for my family waiting to embrace and love me on the other side.

Nikolaj's gaze meets mine.

I grit out, "The difference between us, Nikolaj, is, when I die, Runa will *want* to see me. Runa will still love me. *Not* you. *Never* you."

My strength weakens as I reach to grab the hilt of the dagger, my fingertips brushing along Nikolaj's skin.

Warm liquid trickles down the center of my chest, and the pressure tugging my scalp slackens as a startled hiss is directed in my ear.

The momentary freedom is nothing as I am released, my hands catching myself from forcing the dagger farther into my body.

On my hands and knees, I barely have the strength to gaze up and catch the frost transforming to ice over Nikolaj.

His right hand grows with frost, streaming up his arm and down his body in rapid succession.

My magic at play is horrifying to see, the past repeating itself as Nikolaj loses movement.

He withdraws another dagger, attempting to hack away my powers molding to him and the speed of it multiplies. His tanned skin alters to a sickly pale tone as the ice splinters and bursts up his chest.

It cracks with each new angle he shifts into, the crystals freezing him to the ground. His movements turn frantic, cleaving and sawing at his own body, with the hope of escape.

But as the puddle of blood grows underneath me, I collapse on my right side, weakly wrapping my arms around myself. I shake uncontrollably in agony as I watch my magic right one of my endless wrongs.

Terror etches itself in Nikolaj's features and body as the Snow Queen's touch steals his life.

I close my eyes at the end of a man I thought I knew, expecting grief to hit me, but instead, there is a void.

With one problem gone and one more left, I seek my own peace, begging my magic to numb the pain and to finally remove the threat I am to everyone.

I pray hard, hoping the Deities will let me return to my family.

My head droops, seeking to rest against the stone floor, but it meets something soft.

A tender hand rests on my hip, and I groan in pain from the movement, the blade shifting in my chest.

When pale blue eyes meet mine, I immediately wish to cower to my early grave.

"*Tove*," Jerrick chokes out.

His audible pain sends a tear down the side of my face.

I never thought I'd hear him say my name ever again.

But a coppery tang is in the air, my attention on the blade and the vast amount of blood seeping from my body. It trickles down my arm and pools around me.

Jerrick cups my face, directing my focus to him.

"Don't look. I'm here, my love. I'm here," he soothes. "I've always got you, remember?"

My chest hollows, and I wheeze, seeking to fill my lungs with what my body needs. But the air is too far away...

"I-I'm so, s-so, s-s-soooorry." I shiver and pant.

I never wanted to hurt him.

I never meant to lie.

I hope this... This is enough.

The ceiling above me moves down as the frost, the chill, and the cold seep around me, changing. It is not a glimmer of power nor a small kernel of home when I reach for it.

This coldness is dark, gloomy—*grave.*

Jonas, Viggo, and King Beauvais come into my line of vision.

Jerrick analyzes the blade in my chest and turns to the now frozen statue of Nikolaj.

A numbing sensation pricks itself along my fingertips and toes as Jerrick looks at King Beauvais.

"*Please,*" Jerrick begs the man hovering above.

Blinking is too strenuous to do at this point.

I lean into Jerrick, warmth soothing me as the numbness creeps up my arms, weighing down and reducing the use of my hands and fingers.

"It's okay," I murmur up to Jerrick through a pained smile.

He looks down, his entire expression forlorn.

I seek his hand, not knowing if he can feel the circles I am drawing along his skin to comfort him. "You get to find someone to break your curse. You get to find *love*—you get to find your happy again, Jer."

I inhale the mixture of cologne, leather, and blood.

One last time.

A presence lowers as everything feels heavy—so dark.

I can't tell who it is, and I don't even want to look. I keep my attention on Jerrick as long as I can, smiling faintly at him.

But I just want to rest my eyes.

"*Tove,* you fool," Jerrick whispers.

A beam of light shines in the darkness, the sense of something foreign leaving my body. It scrapes my skin, feeling just as painful, if not more so than when I was stabbed.

I slowly blink, yellow light in full view. It is blinding and warm.

"We need to move her," someone says.

"But what about the frost coming from Lord Nikolaj?" a man asks.

"We need to warm her first," another declares.

"What about—"

My mind drifts...

A warm comfort grazes my chest, my arms, my legs, and my feet. It spreads along my body, light and sweet.

It reminds me so much of Jerrick's magic.

Maybe when I wake, I can compose a melody to remember how sweet and serene this warmth is, too.

Cologne fills my senses as a hard solid cushion barricades me. Nuzzling in close, the nostalgic fondness of home draws a smile from my lips.

Images of Jerrick's face blur in my mind.

His face swirls and swishes away, converting into a room adorned in candlelight.

A beautiful vision of a couple sitting on a piano bench together, heads resting against one another. One, a woman with long silver-blonde locks, runs her hands up and down the entirety of the piano, laughing. In the other, a man with black shoulder-length hair loops an arm around her and scoots closer, lifting his head to kiss the top of the woman's. The vision is one of what I wish for in my own life, wishing I had the strength to utter those three precious, tenderly *perfect* words to a man who never once believed I was a monster.

A man who stole my breath away when I first laid eyes on him.

A man who stole my heart, connected my soul, and gave me the briefest of glimpses of finding my happy again...

I love you.

Darkness surrounds me as the phantom pain drifting through me dissipates. I revel in the void's embrace, descending into the abyss. Warmth blankets itself around me as I take in fuzzy auras that flash to life with familiar faces. *Three* familiar faces.

One female, long silver-platinum hair, eyes pale and blue like mine, holding the hand of another woman, whose dark strands matches that of the last person, a man, resting his hands on the two women's shoulders.

Warm, familiar hazel eyes come into focus, and my lips tremble.

"I'm home," I whisper, running into the arms of my mother, my father, and my sister.

The impact of my embrace has them all grunting. They wrap their arms around me, my father's wise, tender voice filling the darkness.

"You're home, dear."

I nuzzle into each of them, squeezing them as if they are my own air—my own breath.

A small flood of light beams from behind my family, forcing us to break apart. We turn, the light glowing and expanding, bright enough to fill and diminish the darkness surrounding us.

The lightest of white borders the warm yellow hues, reminding me of a crisp winter's snow or a soft, delicate cloud. As if the light knows my thoughts, the sensation of wind, cold and calm, floats across my face, blowing hair away from my vision.

The bright rays of light shine around us. I am in awe and filled with curiosity, desiring to explore this space.

My father holds my hand, squeezing it tight enough for my eyes to look up at him. His wrinkles are thick on his forehead, eyes, and cheeks from years of raised brows and full smiles.

He bends down, kissing my head before letting go and walking toward the rays of light.

A surge of his love vibrates through me, comforting me and soothing me with the promise of more hugs and reunions soon. He vanishes into the light, and a surprising comfort warms me.

I rub the heat in the center of my chest as my mother faces me.

"Thank you, my sweet girl," she says.

I tilt my head. "For what? Mother, why did you do all of this?"

She grins at Runa and me, pulling us close. "Because it is what the Makers wanted from me and from you."

I blink rapidly, not understanding her. "What did they want?" I keep a tight hold of her, needing answers.

"For you to be the start of helping us all find peace," she whispers before pulling away.

Her maternal love radiates as she kisses my cheeks, holding them and staring intently into my eyes. Tears line her vision, a direct reflection of me.

"I'll see you soon, my sweetheart," my mother whispers, looking at Runa and glancing back at me once more.

The right side of Mother's lip lifts, her hands drifting down my arms, lingering before she walks toward the light.

Runa laces her fingers with mine.

When I look down at our connection, my lip trembles at the soft circles she runs against my skin. And when I meet my sister's jade-green eyes, I am met with her beautiful smile.

Regret surges forth, my guilt and shame for ending her life leading me to avert my gaze as tears fall.

"I-I'm so sorry, Runa," I sob, covering my face.

My cries are the only sound between us, and I pour my heart and soul into repeated apologies, begging for her and the Makers' forgiveness.

Runa embraces me. "Tove, it's okay." She tries reassuring me, but the shame is too overwhelming. "There is nothing to forgive."

"H-How can you say that?" I ask, clutching her tight. "I am a monster."

She pulls us apart and inclines my head to look at her. "Tove, it was my fate. The Makers had spoken that day, as they do now."

I remember some of Runa's last words on that fateful day, not understanding. Still not understanding now. "Runa—"

"*Tove.*"

I snivel, feeling unworthy as she helps dry my tears and holds my cheeks, as our mother did.

She combs my hair away from my face and holds my cheek. "There is no monster inside of you. There is no Snow Queen inside of you. Only Tove. Only my sister. My kind, passionate, inspiring sister who is sunshine itself."

I shake my head as my lip quivers, undeserving of her kindness. "Runa, *you* are the sunshine. I never have been."

"Your sunshine has always been there. You just struggle to see it. And while your light dimmed for a brief duration, you shone brightly again when you met him." She smiles.

Jerrick's features etch to life, and my heart fills with love and joy. A passion and bond deeper than I had imagined, a relationship I had hated but came to love.

I sigh at the memory of his eyes matching mine, his scar, and how it would perk up whenever he smirked or laughed. How he always tied his hair up when he was training. How he would rub my hand in soft circles...

Lifting my hand to inspect it, I swear a warm spot lingers where Jerrick would always comfort me.

Runa leans in, her voice pulling me from my thoughts. "Go to him."

I lift my brows.

She nods with pure joy in her features.

I look between her and the light and the tugging warmth in my palm. "I-I can't. He needs to find someone to break his curse. It is less of a mess without me."

Runa's soothing voice surrounds my senses. "You two were fated to meet. You were meant to break his curse, Tove."

My mouth falls. "Th-The curse is broken?"

Runa brightens and nods happily. "Yes."

"B-But how?"

"I think you know," she says, wiggling her eyebrows before taking one step back, then another.

Once more, she fades from my existence, this time shining bright, free of pain, and smiling. Our bond as sisters marks and instills love from her—love from my family—love for myself.

Her voice echoes, "Go be the sunshine. Go be the queen we know you to be. Go to your happy, Tove."

48

Judgment

Muttered voices cloud my senses, and I hate how I listen to each of them, disappointed I cannot find the one I desperately long to hear. My eyes remain shut, my head tossing from soreness in my chest.

I move my hand and someone gasps, all conversations halt.

I squint through the light as my vision clears, a group of people standing a few feet away. Scanning my surroundings, I am in a bed. Am I in a bedchamber or the healing wing?

"Tove?" a female asks with reverence.

I move toward the voice, recognizing the long brown hair and chocolate eyes staring at me, filled with tears.

Sunshine surrounds Dorit, and the rays form a halo around her as she hugs her sides. Dorit muffles her sobs, Cordelia and Ophelia doing the same. Their worried expressions and tears dampen their cheeks.

Pain tightens in my throat at their concern, seeking to comfort my friends.

Dorit breaks down, and my face falls.

A man steps up, and I recognize him. *Viggo.*

Ophelia, Cordelia, and Dorit all look at Viggo, who motions them to step back. He looks over, offering me the same bashful expression.

I work up a soft smile for him.

The four of them shuffle away as two more people come into view.

But my brows furrow at the sight of Jonas and King Beauvais. Jonas's arms are crossed as King Beauvais perches on the side of the bed, reaching toward me.

I try to lean away from his touch, and he notices and pauses.

"I'm here to help," he says reassuringly.

The tension and apprehensiveness relax in my system. I still feel as if words are hard to reach for in my mind, so I nod.

He touches the top of my brow, and he peers over me. Alarm has me wanting to cover my chest, but my arms don't budge. They are too worn, too weak.

King Beauvais meets my gaze, his golden eyes tinged with more yellow than an orange I remembered seeing somewhere. "I wasn't able to heal you completely, so expect a little soreness. But you will make a full recovery, Queen Tove." The King of Torgem smiles.

Heal?

A few memories rush in, gripping my heart tight as emotions pair with each one. The visible hurt in Jerrick's pale blue eyes, borrowing Ophelia's boots—Nikolaj stabbing me.

A flash of ice and frost dances across my mind as everything pieces together.

But the dread of facing Jerrick for my judgment hits me hard.

Fuck, maybe I should have stayed dead.

The door to my left swings on its hinges.

I am stunned that, of all the people in the world, I would not have expected *him* to come barreling in. His blond hair and high cheekbones are cut and disheveled, and his eyebrows lift when he sees me.

"Your Majesty!" Ulrik Albertsen says with what sounds like genuine relief.

He rushes in the bedchamber as Betina's father hovers in the doorway. I offer her father a polite nod, surprised the noblemen of Axidoria are freely roaming and not in a dungeon.

Ulrik rushes to my side, shooing away and waving at King Beauvais.

I glance sideways at King Beauvais, Jonas, and the others, perplexed.

Ulrik lowers to a knee and takes my hand, kissing my knuckles before he meets my gaze with worry. "Queen Tove, it brings me such joy to see you are well and are recovering." Ulrik glances to Jonas.

I arch a brow as Jonas studies Ulrik carefully before inclining his head. Ulrik faces me as Jonas's eyes land on me.

What the—

The smell of tobacco hits my senses when Ulrik shifts closer, speaking in a hushed tone. "Can you dismiss everyone except Prince Jonas? We have some business to discuss." His expression is encouraging, not one of scheming.

I eye him skeptically, even though he appears genuine. I pick at my nails in contemplation, feeling wary.

I look at the group in the room. "I'd like a moment alone with Lord Ulrik and Prince Jonas, please."

My friends bow and exit, passing by Betina's father and King Beauvais. They leave one by one, with King Beauvais stopping at the door to peer back.

"Shall I?" he asks Jonas.

Jonas stops him. "I will."

King Beauvais tilts his head to Jonas before meeting my stare with a bright smile. "I'll return to check on you later. Rest well, Queen Tove."

I touch my chest with gratitude. "Th-Thank you, King Beauvais."

"Please, call me Beau. It is what my friends call me." He beams back.

I smile at the kindness Beau offers before he closes the door behind him.

My attention remains on the door, somehow hoping—*praying*—desperately Jerrick would come running in as Ulrik did. But the longer I stare, the harsher my torment sets in.

He isn't coming. I lied to him, and I betrayed him.

And I am in love with him.

I'm such a stupid, stupid, fool.

I turn to Ulrik, who's still on his knee, and Jonas, who's a few feet back, wearing the face of a prince. Why is Ulrik, of all people, still here without guards or shackles around his wrists?

I swallow thickly, realizing that, without me, he is the closest person the people could have pass as a ruler in Axidoria. A horrid thought comes rushing in, one where Jerrick divorces me only to broker me in a marriage to Ulrik. That could be the only reason why I am still alive, why I am not locked away in a dungeon, or why I'm not at the torturing whims of Jerrick right now.

I swallow those dark thoughts, gathering my emotions, and brace for the impact of my world truly falling apart.

I deserve it.

Jonas steps a little closer to the two of us. "Lord Ulrik fought on our side the morning after the masquerade ball and has been very... *insightful* with the events of what happened after you left Axidoria. Most of the bannermen Lord Nikolaj had gathered were criminals instead of actual nobles and guardsmen."

I pinch my brows in confusion.

Jonas seems perplexed himself as he continues, "Apparently—and I am only saying this because this is still speculative in my opinion—the noblemen had agreed to fight with Lord Nikolaj because they knew he would lead them back to you."

I drift back to the night of the ball when Nikolaj had approached me with a few noblemen from Axidoria behind them, one of them being Ulrik Albertsen. He looked away quickly, and when we danced at the Celebration of Spirits, he was kind. Ulrik has always been pleasant to me, unless intoxicated, but Nikolaj said he and many other noblemen despise me and hate me.

My gaze lands on Ulrik. "I-I thought you all hated me," I state bluntly, bypassing all formalities.

Ulrik huffs a disbelieving laugh. "*Hated* you? How could we, Your Majesty?"

"The rumors. You *all* spread them."

"We never started those rumors. That was Lord Nikolaj."

Nikolaj.

A pang sears deep into the pit of my gut, a knot twisting my insides at more betrayals and lies from Nikolaj coming to a head. I glance away, tears already rising from the sting.

Deities, was I really that blind?

I blink my tears away, taking a careful breath before gazing back at him.

Ulrik takes my hand. "Your Majesty, we understood everything you were going through with your family's passing. We all tried to put our best steps forward to help you when you stepped into power. But Lord Nikolaj said you didn't need us. He was always with you, and we saw him more than you. It became difficult for everyone. And pardon me, but he was a pompous asshole in every meeting you were not a part of.

"We did not know if the decisions made were coming from you or coming from him. We were not sure how to tell you, how to approach you, because we did not want to speak treasonous thoughts against the crown. And when you appointed him as proxy, we lost hope. But then he announced your safety to the kingdom and started carrying out plans. We felt something was amiss and were biding our time, wanting to gain proof of his dealings to show you."

Filled with skepticism, I look at Jonas, and he speaks up. "We interrogated every nobleman from Axidoria, and they all had the same story."

I incline my head slowly, still unsure of Ulrik, given the information Betina had told me about his family and Nikolaj's. I want to find a way to wrap my mind around everything, even though I wish I was sleeping.

Ulrik nods, still holding my hand as he clarifies. "If it wasn't for King Jerrick vouching for us, I don't think any of us would be here."

Jerrick.

My soul fractures, emotions clogging my throat. "That was..." I hesitate, the thickness of emotion building more. "That was kind of him."

"It was," Ulrik agrees. "Your Majesty, I am so sorry we failed you. Please accept my sincerest apologies for not pushing hard enough to help you. And please extend that apology again to King Jerrick. We did not want to fight either and tried to contain as much of it as we could. And I am more than happy to discuss future imports and trades as soon as you are recovered."

Overwhelmed with this information, I'm still unsure of what to trust, what to believe. Not to mention I doubt I will ever have a chance to speak to Jerrick. But I need to get to the bottom of my own demise and figure out the best plan to help my people when I am truly gone.

All I can manage is squeezing Ulrik's hand.

Removing my indifference, I offer him a glimmer of me and not live up to the rumors Nikolaj spread. "Thank you, Lord Ulrik. I appreciate your kind words. Please extend my gratitude to the noblemen for me. I'd truly love to have a full meeting with all of you to discuss and make better arrangements for Axidoria—"

I stop, unsure of if I am still the Queen of Palaena.

Ulrik kisses my knuckles once more before rising. "Is there anything the noblemen can do for you?"

I think momentarily, looking at Jonas. Regardless if he hates me, I still would trust him more than anyone to run my kingdom. And with a divorce inevitably coming or my impending death, I still have faith he would see my wishes through.

"Please keep Prince Jonas updated with everything," I decide.

Ulrik nods to leave, but before he can, my own misgivings have me reaching for his tunic, halting him and drawing his attention back to me. "Should anything—and I repeat, *anything*—go amiss while I am recovering, you and all the persons responsible will be dealing with me. *Personally*. Am I understood?"

Ulrik's eyes widen at the menace in my tone, but it vanishes as he nods again, more earnest than before.

I release my grip on his tunic. "Good. Now, if you don't mind, I need to speak with the prince."

The lord bows without another word, leaving me alone with Jonas. The silence is awkward as we stare at the other. I am unsure of what to say, what to ask, and what to do.

Jonas releases a long sigh, uncrossing his hands to scratch the back of his head.

I rush to blurt out my apologies.

"I'm so sorry—"

"I'm sorry—"

I sheepishly curve my shoulders inward as my cheeks heat with embarrassment. Jonas tightens his lip and gestures for me to speak first.

My skin is hot and clammy, my betrayal hangs heavy between us, making my emotions thick in my throat. I swallow the bile threatening to force its way up as I beg for forgiveness I know I will never get and will never deserve.

"There are not enough apologies in the world to say to Jerrick and you, Jonas. I am sorry I lied. I am sorry I dragged everyone into this mess. And once I am deemed well, I am more than willing to accept my judgment and execution or allow Palaena to dictate the terms through the divorce process and discussions of trade and borders. I am willing to redefine Axidoria's borders and anything Palaena needs to atone for my actions," I say through shaky breaths.

"Execution? Divorce?" Jonas asks, brows furrowed.

I nod as tears line my vision.

Stupid tears.

"I completely understand coordinating one or both because of what I did, what my kingdom did," I tell him.

Jonas shakes his head, sighing. "Tove, why are you thinking about any of that?"

My lip quivers as more tears fall. The pain in my chest tightens as I fight to keep my emotions at bay.

"I-I assumed—"

Jonas steps up and lowers to a knee, reaching for my hand. His stoic features have softened, drawing forth the enthusiastic and patient Jonas I've come to know and admire.

"Tove, we don't care about any of that. We only care about you and making sure you're alright," Jonas says, scooting closer.

"But—" I break off, disbelieving his compassion and care for me. "After everything I did? You *should* care. You *all* should care. I should be executed or shipped off to Axidoria and away from you all."

Jonas's brows pinch, shaking his head softly. "I heard everything, Tove. Well, almost everything."

I do not know *everything* he refers to, but Jonas continues, "Beau found me first, told me you went off to the throne room and that he was going to find Jerrick. I stormed off to find you and help you, but when I neared the throne room, I heard conversation instead of fighting, and I listened." He sighs and looks away. "I should have found Jerrick and brought him and a group of men sooner."

"You couldn't have known what he had planned. I didn't even know," I force through a breathless sob.

He turns back to me, eyes filled with tears. "I know you didn't, Tove."

We squeeze each other's hand. I look up at the ceiling, trying to work through my blurred vision as I struggle to not ask the one question I need an answer to.

I can't hold it in any longer.

"Is Jer—" My courage wavers.

Jonas takes a long breath. "He's—he's in bad shape."

Alarm scatters up my spine. "Wh-What? What happened? What's wrong?"

Jonas closes his eyes. "H-H-He—" He pauses, seeming lost for words.

I refuse to believe something happened to him. "Where is my *husband*?"

He can hate me and want me dead, but that won't stop me from making sure he is okay.

I move, but Jonas halts me and tries to reassure me. "He's here. He's here."

It does nothing to comfort me. He did not say Jerrick was okay. I *need* to know he is alright.

Jonas gulps slowly. "He's watched you almost die, Tove. *Multiple times*. And while Beau helped heal you, you weren't waking up—" Jonas wipes his eyes, sniffing. "Jerrick was *inconsolable*. We moved you to rest and wake up, but he just... *left*. He locked himself in his room."

"Has anyone told him I am awake?"

Jonas shakes his head. "He said he only wanted to hear news from me."

I slump, muddling through Jonas's words.

Jerrick is inconsolable because I betrayed him. And he wasted all this time helping me and saving me multiple times, only for me to break his trust and everything we built and throw it in his face. And even if Jonas cares about my well-being, it does not mean Jerrick does.

Jerrick has every right to execute me or divorce me, and only he will be able to make that decision. The only way a choice can be made is if I see him and ask for his judgment myself.

I look at Jonas, setting my eyes in determination, no matter how much I am dying on the inside all over again, this could be my last chance to see Jerrick.

"Take me to him," I order.

"I can go get him and bring him here."

I wave him off and roll on my side, hoisting myself up. "No, I need to do this. He has done too much for me. The least I can do is go to him."

Jonas offers me his hand.

I take a hold of it, indebted to him and his help, and nudge my head toward my vanity. "Help me with my dress robe?"

"Wait here."

He grabs my long blue silk dress robe, opening the sides to help ease my arms into it. I have a white undergarment on, but the robe is enough to cover me without too much effort of clothing beyond that.

Jonas helps wrap the lace around me, tightening the tie at my waist before lifting my hair from underneath. He smooths my locks as I look up, catching my appearance in my mirror.

My skin is pale and slightly discolored, my cheeks sunken from the lack of food. I linger on my eyes, taking myself in and not hearing cracking noises. I don't see Runa's reflection staring back, and I don't see a monster thrashing to escape.

I see me.

I see a broken person, but that broken person is me.

It's okay not to be okay, Jerrick's voice whispers in my mind, and my features scrunch up, his words settling into my bones as I wipe my tears away from my cheeks and smile at my own reflection.

When I am ready, Jonas holds my hand and supports me. I lean into him as I seek out my husband.

49

SIDE BY SIDE

Jonas looks at me in question, and I incline my head once. He exhales quickly, reaching forward to knock three times.

I hold the food tray in a death grip, grateful Jonas and I caught Dorit with a plate of food. I stole it from her, knowing I needed it for Jerrick. I tremble with exhaustion and foreboding as the last and final knock echoes in the hall.

"I said go away," someone says on the other end, quick to dismiss us.

Jonas clears his throat and says with trepidation, "Jer, it's me. It's about Tove." He helps me a step when he hears footsteps on the other end rushing toward the door.

I move tentatively, watching my footing and catching wind of the door.

The frame fills with Jerrick.

My heart sinks at him so disheveled and so... *broken.*

He looks bewildered and angry, no sign of flirtation or charisma. Not even a sign of the King of Palaena. Just a man who was betrayed by someone he thought he trusted.

I hurt him. So much.

"Wha—"

Jerrick's anger ceases, and he goes rigid.

Disbelief is visible as he looks at Jonas, me, then the tray of food. When our eyes lock again, his entire posture slackens. So many apologies surging forth, and I tremble, my determination faltering.

I take a small step forward, Jonas helping me as I extend the food tray Jerrick.

"I-I hoped food could h-help with my ap—"

Jerrick lunges forward, snatching the tray and shoving it into Jonas's hands.

The swiftness of his movements sends me off kilter. I sway, but Jerrick catches me, pulling me to him.

I'm frozen in a state of shock, unsure of what I did to deserve his embrace.

Jerrick pulls away, his hands finding my cheeks as he hunches over me. Emotions are thick in his expression, and I cannot help tears from lining my vision. His face pinches, and he tucks himself into the crook of my neck, shuddering.

Tears run down the sides of my cheeks despite wanting to buckle from exhaustion. I do not know how I remain standing, but I fight it, smelling salt in the air mixed with the leather and cologne.

"*Frostbite,*" Jerrick murmurs against my skin.

I close my eyes at the damned nickname I've grown to love, my heart breaking as I realize this could be the last time he says it to me.

I remain silent through my fears, needing to commit it to memory, too.

Jerrick glances at his brother. "Jonas, could you?" he asks, with pure kindness brightening his features into a smile.

"On it," Jonas says, walking into Jerrick's room.

Dizziness makes me sway again and Jerrick is so in tune with me. He lightens his hold to pick me up with ease.

I don't protest, too tired, as he carries me into his room, placing me on his bed.

Jerrick remains in front of me while Jonas sets the tray down. From over Jonas's shoulder a closed-lip smile lights his features as I mouth, *Thank you.*

Anytime, sis, Jonas mouths back, closing the door behind him.

The disarray of Jerrick's bedchamber is the first thing that draws my attention. The moment of tidying Jerrick did on our wedding night was light. Cleaning the room now would require more than that.

Rumpled sheets are piled by the bathing area, discarded, and barely covering full trays of food. The chair by his working table is broken, with fissures on the back end where the legs are slanted from one of the legs being broken off. Papers are scattered across the floor near the mess, crinkled and torn.

And when my attention finds Jerrick, the same neglect of the room reflects in his appearance.

Oil builds up in his onyx hair. The small wisps that typically escape throughout the day are many and cover his face. His black tunic is half tucked, half open, as if he did not know whether to keep it on or change. The shadow of stubble on his jawline is fuller, covering the red undertones from him scratching it insistently. No dimple or smirk, only features pinched and pained.

And when his cold blue eyes meet mine, all I can think is how sorry I am for being the one to cause him such pain.

My fault.

Jerrick touches my cheek, and I melt into it, caressing it as tears stream down my face.

I reach for him, and he obliges.

He sits beside me, resting a leg on the bed and turning our bodies to each other. He tugs me to him and closes the gap between us. His hand remains tight on my hip as his voice lowers.

"Forgive me."

I shake my head, not understanding why he is apologizing. "I should be the only one apologizing, Jer."

He rests his head against mine as my heart constricts, needing to share everything I meant to the night before disaster struck.

I take his hand, looking down to draw circles with a trace of my fingertips. "I-I should have told you. The second I knew how to break the curse, I should have raised a party to find you in the woods and tell you. And I should have told you about Nikolaj. I should have. But I thought he loved me, and like a fool, I thought it would have been enough for him to stand down. I know it was stupid of me to believe that. And I know I betrayed you and used you. There are not enough food trays in the world that I can give to tell you how sorry I am. Jerrick, I am *so* sorry."

Tremors shake through my body. I fight the tears, trying to get everything off my chest.

But it hurts so much.

"There will never be a day that I am not sorry for what I did to you, to Jonas, to everyone—"

Jerrick moves and grips my chin, jerking it up to meet his stare. "You are not stupid, Frostbite. You trusted in your royal advisor. He wanted a fight and convinced you. But when you changed your mind, he didn't listen. I can't fault you for that."

I hold his wrist. "But I lied to you."

"You withheld information," Jerrick says, trying to make my deception lighter than what it really is. "I withheld information from you as well. Do not think you are the only one that has done that. You didn't know what I was dragging you into when you arrived here. I would have done the exact same thing if I had been in your position."

I shake my head. "I still withheld information from you for *months*, whereas you didn't." I pull his hand away from my chin and lower my head in shame. "I know we got off on the wrong foot, Jerrick, but you put your trust in me to help you break your curse. And then you were kind enough to help me understand Palaena was not behind my parents' deaths, and you helped me with my magic. And you did so much more, too. I never deserved any of that."

"You deserve the world," he gushes.

"No, *you* deserve the world, Jer!" Tears still run down my cheeks, knowing he doesn't understand me.

Jerrick's eyebrows lift in surprise at my vigor.

I keep at it, *needing* him to understand his value and not try to give me any. "You deserve to be surrounded by good people! You deserve to pave a path that is separate from your father! You deserve to find your happy, to find love, and have your curse broken. You did nothing wrong to be cursed. And you deserve the world. *You*"—I poke the center of his chest and push hard before laying my palm on him—"you deserve *everything*."

Resigned at the dreadful choice he has to make, I utter, "And I need to be out of your way in order for that to happen." The death of my life stutters in my soul as I force out, "I need you to decide whether to execute me or divorce me. I won't keep you from finding your happy, Jer."

The silence fractures my heart more, the knowledge of losing him hitting me like a forceful wind. A choked sob escapes, and I cover my face, pinching my eyes shut and concealing my shame and rejection.

Jerrick pulls down my hands and softens his voice. "Is it my turn now?"

His question catches me off guard. But I nod twice, since hearing him out is the least I can do.

Jerrick takes a deep breath, his fingers moving to my chin. "Open your eyes."

Our eyes meet, and I take this last chance to appreciate his face up close.

His features are hard and serious and yet so damned handsome. His scar and dimple tug at my heart, and I curse this heartbreak.

It is an out-of-body experience with how many tears I shed. Even if I tried to breathe, I do not think I could stop. I fully embrace being the epitome of sorrow and despair now.

A fitting punishment.

I struggle to blink the tears away, annoyed they are ruining the image of Jerrick I am desperately trying to etch in my mind. I try to focus on him, but the more I try, the more my soul is breaking.

Each crack is its own fracture, an open wound that will break again and again and again. I know what comes next, and my heart shatters repeatedly.

I turn from his stare, covering my face once more before even giving him a chance to speak. I tremble through each sob. "I-I-I am so sorry."

I just need to let the tears run their course. And then maybe I can look at him again. Deities, will I ever be deserving of even that?

I lose myself deeper into my own personal Oblivion.

"Look at me, Frostbite. *Please*," he urges.

I sniff, trying to brave through meeting his gaze once more.

Jerrick cradles my face, his thumbs drying away my tears. His blue eyes stare deep into me, his gaze softening.

"Don't you understand?" I shake my head as Jerrick lifts his lips. "I already have it all."

"But you don't. You need to leave me and go be free."

"No, Tove. I told you I wasn't going anywhere, and I meant it."

"You're *still* cursed, Jerrick," I sigh, hating he is making this harder than this is.

"Not anymore."

My mind goes blank, unease settling in my gut. "H-How do you know?"

Jerrick breathes, taking a more pleading, serious tone. "I know because, when I came to check on you that one night, I was *scared* when I heard you screaming and found you on that ledge. And then when we went hunting? I watched the only person I've ever truly cared about these last five years drown. Sweet Makers, I can't even begin to tell you the sheer terror that ran through me when I reached you in the water." He closes his eyes and looks away. "Your skin was so gray. Your lips were so blue. And all I could think was, *What if I never get to see her eyes open again?*"

The break in his voice makes me wish I never caused him so many problems.

Jerrick turns to me, eyes rimmed with tears.

He swallows, pressing on. "I know because, even when the night of the ball arrived, I was shaking the entire day, filled with nerves and a weird unfamiliar feeling I couldn't put my finger on. I know because my entire world illuminated when you laid eyes on that piano, and something inside of me lit up, too. And I know because, when I spent an entire night with you, I woke the next morning with a peace I hadn't felt in a long time."

My eyes widen. "But—"

He stops me, holding my hands and leaning in. "Even when Jonas told us everything the following morning, even when I asked you if this was all a distraction."

My heart pounds in my ears as I try to wrap my mind around everything he is saying.

"I woke that morning, and you shifted before my very eyes. And after news broke about the fighting? That—that fucking sucked. And no matter how much it tore me apart to watch you deflect my questions, what really broke me was your hope of a divorce."

"I was trying to help you!" I blink away my tears. "Even if I broke my own heart in the process, I wanted you to have the chance to break your curse. I never wanted to hurt you."

He consoles me, pure understanding in his gaze. "I know. I never wanted to hurt you, either. But my powers just... *surged*. I didn't know how to handle it, and I didn't understand what was happening. So, I was stupid and reckless and hid it away from you, as you did me."

I sniff, remembering my own mask slipping when his showed.

Seeing him fighting his tears, the two most injured people from the battle are me and him, and I hate that sharp-edged truth.

Jerrick strains to keep his composure, and my soul breaks to see him like this.

His voice wobbles as he explains, "But even when I was heartbroken with what happened, I knew when *he* held you hostage and when I was too far away to stop him. I knew when I held you as you were dying that my curse was broken, and it was broken because of you."

My heart stops.

Jerrick caresses my skin softly as tears stream down our cheeks. "I am utterly and fiercely yours, Frostbite. My mind, body, heart, and soul are yours, my love. And I think a part of me knew when I first saw you, you were meant to be my queen—even beyond the marriage arrangement. My heart loves you. My soul loves you—*I* love you, Tove. Even when I am absolutely out of my mind with anger, hurt, and confusion, I will *never* want to leave you because I did find my happy again. I found it with *you*."

His words—*his love*.

My soul tethers itself to Jerrick, melded together again. Melded by *love*.

A love I cannot help but fear some unknown force in the future will try to use to wedge us apart because of my own mistakes.

"But what if—"

Jerrick crashes his lips against mine.

I melt in his hold, opening for him as our kiss deepens. I tug him closer, and he, once again, obliges me.

This damned man.

I don't deserve him, but I cannot deny how much I fucking love him. I clutch his tunic, his body heat warming my own cold hands.

Jerrick breaks our kiss, pulling my hands to his chest. He leans in, giving me a soft peck as if we both needed it. Jerrick's tear-filled gaze pierces into my own.

"There is no *what if* this or *what if* that, Tove. I am here, my love, and I've always got you. I am not going anywhere. The Makers themselves will have to tear me to shreds before taking my soul away from yours."

Tears stream down his cheeks as I weep silently. I move, my soul leaving my body and reaching for Jerrick. I pull him in and wrap my arms around his neck, keeping him close.

My tears are that of joy, happiness, and—*love*.

Love and admiration and devotion to this man.

My king, my husband—my *Jerrick*.

I pause our kiss, uttering the words I've longed to tell him. "I love you."

Jerrick's smile brightens the entire room before he kisses me again.

The kiss shifts, deepening from joy into passion. The sweetness of his tongue works through mine, sending desire straight to my core.

I nibble lightly on his lip, hearing a rumble vibrate from him.

I sigh contentedly.

Even when our kissing slows enough for him to break away, his entire demeanor shifts into that of ease and comfort.

"I also think I may have solved your predicament," he adds.

Confused, I ask, "What predicament?"

"Do you feel well enough for a little trip?"

I shrug, unsure. "I guess?"

He pats my upper thigh gently, standing and offering me his hand. "Come with me."

I take his hand, the heat coming off him in waves, and he smirks. He scoops me into his arms, catching me off guard.

I can't help the giggle escaping me. With my arms draped around his shoulders, he winks, and I lean in and kiss his cheek.

Jerrick carries me from his room, guiding us down the hall and the staircase leading to the other levels of the castle.

When we reach the ground level, I study him with anxiety as he guides us to the throne room. Dark thoughts crawl to the forefront of my mind, and I can't help but think this is all too good to be true.

Maybe Jerrick isn't in love with me and is taking me to a group of people to kill me on the spot for my part in the catastrophe.

My grip on his tunic tightens with each step he takes.

The guards are armed at both sides of the throne room, smiling at us as the doors open, and I brace myself for the crowd, an executioner, something.

"Are you alright?" Jerrick asks when a whoosh of breath leaves me at the very empty room in front of me.

"I-I..." I chuckle. "I thought you were taking me to my death."

Jerrick rubs the underpart of my knee in his hold. "We might need to work on removing that fear of me killing you," he jokes, kissing my brow gently and easing me down.

I look at a frozen section of the throne room in confusion. "Where is..."

"Nikolaj?" he finishes my question, guiding me closer to the frozen area. "I hacked his frozen carcass out with my sword and a few other weapons, used my magic to make sure there was no chance of him living, and got others to help cut him down and carry him away to burn his body."

Nikolaj and I did the same with Runa.

I wanted to clear the ice from her frozen state, and I'd tried for months before Nikolaj convinced me to give her peace and remove her body from any prying eyes. The memory returns of us having to make a pyre. Nikolaj constantly retreated into the woods to ensure we had enough fuel to feed the fire.

The stinging sensation has me rubbing my chest.

I try to block Nikolaj from my thoughts, crafting Runa's features instead. When her image runs to the forefront of my mind, I can't help but feel a surge of love flicker at her memory.

I try not to think too much at the odd sensation, directing my attention to where I had frozen Nikolaj.

The floor is cracked and broken into various chunks, some from the brunt force of removing a block of ice atop it and some from the pressure of frost and ice looming from this one spot.

I can't help but stare at the bloodstains across the ice. *My blood.*

Jerrick catches my line of sight. "Have you tried calling forth your magic since you woke?" he asks carefully.

I shake my head and look up at him. "No." I had not even thought about my magic.

He lifts my hand to his lips, kissing it softly. "I have a theory I would like to try. Do you think you could call your magic?"

"I can try," I reply, closing my eyes, trying to find my concentration.

Jerrick touches my upper arm encouragingly before leaning in. "I can always use my magic to help speed it along," he teases, earning a peek from my right eye.

"Already wanting to kiss me again?" I taunt.

Jerrick smirks, pulling me closer. "*Always.*"

I sigh joyfully as he draws my breath into his. I relax in his hold, trusting the heat running down my throat and skipping across my skin, reveling in the energy coming alive.

Jerrick's magic is warm and companionable against mine as he draws it out, a small tentative spark of power within me, stretching, yawning as if it, too, was in a deep slumber. And then a familiar, loving ripple of a chilled magic perks its way up along my spine as Jerrick breaks the kiss, our eyes opening to the frost drifting across my skin.

"I don't think I'm ever going to get over how magnificent you are," Jerrick sighs, watching the swirls of snow flurries appear on my hands, a cold breeze of air manifesting in my palms.

I smile at the sight, appreciation and a fondness deepening for my abilities. "What is your theory?"

Jerrick eases us both to the floor, touching the frost near us. His eyes meet mine with mischief.

"Kiss me while you try to melt the frost."

"Wh-What?"

Melt? I can barely remove my own powers.

"Just trust me," he says across my lips, kissing me deeply, wildly, and *very* thoroughly.

I almost lose my balance from the force of his lips on mine, a snicker escaping in between our kisses. But I indulge in Jerrick's theory, concentrating on the task at hand.

I count our kisses instead of my breaths, letting my mind wander in meditation as his magic streams through me. Recognition of my own powers is quick, and I tap into them, breathing through kisses, love pulsing through me.

Jerrick's power runs down my arms as the frost pours outward.

I nip at his lip, teasing him in my distraction. He growls wickedly against my mouth, and it sends a shiver up my spine. The sensation of warm and cold from our magic intertwining is nearly forgotten.

But when Jerrick whispers "*Look*" against my lips, I break away, balking at the sight.

There, on the marbled floor, is my own melted handprint.

I cover my mouth in astonishment as my eyes line with tears.

I-I removed the ice—no. I melted it.

I didn't pull it back into me, but I *melted* the ice.

"H-How did you know this would work?" I shake my head in disbelief, glancing between Jerrick and the handprint.

I gasp when the magic expands, melting more ice and frost surrounding us.

He rubs the back of his head as his cheeks redden. "I thought your power might have been too cold, so I thought if I was able to help warm your blood while you are using your gifts, it would help your magic recognize the difference, allowing you to melt rather than try to pull the frost back into you."

I... I can *finally* remove winter from Axidoria.

Sobs wrack through my body from relief at the miracle bestowed upon me.

A comforting touch has me smiling up at an already beaming Jerrick, my husband, my king, my love, illuminating my entire world.

Each of my wishes to Yeva was granted before I even realized it. I've found a way to save my kingdom. I've found there is more to life than grief. I've found it all through my friends and my family.

And I've found my happy again with Jerrick.

My husband kisses me tenderly through my tears, letting my emotions be what they are, simply existing beside me, supporting me, and loving me.

"And I know, with time, you'll be able to do this and more without me," he says when he pulls away.

"Oh, already tired of kissing me?" I flirt.

Jerrick's eyes twinkle with mischief. "*Never.*"

A giggle escapes me as his lips find mine, and the energy between us buzzes with our power.

Our love.

I adjust my position, straddling him and kissing him deeper.

He cups my backside as he leans into the kiss once, twice, and a third time, allowing us to sink together in perfect harmony. He rests his forehead along mine, my eyes closing and taking a long, selfish inhale of him. Jerrick's lips meet my brow, and my soul shines in happiness I didn't know, didn't think I would ever find. It cocoons me, rooting itself deep inside of me.

I gaze at Jerrick, the two of us infectiously making the other smile brighter, and I can't help but hold his cheeks and kiss him again.

He laughs. "My conscience is telling me we need to pack our bags."

"Pack our bags?" Worry etches across my features.

"We need to go melt the winter in Axidoria too, right?"

I gasp with excitement, drawing my hands over my mouth as he chuckles lightly. I pull him in tightly—eagerly—baffled this day is truly here.

I am finally returning to help my people—*our* people.

I kiss him. I squirm to escape his hold, desperate to sprint to my chambers to pack my bags. But Jerrick applies a light pressure, giving me pause.

He smirks, patting my thighs.

I move awkwardly as he guides my legs to wrap around his lower back.

His hands drift under my backside, and he squeezes it before pushing our weight to help himself get enough momentum to stand.

I lock my legs tight as my butt loses the comfort of solid ground. But I know I am safe in my husband's arms, especially when Jerrick keeps his hands on my ass. I lean in, brushing kisses across his cheek.

"As much as my conscience tells me to pack our bags and head out, I can't help but think it might be in our best interests to leave tomorrow," he whispers seductively as he squeezes my ass and we exit the throne room.

I bite my lip as it curves into a smile at his promise.

"Oh?" I ask, leaning into his ear and nibbling the lobe in response to his touch.

He groans before whispering, "Tonight, I am in desperate need of exploring every inch of your body."

Thrill creeps down my spine at his declaration, and I can't help myself as I lean in once more with lust pouring into my next words. "Tomorrow, it is."

EPILOGUE

HAPPY AGAIN

One Year Later
Jerrick

My boots are caked in mud from my trek to the front of my home from the stables. Approaching the entrance, I diligently drag each footstep, hoping to remove as much mud as possible prior to stepping over the threshold. If I leave tracks throughout the castle, my wife will scold me.

My wife.

Her eyes, her smile, and her sweet scent linger in the air.

Fuck, two weeks away on business for Axidoria was long enough. I left to inspect the progress of the revised borders and trade routes we had created a year after *Nikolaj*, the fucking bastard, tried to invade our lands.

I grind my teeth in irritation at the memory of that day, the countless number of men I slaughtered without a second thought because they were dividing themselves amongst Yadir and my home, trying to create as much carnage as possible in their wake.

They all deserve to be stuck and trapped in Letum's Oblivion.

Since then, Axidoria and Palaena have made strides on uniting. Of course, there were complaints from the other kingdoms, angered our marriage had increased our lands and resources. But we grouped together, calling a meeting of all six kingdoms, and revamped the kingdom's borders to showcase five instead of six.

I remember the group breaking for a meal during the day, and I was earnestly trying to find a solution for each of them. It was enraging how no one was willing to offer new ideas aside from their own selfish desires to protect their borders.

My fists remained tight knuckled that entire morning through early afternoon, and my magic sensed my frustration.

A humming, buzzing suggestion cooed and tried to lure me into touching someone, any one of them, to persuade them.

But Tove was quick to catch on to my struggles that day, taking my hand and squeezing it twice before a little spark of her own magic distracted mine. It caught me off guard, and my cunning Frostbite only smiled as if it was our own secret to share.

And indeed, it was.

None of them knew of my gifts, and I wanted to keep it that way. I didn't need any more attention drawn to Palaena or Tove.

I only wanted us to enjoy life with the happy we found again.

When everyone eventually compromised, we began the draft for a declaration of new borders.

With two castles in our lands, we decided it was in our best interest to pick one as a permanent home. I'll never understand why Tove chose here instead of Axidoria.

After we successfully removed the winter from her lands, the soil and grass that bloomed the following spring was lush, rich, and plentiful. A valuable resource, all the more reason why we had to divide and somewhat dissolve Axidoria.

She even agreed to use her gifts during the colder season to make it a little longer than a month, allowing the earth extra time to rejuvenate and improve the quality of crops.

Tove is not even fully trained, and I know her power will be one of the greatest.

Deities, the magnitude of her gifts is still unfathomable to me.

Watching her remove the winter the first time with my help was a sight to behold, and the reunion of her with her friend Betina and the joy and worship exclaimed by her people were inspiring.

And this last winter, when we did it again, the joy on her face only made my love grow.

The image of her lighting up my world envelops me, carving deep into my heart and etching itself into my soul.

I never believed love would happen to me. I never believed I would meet someone who took me by surprise and peeled away the layers I buried myself under for so long.

My magic stirs at the emotion in my throat, the absence of my wife hurrying my stride into a sprint.

Heading to the far alcove of home, I wave off anyone acknowledging me. Everyone knows where I'm going. Everyone also knows it is in their best interests to leave the entire floor and section of the castle because, when I finally see her—my cock twitches at the thought.

I take the stairs two at a time, bouncing off each one as music echoes down, filling the stairwell. I smirk at the soft, strenuous ballad my wife plays, wondering if it is one she has composed or one she learned.

My lungs focus on evening my breathing, my stomach flipping the closer I get to Tove's second favorite place in our home.

The song builds momentum as I reach the doorway.

My wife's back is to me, but I can't help but stop and lean against the threshold to admire her.

She sways, fully absorbed in the moment.

The peace and vulnerability she releases when she plays is fierce and wonderful, another quality of hers that takes my breath away. Seeing her here, with me, and happy, is something I never thought was possible.

But our comfortable silences, our discussions while reading, our shared stories and passion are a craving I have to indulge in every day.

My heart and cock jolt in tandem as the air whooshes from me, the love I have for her constantly growing and fortifying itself.

The scar on the side of my face pinches against my skin. Smiling is not new to me, but it is a norm I am growing used to whenever I am in her presence.

Tove finishes the song, her hands lifting from the keys, letting the final note string itself upward and bounce around the marbled acoustic walls. She shifts her foot off one of the pedals, and her posture slackens at the song ending. She waits momentarily before jumping back in. This time, the melody is one I recognize.

It is one she has been working on for a while.

I use this as a chance to close the door quietly behind me and enter, approaching and sitting beside her. As much as I expect her to stop and give me her undivided attention, I know her too well.

She keeps her focus on the melody, playing it softly as a smile dances along her features.

Deities, even the side of her face is beautiful. I cannot help but scoot closer, looping my arm along her backside.

She leans into me, and I rest my head on hers. She pauses mid-playing, snickering and lifting her hand, holding my cheek. Tove bites her lip in a stupidly adorable way.

"What?" I chuckle, wanting to be part of whatever it is she is thinking.

She simply shakes her head, still smiling. When she faces me, her ice-blue eyes brighten, illuminating my world every time I look at them.

"It's nothing," she beams, guiding her lips to me.

I take my wife in, kissing her slow and sweet before pulling away, skepticism furrowing my brow. "That's not nothing," I tell her, always wanting to know what is on her mind.

A lustful smirk plays across her face, and it makes me want more.

Tove leans in, resuming our kiss, whispering some of my favorite words. "I love you."

I pounce, moving her to straddle me as I push the bench away from the piano, ensuring my mouth remains on hers. Fuck, two weeks is too long without savoring every part of my wife's body. I've craved her, and being here sends me into a needy frenzy.

Tove hums her approval, feeding into my desire and grinding against me. She usually wears gowns for meetings and special occasions, and I thank the Makers she is wearing one now instead of pants.

While she prefers wearing trousers, I prefer when she wears dresses.

Easier access.

"I missed you," I murmur lazily.

She drags her hands up the base of my skull, combing through my hair and massaging my scalp. Tove yanks my head back, flirtation filling her lustful gaze.

"You did?"

I groan, reaching under her dress and seeking her perfect, round ass and find her completely bare.

All for me.

"Your nakedness tells me you feel the same," I say, squeezing her backside tightly, earning a gasp from her.

Deities, the hitching of her breath undoes me.

I smack her ass, my growing need to be inside of her has me covering the piano keys and lifting Tove to perch her ass against the piano as our mouths clash. I squeeze her hips as my wife's arms spread across to the sides of the instrument, holding herself in place as I kiss down her neck.

I trail my lips down to her chest, her bodice loose and begging to be removed. Hunching over, I use my teeth to drag her top to her stomach.

Tove's full breasts fill my line of vision, and my mouth waters.

My wife's eyes study me, her breathing ragged and skin flush.

I smirk mischievously, needing to hear what she wants. "Tell me what you want, my love."

My eyes remain fixed on Tove as my hands run along her thighs. I have been starved for too long without her. I offer a few glimpses into suggestions that allow me to thoroughly relish being home and here with her.

"Do you want my mouth on your breasts?" I ask, bringing her nipple into my mouth and sucking hard.

Tove moans, convulsing in pleasure.

I pull her breast out of my mouth, running a hand down the outside of her leg, circling back to her core. I lightly drag my finger through the center of her clit.

"Do you want my hands or my mouth to feast on your pretty pussy?" I draw her breast into my mouth again, unable to control myself.

Tove whimpers and fastens her hold on me, keeping me in place.

I study her, admiring her in exaltation as her heated gaze and desire keep me under her spell.

"I want your dirty mouth to suck and bite my nipple so hard it leaves a mark," she pants.

Her grip on my hair loosens, and I remove my mouth, still gazing at her with a smirk.

Tove hunches forward, keeping me focused on hearing her every wish and desire. "And I want you to fuck me against this piano. *Hard.*"

Her words barely leave her mouth before I spring up to kiss her, fumbling for her skirts as she reaches for my trousers. She frees my cock faster than I can remove her clothing, and Sweet Makers, when she takes me in her hand.

"Fuuuck," I rasp.

Tove nips at my lip in response, her hand twisting my dick in her grasp as I help her out of the dress and remove my tunic.

I return to her breasts the second her dress is discarded, one hand dragging along her sex and rubbing her pussy. My cock pulses at the thought of driving into her when I feel how aroused she is.

"Are you wet for me?" I ask, kissing her breast before latching my teeth along her nipple.

I suck her breast and pinch her clit in tandem, Tove rewarding me with another whimpered moan as her head falls back, her hands gripping the piano for support.

My own need takes hold, seeking to achieve my wife's desire of being fucked hard. I lift her legs around my waist, bracing her further against the piano and thrusting my dick inside of her without a second thought.

We both gasp, Tove's eyes widening with pleasure. Her cunt is so tight, its begging me to fuck her harder.

"So fucking wet for me, my wife."

Her features warm at my acknowledgment. "Always, my husband," she breathes.

I kiss her deeply, thrusting hard and deep, my hand rubbing her clit.

Tove arches against the piano, her hips grinding. Each of us holds one side of the instrument, and Tove's legs flex, her nails digging into my hip.

"More," she pleads greedily.

I am happy to oblige. I drive deeper, savoring each thrust as it pleases her flawless body.

She arches further back, almost laying on the top of the piano, allowing me the perfect chance to savor her.

I suck the tip of her nipple, and I rub her clit faster. The tension of her walls tighten around my cock, and I take her in, loving the sounds escaping her and the tightness in her face when she gets closer and closer to her climax.

Her chest rises and falls with mine, her gorgeous body displayed for only me to revel in.

"I'll never get tired of this," I promise her as I trail kisses along her skin. "Seeing you writhe as your pretty little cunt takes me makes me harder."

Her eyes meet mine as I increase my pace, moving my hand and cock in tandem with her breaths, watching her reactions and making sure her needs are thoroughly met. She moans with the change in rhythm.

I praise her, knowing it unravels her in the best of ways. "The moans escaping your lips are my own composition I play through in my mind every second of every day."

"Jer—" she pants.

Tove's body convulses, tightening around my cock.

She is so close.

I lean in and kiss her with passion and love, keeping my momentum steady and true, ensuring she reaches ecstasy.

"Watching you completely shatter," I breathe into her through grunted thrusts, "that is what undoes me."

I kiss her again, calling forth my magic to send a wave of heat into her.

She senses it within seconds, drawing her own power to meet and join mine.

We breathe our magic into the other, a soothing chill kissing up my spine.

I know it does the same for her from the countless times we have done this, using it for our pleasure.

"I-I'm—" she stutters, releasing another delicious moan I am going to repeat over and over in my head.

I keep her close.

"That's it, My Queen." I grind into her.

She mewls, biting her lip as our foreheads press together.

"That's it, my wife."

"I'm going to—" Tove pants, her words replaced with a guttural groan.

I go deeper and harder, applying added pressure to her clit.

She moves, her rhythm shifting, and I stay in tune with it, in tune with her. I meet her rhythm, conducting her to shatter to the perfect melody of our love.

"Come, my love." I finish for her, fully sheathing myself inside of her. The insatiable need to feel her coming on my dick has me begging. "Come for me, Tove."

Her mouth slackens, the cusp of her orgasm so close.

I press my thumb hard against her clit, rubbing frantically to hear her screams. Tove's walls clench around me, and she cries out my name.

It sends me over the edge. A harsh moan escapes, the two of us coming apart in rapture as we seal it with a fevered kiss.

I slow my thrusts, aware of her exhaustion through staggered breaths.

She loosens her legs from my waist, but I pull my wife close, helping her off the piano. I keep a hold of her, easing us to the ground, choosing to lay down on our clothes instead of the cold floor.

Facing each other on our sides, she still trembles.

I draw on my magic once more, hovering closer as I kiss warmth into her skin. Peering up at her, she beams, reaching for me as her breathing evens out.

She holds the sides of my face and kisses me passionately.

I wrap my arm under her, drawing our bodies close. Having Tove here in my arms is like reuniting my soul to its missing half.

I don't know how my soul existed for so long without her. And I don't know what I ever did to earn her trust, her kindness, her love. It was something we both believed impossible, given our pasts, our traumas, and our perception of each other.

But I would not change anything about our story, no matter how much I still, to this day, cannot fathom what I did to deserve her.

Tove pulls away from our kiss. "What is it, my love?"

The keen awareness we have of one another has only grown since we've been married, the ease of conversation and being vulnerable with each other strengthening our bond. But I defer to teasing, always seeking new ways to make her laugh.

I mock the giggle she gave me earlier.

"It's *nothing*," I tease with a wink.

Tove rolls her eyes, her smile contradicting her annoyance. She playfully smacks the side of my arm, earning a chuckle. She huffs her own amusement.

I kiss her brow, murmuring the only words perfect for this moment. "I love you, Frostbite."

She beams at the nickname I use for her and only her. A blush breaks out against her cheeks before she drags me back into our sweet, perfect bubble, kissing me senselessly through my smile.

We remain entangled with one another, safely tucked away from tomorrow's problems and today's stresses, enjoying the discovery of our happy again with each other.

THANK YOU FOR READING!

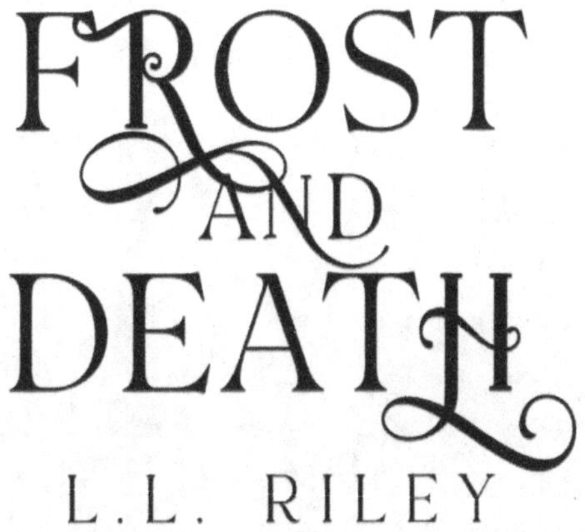

Did you like it? Love it? Want some more of it?

Feel free to share your thoughts on Amazon and be sure to subscribe to my newsletter to gain access to an *exclusive* character art scene and be the first to know about book 2, which will be Princess Vivienne's story!

Subscribe today at:
https://www.llriley.com/

Acknowledgments

First and foremost, if you're still reading this, I want to extend a HUGE thank you for reading. This was A LOT for me to do, and there were a lot of people who helped make this book happen. I wouldn't be where I am if it wasn't for them.

To my Boo Thang, this book TRULY would never have seen the light of day if it wasn't for you coming into my life and encouraging me in everything I have ever hoped for. There will never be enough words to express how important you are to me. There will never be a character I read or write that will replace you. You are my person who sees me for me, and I would not be who I am if it were not for meeting you. You are my goofy goober, rock! I love you lots, like polka dots.

To my sisters, being your sister is one of my greatest achievements. Our love for fairy tales as kids was the key foundation of this story and series. Each of us finding our happy again after the trials we have endured together and individually is what kicked me in the butt and ultimately pushed this entire fictional world beyond what I originally thought. Thank you for seeing me through everything. And thank you for being my sisters. Love you.

To Kyrsten and Sarah, the friendship we have had throughout my life is one I know will never change, no matter the amount of time or distance that separates us. I love you both to the ends of the earth and am truly honored to be called your friend.

To Sara and Mandie, my badass babes, y'all were the first ones to ever see the real beginnings of this book. You two are my original hype girls who are a constant support in all parts of life. You both constantly inspire me and make me strive to being a better human. Our friendship is a true treasure I discovered in my adulthood, and

I intend to keep you both as long as you'll both have me. Love you both to the moon and beyond.

To my husband's friends—weird, I know—I have to thank you for entertaining and nurturing my spouse while I spent my time writing this novel, and even before. The friendship you have with each other is a delight to witness and thanks for having amazing partners that I love and being amazing people yourselves. Thank you for always keeping things lively and hilarious whenever we all get together and hang out.

To my Polka Dot BFF's, my neuro-spicy babes, wow. The love I have for our lil group. Not to mention each of you individually. I will forever be in debt to each of you for constantly calling me an author even when I wasn't writing or believing in myself. You all set the bar high in being an author, and I can only hope that this book will be the stepping stone in me playing catch-up with the rest of you. The love and adoration I have for each of you knows no bounds. Seriously. Don't ever doubt that. Ever.

To my editors and my beta readers, words SERIOUSLY AND TRULY cannot even express the amount of gratitude I have for each of you. Thank you from the bottom of my soul for everything you did to help me learn and grow as a writer and make this story visible to the world.

To my artists, thank you so much for the cover art, character art, and long chains of emails and DMs that helped bring this vision to life. Your talent is truly inspiring, and I am eternally grateful to each of you.

To Sarah—I know a lot of Sarahs and Saras—thank you so much for taking a chance on me. You've been such a delight to have in my corner, and I've truly enjoyed the work we have done together, and I can only hope we can continue to do so. Your calming presence, knowledge, and insight for the book community have helped me learn so much as well as increased my own personal TBR. You are a gem, a rockstar, and anyone who knows you is lucky to have you. I know I sure am!

To the Bookish Babes Get Lit Book Club, creating our Discord server has been life-changing for me. The friendships I have made with each one of you are phenomenal. I love our little book club and love how welcoming and kind everyone is. Whether you have just joined or have been there since the beginning, each of you are gems in my book, and I am truly grateful to call you all my friends.

To the rest of my family and friends—because let's be honest, there are a lot of you, lol—I am truly honored to have so much support. I know I am terrible at reaching out, but that will never change how much love I have for each of you. My love is always there and will never go away.

And lastly, I can't forget about the book community. Thank you for being a haven for me when I was venturing into a new reality. Discovering books has truly changed my life and making my Booktok and Bookstagram account allowed me to escape reality. Creating content has been such a blast, as well as meeting and interacting with some incredible human beings online. It has been such a joy and pleasure, and I can only hope I've pleased you. I pray to the Makers that you'll stick around because I have more stories to write and share with the world.

Cheers to all of us trying to get through our never-ending TBR.

About the Author

L.L. Riley grew up in California and decided, in her later years, to switch it up and explore the slow life of the Midwest. Something about seeing if Kansas really was "no place like home." While she physically found a home in Kansas, she found her true home through reading and writing. She loves to be silly and goofy, always wanting to make someone smile. She lives life to the fullest with her husband and four precious cats who all spoil her senseless with love.

Follow L.L. Riley on social media and subscribe to her newsletter for more news on Princess Vivienne's story!